I0761259

bluebird
GOLD

OTHER TITLES BY DEVNEY PERRY

Shield of Sparrows Series

Shield of Sparrows

Haven River Ranch Series

Crossroads

Sunlight

The Edens Series

Indigo Ridge

Juniper Hill

Garnet Flats

Jasper Vale

Crimson River

Sable Peak

Treasure State Wildcats Series

Coach

Blitz

Rally

Merit

Clifton Forge Series

Steel King

Riven Knight

Stone Princess

Noble Prince

Fallen Jester

Tin Queen

Calamity Montana Series

The Bribe

The Bluff

The Brazen

The Bully

The Brawl

The Brood

Runaway Series

Runaway Road

Wild Highway

Quarter Miles

Forsaken Trail

Dotted Lines

Maysen Jar Series

The Birthday List

Letters to Molly

The Dandelion Diary

Lark Cove Series

Tattered

Timid

Tragic

Tinsel

Timeless

Jamison Valley Series

The Coppersmith Farmhouse

The Clover Chapel

The Lucky Heart

The Outpost

The Bitterroot Inn

The Candle Palace

Holiday Brothers Series

The Naughty, The Nice and The Nanny

Three Bells, Two Bows and One Brother's Best Friend

A Partridge and a Pregnancy

Standalones

Clarence Manor

Rifts and Refrains

A Little Too Wild

DEVNEY
PERRY

Published by Montlake, Seattle
www.apub.com

EU product safety contact:
Amazon Media EU S. à r.l.
38, avenue John F. Kennedy, L-1855 Luxembourg
amazonpublishing-gpsr@amazon.com

ISBN-13: 9781662536724 (paperback)
ISBN-13: 9781662536731 (digital)

Cover design by Hang Le
Cover image: © Krista Taylor / Getty; © charnsitr, © evlmint, © goran cakmazovic / Shutterstock

Printed in the United States of America

Author's Note

My father was a music teacher by trade and a Montana historian by heart. I've lost count of the number of tales he's shared with me over the years about ghost towns and gold mines. Most of the stories I've forgotten, but there are a few that have lingered in the far corners of my mind.

This story is loosely based on one of Dad's "research projects." I've taken many liberties in the name of fiction, and this story is in no way historically accurate. But beneath my embellishments, there are a few golden nuggets of truth and history.

So with that, I invite you to take a trip to the past and visit my beloved Montana.

Prologue

Dear Ilsa,

Remember those days when you were little, and I used to tell you stories? We'd go fishing, and I'd tell you a story so you wouldn't get bored. I'd be cooking dinner, and you'd be sitting on the counter, kicking your bare feet as I told you about cowboys and bandits. Or we'd be on the dock, watching the sunset, and I'd give you the short version of whatever book I'd just finished reading.

I miss those days. I miss the way you'd lean your head on my shoulder and hug my arm. I miss the sound of your laugh. I miss counting the freckles on your nose.

You're long past the age of enjoying my stories, but there's one I never told you. It's a favorite legend of mine, and it goes like this.

Montana was a wild place during the gold rush days with some of the purest gold in the nation. Pioneers flocked here with dreams of striking it rich. Miners, outlaws and businessmen arrived on horseback or by wagon and stagecoach. Some traveled with only the clothes on their backs, and the only way they survived our punishing winters was by sheer grit and determination.

Montana only keeps the iron willed. And those miners and early settlers were tough as nails, living on next to nothing. Surviving day to day on hopes and prayers.

Picture towns made of tents and ramshackle buildings. Shanties and dugouts. Saloons with hitching posts and swinging doors. General stores selling sacked flour, canned cow's milk and hard candies for a penny.

Every man wore a pistol on his belt and there weren't enough women to keep those men tame. There were corrupt lawmen secretly leading gangs of road agents. And masked vigilantes stepped in to uphold the peace.

Here's where the legend gets interesting. What if those vigilantes were not always on the right side of wrong?

There's a lost legend from Garrack, one of the more prominent mining towns in those days, that once, a wagon of gold was stolen by a notorious gang. After the robbery, a band of vigilantes went after the thieves. Except they returned empty-handed. And the gold was gone forever. Or was it?

Rumors began to trickle through Garrack that the vigilantes had in fact found the thieves. And rather than return the gold to its rightful owners, the vigilantes had taken it for themselves, hiding it away, biding their time until they could leave town without suspicion.

Only they waited too long. Speculation turned to accusation, and the townsfolk turned on their peacekeepers. Each of the vigilantes who'd gone in search of the stolen gold was hanged for their betrayal. The secret location of the stolen gold was buried with them in unmarked graves.

The gold was truly lost, never to be seen again.

And that's the story of Garrack's legendary lost gold.

I should have told you more stories, honey bear. Come to Montana. Come and see me so I can tell you more stories.

Love,

Dad

Chapter 1

Ilsa

January 1983

Once upon a time, I called this cabin on Cotters Lake home.

As I spun in a slow circle, past swirled with present. Then and now.

Then.

A crackling fireplace and the steady clicks from Mom's knitting needles. The scents of cigars and sugar cookies. A small living room, but a clean, happy room. A little girl with dirt under her fingernails, curled on her father's lap as he read her a story.

Now.

Dust motes floating past dirty windows. Stale air with the faint stench of a long-dead mouse. Clutter beyond clutter to the point of chaos. A tattered recliner and lonely, quiet rooms.

Dad's cabin was smaller than I remembered. The ceilings seemed too short, the walls too close.

Probably to be expected, considering the last time I'd been in this house, I'd been sixteen. A lot had changed in the past ten years. Yet if I closed my eyes, I was that little girl again, curled on her father's lap.

My earliest memory was in this cabin. In this living room. I'd been three, maybe four.

There was a fire burning in the stove. Dad had built it for Mom before he'd left to go ice fishing on the lake because Mom didn't like building fires. She got splinters from the wood.

Frost trimmed the windows. The couch was pushed into a corner to make space for the Christmas tree. Mom and I were decorating it with ornaments while she complained about the *insufferable* snow.

That was the day I'd learned what insufferable meant.

Mom was upset because we'd had to cancel our shopping trip to Missoula when they'd closed the roads. I'd been too young to remember her exact words, but the way she'd spoken about Montana had always been such a contrast to Dad's feelings.

He'd been sunshine. She'd been gloom. His lifestyle had been her misery.

Until the spring I'd turned six, when the snow melted, the daffodils bloomed, and Mom loaded me into her olive-green Oldsmobile and left Dalton.

Left Dad.

Mom had been lighter after that. Happier. But her joy had been the death of his laughter. Their roles had switched. She'd blossomed. He'd withered.

Daylight and despair.

And somewhere in the middle: me.

Always in the middle. Until now. Dad was dead and there wasn't a middle to occupy.

A shiver chased down my spine. Goose bumps dotted my forearms. The fire I'd started in the hearth was rushing to a roar, but it hadn't chased away the cold yet.

It had been twenty years since I'd spent a winter in Montana. I'd forgotten just how bitterly cold it could get. I'd been back in Dalton for a week, and the temperatures had dropped lower and lower each day. But despite the cold, the winters were beautiful. Even Mom couldn't argue the splendor of Montana covered in snow.

Beyond the filmy windows, the sun had dipped below the jagged mountain horizon. Its fading light tinged the world in blues and violets. The trees looked more indigo than green. Beneath their trunks, the yard was blanketed with snow. Past the boat dock, the frozen lake stretched from one icy shore to the next.

Once upon a time, I'd loved that lake. I'd spent countless hours swimming, playing on the gravel beach, and floating on an old inner tube.

Strange that I could remember a Christmas from decades ago, but I couldn't remember who'd taught me to swim. Was it Dad? For as long as I could remember, I'd just known how to swim.

He'd been a good swimmer too.

Just not good enough.

My heart twisted, the pain a constant companion this week. I'd spent most of the past week avoiding this cabin, throwing myself into my new teaching job at Dalton High School. And when I was here, I'd hidden in my childhood bedroom, huddled beneath blankets, blocking out the memories and cold. But a week of surviving in this clutter was enough.

I'd come to Montana to settle my father's estate. To clean this cabin and sell it in the spring.

To say goodbye.

Yesterday, I'd tackled the kitchen. Tonight, maybe I'd find the living room couch. It was buried somewhere beneath a mountain of boxes and bags and whatever else Dad had been collecting over the last ten years.

When I'd arrived last weekend, I'd barely been able to get into the cabin, so I'd focused on cleaning the essential rooms. The bathroom. My bedroom. The spaces I'd needed to survive my first week in Dalton.

Everything else, well . . . ignorance wasn't bliss, but it was my favorite hobby. Except there was simply no more ignoring the hoard of junk my father had amassed in this tiny house.

Dad had piled boxes nearly to the ceiling, leaving only narrow paths to move from room to room. The entryway was still overloaded, mostly from stuff I'd moved off my bed so I could sleep.

Was this mess my punishment for not visiting Dad sooner? How long had he been living like this?

I should know the answer. But Ike Poe had always been a bit of a mystery, even before I'd stopped coming to Montana for my summer vacations. That mystery would remain unsolved now that he was gone.

Maybe in this sea of boxes, I'd learn more about the man my father had been before his death.

I walked to the closest stack, stretching onto my tiptoes to heft down the box at the top. A puff of dust billowed off the cardboard as I set it beside my feet. Whatever was inside gave a tinny clatter.

Prying open the box's flaps, I did a double take at the contents. "Cans."

Empty cans. From the looks of it, Dad had been surviving on Campbell's Tomato Soup and Western Family Whole Kernel Corn.

I pushed the cans aside, making sure there wasn't anything else in the box. Then I carried it outside, adding it to the growing pile in the snowy driveway. The next three boxes were more empty cans. They joined the heap, destined for the dump.

As I lifted down the fifth box, heavier than the others and hopefully not full of cans, the phone rang, interrupting my cleaning.

It was a Sunday. Troy always called on Sundays.

Dread swirled with excitement—excitement that felt more like a habit than genuine interest.

For years, I'd looked forward to these Sunday calls. I'd made sure, no matter what, I was home whenever my phone rang. I'd loved the familiarity of Troy's voice on a Sunday evening. I'd loved the consistency of talking to my friend. My best friend.

Were we best friends? We had been once. I wasn't sure what we were right now.

Maybe we were two people who needed to stop talking on Sundays.

Yet I set the box aside and walked to the phone, lifting the handset from its cradle. "Hello?"

"Hello." Troy's one word was laced with enough pity to fill a thousand of Dad's empty soup cans.

Did all grieving people reach the point when they were fucking tired of receiving sympathy?

"How are you?" he asked.

"Good," I lied.

"Ilsa." My name in that smooth timbre, and my shoulders sagged. He knew me well enough to hear through a bad lie.

"I'm taking it one day at a time." I walked to the closest window, stretching the phone's spiral cord to its limit.

Beyond the filmy glass, night was falling. It was still early, just after five o'clock, but the short winter days meant the sun had already set, giving way to long winter nights.

Dad used to say there wasn't a place on earth that had as many stars as the shoreline of Cotters Lake after dark. Maybe after I got these windows cleaned, I'd actually be able to see them.

"How was the first week in Montana?" Troy asked.

I groaned. "Rough. But I've got a job."

"Yeah? That's great. How's it going?"

"Well, I'm not exactly sure what the previous teacher was doing with these kids, but it wasn't teaching them math."

"That bad, huh?"

"Beyond bad. I gave everyone a review test on last semester's material. Only half of the juniors and seniors passed. A third of the sophomores. And of the fifteen freshmen, only two passed. And when I say passed, I mean they each got seventy percent."

"Ouch. Sorry."

"There's nowhere to go but up, right?"

Troy chuckled. "There's that sunny optimism."

A smile tugged at the corners of my mouth. "You know me. I'll never give up on a kid."

"As you shouldn't. And the house? How's it coming?"

"I haven't made much progress yet."

My focus this past week had been on work. I'd driven into town early each morning and stayed late at the school each evening, trying to make sense of the previous teacher's notes and chaotic filing system. Every student seemed to have a different version of the curriculum textbook, and either they were all putting me through some sort of strange hazing ritual or none of them actually knew what chapter they'd been on when she left before winter break.

It was a thirty-minute trip from Cotters Lake to Dalton, and by the time I'd gotten home each evening, I'd been too tired to tackle the cleaning. Though this weekend, I'd made some progress.

Yesterday, I'd scoured kitchen cabinets and washed dishes and scrubbed countertops so that I could cook and use the sink and stove. This morning, I'd spent hours in the laundry room, clearing out old boots and coats and Dad's collection of fishing gear, moving it to the shed. The door to his bedroom had stayed firmly shut. I wasn't ready to go in there yet, to sort his clothes.

"I don't know what to keep," I told Troy. "And the fact that I don't know what to keep and what to trash makes me feel guilty."

A good daughter who knew her father wouldn't have hesitated. She would have known what he'd deemed important. What he would have wanted me to have.

A good daughter would have cried for the loss of her father.

It hurt being here. Missing him. Regretting him. But I hadn't cried, not once. Not yet.

"Are you sure you want to do this alone?" Troy asked. "We can hire someone to do the cleaning. Then you can put it on the market and leave it behind."

"No," I whispered.

Not that the thought hadn't crossed my mind. But the idea of letting a stranger sort through my father's possessions would only make the guilt worse.

Maybe I wasn't much better than a stranger. But at least I was his. And he'd been mine. Besides, where else did I have to go?

"I need to do this," I said.

"Then please, let me come and help." It was the tenth time he'd offered to come to Montana.

And for the tenth time, I said, "No, I'm fine."

"Ilsa."

There was my name again. No pity this time, just scathing disapproval. Like I was a child in need of scolding.

I hadn't heard that chiding tone from him before. Or maybe I had but I'd been so blinded by my love for him that I hadn't noticed.

"How's Lori?" I forced as much sincere curiosity into my voice as I could muster.

"Don't do that. Don't change the subject."

"I'm not doing anything. I appreciate the offer to help, but this is something I need to do on my own." I'd go through each and every box. I'd deal with the cans and dust and whatever else I uncovered beneath this roof.

Because maybe if I could learn who Dad had been in the last years of his life, I could retrace his footsteps. All the way back to that early memory, when I'd been a happy girl who looked at her father like he hung the moon.

If I started at the beginning, maybe I'd find the point when I'd gotten lost.

"I want to be there for you," Troy said.

"I know."

That was the worst part. If I asked him to be here tomorrow, he'd drop everything to drive from Arizona to Montana.

But being here? That was only geography. Whether he was in my living room or his own, whether we were thousands of miles apart or a few short feet, nothing would change. He could *be here*. And not be *with* me.

"You didn't answer my question," I said. "How is Lori?"

"She's good. At Jazzercise tonight."

"Sounds fun." My molars ground together. Asking about his most recent girlfriend was akin to torture, yet I'd asked for the past three months, ever since I'd found out they were dating.

The same night I'd come home from dinner to find a police car waiting outside my house and an officer poised on my porch to tell me that my father had died.

Troy and I had been out to dinner before that. He'd told me that he'd met someone, that Lori might be *the* one.

Maybe the reason I hadn't cried when that police officer told me about Dad was because my heart had already been broken.

It would be easier if Lori weren't a lovely woman. She was sweet, and the few times the three of us had met for drinks, she'd been nothing but kind. She'd fawned over Troy, always touching him, praising him, boasting about him like I didn't already know he was smart and funny and charming.

Like I didn't love him too.

I'd met Troy first, but it just didn't matter. Timing had never been on our side.

For years, we'd dodged and denied a mutual attraction. In the beginning, I hadn't wanted to risk our friendship, and by the time I'd been brave enough to tell him how I felt, it was too late. He'd met someone else.

Suzie. Then Hollie. Then Brenda. Then Tiff.

I hadn't waited. I'd moved on, dated and tried to find my own someone special. And neither of us had ever admitted we wanted more than friendship. But there were feelings. A hope that eventually, the timing would work.

Three months ago, for the first time in years, I'd been single and he'd been single. When Troy had asked me to dinner, I'd thought it was a date. Finally.

Silly me.

He'd told me all about Lori over breadsticks at my favorite Italian restaurant.

"Have you talked to your mom?" he asked.

"Not since I called to tell her that I made it to Dalton."

Mom didn't want updates about my time in Montana. She was irritated that I'd moved over a thousand miles away to clean up Dad's mess. She hated that I hadn't simply taken a week off work, dealt with this cabin lickety-split and returned home. She blamed him for my leaving Arizona. But it was all a ruse to hide her heartbreak.

Her entire life she'd been in love with my father, even after she'd filed for divorce. Mom had never remarried. She'd never shown any interest in another man. Yet for as much as she loved Dad, she hated him too.

She hated that he'd chosen Montana over her.

Twenty years ago, when she'd told him she couldn't live here anymore, that she couldn't do another harsh winter and needed more than his small town had to offer, he let her pack our bags. He'd watched from outside this very cabin as we'd driven away.

Mom had told me countless times that it was a mistake to come to Montana. That Dad hadn't cared enough about me to leave Dalton in decades, so why would I uproot my life to tidy up the remains of his?

Maybe she was right.

Maybe if Dad hadn't written me that letter, I would have stayed far, far away.

But since the day it had arrived in my mailbox, exactly two days after he'd died, I hadn't been able to let it go.

So when I'd finished the past semester at the high school where I'd been teaching in Phoenix, I'd packed up my life, putting most of my belongings in storage in my mother's garage. Then, despite the protests from both Mom and Troy, I'd moved to Montana.

By some miracle, I'd managed to get a job teaching. It was only temporary while another teacher was on maternity leave, but I wasn't staying in Dalton.

Maybe once I finished the school year, once I finished cleaning and selling Dad's cabin, I'd move to the East Coast. Maybe I'd try California or Colorado or Connecticut. Where? That was another day's problem. All I knew was that Arizona was history. Mom could keep her sunshine and scorching summers. I wanted to live in a place with all four seasons.

"Any idea when you'll be able to come home?" Troy asked.

Telling him I wasn't moving back was another day's problem too. "No. But I'd better let you go before this call gets too expensive."

"I can afford long distance, Ilsa."

"I know. But I'd like to get more work done before I call it a night."

"All right. Don't work too hard."

"No promises."

"Next Sunday?"

"I'll be here." Despite the nagging feeling that our friendship was coming to an end, I'd be here on Sunday, answering the phone the moment it rang.

"I'm worried about you," he said.

"Don't be. I'll be fine."

He scoffed. "Of course I'll worry about you, Ilsa. I love you."

It was a knife through the chest. Did he love me? Did I love him? Or was Troy simply comfortable, like my favorite old T-shirt?

Even if it was love, none of it mattered. A long time ago, in this very house, I'd learned that love wasn't enough.

"Have a good week." I carried the phone to its cradle and hung up.

No matter how many calls he made, I never ended them with a goodbye. Deep down, I was too afraid he'd take it as permission to stop calling.

"God, what the hell am I doing?" The wall of boxes didn't have an answer as I turned toward the living room. "What are the chances you're all cans?"

Only one way to find out.

The next box I pulled from the stack was full of photographs. I carried it to the kitchen, lifting them out and spreading them across the countertop.

They were Polaroids, most faded to black and white and tan and gray. But the face in each square, white frame was mine. Every single picture was of me during my summer visits.

My nose began to sting, a lump forming in my throat, but my eyes stayed dry.

I hadn't cried when the cop told me about Dad's death. I hadn't cried during the two-day drive from Phoenix to Dalton. I hadn't shed a single tear since I'd arrived in Montana, not even when I'd walked through the front door.

Ike had been an absent father to a shitty daughter.

Neither of us deserved tears.

I picked out a stack of my favorite photos from the massive pile and slid the rest off the counter's surface, pushing them into the empty box. Then it joined the others outside.

The next box was full of socks and white T-shirts. Everything had been folded perfectly, the shirts in tidy squares.

Dad had taught me how to fold clothes. Mom was hopeless when it came to laundry, content to pluck clean clothes out of a basket rather than put them away in her neglected dresser drawers. The summer after we'd moved to Arizona, the first summer I'd come to visit Dad, he'd seen my haphazard suitcase and a pile of clothes on the floor and taught me how to fold.

That sting in my nose returned with a vengeance.

I closed the lid, leaving everything inside untouched. There was no point in me keeping his shirts and socks, but instead of taking them outside, that box went to the laundry room shelf. It couldn't stay beside the detergent and bleach indefinitely, but for now, I wasn't ready to throw out his clothes.

The next box was as mysterious as the cans. White paper napkins filled it from top to bottom, and every single one was adorned with Dad's neat script. I plucked one from the top of the pile.

It was a to-do list, the first word capitalized and the tasks punctuated. Each item was crossed out with a straight line, except for the last.

Buy oranges.
Mow lawn.
Change oil.
Write Ilsa's letter.

The letter.

It wasn't crossed off, not on this napkin. Would I find one in the box where he'd checked it off? Because he'd written that letter. It was in my purse, tucked safely in the envelope in which it had arrived.

Why had he kept these napkin lists? Making them was normal, sort of. Keeping them? Not so much.

The cans. The lists.

The junk.

All signs that my father's mental health had been deteriorating in his final days. Signs I'd missed because I hadn't been around.

Dad had called me this past summer and pleaded with me to take a trip. It was the first time in years he'd invited me to Dalton. *Come and see me, honey bear. Spend a week on the lake. There's a lot I'd like to talk to you about.*

A good daughter would have made the effort. Instead, I'd been too busy making excuses. Too busy proving a point.

Dad had never once come to see me in Phoenix. Not in twenty years. He'd missed my high school graduation. Birthdays. Christmases. Why should I rush a trip on my summer vacation to Montana?

Saying no had been my form of revenge.

Guilt and regret as thick as black sludge crept through my veins. Would it have made a difference? Would I have been able to get him help? Questions I could never answer.

A blast of cold swept into the cabin, so I walked to the fireplace, adding another log to the stove.

At least I didn't have to chop wood. Dad had built up a stash of wood by the front door that would last me through two winters. Not that I intended to stay for more than one.

As the new log caught fire, I stood and took in the plethora of boxes, my energy waning. God, there were so many boxes. Tomorrow, after work, I'd unearth the couch.

I navigated the narrow path through the mess, about to slink into my bedroom and pull on a pair of warm socks and flannel pajamas to read for a few hours before going to bed. With my hand hovering over the light switch, I gave the boxes one backward glance.

And saw a person wearing a dark ski mask in the dirty kitchen window.

Chapter 2

Cosi

A click of static buzzed through the CB radio in my truck before Chuck's voice came through the speaker. "Cosi Raynes, you got copy?"

I sighed and plucked the mic from its cradle, pressing the button as I held it to my mouth. "Yeah, I'm here. Over."

"We've got a problem out on Cotters Lake. I sent Larry but he just called in. Needs a hand. Over."

"Damn it," I muttered, off radio. Why was it that my deputies could handle anything that came through during the week, but Sunday evenings they needed my help?

I raised the mic to my mouth. "What's the problem? Over."

"Lady called in and said there was a man sneaking around Ike Poe's cabin. Over."

So what if someone was sneaking around? That cabin was empty. As far as I knew, no one had been out there since Ike had died a few months back. I doubted there was much inside worth stealing. Was it a neighbor complaining? The folks on Cotters Lake didn't like traffic or visitors on their road. Or maybe someone was breaking in to cause trouble? Either way, Larry should be able to handle this on his own.

"Who called it in? Over." My money was on Sue Anne Holmes. She was one of Ike's neighbors and didn't understand the concept of *mind your own goddamn business*.

"Ilsa. Over."

"Ilsa who? Over," I asked, waiting for a last name. And I didn't get one.

Meaning Chuck, who was manning the station's phone today, hadn't bothered to ask. "For the last time, Chuck. You've got to get last names. Every call. Over."

"Sorry, Sheriff. Over."

I sighed. *Shit.* At this point, tracking down details myself would take less time than trying to relay them through Chuck. "Tell Larry I'm on my way. Over and out."

The grocery bags in the back of my Bronco rustled as I slowed to make a U-turn on Main Street. So much for dinner at home tonight.

I reached for the radio, changing the channel before I lifted the mic again and said Mom's handle. "Knitting Needles."

Linda Raynes loved to knit. The woman went nowhere without her needles, hence her handle. It took her a minute to answer. "Knitting Needles here."

"Sorry, Mom, I'll be late for dinner. Over."

"Again?" Her disappointment was as cold as tonight's below-zero temperature. She was sick of me getting called in on Sunday evenings too. "Well, that's how it goes, I guess. I'll feed Spencer. Over."

"Appreciate it. Hopefully, I won't be long. Over and out." I hung up the radio and hit the gas pedal, speeding past the remaining buildings in town.

The highway stretched ahead, bordered by towering evergreens as it curved through Dalton's mountain valley. Of course, this call meant I'd have to drive out to Cotters Lake. Heaven forbid it was somewhere in town, somewhere close.

"Son of a bitch." I promised Spencer we'd have fried chicken tonight. That Mom could spend the evening with him as a grandmother, not babysitter. We'd planned to play a card game, then watch TV.

There was a playoff game Spencer and I wanted to watch. Neither of us were diehard Miami Dolphins fans, but we both enjoyed watching Dan Marino play. Maybe if I hurried, I could salvage part of the evening. At least spend an hour or two with my kid.

Except the moment I turned off the highway, I knew this wasn't going to be a quick trip. The narrow road that led to Cotters Lake was covered in snow, and there was only so fast I could drive on the icy ruts.

There'd be no hurrying, not tonight.

My hands strangled the wheel as I followed the road, deeper and deeper into the forest. My headlights bounced from one tree trunk to the next. A few overgrown branches smacked the Bronco's side mirrors.

There weren't many people who lived on Cotters Lake, even fewer who stayed through the winter. Most houses up this way were summer cabins.

Those few who did stay year-round were, well . . . reclusive. People who didn't need to come to town often. Who didn't care when the road was snowed closed and they'd have to wait a week or two for the county to send up a grader to get it plowed.

Who was this *Ilsa?* I didn't know anyone up here named Ilsa. But the name . . . it was familiar.

By the time I made it to the lake, I still hadn't placed it. Maybe a relative of Sue Anne's? She was always yapping about her many, many cousins from Idaho whenever I bumped into her at IGA.

A solid stream of smoke billowed from Sue Anne's chimney as her log A-frame came into view. Her round face was pressed against the glass in her living room.

The next house I came to was Robert Aaron's place. Every light seemed to be on, illuminating his home like a torch.

Five hundred yards later, tucked into a cluster of trees and perched beside the lake, was Ike's cabin. The last on the road along Cotters Lake.

I'd expected it to be dark, but golden light spilled from the windows. A plume of smoke trickled from the chimney. And parked beside Ike's two-tone teal and silver Ford Ranger truck was a mint-green Volkswagen Rabbit.

"Ilsa." I snapped my fingers as it clicked. Ike's daughter.

He hadn't talked about her much, at least to me. The last time had been years ago. From what I'd gathered, they were estranged. Her choice, not his.

What was she doing out here? I parked beside Larry's cruiser, then stretched for the jockey box, snagging a flashlight and the pair of leather gloves Spencer had bought me for Christmas. With them on, I stepped outside, just in time to hear a woman's voice carry from the cabin's open front door.

"That window. Right there." She pointed to the side of the house as she barked at Larry. "He was standing right there, staring at me."

"Ma'am—"

She growled. "Deputy, please stop calling me ma'am and find the creep spying on me."

Hell. I did not have the energy to deal with a pissed-off woman tonight.

I blew out a long breath and made my way toward the cabin, glancing around as I walked. Footprints littered the snow. Some small. Some large.

"Larry," I said as I came up behind him.

He whirled from his position on the stoop, his eyes wide and his belly straining the zipper on his black department coat. His frame sagged when he spotted me. "Sheriff."

"What's the problem?"

"I, uh . . ." He shifted his large frame out of the way.

"Are you his boss?" The woman inside stepped forward, crossing her arms over her chest. She was dressed in a cable-knit cream sweater and a pair of jeans that accented her long, toned legs.

Her dark hair was pulled into a ponytail, the curls thick and silky draped over one shoulder. Her nose, upturned slightly at the tip, was dusted with freckles. She had a square face, bold but elegant, with full, pouty lips.

I rocked slightly on my heels. This woman was a knockout. Definitely not what I'd expected to find on Cotters Lake.

Her big brown eyes locked with mine, and she arched a delicate eyebrow as she waited for me to answer her question.

"Yes, I'm his boss. Sheriff Cosi Raynes."

"Ilsa Poe."

"Ike's daughter. I didn't realize you were in Dalton."

"I've only been here a week."

A week was plenty of time for news to run through town. Especially considering Sue Anne kept nothing from the prayer chain. Newcomers were always the rumor mill's hot topic in our small town, and no matter how many years I'd tried to avoid local gossip, it always seemed to find its way to the station.

But there hadn't been a word about Ilsa.

Well, after tonight, that would change. Between Sue Anne, Larry and Chuck, the town would be abuzz come tomorrow morning.

Ilsa cast Larry a sideways glare as she stepped past him. "There was a man sneaking around the house. He was staring at me through my kitchen window."

Probably because she was the most beautiful woman to grace Dalton in decades. At the moment, I was struggling not to stare myself.

"Can you describe him?" I asked.

"No." She pursed her lips. "He was wearing a ski mask."

"Cold night." My breath billowed to prove my point.

"Or he didn't want to be seen as he was violating my privacy."

Now I understood why Larry had asked for backup. He could break up a bar fight in less than a minute, go toe-to-toe with any man in Dalton County. His six-foot-five frame was intimidating, part of why I'd hired him, even though he was usually a giant teddy bear. But when it came to spirited, pretty women? He lost his nerve and, more often than not, put his foot in his mouth.

"Would you mind if I take a look around?" I asked.

She swept out an arm. "By all means."

I jerked my chin for Larry to follow me around the corner of the cabin. "Okay, what's going on?"

He pulled off his stocking cap, raking a hand through his curly blond hair before putting the hat on again. His cheeks were ruddy from the cold. "I got here and introduced myself. She was scared and shaking, so I tried to be nice. I told her it was probably a neighbor. You know how Sue Anne and Robert get. Figured I'd find their tracks in the snow and follow them to whoever was nosing around."

Exactly what I would have done. "Then why am I here, Larry?"

"There, um . . . there aren't any tracks."

I blinked. "What?"

"I circled the whole house. Twice. Couldn't find anything. I told her there were no signs anywhere and asked if she'd been drinking."

Oh, hell. I swallowed a groan. "Let me take a look around. Maybe it's best you head into town."

"Sorry, boss. I didn't mean to insult her."

"I know. I'll handle it." I clapped him on the shoulder, then nodded to his cruiser. "See you tomorrow at the station."

As he lumbered across the icy driveway, I stepped into the snow-covered yard and pulled the small flashlight from my pocket. There might not have been tracks earlier, but they were everywhere now. I recognized Larry's size thirteens as I circled the house as well as a smaller pair, probably Ilsa's.

But there were no tracks cutting through the yard. No sign of a visitor coming off the driveway. So I headed for the front door, raising my hand to knock.

It whipped open before I had the chance.

"Well?" Ilsa asked.

"I'm sorry, Miss Poe. I don't see signs of anyone but you and Larry."

Her nostrils flared. "I'm not making this up."

"Didn't say you were."

"He was out there." Ilsa's arms wrapped around her middle. "He was watching me. There have to be tracks somewhere. What about right along the house?"

There was a sliver of space beside the log exterior, six narrow inches where the eaves protected the ground from snow. "Could someone have shimmied along the house? Yeah. But it's unlikely."

There were dark circles under her eyes. Exhaustion written all over her face. Sometimes, when people were tired, their minds played tricks on them.

She rubbed at her temples, doubt filling her expression. "I swear, it looked like a person watching. And as soon as I looked at him, he ran off."

"Probably a neighbor trying to hide the fact that they were here." Though that neighbor still would have left tracks.

"That's what your deputy said."

"You've got two nosy neighbors in Sue Anne and Robert."

"But instead of knocking on the door and introducing themselves, they spy on me?"

"I wouldn't put it past Sue Anne. Look, it's dark. It will be a lot easier to look around come daylight. How about I send someone out tomorrow to have a look around?"

She sighed, shoulders curling in on themselves. "All right."

"Are you going to be okay out here? We haven't seen the worst of winter yet either. Folks can get stranded out here for weeks." This secluded cabin wasn't a great place for a single woman. Plus there were plenty of bears and mountain lions that called these woods home.

"I appreciate the warning, Sheriff. I'll be fine," she said as a slight breeze lifted a few errant strands of her hair. It carried her faint perfume, citrus and vanilla, sweet and clean. The kind of scent a man breathes in deep, holds in his lungs.

Damn. I took a step away. A gorgeous woman who smelled that good? Trouble. I'd learned a long time ago to stay away from women who meant trouble.

"Sorry about your dad." My manners kept me from walking away without condolences. "He was a good man."

"Was he?" The question was asked so quietly I almost missed it.

"Yes, he was."

Ike had been a good man. Sad. Lonely. Withdrawn. But a good man.

I'd been at the station when the call had come in the day he died. His boat had been spotted drifting next to Cotters Island, without Ike at the motor. We'd found his body washed up on shore not far from the boat.

From what we could tell, he'd gone out fishing one morning. He must have slipped and hit his head, then fallen into the water.

The last time I'd seen him, Ike had been at the bar, nursing a beer. He'd worn a haunted look, the expression of a man whose heart was broken.

If Ilsa wanted to know about her father, she'd have to ask. It was cold outside. And I was late for dinner.

"Good night." I lifted a hand to wave goodbye.

She had already turned to lock herself in the cabin.

The drive home was slow, and the fried chicken I'd picked up at the grocery store had been in the back for so long that the Bronco and everything inside, including me, smelled like grease by the time I pulled into my garage. Good thing Spencer and I both preferred our fried chicken cold.

I hauled the paper bags inside, toeing off my boots in the entryway as Mom came storming through the living room.

"Hi. What's wrong?" I asked.

Her long brown hair, streaked with gray, was coming out of its braid, like she'd been tugging on the end. She grabbed her coat from the hook beside the door. "Oh, nothing. My grandson is just testing my limits. Apparently, when I go through his schoolwork because I have the audacity to care about his grades, I'm invading his privacy and now he doesn't trust me."

I missed the days when I'd come home to smiles. "Sorry. I'll talk to him."

"Good luck." She didn't bother putting on her coat. She just ripped open the door and made sure to slam it behind her.

I pinched the bridge of my nose. "Spencer."

No answer.

Damn it. I carried the groceries into the kitchen. A half-eaten plate of beef stroganoff lay abandoned beside the sink. Next to it was a math test.

The red F in the upper right corner was circled twice.

What the shit? Math was Spencer's best subject. Meaning he had a B minus. In everything else he was lucky to get a D. That B minus was carrying his grade point average and meant he could stay on the basketball team. If he flunked math, the coach would sit him on the bench. And if Spencer didn't have basketball to fill up his free time, then he'd find something else to do, something that would likely get his ass in trouble.

"Spencer," I hollered, this time with more bite. This yell, he'd better not ignore.

His bedroom door opened, and he came down the hallway that led toward his end of the house. But when he reached the kitchen, he didn't cross the threshold. He hovered in the hall with a scowl.

His Levi's were rolled up at his ankles. His plaid shirt was unbuttoned, revealing the plain white T-shirt underneath. There was a hole in the toe of his sock, a pair I'd told him to toss ten times.

I lifted the test. "What is this?"

Spencer huffed and crossed his arms. "Ask Grandma. She's the one who went through my things without asking."

"Because she cares. Lay off your grandma." I sighed, dragging a hand over my face.

"She didn't even ask. She just went to my room and dug into my backpack."

"I said, lay off."

His nostrils flared. A *fuck you* was written all over his face—he had the brains to keep his mouth shut. But I was taking Mom's side, which meant now he was pissed at us both.

This kid. Fourteen and we were constantly butting heads.

Mom said Spencer was exactly like me and had been since he was born. We had the same brown hair. The same hazel eyes. The same chin and nose. When he filled out his frame and grew a few more inches, we'd probably have the same build.

All he'd be missing was a mustache.

But when Mom reminded me that my son was mine in every sense of the word, it had nothing to do with our looks. She was talking about attitude.

I was stubborn. My son? Gave stubborn a whole new meaning.

"Explain," I ordered.

"What's there to explain? The new teacher gave us a test. I failed. Seems pretty cut and dry to me."

My molars ground together as I fought to keep my cool. That smartass tone of his was becoming a habit, and it grated on my last nerve. But over the last couple of years, I'd learned to pick my battles.

Mom liked to remind me that when I was fourteen, I'd been a smartass shithead too.

"What new teacher?" I asked. "What happened to Mrs. Riley?"

"She had a baby."

"Already? I didn't think she was due until spring."

Spencer blinked.

"Okay, so this new teacher flunked your test."

"Says F, doesn't it?"

"Easy," I warned.

That earned me an eye roll.

I fucking hated eye rolls.

"Did you try?" I regretted the question the moment it flew out of my mouth.

Spencer's eyes narrowed. His arms uncrossed and his hands balled into fists at his sides. Then he was gone, stomping to his bedroom and slamming the door.

"Shit." I flung the test through the air, letting it float to the floor.

He couldn't fail math. It wasn't an option. Getting benched wasn't an option. Basketball was the only time Spencer smiled. He loved that team and sport. He was good too, the only freshman on varsity.

How could he fail? Spencer was smart. A lack of intelligence wasn't the problem. But when it came to schoolwork, he applied the bare minimum.

Maybe another father would have pushed harder. Would have hounded his son to get perfect grades. But Spencer and I were at each other's throats lately. At this point, I just wanted him to graduate.

I picked up the test, setting it on the table in the corner of the kitchen. Then I made my way down the hall, knocking on Spencer's door.

"What?" he snapped.

I turned the knob, surprised he hadn't locked me out. "Can we talk?"

He was on his bed, tossing a baseball toward the ceiling. "What's there to talk about? I flunked. I don't want to talk."

"About math? Or the letter?"

Spencer snatched the ball from midair, shoving up to his feet so fast, a move like that would have made me dizzy. Then he threw it at the wood-paneled wall so hard it filled the room with a *thwack*. "No, Dad. It's not about the letter."

"Okay." Definitely about the letter.

"I failed a test. The new teacher is a hard-ass, and now I'll probably get kicked off the basketball team." Spencer's voice cracked.

And with it, my heart.

"I'll talk to your teacher," I said. "Find out if there's some extra credit or something we can do."

He scoffed. "We?"

"I'm decent at math."

Spencer picked up the ball from the floor and flopped back on his bed, tossing it in the air again. "Whatever."

Whatever pissed me off almost as much as an eye roll, but I bit my tongue. "I'll stop by the school tomorrow."

"Good luck," he mumbled.

I sighed, backing away from the door, but before I retreated to my room to change and fold laundry, I paused. "What's this teacher's name?"

"Miss Poe."

Of course it was. *Fuck.*

Chapter 3

ILSA

"Bitch." The kid in the last row didn't even bother saying it quietly. He didn't bother waiting until my back was turned to the chalkboard either.

The brat said it right to my face after I'd told him he was going to have to stop talking in my class if he wanted to pass and graduate.

He was bold, I'd give him that. Part of me wanted to let it go. Pretend I hadn't heard the insult. But I knew that if I let him walk all over me, not a senior in this class would show me an ounce of respect for the rest of the year.

"What's your name again?" I asked.

"Paul Johnson." He chomped on a piece of gum, his jaw flexing as he chewed.

The cluster of boys who sat around him shared his arrogant smirk.

He was tall, his knees knocking on the underside of his desk. The collar of his polo was popped, the sleeves tight around his biceps. I might only have spent a week at Dalton High School, but if I had to guess, I'd say he was the quintessential cocky senior. Probably captain of some sports team. The guy crushed on by most girls. The guy revered by other boys.

A kid who was undoubtedly going to be a pain in my ass.

"Paul Johnson," I drawled his name from where I stood at the front of the classroom, "go away."

His nostrils flared as he kept chewing that gum. "Go where?"

I flicked a wrist toward the open door. "Anywhere but here. Bye."

He hesitated for a moment, chomping that gum so loudly it was the only sound in the room. The other kids swung their attention back and forth between us.

Paul glared. "You'll be sorry for this."

I arched an eyebrow. Threats only pissed me off.

He called me a bitch again before he walked out the door.

First period this semester was going to be rough.

I reached for the coffee mug on my desk, lifting it to my lips, only to remember it was empty. "Ugh," I groaned.

I'd gulped the last cold swig during eighth period when one of my junior students, a boy with blond hair and a short buzz cut—Harry? Henry? I was struggling to put names with faces—had asked if I would be his prom date.

I'd told him if he aced my class, I'd be his date.

Given a quick review of the assignment he'd set on my desk after the dismissal bell rang, I didn't need to worry about finding a dress.

A yawn tugged at my mouth.

There was probably a fresh pot of coffee, hot and strong and deliciously bitter, in the teachers' lounge. But I'd rather suffer a caffeine headache than venture to that miniscule lounge again. Not only was the tiny room cloaked in a thick fog of cigarette smoke, but I couldn't stand the thought of another forced smile or awkward wave with a colleague clearly not interested in getting to know the *temporary* math teacher.

The last time I'd ventured into the lounge today, the table had been crowded with a handful of men, all sharing an ashtray. As I'd filled my coffee mug, I'd listened to them talk about the Cold War and the farm crisis while speculating what Ronald Reagan would discuss in his upcoming State of the Union address.

Personally, I hoped President Reagan would cover social security reform, an opinion I would have shared had a single person made eye contact with me when I'd walked into the lounge.

The faculty at Dalton High School was as chilly as the draft blowing through my classroom window.

Setting the empty coffee mug aside, I grabbed the jar of water on my desk, taking a sip. The sour taste of pickle brine spread across my tongue, and I grimaced. Not that I had anything against pickles, but I preferred my water flavorless.

This jar was one of many that Dad had kept in his kitchen cupboard. In all my life, I couldn't remember ever seeing him drink out of an actual water glass. If he owned any, I hadn't found them at the cabin. But he'd had jars and lids aplenty. After he emptied one of pickles or jam, he'd turn them into his cups and glasses.

I'd tossed out those tinged red from spaghetti sauce, but I should have trashed anything with a pickle label too.

I yawned for the hundredth time today, checking the clock. Another hour to finish up some work, then I'd be calling it quits. Sixty minutes, then I could go home, swap this caramel corduroy dress for a pair of cozy sweatpants, curl up in bed and sleep for at least ten hours. *If* I could sleep.

After Sheriff Raynes had left last night, I'd been so freaked that I'd locked myself in my bedroom with a kitchen knife on my nightstand. Every time I drifted off to sleep, I'd imagine that masked face in my window and pop awake.

Someone had been in my window, right? The deputy hadn't explicitly stated that he didn't believe me, but when he'd wandered around the house and found nothing, the skepticism had been written all over his face.

Maybe my eyes had been playing tricks on me. It had happened so fast. He'd been in the window, and then nothing. I'd blinked and he was gone.

Or no one had been there in the first place.

God, I was tired. Eight days in Montana had zapped me dry, and the exhaustion went bone-deep.

Maybe I *had* imagined a person in my window.

Another yawn stretched my lips.

When I'd finally given up on sleep at three this morning, I'd gone through more boxes in the living room. A few had been packed with Dad's clothes. Another had been tools—when I'd gone to lift it off a stack, the cardboard bottom had fallen out, and I'd nearly lost a toe to a crescent wrench.

Tonight, I'd sleep with that wrench instead of the knife.

The tick of the wall clock seemed to get slower and slower and *slower*. I slumped in my chair, the wheels rolling away from the desk. This was officially the longest Monday of my life, and I was blaming my shitty mood on Paul. My rage had fueled me through lunch, but now I was simply dreading seeing him again in the morning, the little shit.

His bad attitude had infected the other seniors, some of the juniors too. Somehow, I had to turn this around. I couldn't be loathed by my students. They were the entire reason I loved my job. Seeing joy on a young face when a child solved a problem fed my soul.

Except Paul had called me a bitch. He hated me. It hurt more than I wanted to admit.

School had ended twenty minutes ago, and the kids were gone, the halls quiet.

In Arizona, this was the time of the day I'd spend tidying up my classroom and grading papers. Preparing for tomorrow. Chatting with teacher friends.

In Montana, I didn't have any teacher friends, not yet. And the very last thing I wanted to do was go through the stack of homework sheets on my desk.

The idea of seeing all the wrong answers made my skull throb.

A throat cleared from the doorway. "Miss Poe."

I swiveled my chair forward, my spine straightening as my boss walked into the room. "Hi, Principal Harlan. How are you?"

Stupid question. The frown on his face was indication enough.

"Fine." Harlan took a seat on the corner of my desk, crossing his arms over his chest. He was dressed in brown polyester pants and a starched beige button-down with a narrow taupe tie. His thinning dark hair was slicked back.

He was five foot two, if I was being generous, and whenever we met, Harlan made sure to put himself in a position where he could look down his hawkish nose at me.

During my interview—Monday morning last week, exactly seven days ago and coincidently the same day I'd started teaching—he'd paced his office while I'd sat in a chair feeling like I was being interrogated.

Thankfully, it had been the shortest interview of my life. Ten whole minutes, and I'd gotten a job.

The day after I'd arrived in Dalton, I'd come into the school, hoping they'd need an occasional substitute teacher. I had some money stashed away, but I didn't want to deplete my savings in case I needed the cash for my next big move. So I'd figured substitute teaching could pay for groceries.

Harlan's secretary had brought me into his office, and after a few questions and a quick scan of my résumé, he'd offered me a job as the high school math teacher.

Temporary math teacher.

Full-time. Starting immediately.

Since they hadn't been able to find a teacher to cover classes during Mrs. Riley's extended maternity leave, Harlan was the person who would have had to teach math. And apparently, I was the better alternative.

Beggars can't be choosers. His exact words.

Principal Harlan was a real peach.

"I just received a call from Dean Johnson," he said.

"Ah." Now this visit and his frown made sense.

Dean was Paul's father. He'd called earlier today to chew my ass for kicking Paul out of class. Dean hadn't called me a bitch. No, he'd used bigger words. Incompetent. Unprofessional. Ignorant.

That phone call over my lunch hour had been the low point in my day. Though I had a feeling this discussion might take me to rock bottom.

"He's rather upset at the grade you gave Paul on a recent test," Harlan said.

Ah, so Dean hadn't tattled about me booting Paul from first period. He'd called about the failed test.

"Well, he got the questions wrong." Which was exactly what I'd told the two other parents who'd called me today to complain about their kids' grades.

Math was a beautiful thing.

There was a single correct answer. No subjectivity. No gray areas. Algebra seemed to be the only constant, dependable part of my life these days, and if Harlan wanted to take that away from me, he'd have to pry it from my cold, dead hands.

"How is it that Paul had one hundred percent before winter break, but then he comes back to a new teacher and he's failed the first test in his senior year?" Harlan tapped his chin. "Explain that to me, Miss Poe."

I really, *really* hated the way he said my name. Mizzz Poe with the *p* stressed so hard, I was afraid a glob of spittle would come flying out of his mouth and land on my face.

"Do you want me to be honest or tell you what you want to hear?" The words came out so fast, I didn't have a chance to stop them. *Shit.* Normally, I kept those snarky comments inside my head.

Harlan's mouth fell open, his eyes flared. Then his cheeks turned an ugly shade of red. "Excuse me?"

Beggars can't be choosers. I swallowed the urge to throw his own statement into his flushed face.

This temporary job might be more temporary than planned. If Harlan did fire me, I guess I'd spend the next six months unemployed and leverage my savings. Dad had left all of his estate to me in his will—I hadn't gone to the bank, so the value was still a question mark.

But money wasn't the only driving factor here. The idea of spending all day, every day, in Dad's cabin? *No.* I wanted this job simply for an excuse to leave that house.

And I loved teaching. I loved kids. But I wasn't going to do a shitty job just because shitty had been Mrs. Riley's standard of excellence.

"I've already decided to make it a practice test," I told Harlan. "The students will be able to retake it again next week. But, Mr. Harlan, I tested the students on the material they were supposed to have completed last semester according to Mrs. Riley's notes. None of these kids are at the level I would expect for their respective grades."

From the freshmen to the seniors, all of my students were missing fundamentals they should have learned in junior high.

"Mrs. Riley has been with us for years," he said. "She's beloved in this school and community."

"That's wonderful." I gave him a saccharine smile. "But it doesn't change the fact that these students are behind."

Harlan's lip curled. "According to who? You?"

"Yes. I've spent years—"

"You're the teacher. Catch them up."

My hands fisted on my lap.

To quit. Or not to quit.

Damn it. I was not a quitter. "Fine."

Harlan hopped off my desk, jutting up his chin as he headed for the door.

"Could I please get a student roster for each class?" I asked.

"Why?" He didn't even turn around as he spoke. "You see the students every day."

I tucked my hands between my thighs so I wouldn't flip him my middle finger. "How about some new textbooks? The sophomores' books are falling apart. Most of the seniors don't even have one."

"Mrs. Riley didn't use them," he said, then walked out.

The irony of that statement was stifling. I waited until the sound of his footsteps faded in the hallway before I folded forward, letting my forehead rest on the desk. "Asshole."

"Is that how you greet all your visitors, Miss Poe?" The deep, gravelly voice made me jump.

I straightened as none other than Dalton's incredibly built, incredibly attractive sheriff walked into my classroom. "Sheriff Raynes. Sorry. I thought I was alone."

He walked with unhurried confidence. It wasn't arrogant or swaggering, just the stride of a man who was entirely comfortable in his own skin. That confidence was almost as attractive as his chiseled jawline and the thick, dark mustache above his upper lip.

The features I'd missed last night in the dark, in my fear and panic, were on full display beneath the fluorescent lights.

Broad shoulders covered in an open flannel with a white Henley beneath. Faded jeans that molded to long legs and bulky thighs. Scuffed cowboy boots and a tooled leather belt that held his badge and a gun.

His nose was perfect, a classic shape that would make a sketch artist drool and positioned exactly in the center of his face. His hair was a rich brown, and the strands curled slightly at his nape. Loose curls that were practically begging to be threaded through a woman's fingers.

Just not my fingers.

After all the ups and downs with Troy, after losing my father, I was in no place for a relationship. So while Sheriff Raynes was, without a doubt, the most handsome man I'd ever seen in my life, I'd appreciate his good looks from afar.

"Did you find out anything about last night?" I asked.

"No." He shook his head, taking a seat on the edge of a desk in the front row. When he crossed his arms, his biceps strained the fabric of his shirts. "I sent a deputy to look around. But other than your tracks and Larry's, he couldn't find anything."

So I was losing my mind and imagining masked faces outside windows. *Cool.*

"Well, all right. I appreciate the effort."

With his update complete, I expected him to leave. But he stayed put, staring at me for a long moment. Long enough for me to take in the gray and green striations in his hazel eyes. Long enough that I began to squirm. What Principal Harlan lacked in natural intimidation, Sheriff Raynes made up for in spades.

"Was there something else, Sheriff Raynes?"

"Cosi."

Now that was a great name. Unique. Bold. Fitting for a man so striking. *Cosi Raynes.* I couldn't imagine him being named anything else.

He shifted, digging a folded piece of paper from the back pocket of his Wranglers.

I didn't need him to bring it closer to recognize last week's test. "Yikes. It's bad if parents are calling local law enforcement to reprimand a high school math teacher."

Cosi stood, bringing it over. With him, a hint of cedar and juniper and cloves.

Of course he smelled incredible. That scent was as bold and unforgettable as the red F circled on the test.

"Spencer Michael," I read the name aloud.

"Spencer is my son."

"Ah." So this visit wasn't really about my call to the police last night. He was here to talk about his son's grade. With the different last names, I hadn't put that together.

"His last name is Raynes," he said, like he had a direct line to my thoughts.

"Then why did he put Michael?"

"That's his middle name. He likes to forget the Raynes whenever he's pissed at me."

I opened my mouth, about to ask why Spencer was pissed at his father, but stopped myself. Not my business. Not my problem. I had plenty of my own at the moment.

"Don't worry. Now that I've seen everyone's work, I'll be making it a practice test. Students will get another chance. That said, Spencer is behind in math."

"It's his best subject."

Ooof. That didn't bode well for his GPA. I laced my fingers together on my desk. If he was hoping I'd bend the rules so Spencer could keep a decent grade, he was poorly mistaken. "What exactly can I do for you, Sheriff Raynes?"

"Cosi," he corrected again.

A fantastic name that I'd love to use, but at this point, it seemed safer to keep titles in place.

He stared down at the paper in his hand, a crease forming between his eyebrows. "Spencer is a smart kid. But somewhere along the way, he decided to check out. He gives school the bare minimum. Enough to stay on the basketball team."

"And if math is his best subject, a bad grade means no more team. I understand that sports often trump academics for kids, but I'm not one for making exceptions. He'll have to put in the work to understand the material."

"I'm not asking for a favor."

"Then what do you want?"

He studied me for a long moment. "You're direct, aren't you."

"I'm tired. I didn't sleep well last night. Direct is a side effect."

"Fair enough." He folded the paper in half, returning it to his back pocket. "Honestly, I'm not sure what I'm asking for at this point. I guess . . . I wish my kid gave a shit about school."

"Well, if it makes you feel better, most kids at this age don't. They're too worried about girlfriends or boyfriends or sports. It's normal. I'll do what I can to help Spencer catch up in class, but education doesn't end in this building. I'm happy to send home worksheets to help reinforce lessons."

"Appreciated."

There was no ring on his left hand. Where did Spencer's mother fit into this puzzle? Also not my business. I'd learned early on in my teaching career that homelife meant something different for each and every student and stopped making assumptions.

With a short nod, Cosi walked to the door, but before he stepped into the hallway, he turned back. "Don't know how much you know about Dalton, but people around here talk. You're making a name for yourself already."

My eyes narrowed. "Is that a warning or a threat?" I wasn't really in the mood for either today.

"Let's call it an observation."

I didn't give a damn about his observation. I was leaving in six months. In exactly one hundred and seventy-four days, when this semester was finished and Dad's cabin was cleaned and listed with a realtor, I would be gone.

"How about you stop worrying about the name I make for myself and focus on finding the person creeping around my house at night?"

Cosi's mouth flattened into a thin line, then he was gone, the echo of his boots in the hallway fading with each step.

"Great." The air rushed from my lungs as I sagged in my chair.

Who else in this town was calling me a bitch? I'd been here for a week. Was this all because I'd given a test on the material the kids should have already learned? How was this fair? Or my fault?

Why was no one questioning Mrs. Riley?

Well, I guess I'd have to live with this *reputation.* I wasn't going to do a half-ass job when the people who'd suffer most were kids.

I glanced at the clock. Forty minutes to go.

Reaching for my red pen, I was about to start grading the worksheets on my desk when a knock came at the door.

Another parent stormed into the room, her daughter's test wrinkled in her grip. "Are you Miss Poe?"

"Yes." Unfortunately. I set my red pen aside. Forty minutes.

Then one hundred and seventy-four days until I put Dalton in the rearview mirror and said farewell to Montana forever.

Chapter 4

Ilsa

My fridge was nearly empty. I had a block of mild cheddar cheese and a roll of Ritz next to my gallon of milk and jar of salsa. The tortilla chips, also something I'd kept in the refrigerator with the crackers, were long gone.

I closed the door and surveyed the freezer next. One turkey pot pie and a Banquet TV dinner—Salisbury steak. None of those options were particularly mouthwatering, but my stomach growled, so I went back for the crackers, opening the sleeve and popping one in my mouth.

Rather than venture into town and hit IGA today, I'd chickened out and stayed at the cabin. Hiding on a Saturday seemed safer than risking an encounter with an angry parent in a grocery store aisle.

It had been a miserable week at school. Sexy Sheriff Raynes was one of many parents who'd visited my classroom in the past five days. Though unlike my other visitors, Sheriff Raynes was the only guest who'd been respectful. Everyone else had been pissed at me over what was now a practice test.

My intelligence had been called into question. One father had demanded to see my résumé. And Principal Harlan had made three additional visits with veiled threats about my employment.

I suspected the only reason he hadn't fired me yet was because he didn't want to teach math. Otherwise, I'd be history.

Yesterday, I'd overheard Mrs. McNally in the teachers' lounge say that Harlan was hoping to convince Mrs. Riley to shorten her extended maternity leave and return before the semester was over.

The lounge truly was a miserable place.

So much of me wanted to quit. To force Harlan to take over math education and say screw you to Dalton High. But I was too stubborn to walk away now. Besides, these kids needed me.

One of my sophomores wanted to become a pilot. A junior had told me her dream was to be a doctor. For the safety of his future passengers and her future patients, I'd do my best to impart any and all mathematical wisdom possible for as long as I had the chance.

Why was this so hard? I'd known coming to Montana wouldn't be easy, but this was more than I'd bargained for. So much more.

This was a solitude I'd never felt before. No family. No friends. Not even a kind smile when I crossed paths with the other teachers in the hallways.

Was this what Dad's life had been like? Isolated and lonely?

I put the crackers in the fridge and closed the door, moving to the cupboard where Dad had kept his jars. As I filled a clear Mason jar with **Ball** written on the side with water from the tap, I stared out through the window above the sink.

Afternoon sunlight spilled through the spotless, clear glass. Of all the cleaning projects that this cabin needed, washing windows shouldn't have been at the top of the list, but after last weekend's masked visitor—or my grand delusion of a voyeur—I'd made the windows a priority, and every pane in this cabin gleamed.

Well, almost every pane. I hadn't gone into Dad's bedroom yet, so only the outside of those windows was sparkling.

Sipping my water, I stared over the snow-covered yard to the dock. Where was Dad's fishing boat? I assumed the police had taken it for evidence. But where was it now? As far as I was concerned, they could keep the damn thing.

I turned away from the window and leaned against the counter, assessing the living room. There were still boxes pushed into the corner, but I'd made a dent in Dad's mess. Five more boxes and I'd actually be able to sit on the brown upholstered couch.

Finishing the last of my water, I set the jar down, about to get to work, when the phone rang.

I gave it a sideways glance as the trill filled the cabin, sharp and piercing. Not many people had the number to the cabin, but one of those people was Principal Harlan.

Was this the call when he told me not to bother coming to work Monday?

I plucked the handle from the cradle, pressing the tan plastic to my ear. "Hello?"

"Hey." The man's voice didn't immediately register.

"Who—" I blinked. Wait. "Troy?"

"Yeah, it's Troy." He chuckled. "Is there another guy who calls you every week?"

"No. But it's Saturday." It was Saturday, right? Or had I blacked out from too much ammonia in the glass cleaner and missed a day this weekend?

"Am I not allowed to call you on Saturdays?"

"No, you just normally call me on Sundays." Even when we lived in the same city, even when we'd see each other for dinner or drinks during the week, Troy always called me on Sundays.

Troy and I had met at the Italian restaurant where we'd both worked during college. I'd been a freshman, he'd been a senior, and our friendship had sparked over a love for pasta and garlic bread. One late night, while I was rolling silverware and he was sweeping the floors, I told him about Dad.

How when I was a kid, my dad had called me on Sundays. Every Sunday until I was seventeen.

The Sunday calls had stopped when I'd told him I couldn't come to Montana that summer. I'd gotten a summer job in Phoenix at a movie theater to save up for college and a car. That, and I hadn't wanted to leave my friends.

Dad and I had gotten into a fight. It was the one and only argument I could ever remember having with my father.

He'd told me I had no choice, that I was coming to Montana. I'd told him he'd have to come get me—he hadn't.

After that, the Sunday calls had changed. They'd become tense and awkward, dwindling to weeks, then months in between. Until they'd stopped altogether by the end of my senior year.

When I told Troy that I missed those phone calls, he took over Sundays. Even when he spent three years in Nashville for law school and I stayed in Phoenix to finish college, he always called, no matter what.

"I know we normally talk on Sundays, but I wanted to tell you, I won't have time to call tomorrow."

"Oh." The disappointment was instant, like being shoved to the ground. Even though I'd known, deep down, these calls would eventually end, even though I'd known it was better for my heart to let him go, it stung. "Is, um . . . is everything okay?"

"Yeah, it's great. I'm meeting Lori's parents. We're spending the day and night at their place in Scottsdale."

He'd never not made a Sunday call, no matter who he was dating. No matter who I was dating.

"I'm sorry, sweetheart." The endearment was salt on an open wound.

"It's fine." I made myself smile in the hope that some cheer seeped into my voice. "How is Lori?"

"Good. Excited for tomorrow. She's very close with her parents, especially her mom."

"That's great. Are you nervous?"

"A little." He laughed. "Can you believe it? Twenty-nine years old, and I'm nervous to meet my girlfriend's parents."

"They'll love you. I'm sure of it." I swallowed hard, my grip on the phone tightening as I squeezed my eyes shut.

I refused to let myself cry, not over a silly phone call. Troy was happy, and that's all I'd ever wanted, right? Sure, I'd assumed that eventually, when the timing was right for *us*, I'd be the woman who made him happy, but I guess that was Lori.

"I miss you," he said. "It's not the same here without you."

"Miss you too." It wasn't a lie and it wasn't the truth.

Did I miss Troy? Yes. But not as much as I'd thought I would. Mostly, I missed that he was a person I could talk to. No one talked to me in Dalton.

"How are things in Montana?" he asked.

"Still a mess. But I'm sorting through it. Box by box."

"What if I came out in a few weeks? I'm almost finished with this case I've been assisting on for months. The jury is going into deliberations soon. Once it's over, the whole team is taking a break. I could drive up in February. Help with whatever you need. Give you a hug. Sounds like you might need one."

"It takes two whole days to get here, Troy. It's twelve hundred miles. That's a long drive."

"And I'd make that drive for you."

Yes, I wanted some help. Yes, I needed a hug. But what I wanted more than anything else was to let these feelings go. To go back to the beginning and simply be his friend. And for that, for now, I needed those miles between us.

"I appreciate the offer. Truly. But I need to do this on my own."

"Why?"

"Because it's more than me cleaning out boxes and sorting through Dad's belongings. This is my chance to know him. My last chance."

"And you can't do that if I'm there?"

"It's not . . ." I sighed. "It's not pretty, Troy. You know the last few times I talked to him, he sounded different. Now that I'm here, it's worse than I realized. I don't want you to think badly of him."

"Too late," he muttered.

Troy had never met Dad, never spoken to him, but he had nothing but anger and bitterness where my father was concerned. Emotions I'd harbored once too. I'd spent years nursing resentment for Dad's absence in my life.

But at some point in the past few years, those hard feelings had softened. Dad had made an effort to call from time to time. To send birthday and Christmas cards. And I'd accepted the fact that my father wouldn't leave Montana.

This was his home.

I hoped that someday, I'd find the place where my heart belonged too.

"How about we talk about a visit in a couple of weeks?" I asked. "Finish your case. And then we can decide."

"All right. Talk next week?"

"Sure."

Except before I could hang up, he stopped me, a seriousness in his voice.

"Hey, Ilsa? I, um . . . about tomorrow. And Lori. I've never met a girlfriend's parents before."

"You'll be great."

"Yeah, it's not that. The only mom I've met before is yours."

"And she loves you to pieces. So no need to be nervous."

He sighed. "It's a big step. Meeting the parents. It's serious."

"It is."

"Lori and I. We're not . . ."

I waited, hanging on every passing second, hoping he'd say something—anything—that would make the pining stop.

Either tell me he loved me.

Or that he never would.

"What?" I whispered.

"Nothing."

Was that what we were destined to become? Nothing?

This had to stop. Before I wasted my entire life on a man who was meeting Lori's parents tomorrow.

"Bye." It wasn't loud. It wasn't firm. But it was the first goodbye I'd said to Troy.

I hung up the phone before I could take it back.

It was time to start saying goodbye to Troy, no matter which day of the week he called.

My heart was too heavy, and I was afraid that if he called back, I wouldn't have the courage to ignore the ring. So I hurried to the entryway and grabbed a coat off the hook, then went outside, letting the fresh air fill my lungs.

I tipped my face to the blue sky, to pure white sunbeams and evergreen treetops. With every inhale and exhale, the pressure in my chest eased.

What did that say about my feelings for Troy? A year ago, that phone call would have left me in tears. Today, all I'd needed were ten deep breaths and it was done. Over.

It wasn't going to take long to let him go, was it?

I tucked my hands in my pockets and started across the yard. Since I'd been back in Dalton, I hadn't spent much time outside. Other than a few trips to the shed, I'd mostly stayed indoors. Partly because it was so damn cold. Partly because the winter days were so short. But also because I hadn't been ready to face the past.

Summers with Dad had been spent outdoors, and the memories inside paled in comparison.

My boots crunched on the snow as I walked toward the dock. It was like walking back in time, to the summers when I'd start and end my day with a swim. The dock itself was built on the gravelly shore, about fifty feet from the house, and stretched far enough into the water that I could do a leaping cannonball as a kid and not touch the bottom of the lake.

I walked in no hurry across the yard, my breath puffing around me in tiny clouds. Then I stepped onto the dock, taking it slow until I stood at its end, overlooking nothing but a sheet of white that stretched from shore to shore.

And a small island, covered in thick trees, in between.

I tore my gaze away from the island, not ready to face it yet, and surveyed the opposite side of the lake.

The road didn't wrap all the way around Cotters, so there was nothing but untamed forest. Someday, someone would probably build a cabin over there, but for now, it was rugged and raw, the trees growing all the way to the water's edge.

Cotters was a true mountain lake, surrounded by tall peaks in all directions. The lake wasn't big, with only about three miles of shoreline in total, but as a kid, it had seemed like the most magical place in the world.

When I closed my eyes, I could picture myself racing off this dock, feet bare and hair wild as I went splashing into the lake. Shrieking at the chill, because even in the peak of summer, Cotters was cold.

I could hear Dad laughing from this very spot. He'd sit here, jeans rolled up his calves, toes dangling in the water. I could smell moss and dirt and cigar smoke.

The air was still and quiet. Not a breath of wind touched my face, almost like the lake and mountains knew I needed a moment of peace to lose myself in those memories.

I wished, more than anything, that I had spent one last summer with him on Cotters Lake.

The regret was something I'd have to learn to live with. For the rest of my days.

It was tempting to stand here, to lose myself in happy memories, but I was only dressed in jeans, and these boots weren't made for hours in the snow. The cold was already seeping through the leather.

So I opened my eyes, about to retreat inside, except the moment my lashes lifted, I gasped.

I wasn't alone.

A man stood on the frozen lake, about twenty feet away. A trail of footsteps led to the island at his back.

He stared at me with clear blue eyes and a blank expression.

A shiver rolled down my spine. How had he come up on me so fast? How had I not seen him earlier? How long had he been standing there?

I took a backward step, about to hurry inside, when he held up a gloved hand. My heart climbed into my throat as he walked forward, extending that trail of footprints across the ice.

He was about my height, five six, but since the dock was lifted off the water, when he stopped in front of me, I had to tip my face down to hold his gaze.

Tufts of stark white hair poked out from beneath the band of his green stocking hat. His face was carved with deep, weathered wrinkles, and his nose was round, the skin red at the tip. His bottom lip was chapped and cracked in the center.

"You're Ike's daughter." His voice was quiet and hoarse, like he didn't use it often.

"Yes," I murmured.

He reached a leather-gloved hand into the pocket of his faded black winter coat, pulling out a creased envelope. "He said you'd be comin' back."

"W-what?" Why would Dad think that? I'd told him I couldn't visit. That it would have to be another time. Yet he'd told this man I was coming to Montana?

"Said that when you came home, if he was gone, to give this to you." He held out the letter.

I slipped my hand from my pocket, taking the envelope. "What is it?"

The man didn't answer my question. He turned and followed his footprints away.

"Wait," I called, not sure what to say, but here was a man who'd known my father. A man Dad had trusted to deliver this letter.

He stopped and glanced over his shoulder.

"Is that safe? Walking on the ice?" I raised my voice so he could hear. It seemed to carry across the entire lake, disturbing the peace and quiet of the day.

"Safe to walk on. Wouldn't drive on it though. There's enough of a current it's got weak spots."

I'd skip walking and driving on the ice. "What's your name?"

His feet shuffled in the snow as he faced me again. Then he cocked his head slightly to the side, like he wasn't sure if I could be trusted with his name.

"I'm Ilsa," I said.

"Jerry." His voice cracked. He coughed and said it again. "Jerry."

"Thank you, Jerry." I offered a small smile, lifting the letter. "When did he give this to you?"

"Last summer."

"Months before he'd died? Why?"

"Don't know. I'm just doin' as he asked." Jerry looked around in every direction, making sure we were alone. Then he came back, leaning in close and waving me to bend down as he whispered, "Ain't no accident."

"What do you mean?" I asked even though the tremor that swept through my bones was answer enough.

"Ike wouldn't drown." His eyes flooded with tears and he sniffled, wiping at his nose.

"W-what are you saying?"

Jerry looked side to side, his eyes narrowing at something over my shoulder. Something in the trees.

I twisted, following his gaze, but didn't see anything but snow and branches. "What is it?"

When I turned to face Jerry, he was already gone, jogging away and moving more quickly than I'd expected from an older man.

"Wait," I called but he kept going.

My head was spinning so fast I was dizzy as I stood on the dock, watching as he reached the island, leapt onto its shore, then disappeared into the trees.

The only sign of him was the footprints across the lake.

A crow took flight from a tree at my side, its caw making me jump.

"Shit." I spun away from the lake and hurried toward the cabin, checking over my shoulder as the hairs on the back of my neck stood on end.

I hesitated at the door, searching for anything in the forest, but the quiet had returned, eerie and unsettling. The moment I was inside, I slid the deadbolt into place. Then I pressed my forehead against the rough wooden surface, breathing through my mouth as my stomach knotted.

What the hell was that? What had Jerry meant, it wasn't an accident? There weren't many ways that people died. Old age. Accidents. Murder.

Suicide.

No. Not possible. The police had investigated. Dad had died from a head injury and subsequent drowning. They were certain he'd tripped on something in the boat, hit his head and fallen into the water. They would have done an autopsy to prove it. Should I have asked to see the report?

My heart was beating so hard it hurt. Sweat beaded at my temples as I pushed off the door and carried the letter to my room, not bothering to take off my coat as I plopped onto the edge of my bed.

With trembling fingers, I tore open the envelope's flap. The paper inside sliced into my skin as I slipped it out, but I didn't feel the sting of the paper cut, too focused on Dad's messy scrawl.

Normally, his handwriting was neat and clean. In the letter he'd mailed with the Garrack gold story, it had been nearly pristine. Even his script on those napkin lists had been tidy.

But this he'd scribbled in all caps, like he'd done it in a rush.

FIND THE ATLAS AND THE KEY
THE TRUTH IS BENEATH A TAP DANCE

I read it ten times before I set the letter on my lap. My hands came to my heart, pressing against my sternum like I could push the pain away. Tears flooded my eyes.

This was nonsense. This didn't even have my name.

What was he talking about? Why would he ask Jerry to give me this?

I wanted to ask Dad. I wanted the whole story, not some garbled note. I wanted to smell Dad's cigars and go fishing with him on the lake. I wanted to sit on the kitchen counter and listen to his stories as he fried Spam on the stove. I wanted to hear him call me honey bear. To thumb wrestle with him on the drive into town. To feel his chin rest on the top of my head whenever I gave him a hug.

I wanted my dad.

But he was gone. Forever. And all I had left were questions and regrets.

This was why Mom never came back. This was why she'd told me to stay away from Montana. It hurt. It hurt so much I wanted to scream.

Instead, I curled up on my bed, clutching this strange letter to my chest. And for the first time in months, I didn't stifle the sobs. I didn't blink away the tears.

I stopped caring that we'd drifted apart. I stopped feeling guilty for not being here when he died. I stopped trying to put a lid on the jar of grief and let it spill free.

Chapter 5

Cosi

Somewhere beneath a scattered pile of deputy reports, a handful of manila folders and yellow carbon copies of traffic tickets, was my desk. Today, I needed to find it.

Mondays were reserved for putting my office to rights.

I hated Mondays.

If I'd known that becoming the sheriff would mean so much paperwork, I might have withdrawn my name from the election three years ago.

There were folks in Dalton County who thought I was too young for this job. That I didn't have enough experience. Most of those individuals had been good friends with my predecessor and former boss, so when I'd won the election in a landslide, their only recourse was complaining about me over coffee at the Grizzly Café.

Maybe those complaints would mean the outcome of the next election would be different, but for the most part, people seemed satisfied with the job I was doing. If I was lucky, I'd get reelected for another term and keep my job for a while longer.

If not, well . . . I wasn't leaving Dalton. Mom and I had moved here when I was ten, after my dad had died, and other than the years when I'd left to go to the academy, this was home.

If another sheriff was elected in my place, maybe he'd take pity on me and let me stay on as a deputy or his undersheriff. Or maybe I'd have to find a new career. That was a worry for another Monday.

At the moment, I had plenty to occupy my mind.

I started with the traffic tickets, plucking the canary-yellow sheets from the mess, scanning them as I placed them in a stack for my assistant, Pamela, to process later.

As the county sheriff, my primary focus was overseeing my deputies and the other staff members in the department. It meant I was behind this desk more often than I'd like, but it also meant I set the bar for standards. Dalton County was a safe place to live, and I liked that I had a hand in keeping it that way.

"Cosi." Pamela knocked on my door as she breezed into my office with another manila folder in her hand.

Her pumps clicked on the linoleum floor. Her thick, brownish-red wool skirt swished around her ankles, and her cream turtleneck sweater came all the way up to her chin. It was almost exactly the same shade as her pearl necklace and matching earrings.

"Here are the applications for the deputy position," she said. "I reviewed and added a few notes. Let me know who you'd like to meet with and I'll get them scheduled for an interview."

"Thanks." I took the folder, adding it to the pile on my desk. Then I gave her the speeding tickets. "These can get filed in pending payments."

"Will do." She tucked the stack under her arm. "Looks like you've got a mess here."

I chuckled at the disapproval in her gaze. "I promise it'll be clean before the end of the day."

"Good. Can I get you another cup of coffee?"

"No, I'll get it. But thank you."

No matter how many times I told her I could walk my ass to the break room and refill my own mug from the pot, she always offered. And I always declined.

"Your hair looks nice, Pam."

Her short gray curls were tighter than they had been on Friday.

"Thanks. Got a fresh perm this weekend." She smiled, lifting a hand to touch a strand beneath her ear. Then she swept out of my office, leaving me to get back to work.

Pamela had been the department secretary for twenty years. Lately, she'd been making a few offhand comments about retirement. I wasn't sure I could function without her, so I pretended like I didn't hear those comments.

She was irreplaceable. Calm and steady. A regular voice of reason. Everyone, including me, feared her temper enough that when we were in the building, we were on our best behavior. She wasn't afraid to smack a guy on the back of his head if he cursed in her presence.

I flipped open the folder of applications, scanning the names and Pamela's notes.

She thought four of the seven would be worth an interview. I agreed.

I was just about to go refill my coffee and give her the applications, when she appeared in my doorway again.

"There's someone here to see you."

"Who?" I asked, shuffling the mess on my desk into a single pile to sort later.

"Ilsa Poe."

My hands stilled.

I hadn't seen Ilsa since last Monday when I'd stopped by the school to discuss Spencer's test. Either she was here to talk about the person she'd thought was sneaking around her house. Or my son had done something stupid. But if it was Spencer, wouldn't she have called me into her office, not visited mine?

"Send her in, please."

Pamela nodded, and as she left to get Ilsa, I ran a hand through my hair, combing it away from my face before I smoothed my mustache, making sure there weren't any toast crumbs from breakfast left behind.

"Right this way." Pamela stopped outside my doorway, arm extended as she waved Ilsa into my office.

"Thanks, Pam." I stood as Ilsa walked inside and hell if my knees didn't wobble.

She really was stunning. A flawless face with exactly the right amount of makeup to accentuate her pretty features—the delicate nose sprinkled with freckles and a pretty, heart-shaped mouth. A lean, lithe body that moved with a fluid grace, like she floated more than walked. And those eyes.

Damn, did she ever have beautiful eyes. Chocolate brown with striations of gold and cinnamon that made her irises sparkle.

In another life, I would have given Ilsa my best smile. Dusted off some of the charm I hadn't used in ages and asked her out for a date. Taken her out to dinner, then dancing at the bar.

In another life, I would have followed this woman around like a lost puppy until she'd given me the time of day.

It had been a long, long time since a woman had intrigued me like Ilsa.

Except this wasn't another life, this was reality. I was a single father, and Spencer was my priority. I couldn't afford to be intrigued, especially by his teacher.

"Have a seat." I nodded to the chair opposite my desk as I sank into my own.

Pamela closed the door before I could tell her to leave it open, and as Ilsa took the chair, crossing one long leg over the other, the room became too small.

She was dressed up today, probably for school. Her gray button-down shirt was tucked into a fitted tweed skirt that hugged her hips and thighs, the hem stopping just below her knees. She had on a pair of leather boots that covered her calves. Her coat was pressed wool, black with a wide collar.

This woman was too fancy for Dalton. Not that she was dressed much differently than the other female teachers, but the way she carried herself, the poise and elegance, was not something I saw often around this small town.

Ilsa glanced around the office, taking in the framed documents and photos hung on the wall to my left. The oversized map of the county to my right. The potted snake plant in the corner.

None of it was my doing. About a year after I'd started as sheriff and moved my things from a desk in the bullpen in here, I'd come to work and found the office decorated. Pamela had told me she was sick of staring at empty white walls.

"Not teaching today?" I asked.

"I am. This is my free period."

"What can I do for you?"

She clasped her hands on her lap. "I'd like to know more about the investigation into my father's death."

Definitely not what I'd expected her to say. "Has no one told you about it?"

"The police officer in Phoenix who came to my house to tell me that Dad died shared the information he was given. It wasn't much."

"What do you know? I'll fill in the gaps."

"Dad went out fishing this fall and must have tripped and hit his head. He fell into the lake and drowned."

"That's right."

We stared at each other for a long moment, the silence in the room getting heavy. Her perfume filled the space, vanilla and citrus. Sweet and fresh, like those orange ice cream bars I got from time to time in the summer.

"There have to be more details," she said.

There were plenty. There were photographs of Ike's waterlogged body. Gray, wrinkled skin and blue lips. A gash along the side of his head that would have required at least ten stitches. After his body had spent so many hours in the water, his skin had softened and the wound had split open, all the way to his skull.

Details I would not be sharing with his daughter.

"There's not much more to report," I said.

"Did anyone see him fishing? Was he alone? I'll take the smallest of details. Please."

Was this about closure? About curiosity? "Why?"

She lifted a shoulder. "Because."

I frowned. "My mother does that. Why do women think *because* is a full-fledged explanation?"

A faint smile crossed her mouth.

A full version probably would have stopped my heart. Which meant it was time for Ilsa to leave.

"I'm sorry. But there's really nothing—"

"I don't think it was an accident," she blurted.

My gaze locked with hers. "It was."

"Are you sure?"

"Yes," I drawled. "I oversaw the investigation myself."

"But what if you missed something?"

I leaned forward, elbows on my desk. "Are you questioning my ability to do my job?"

"Did you not march into my classroom last week and do the same?"

Well, fuck. "Fair point," I muttered.

"I just . . . I would appreciate any other information you can share about the day my father died."

I leaned back in my chair and studied her for a long moment.

She pinned her shoulders and lifted her chin. She was a picture of steely determination. It only made her that much more attractive.

No matter how many times she asked, I wasn't giving her the gory details. But maybe all she needed was to hear the report from someone who could answer questions.

"Your father went fishing that morning in October. It was cold, but we didn't have snow yet. Certainly no ice on the lake to prohibit him from taking the boat. One of the neighbors, Robert Aaron, was out that morning too. They crossed paths on the water. They didn't see each other again. Robert went home before lunch. His wife was making goose and cornflake casserole. His favorite. He didn't want to be late."

Ilsa nodded, her fingers threading on her lap. "Was Dad alone?"

"Yes. Robert said Ike was alone. And it was Robert who spotted your dad's empty boat later that day. He called the station. I went up with three of my deputies and we recovered his body. I hauled in his boat myself. There was a sharp metal edge on the hull. And an anchor rope on the floor beneath his seat, likely what he tripped on."

Ike must have gotten his feet tangled and, when he'd fallen, hit his head on that sharp edge. I'd found the blood left behind.

Ilsa swallowed hard, her face paling. "Anything else?"

"No."

I wasn't just the sheriff. I was also the county coroner and had seen enough injuries and dead bodies to know a head wound like that would have knocked Ike out. The medical examiner I'd brought in from Helena had found lake water in his lungs and stomach, confirming the ultimate cause of death was drowning.

"Where is his boat?"

"We've got a small impound lot outside of town. It's on a trailer. Covered. You're welcome to it whenever you'd like."

She shook her head. "I'd like to sell it."

Couldn't blame her for that. In her position, I wouldn't want it either. "Pamela can help with that, if you'd like. Just talk to her before you leave."

Ilsa opened her mouth, but closed it before she could speak.

"What?" I asked.

"Dad was . . . acting strange. We didn't talk often. Our relationship was . . ." She gave me a sad smile. "We didn't talk often. But the last time he called me, something felt off. He begged for me to visit. He hadn't done that in years. About a month before he died, he sent me his will with a note that said he didn't want a funeral. He wanted to be cremated and have his ashes scattered on the island at Cotters in the spring. Two days after I learned he was gone, a letter arrived in the mail. He wrote it before he died. I guess I just find it all odd. Don't you think? Like he knew he was going to die?"

"Yes and no. Considering what happened with Donnie, it doesn't surprise me that Ike was, for lack of a better word, preparing."

"Donnie?" Ilsa's eyebrows knitted together. "Who's Donnie?"

Oh fuck. She didn't know? I guess she really hadn't had a great relationship with her father. "Donnie was, um . . . Ike's friend. Special friend. She died of a sudden heart attack about a year ago. Around Christmas."

"Special friend." Ilsa's mouth parted. "You mean . . . girlfriend."

"Yes." They weren't the kissing-in-public type, but when they walked side by side, he'd have his hand on the small of her back. I'd seen his truck parked outside her place on many occasions.

"Oh." Ilsa's exhale was audible. "I had no idea."

"For what it's worth, I don't think he kept it from you intentionally. Ike seemed like the type to keep personal matters to himself."

"Personal matters? I'm his daughter." She stared, unblinking, at her lap for a moment. "Wow. I can't believe he never told me about her. Especially if she died."

"It rattled him when she passed. Hard. He seemed to come to town less and less." And the times he did venture into Dalton, he'd been jumpy and standoffish. Ike had never been the jovial, chatty type, but he'd become even more withdrawn in his grief. "My guess is he started to think about his own mortality. Hence him sending you his will and last wishes."

Ilsa plucked at a tiny fuzz on the fabric of her skirt. "Do you have any idea who might have been outside my house?"

"No." My answer was the same as it had been last week and the night we'd met. "I still think it was a neighbor."

"Who didn't leave any footprints?"

"Could have walked down the road on the tire tracks. Came to the house by the driveway and was poking around. I'm sure they're all very curious about you."

"Well, if Dad was as secretive with them as he was with me, then I guess they have cause to be curious." Her expression tightened before she stood. "Thank you for your time, Sheriff Raynes."

"Cosi." Everyone in this town called me by my first name. She should too.

Ilsa opened the door and was gone.

Beyond the threshold, chatter drifted from the bullpen. Pamela's voice echoed in the hall as she escorted Ilsa out of the station. Hopefully they were talking about that boat.

Ilsa wasn't the first visitor I'd had in my time as sheriff wanting more information about a loved one's death, but this was the first time that a feeling of unease crept into my mind when the meeting was over.

The feeling wasn't doubt. I had no reason to question the investigation. It was more like I wanted to triple-check that all of my *t*s were crossed and *i*s dotted.

Ike's death was an accident. I'd been there. I'd seen his body with my own eyes. He might have been reclusive, but he hadn't had enemies. Who would want to hurt an old man out fishing? For what reason?

None.

I stood from my desk, needing to smell something other than Ilsa's lingering perfume. Needing a moment to push the unease away. With my coffee mug in hand, I went to the break room, refilling my cup. Then I wandered into the bullpen to check on how things were going with the deputies doing their own paperwork today.

By the time I returned to my office, my cup was nearly empty again. Except that seed of doubt hadn't vanished. Instead, it was sprouting.

I found Pamela in the filing room, a drawer open as she rifled through folders. "Hey, Pam?"

"Yes?"

"Did Ilsa talk to you about Ike's boat?"

"She did. I told her I knew someone who might be interested. I'll make a few calls, see if I can't help her sell it."

"Appreciate it."

"She seems sweet, and with her new in town, I'm happy to help."

"Yeah." I frowned, already hating what I was about to ask. "When you get a minute, would you bring me Ike Poe's file?"

"Sure." Her forehead furrowed.

Ten minutes later, the file was on my desk, my other paperwork forgotten.

And I was staring at the morbid photographs we'd taken of Ike Poe's corpse.

Chapter 6

Ilsa

Snow was falling outside in fat, pillowy flakes. They floated to the ground, adding to the thick, white blanket that covered the forest and lake. Only four windows in the house, those on the yard side of the cabin, weren't blocked by massive drifts.

It had taken me an hour this morning to dig and shovel out the front door. Even longer to cut a path to the shed behind the house and another to my car. Not that I was driving anywhere. My little Rabbit wouldn't be able to get out of the driveway.

I was well and truly stuck in this cabin and had been for two days. The storm that had blown in Monday had made me its prisoner.

When I did finally decide to venture into town, I'd have to take Dad's truck, if I could find the keys. They hadn't been in any drawer or cabinet in the house. Hopefully, I'd find them in the ignition. But even if I found the keys, I wasn't going anywhere until the county transportation department sent a grader to clear the road.

Though I doubted they'd plow until this snow stopped. At least the howling wind had calmed. It had blown hard enough last night to shake the walls.

The school was closed this week as all of Dalton hunkered down to wait out this storm. According to the radio broadcast I'd listened to before it had started to snow, it was predicted to end today. I would have loved another update, but the radio and the television weren't getting any reception at the moment. Both gave off static and a blaring hiss. At least my phone still worked.

I turned away from the window, sipping from the cup of coffee I'd poured myself after lunch. When I'd heard warning of the storm, I'd made sure to stock up on food and essentials. Part of me had worried the water pipes would freeze, so I'd left every faucet on a slow trickle, and thankfully, those drips hadn't stopped.

Maybe this storm was a blessing in disguise. With nothing else to do, I'd stopped procrastinating and cleaned this house.

I'd sorted through boxes. I'd scrubbed away years of dirt and dust and soot. I'd even ventured into Dad's bedroom to sort through his things and stow the box of his cremated ashes in the trunk at the foot of his bed, crying the entire time.

Ever since that day Jerry had brought me Dad's cryptic letter, I'd stopped fighting the tears. Surrendering to the sorrow, giving myself permission to grieve, had been cathartic. And when I wasn't cleaning or sobbing or watching it snow, I was replaying my conversation with Sheriff Raynes from last week.

I wasn't sure what to make of Donnie.

Every time I imagined Dad heartbroken and alone after her death, my insides twisted. How long had they been together? What had she been like? If he'd loved her, why hadn't he told me about her?

It hurt to know I'd been left out of such an important part of his life. Though it wasn't like Dad had known Troy or any of my boyfriends.

Donnie was simply another shard to our broken relationship.

As hard as it had been to learn about her from Cosi, his recounting of Dad's death had been just as difficult to hear. Though I suspected he'd kept the more horrible details to himself.

Jerry had said Dad's death hadn't been an accident. Knowing now that Dad had been suffering through his own grief, what if it had been—

I shuddered, refusing to let myself go down that path. I didn't want to believe that Dad had been in a place dark enough to take his own life.

Besides, if there'd been any hint of something other than an accident, Cosi would have investigated, right? I'd only spoken to him a few times, but he seemed like an honest person. He seemed like a man who cared about truth and justice.

Maybe that was me being blinded by his handsome face, but my intuition about people was usually right, and nothing about Cosi Raynes struck me as lazy or deceitful.

As much as I wanted the truth about that day in October, the reality was . . . I'd never know what had been going on in Dad's mind during his final hours. All I could do was say goodbye.

So I'd focused on the task at hand. As the snow had fallen outside, I'd finished going through every box in this house. Most of Dad's things would be trashed. Anything I'd deemed worth selling at a yard sale this spring, I'd carted to the small shed behind the cabin. And the few items I'd decided to keep were now stowed in the closet to take with me when I left Montana.

The reason I'd shoveled a path to my car was because I'd needed a place to put the junk. Anything that was going to the dump was now stuffed into the Rabbit, where it would stay until my next trip to town.

With the cabin cleaned, it was like the home from my childhood. The furniture was polished. The floors were mopped. The couch was exactly as I remembered, cozy and comfortable. And on the coffee table, I'd left Dad's glass ashtray and a box of his cigars so that when I sat down to read or grade papers in the evenings, I could smell the tobacco.

Now that the house was in order, it was time to turn my attention to Dalton High School. To the students who so desperately needed me to teach them basic math. Maybe I'd even win over Paul Johnson. Unlikely, considering he'd started calling me Miss Crone during each and every first period class, but a teacher could dream.

I refilled my coffee mug, and carried it to the small, round dining table that separated the living room and kitchen, where a stack of tests and my red pen waited. These tests were the same as I'd given that first week at Dalton High, and I prayed that the extra time I'd spent reviewing with students would mean the grades would be better.

Regardless, this storm had given me a welcome break from the classroom and time to formulate a plan for the rest of the semester.

Next week, we'd be going back to basics in every class. We were going to start with the fundamentals and work our way up. Together.

It might be too late for some of the seniors—Paul wasn't going to learn anything just to spite me. And a single semester simply wasn't enough time for most. The kids going off to college next year might struggle in future classes, but I'd do whatever I could to get them ready.

Except before I could dive into the tests, the phone rang. The chime was so much louder now that the house wasn't filled with boxes.

I crossed my fingers as I hurried to answer, hoping it was news about the county snowplow. "Hello?"

"Hi, cutie." Mom's voice was as familiar as it was surprising.

"H-hi, Mom." We hadn't spoken since the day I'd called to tell her I'd arrived in Montana. The day she'd informed me she was mad, and when she was done being mad, she'd call.

I guess that was now.

The thing I loved most about my mother was that she was real. Where my father hid his emotions—himself—from the world, Mom was an open book. She didn't pretend things were okay when they weren't. And I never had to guess how she was feeling.

That openness had made for a few dicey moments during my late teens when we'd fought and I'd threatened to move to Montana—we'd both known I was bluffing. But I could always be honest with Mom, in all things. Even in our disagreements.

"I figured you would have erased this phone number from your memory," I teased, stretching the phone's cord so I could hop up and sit on the kitchen counter. "I guess this means you're not mad and pouting anymore."

"Oh, I'm still pouting, cutie. I still don't understand why you're in Montana. But no, I'm not mad."

"Good."

"I'm sorry, Ilsa. You know when it comes to your father, I tend to overreact."

"I know. And it's okay, Mom." Even if I hadn't moved away from Phoenix, me being in Dalton was always going to be a hard pill for her to swallow.

She understood that I had to be the person to settle his estate. She also knew that it would be painful. And even though now he was gone, Mom was tired of me being hurt by my father.

When Dad would promise to visit for my birthday but cancel last minute, it was Mom who'd make sure I had a cake with candles and an extra present to open. When he'd vow to visit for a dance recital or junior high band concert to see me play the flute, but never show or bother to explain, Mom would be the person to clap twice as loud and make up for his absence. When he'd stopped calling on Sundays, it was her shoulder I'd cried on.

She blamed him for my tears. And he blamed her for robbing him of the chance to be a father.

And standing somewhere between their pointed fingers was me.

"I miss you," she said. "I went to JCPenney yesterday, and I didn't have anyone but the clerk to tell me if the pants I bought made my butt look big."

I laughed. "Your butt is not big."

"But does it look big in my new pants? I guess I won't know until you move home."

Except I wasn't moving home. A conversation for another day. A conversation I wanted to have with her in person, not over the phone. "I miss you too."

"So how's my girl? How's teaching? How's that cabin? Are you okay?"

"Well, I'm currently snowed in," I said.

She gasped. "You are? Do you have food? Water? Can you make it to a neighbor's house? I don't like you stuck out there all alone."

Probably because she'd been stuck out here alone once too. It was years ago, when she'd been pregnant with me. Dad had driven to Missoula for an engine part to fix her Oldsmobile. He'd only planned to be gone a day, but a nasty storm had blown in and they'd closed the highways.

When he'd finally made it back to Dalton, the road to Cotters Lake had been snowed in too, which had kept him away another night.

Mom had been scared and alone, trapped in this cabin with no word from Dad because the phone lines hadn't been run to this remote stretch of the county until two years later. And the storm had knocked out her power. It would have freaked me out too.

"I'm fine. I still have power and water. And they closed the school all week, so I have nowhere to go."

Mom hummed, a sound I'd heard a thousand times. The sound she made when she was worrying her bottom lip between her teeth.

"Really, Mom. I'm good. I promise. It's actually been fairly productive. I think I've got most of the house cleaned. The only drawback is being alone with my own thoughts."

She didn't laugh at my joke. "I want you to call the county office. Make sure they know they can't wait too long to get that road opened up."

"I will. As soon as it stops snowing."

Another hum.

"Mom, relax."

"When you have a daughter trapped in a cabin like the one where you're living, you'll know there's no chance I can relax."

"I'll be fine."

"Yes, you will be fine. And I'll be calling you daily until that road is open."

"That's too expensive."

"I'll spend my hard-earned money however I want, thank you very much."

"Okay." I smiled. "I'd like that."

"Have you talked to Troy?"

My shoulders slumped. "A couple times. He's been busy."

I had no idea how the meeting of Lori's parents had gone. When the phone rang last Sunday, for the first time, I hadn't answered. I'd stared at it while it rang and rang with my hands tucked in my jeans pockets.

It should have been harder to ignore him. It should have been agonizing to hear it go quiet.

Yet the moment the last chime had faded to nothing, I'd exhaled and gotten back to work cleaning the bathroom. That I'd prefer to scrub a toilet over talking to my best friend was proof enough our relationship was falling apart.

"Is he still dating that girl?" Mom asked.

"Yes. Her name is Lori. She's nice. Pretty."

"Not as pretty as you."

"You've never met her. And you're biased."

"Yes, cutie. I sure am. But I also know there aren't many girls in this world as pretty as mine. And he's a fool if he doesn't see that too."

I wasn't the only person who'd thought, eventually, Troy and I would find our way together when the timing was right. Even though I'd always told Mom that we were simply friends, she'd always seen through the lie.

Mom adored Troy, but her patience was running thin.

"I wish I was there to give you a hug," she said.

"I wish you were too."

"You know I'd get in my car and drive to Montana if you asked."

"I know." Maybe if I hadn't learned about Dad's *special friend*, Donnie, I would have asked Mom to visit Dalton. For her own good, more than mine.

Mom had a lot of heartache wrapped in this town and part of me wondered if a visit would help her heal old wounds.

At some point in her life, she'd been enchanted enough by this small town to live here for a decade. Most of that enchantment had been centered around Dad. He'd been ruggedly handsome. The strong, silent type. Moonbeams to her sunshine.

I wanted her to find closure. To say goodbye to Dad too. But if she came here and learned about Donnie, it might only make the pain worse.

For better or worse, her heart belonged to Ike Poe. It would crush her to realize he'd moved on.

Literally.

The boxes in this cabin had stumped me from the moment I'd walked through the door. Mostly because their contents were . . . normal. Well, except the cans. Dad had packed up his clothes. Photographs. Tools and tackle boxes.

Dad had packed up his life.

To move. It was the only explanation I could come up with.

He must have been moving in with Donnie. He'd fallen in love with a woman and planned to share the rest of his life with her. Until she'd died.

Maybe I had it wrong. But I had a hunch I was right. Dad had packed up his life to be with Donnie. To leave this cabin for her when he wouldn't for Mom and me.

Granted, Donnie had lived in Dalton. Still, it was another wound that I hoped wouldn't leave a scar.

I wasn't sure why he'd never unpacked. Maybe it had been too heartbreaking. Maybe he'd gotten lost in his grief and that's when the strange behavior had begun.

Was that why he'd scribbled that letter for Jerry to deliver?

FIND THE ATLAS AND THE KEY
THE TRUTH IS BENEATH A TAP DANCE

"Mom, can I ask you something?"

"Always."

I closed my eyes, steeling my spine. "Does an atlas or a key or a tap dance make any sense to you?"

She was quiet for a few minutes. "What are you talking about?"

"Nothing," I muttered. "Just some strange notes I found in the cabin. Wondering if they meant anything to you."

"No, sorry," Mom said. "You know I hadn't talked to your dad in a long, long time."

Not since she'd invited him to my college graduation and he hadn't shown. That was the last time she'd called this number until today.

"It's okay," I said, hopping off the counter. "It was a strange note."

"I don't know about the atlas or a key. But the tap dance. Maybe he was talking about when you were little."

"What do you mean? I've never tap danced."

"Well, you have but you were tiny. You probably don't remember. When you were two or three, there was a dance teacher who moved to Dalton. She only lasted about four months. But while she was there, she did a little dance class for girls around town. Tap dancing. You were so adorable. Your dad would push the furniture aside so you could have the whole living room to practice."

My gaze whipped to the coffee table.

"I didn't remember."

"It was a long time ago."

"Thanks. I'd better let you go."

"All right. I love you. Please stay safe."

"I will. And I love you too, Mom."

"Call the county about that road. Right now."

"I will. Promise."

She made a kissing noise in the phone. "I'll talk to you tomorrow."

"Okay. Bye." I returned the phone to its cradle, then faced the coffee table.

I hadn't moved it while cleaning the living room. There was plenty of space beneath its legs to mop and sweep without having to shift it out of the way.

With a few long strides, I was across the room, sliding it out of the way. I stared at the wooden floor, not sure exactly what I was searching for.

A tap dance?

"This is ridiculous." I closed my eyes and did a tiny dance, clicking the heels of my boots on the floorboards.

There was nothing. No mystery to unfold. Just me looking like a fool as I danced around my father's living room.

I sighed and reached for the coffee table's edge to pull it back into place. But as I tugged, the leg caught on the lip of a board.

"No way," I whispered, dropping to my hands and knees.

At first glance, it was identical to the others, stained brown and marred with a few knicks here and there. Except at the end, that raised edge, there were two small notches equal distance apart. Notches that reminded me of the hammer I'd put in a kitchen drawer with a few of Dad's other tools.

Scrambling to my feet, I rushed to get the hammer and bring it back. The claw end fit perfectly in those notches.

My heart leapt into my throat as I carefully pried the board up from the floor.

The scent of earth and wood filled my nose as I lifted the board, just enough for me to slip my hand underneath. My pulse raced as I carefully splayed my fingers, hoping I wasn't going to lose all five by reaching into a hole beneath the house.

I touched something soft, smooth and cold stashed beneath the floor. With tentative movements, I picked it up, letting its familiar weight and shape settle into my hand, exhaling when I realized it was a book.

Except it was a leather-bound journal, not a book, that I fished out from beneath the floor.

When I reached beneath the floorboard again, the only thing I touched was dirt, the loose grains wedging beneath my fingernails.

Pulling my hand free, I wiped my palm on my jeans, then freed the journal's snap button, flipping the cover back to fan through the book.

Dad's handwriting filled the beginning. Newspaper clippings were glued onto a couple pages, and on another, a Polaroid of a woman with dark hair was tucked into the spine. Was that Donnie? Why would he hide a journal beneath the floor?

The feeling of being watched made the hairs on the back of my neck stand on end. A shiver rolled down the length of my spine, and I twisted to the windows.

A person wearing a black ski mask stood on the other side of the glass.

My gasp was instant. A yelp escaped my throat as my hand flew over my mouth. Then the masked figure was gone, disappearing from the window's frame.

For a moment, I sat frozen on the floor, eyes locked on the window, expecting the figure to appear again. Then terror took over and I scrambled to my feet, running across the house to the front door, where I slid the deadbolt into place. The moment it was latched, I dropped to a crouch, crawling into a corner where I was hidden from sight.

Someone had been watching me. Someone had been outside this house.

For two weeks, I'd convinced myself I'd imagined it the first time. But it was real. Someone in a black mask was watching me.

My body trembled as I lifted up enough to see through the kitchen window. The only thing outside was snow.

Snow that had me trapped in this cabin.

I was stranded out here, alone. "Oh God."

A whimper tore from my lips as I dropped to my hands and knees, crawling through the kitchen to the phone. With trembling fingers, I pushed the rubber buttons and dialed the sheriff's office.

Chapter 7

Cosi

Sweat beaded at my temples as I dug my shovel into the snow, tossing a clump onto the heap I'd been building. Spencer and I had been out here for an hour, clearing the sidewalks and driveway so I could get the Bronco out of the garage.

This storm had blown in with a vengeance, burying Dalton in snow. The plows were out but they were struggling to keep Main and the highways clear, let alone any of the side streets or neighborhoods.

When the snow had finally stopped falling midmorning, I'd breathed a sigh of relief. Then I'd gotten to work. First, I'd walked to Mom's place a few blocks over and shoveled her driveway. I'd thought for sure I'd find Spencer still in bed when I came back, enjoying a break from school and sleeping past noon. But he'd been up and clearing the front stoop.

It took three more shovels to finish my side of the driveway. I wiped the sweat from my brow with the sleeve of my flannel—I'd abandoned my coat a while ago, too warm to keep it on. My insulated canvas pants and Sorel boots were plenty to chase away the cold.

Spencer, wearing a pair of my old bibs and his own snow boots, finished his section of the driveway and yanked off his stocking hat. Steam wafted from his sweaty brown hair.

I propped an elbow on my shovel's handle, taking a moment to catch my breath. "I'm going to head to the station next. See if I can't get the truck with the plow started."

The old Chevy was reliable, for the most part, but the storm had come in so fast that I doubted anyone had thought to plug it in, and with the below-zero temperatures, it might not start. But if we could get it going, I could help out around town and blaze a few paths in the roads.

Thankfully, most people had been smart and stayed home during the blizzard. Other than a few people whose vehicles had gone off the road into ditches, there hadn't been many calls to the station. But now that the snow was letting up, more people would be venturing outside. It was just a matter of time before there were accidents.

Having a truck with a plow blade mounted to the front was going to come in handy.

"I'll come with you," Spencer said.

"Really?"

He shrugged. "Nothing else to do."

It had been a hell of a long time since Spencer had willingly come to work with me. When he was a kid, the station had been one of his favorite places. If there was a day when I was off duty but needed to go in to catch up on reports, he'd tag along. He'd kept his own special spot in the bullpen and would spend hours filling coloring books or playing with the stash of Hot Wheels he'd kept in my desk drawer.

Even though my desk was different, I still had those little cars in a drawer. I had the coloring books too because I hadn't been able to throw them away.

"I'm going to get a cup of coffee," I said. "Want anything?"

"Can I have a Coke?"

"Sure." I set my shovel inside the detached garage, then walked down the sidewalk to the door and inside to get our drinks.

Spencer was waiting beside the Bronco when I returned, his hat covering his hair again. "Think we can drive to the station? Or will we have to walk?"

"We'd better walk. I'm worried the plows have created a berm along the highway that'll be pretty tough to break through."

"Okay." He pulled on his coat as I did the same, then together, we headed for the station.

The snow came up to my knees in a few places, but we trudged through it, leaving twin trails as we headed down Pine Street.

As expected, the berm of snow blocking the junction to Main was thick and tall enough that we probably would have gotten stuck. Spencer and I clambered over it, then set out along the plowed edge of the road, sipping our drinks as we passed the café and post office—both closed.

The station was only seven blocks from home, part of the reason I'd bought my house ten years ago. I could be at work or my mother's house in minutes. And Spencer could walk to school, five blocks in the other direction.

Someday, I'd love to have a place out of town. A bigger house with some acreage, a place with room to breathe and where I didn't have neighbors too close. But that was a dream I might never be able to afford.

My salary meant Spencer and I were comfortable. Because my schedule could be erratic, Mom only worked part-time at the hospital in their filing department. She wanted the flexibility to help with Spencer, and I made enough to pitch in with her expenses too. Anything extra, I squirreled away.

Spencer hadn't once mentioned college, but if he actually decided to go, I didn't want him graduating with a mountain of debt, so I'd been saving a little every month for his future.

I didn't need to be a wealthy man. I was rich in other ways. Mostly, I was rich because of the kid at my side.

There was a hint of peach fuzz along his jaw that he hadn't shaved this week. Spencer's face had changed too quickly from little boy to young man. He was growing up, and while I didn't want to talk about Gwen, we couldn't avoid the topic of his mother forever.

"So . . . we haven't talked about the letter," I said.

The easy expression he wore vanished and he shot me a glare. "Dad."

"Sorry, pal. I know you don't want to talk about it."

"I don't," he snapped, twisting to look over his shoulder, like he was going to turn around and go home.

"Hey." I stopped walking and put my hand on his shoulder. "You don't have to see her if you don't want to. No matter what you decide, I'll back you up. But you have to tell me what you're thinking."

His frame sagged, and for a brief moment, I saw my little boy. Unguarded hazel eyes that looked at me like I was his hero. Like I could solve any problem in the world. "Why couldn't she just leave us alone?"

"I don't know."

Gwen had written me a month ago, asking if she could visit Spencer. Apologizing for missing his life. Years ago, I would have tossed the letter in the fire and never thought twice. But he was getting older, and I did my best to treat him like the man he was becoming. He deserved a choice in this, so I'd given him the letter to read.

And I'd been holding my breath for a month, waiting for him to decide what to do.

He stared at our boots, kicking a scuff in the snow. "I don't want to see her, Dad."

"Donc. You don't have to." I hauled him into my side for a hug that he wiggled out of too soon.

I didn't give a fuck that Gwen wanted to see Spencer. She'd given up any right to my kid years ago. She might be his mother, but he was mine.

She'd left. Her choice. She'd left Spencer. She'd left me. She'd left Dalton. And this was the consequence.

She'd lost her kid.

"Will you tell her that I don't want to see her?" Spencer whispered, his voice barely audible over the sound of our boots on the ground.

"Yeah." I nodded. "I'll take care of it."

Gwen had left a phone number and return address on her letter. I'd mail a reply first thing tomorrow.

"Thanks, Dad."

"Welcome, son."

We walked in silence the rest of the way to the station. Only one vehicle passed us, a pickup heading out of town. Its taillights grew smaller and smaller as it passed the point where Main became the highway and stretched away from Dalton.

When we reached the station, I pulled my keys from my coat pocket to unlock the door. The moment I stomped off my boots on the mat, Alan came marching down the hall, dressed in jeans and his tan uniform shirt, pulling on his black Dalton County Sheriff's Department coat as he walked.

"Alan." I dipped my chin. "Thanks for coming in today."

We'd shuffled the schedule once the storm hit so that any deputies who lived out of town didn't need to drive in. Alan and his wife were having their fifth kid this spring and he'd been begging for extra hours, so when I'd asked if he'd cover Larry's shift, he'd volunteered without hesitation.

"You got it, Cosi. I'm actually glad you're here." He frowned. "Just got a call from Ilsa Poe out on Cotters Lake. Said someone is creeping around her place again. Looking in her windows. I just tried your phone and radio. Thought I'd walk over to your place but since you're here . . . I'm not sure how to get there. But she's scared, and I think we ought to try and send someone."

"Miss Poe from school?" Spencer asked, looking between Alan and me.

Hell. I dragged a hand through my hair.

If it was bad in town, it would be twice as worse toward the mountains. A truck with a plow blade would probably only get stuck. That road needed bigger equipment.

"No one is getting up that road until a grader can plow through the snow."

"Yep." Alan nodded. "I already radioed Hank. You can probably guess what he told me."

To piss up a rope.

Hank was head of the Highway Department for Dalton County. He did his best with a limited budget, stretching equipment and manpower to keep the gravel roads in good condition and manage snow removal. That road to Cotters Lake was not his priority, not when so few people lived up there.

"Shit," I muttered.

Ilsa was a gorgeous headache I did not need today. But I couldn't ignore this. If something happened to her, if someone broke into her cabin and she got hurt, I'd never forgive myself.

Was there really someone sneaking around her cabin? Who? And why? She didn't strike me as the type to make false claims. Which meant I'd missed something the first time around. *Damn it.*

Dalton was a fairly safe community. The railroad track a few miles south of town brought in the occasional drifter. Could someone have wandered up to Cotters? Maybe someone who had found an empty summer cabin and was squatting through the winter?

A face like Ilsa's was sure to draw notice. If a guy decided he wanted more than just a look . . .

I shuddered. It would be a pain in the ass to get up there, but I wasn't going to risk Ilsa's safety, the chance that she'd get raped or killed, because of some goddamn snow.

"I'll get ahold of Hank," I told Alan. "You good to hold down the fort here?"

"Of course."

"Thanks." I gave him a nod, then headed down the hallway with Spencer trailing behind.

"Dad, are you going to help her?"

"Yeah, pal." I breezed into the storage room where we kept the spare cruiser keys on a row of hooks mounted to the wall. It was also where we kept the keys to the plow truck.

I snatched them up, then hustled outside, grabbing the snow shovel that Alan had left inside the front door.

"I'll drop you at home."

"Can I come?"

We spoke in unison.

I shook my head. "Not this time."

"Please? I'll stay in the truck. Promise."

If there was someone out there, I didn't want my kid tagging along. And if by chance this person stalking Ilsa had returned, if the unthinkable happened, I didn't want my son as a witness.

"No." I put my hand on his shoulder. "It could be dangerous. The road is a mess. If I get stuck out there, I don't want you with me."

He sighed. "Fine."

"Come on." I steered him toward the plow truck, buried in feet of snow. "Let's see if we can get this thing started."

With the two of us working, it only took five minutes to get the windshield and hood brushed clear. We climbed inside, and with my gloves resting on the bench seat between us, I fitted the key into the ignition and twisted.

Come on, buddy. The engine cranked twice, and for a moment, I was sure the truck wouldn't start. But then it roared to life and cold air blasted through the vents. "Thank God."

I plucked the CB radio's microphone from its cradle and tuned the channel to Hank's frequency, pressing the button to talk.

"Sawdust, this is Cosi Raynes. You got copy?"

It only took a minute for him to respond. "Cosi, I'll tell you the same thing I told Alan. Over."

"You know I wouldn't ask if it wasn't an emergency," I said. "I'll make it up to you. Plow around town myself. Over."

Spencer and I shared a look as we waited.

If Hank said no to a grader, then I'd have to try and make it up there with this truck. It wasn't impossible, but it wasn't going to be fun.

"Meet me at the turnoff to Cotters in thirty," Hank barked. "Over."

"I owe you one. Over and out." I hung up the mic and put the truck in gear. Then I positioned the blade with the hydraulics and pushed a path through the parking lot.

I took the side streets from the station, plowing as I drove. "I should be home before dinner. But if you get hungry, eat without me."

"All right."

I stopped outside the house, letting him hop out. Then once he was opening the front door, I hit the gas so I could get up to Cotters Lake.

~

There were tears in Ilsa's eyes as we stood in her living room. Her face was pale, her hands trembling at her sides.

Those unshed tears were a punch to the gut. I didn't know what to do with crying women. The females in my life—Mom and Pamela—weren't the crying type.

"I'm not making this up," she said.

I wanted to believe her. I really did. But the evidence, or lack thereof, was hard to ignore.

It had taken less time than I'd expected for Hank to clear the road to Cotters Lake. I'd never seen him drive a grader so fast, but he'd been on a mission to bust through the drifts and get back to town. He was probably halfway to Dalton by now.

On the way up, I'd stopped at every empty cabin on the road. Those that had been winterized, their owners in town, didn't show any sign of entry or life. No tracks in the snow. No broken windows or picked locks. Was there still a chance someone could have been hiding inside? Yes. But it was slim, at best.

When I'd gotten here, Ilsa had appeared in the doorway, visibly shaken and panicked. She'd pointed to the side of the house, and without a word, I'd stepped into the snow.

There'd been a shoveled path leading from the front door to the small shed behind the house. Another cut from the door to her car. But nothing next to her windows.

Both shoveled paths were full of tracks in the snow. And from what I could tell, every footprint had the same boot tread pattern.

Boots that were still damp and sitting in a tiny puddle of melted snow in the entryway.

She'd told me they were Ike's snow boots. She'd worn them this morning when she'd gone outside to shovel those paths.

I wanted to believe her. I really did.

But at the moment, the only evidence I had were her own footprints in the snow.

During my first three years with the department, there'd been an older woman who lived nearby a forest service campground along Diamond Creek. Pearl Cline. It wasn't a normal week if Pearl didn't call at least once.

A suspicious vehicle on her road. A plume of smoke in the mountains. A group of teenagers camping and probably doing drugs.

Not once had Pearl's calls resulted in an actual crime or emergency. The vehicles were always legitimate campers. The smoke was from a tended campfire.

Ilsa's calls were starting to feel a bit like Pearl Cline's.

"There was someone here." Ilsa wrapped her arms around her middle as she spoke through gritted teeth. "I swear it."

"Look, there's a good chance that whoever came out here stuck to the paths you shoveled. They probably walked up the road and the grader wrecked any trail they'd left behind. I'm still thinking it's a neighbor. Both Sue Anne and Robert are . . . well, they're interesting characters." That was the nicest way I could think to say they were both incredibly odd. Sneaking up on Ilsa, wearing a black ski mask, was something I could see either of them doing.

It certainly wasn't anyone who'd driven up here. Up until now, the road had been impassible.

"Have you met them yet?" I asked.

She shook her head.

"If I were you, I'd go over and introduce yourself. At least to Sue Anne. If she is the person poking around, you'll satisfy her curiosity."

"Sure," she murmured, those arms wrapping tighter around her waist. "I'm sorry for the trouble."

"Don't worry about it."

She gave me a tight smile that was my cue to leave.

I headed for the door, about to see myself out, when she stopped me.

"Cosi?"

I shouldn't have liked the way it sounded to hear her use my first name. But damn it, I did. I liked it a lot. "Yeah?"

"Indulge me for a moment. What if there is someone out here? And what if that person killed my father?"

Wait. What? Now she was speculating Ike's death was a murder? Where the hell was this coming from?

"No one killed your father, Ilsa. I get grief. My dad died twenty years ago. He went hunting with a friend and that friend shot him on accident."

Her sharp intake of breath filled the room. "I'm so sorry."

"It was an accident. They happen. And I know what it's like to question those awful accidents. Dad and his friend both served. They were both plenty experienced with guns. And both were messed up from World War II. I spent years wondering if it was an accident, so I understand the need to have answers. But sometimes, we don't get them. Sometimes, all you can do is accept that your father is gone."

She swallowed hard, staring at me for a long moment. Then her gaze dropped to the floor. Class dismissed. "Thank you for coming up, Sheriff Raynes."

"You're welcome, Miss Poe."

The drive to town was quiet, and other than the occasional relay between Hank's crew on the radio, my own thoughts plagued me as I steered the plow truck toward home.

Everything I'd told Ilsa held true. I'd bet money that the person lurking around her house was Sue Anne. Maybe I should have stopped at her A-frame on my way out. Confronted her about it myself. Robert too.

But both would have denied it. I'd bet money on that.

At least Ilsa wasn't trapped out there any longer. If there was a silver lining to this mess, she could come and go from Cotters Lake as she pleased.

Even though it was only five, night was falling by the time I parked in my driveway. The sky overhead was turning navy blue as the last faint rays of light limned the jagged mountain horizon.

When I walked inside, the house smelled like burnt toast. Spencer's bedroom door was closed, and there was a charred grilled cheese sandwich on a plate in the kitchen.

I pulled a bottle of Black Velvet whisky from the cabinet above the fridge and poured myself a drink. Maybe it would help get Ilsa off my mind.

Did she really think her father had been murdered? What about our conversation at my office would lead her to make such a leap?

Ike's death was an accident. Just like my dad's. There was no mystery to solve, no killer to apprehend.

Accidents happened.

Accidents changed lives.

End of story.

So why couldn't I get Ilsa's tears out of my mind? Why, when I hadn't spoken about my father's death in years, had I told her about his accident? I could have left those personal details out. I could have simply reassured her Ike's death was an accident. But no, I'd opened my damn mouth and shared too much.

I sipped my whisky as I walked to the kitchen window. In the short time since I'd come inside, it had started to snow again.

Fuck. I didn't like that she was out there alone. But that woman wasn't my problem.

I drained the rest of my glass.

And ate the burnt sandwich my son had made me for dinner.

Chapter 8

Ilsa

With my plum briefcase in hand—a gift from Mom when I graduated college—I slung my purse over a shoulder and tucked an empty Ball jar into the crook of my arm. Then I flipped off the lights to my classroom and started down the hallway for the exit doors.

This was arguably the longest Monday of my life, except it wasn't a Monday, it was a Thursday. Thank God there was only one more day of school this week.

The students had been distracted and irritable all week. After their unexpected break thanks to last week's snowstorm, it had been almost impossible to rein in their focus. Four days in a row of grumpy kids meant I was grouchy too.

Though if I was being honest with myself, my mood had been garbage since last Wednesday.

Cosi hadn't told me straight out that I was losing my damn mind. But what if I was losing my damn mind?

From the outside looking in, I could see why he'd be skeptical. Two calls to the sheriff's office with zero evidence found to suggest a person was creeping around my house. I'd be skeptical too.

But this wasn't my eyes playing a trick on my mind. There was someone spying on me or the house or both. And whoever it was had enough knowledge about the property to not get caught.

The entire incident had put me so on edge that I'd hung up quilts and blankets over every window that wasn't blocked by snowdrifts. By the time I'd emerged on Monday morning to clean off Dad's Ford Ranger and drive to town for school—the keys had been in the visor—my mood was as gloomy as the skies.

What I needed was a change of scenery. Something different to break up the monotonous routine of driving back and forth between Cotters Lake to this school. I needed a date, even if that date was with myself.

So tonight, I was going to brave the local bar.

I was nearly to the exit when the double doors to the gym burst open and Spencer Raynes blew into the hall.

He pulled up short before bumping into me.

"Hi, Spencer," I said, giving him a smile.

The kid only glowered.

That was a look I hadn't seen on his father, but without question, I knew where Spencer had picked it up.

He stormed past me, turning down the hallway that would take him to the freshman lockers.

"Great talking to you too." I heaved a sigh and walked outside. "Have a nice night."

Spencer was long gone.

Cosi had been right about his son. Spencer was smart, but that kid didn't give two shits about school and it showed. His work was sloppy and rushed, the handwriting mostly illegible. I had yet to get a worksheet from him that wasn't crumpled or folded.

It was so frustrating to see a kid squander his intelligence. Every time I called on him in class, he never missed an answer. Not once. Earlier today, I'd asked a question about linear equations, and when no one had volunteered to come to the chalkboard and write out the answer, I'd called on Spencer.

He'd scratched it out without any trouble, then gone back to his desk to glower. If he gave his homework an extra ten percent of effort, he'd have a solid A.

The parking lot was mostly empty as I walked to Dad's truck. Nearly everyone had gone home for the day. The overhead lights flickered on as I unlocked the Ranger, the sky dark even though it was just past five.

I'd stayed a little longer after school to grade papers and finalize lesson plans for tomorrow. When I made it back to the cabin, I had other reading to do. Dad's journal was in my briefcase, and it was time for me to make it past the first entry.

He'd written a letter to Donnie on that initial page. A letter he'd penned after her death. A letter that had ripped out my heart. Tonight, no matter how much it hurt, I was forcing myself to read the next page.

After that date.

Trick and Sully's was the one and only bar in Dalton. It was located at the far end of Main Street, set off the highway about fifty feet, with a glowing red neon sign that read **BAR** mounted to the roof.

There were only a few trucks outside, each caked with dirt and snow. A filthy yellow dog with a clipped ear was inside one pickup. The moment I climbed out of Dad's truck, he started barking through the window.

I stripped off my coat, tossing it on the bench seat to cover my briefcase. Then I smoothed down the front of my favorite green and ecru fair isle sweater and snagged my purse from beneath the black skirt I'd worn to work.

After my last class, I'd gone into the bathroom and changed into jeans in the hopes that I'd blend in at the bar.

"Here goes." I steeled my spine and walked to the door.

I'd never been on a date by myself. Strange how nervous I was to eat alone, something I did every single day.

The dog was still barking as the door swung closed behind me.

It took my eyes a moment to adjust to the dim light. Cigarette smoke singed my nose, and I frowned. It wasn't as thick as it was in the teachers' lounge, but it was close.

The jukebox was playing "Ring of Fire" by Johnny Cash. Two men were shooting pool at the table in the corner, and the clank of cues to balls clashed with the music.

Three other men sat at the bar, each with a smoking cigarette between their fingers. One used his free hand to hold a cheeseburger.

Beneath the smoke, it smelled of grease and beer and liquor.

I weaved past tall tables and red-vinyl-covered stools, making my way to the bar at the back of the room.

The bartender, a guy in his late twenties or early thirties, set down the glass he'd been washing and walked over, greeting me with a charming, crooked smile. "Howdy. What can I get you?"

"Vodka collins."

He winked. "Be right back."

The three men seated at the bar leaned forward to stare. They each had deep wrinkles set around their eyes and bushy beards in various shades of gray. One was wearing a black cowboy hat. Another had his pearl-snapped shirt unbuttoned low enough to display a patch of fuzzy chest hair. And the third chomped on a bite of burger so slowly it reminded me of a cow chewing its cud.

Had I just wandered into Dalton's old man's club? Because I'd never been more aware of being the only female in a room before this moment.

So much for blending in with my jeans.

"Here you go." The bartender set down a square napkin, then my drink. Beside it, he left a plastic cup of maraschino cherries. "You looked like you could use a few extra cherries."

"Thanks." I gave him a small smile. The cherries were my favorite.

"Want to settle up or start a tab?" he asked.

"I'll start a tab, please. I might try a burger."

He grinned. "They're my specialty."

His flannel shirt was rolled up at his forearms. A white towel was draped over his shoulder. His dirty-blond hair was longer, the ends brushing his collar, and his eyes were a rich brown.

His coloring reminded me a bit of Troy. Though Troy would never have gone out in public with scruff on his jaw and definitely not let his hair grow long enough to touch his ears.

"Patrick Dougan." He extended his hand across the bar. "Everyone calls me Trick."

"As in Trick and Sully's?"

"Sully is my partner." He nodded. "Though he's in California at the moment, doing whatever it is Sully does in the winters. He hates the snow."

"After last week, I can understand why," I said, taking his hand. "Ilsa Poe."

"Nice to meet you."

As I returned his shake, it occurred to me I hadn't touched another person in a while.

I'd hugged Mom before I'd left Phoenix. And then . . . nothing. Was that right? Had I really not had physical contact with another person since I'd left Arizona?

No wonder I was lonely.

My students seemed to give me a wide berth. Principal Harlan hadn't shaken my hand when he'd offered me the temporary teaching job. Neither had Deputy Larry when he'd come out to the house the first time I'd called the sheriff's office. And neither had Cosi Raynes.

Why did that last one bother me the most? Did Cosi not want to shake my hand?

I brushed it off and took a sip of my drink. It was the perfect blend of sour and sweet.

"So you must be Ike's daughter." Trick leaned an elbow on the bar, giving me a devilish smile.

It was cute. *He* was cute.

"Yes, I am."

"Truth be told, I knew who you were when you walked through the door. I, uh . . . heard something about a math test that riled up some parents."

I rolled my eyes. "It was a practice test. Sheesh."

Trick chuckled. "Well, things have been fairly boring around these parts. People need something to bitch about."

"And that something is me. Awesome," I deadpanned.

"Don't let it get you down. Gossip around here is as ever-changing as the weather. Just gotta wait until someone else fucks up. Then they'll forget all about your practice test."

"And how long does it usually take before someone else fucks up?"

"It's only Thursday. Give it to Sunday. Last week was an anomaly with everything closed. I'm sure someone will come in here and get rowdy over the weekend."

"So you're saying I should be praying for a bar fight?"

Trick's grin widened. "Considering I own the bar, I'd rather you pray for something a bit less destructive. Maybe Dean Johnson's wife finally realizing he's been cheating on her for months."

I gasped. "No." Paul's father was a cheat? Was that the reason Paul was so angry? Now I felt bad for the kid. Sort of.

"It's not a secret." Trick shrugged. "Part of me wonders if Melody already knows but doesn't want to deal with it, so she turns a blind eye."

"Wow." I took another drink. "Paul is my student. For his sake, I'm going to pray for that bar fight. Sorry."

Trick threw his head back and laughed, and the sound eased something in my chest. I hadn't laughed with anyone in Dalton either. It felt good to share a smile.

Or maybe that was the vodka.

The only liquor at Dad's was a bottle of Wild Turkey, and I'd never liked cheap bourbon. Or any bourbon.

"Paul is a fuckhead," Trick said. "You might be the only person in Dalton praying for that kid besides his mother."

That made me feel better and worse at the same time. I didn't really want to pity Paul.

I shrugged. "So be it."

"What brings you in tonight?"

"It's been a long week. I didn't feel like cooking, and someone said you have great burgers."

It was partially the truth. This date with myself was also an opportunity to start asking people around town about Dad. I wasn't sure if Dad had been a regular patron at the bar, but there was only one way to find out.

"I'm biased, but yeah, burgers aren't bad. Want me to get one going for you?"

"Sure." It was earlier than I normally ate dinner, but the smoke was bothering my eyes and I didn't want to stay too long.

As Trick disappeared through a swinging door that likely led to the kitchen, I nursed my cocktail and took in the bar.

The walls were covered in wood paneling. Tacked around the room were countless tin liquor posters and license plates. There were neon beer signs for Pabst Blue Ribbon, Rainier and Coors. A pair of deer antlers hung above the jukebox. On every prong was a discarded bra.

Behind the bar were shelves teeming with various bottles. And above them all was a gold-framed mirror with **TRICK AND SULLY'S** gilded in its center with a black-letter font.

This was a far cry from the upscale fern bar where Troy liked to meet for drinks. But something about this place felt . . . right. I didn't need fancy cocktails or crystal chandeliers. This rundown bar in nowhere Montana suited me just fine.

It didn't take long for Trick to push through the swinging door carrying a plate with my burger and a heaping pile of french fries. He delivered it to me, then brought over a cardboard six-pack holder, the slots filled with a bottle of ketchup, mustard, hot sauce, and napkin-rolled silverware.

While I took out a knife to cut my burger in half, he went to check on his other customers, first the guys at the pool table, then the men seated at the bar. After opening a bottle of Budweiser for the guy in the cowboy hat, he returned to my corner, leaning on the bar again as I sprinkled salt on my fries.

"So how are things up at Bluebird's place?" he asked.

Bluebird. The nickname was a blast to the past. To summer days when Dad would bring me into town for an ice cream cone or trip to the store. I'd forgotten how everyone used his nickname.

"Things are good." I lifted a shoulder as I set down the shaker. "Maybe a bit strange. I haven't been to Montana in a long time."

Trick gave me a sad smile, like that statement didn't surprise him in the slightest.

"Did you know my dad well?" I asked, eating a fry.

"Yeah. Bluebird was never a regular." Trick nodded toward his other patrons. The regulars. "But he'd come in from time to time. Especially with Donnie."

Hearing her name still felt like a shock. Probably because I hadn't heard it often. But it reminded me that Dad had lived this entire life, had fallen in love, and I'd never had a clue.

"What was she like?" I asked.

"You never met her?"

I shook my head, then lifted my burger, taking a huge bite so I wouldn't have to explain why I'd never met Donnie.

"She was great. Funny. Had a dry sense of humor that I loved. You wouldn't find her without a pack of Virginia Slims. She'd change her cigarette purse to match her outfits. And she really loved your dad. She looked at him with stars in her eyes."

I swallowed the bite, forcing it past the growing lump in my throat. "I'm glad he had that."

"Me too." Trick nodded. "It changed him when she died. For a while, I saw him a lot."

There was something unspoken in that statement. That maybe Dad had used drinking as a way to survive the grief. Maybe I didn't blame him.

"Thanks for keeping him company," I said.

"Not a hardship. It was always entertaining when Bluebird came to the bar." Trick grinned. "He'd have these conspiracy theories and tell anyone who'd listen. Especially after he'd had a few beers."

"Conspiracy theories?" I picked up a fry, trying not to seem too eager. "Like what?"

Like a person sneaking around his house and spying through his windows?

"Oh, he was sure the stock market was going to crash and land prices would plummet. He was planning a trip to Missoula to exchange his cash for silver."

I hadn't found a stash of silver anywhere at the cabin. Maybe Dad hadn't made that trip.

"He'd come in and make a dozen lists on my napkins and tuck them in his pockets," Trick said. "Said he wasn't as sharp as he used to be. The lists helped him remember."

The lists that I'd found on napkins exactly like the one beneath my drink. "What about the cans?"

Trick's forehead furrowed. "Cans?"

"Never mind." Those would remain a mystery. "Any other conspiracy theories?" I popped the fry into my mouth, hoping Trick would keep talking while I ate.

"Well, he thought one of his neighbors was going to burn his house down because they were in an argument over a beaver trap."

"A beaver trap?" I asked, squirting a blob of ranch on my plate.

"Robert Aaron thought the trap was on his property, and Bluebird swore it was on his. I guess it got fairly heated because Ike came in with a shiner." Trick touched his eye. "And I heard from a nurse at the hospital that Robert came in with a broken nose."

Robert Aaron. The person who had allegedly been the last to see Dad alive. A man who also lived on Cotters Lake.

I ate my french fry, mind whirling as I chewed.

"Once, he swore he saw a bull shark in the lake. Told everyone not to go swimming." Trick ran a hand over his jaw. "What else? Oh, he was sure the teller at the bank was going to rob it one day. And he thought someone dug an underground bunker on the island at Cotters."

So much of me wanted to dismiss everything Trick was saying. To chalk this up to the drunk ramblings of a grieving man. Make excuses that Dad had probably been joking around.

But the mess at the cabin and the strange letter were hard to ignore. Maybe once I forced myself to read the rest of that journal, I'd have more answers.

"I don't think he was . . . well. In the end." The pang in my chest was sharp and instant. It was one thing to think about Dad's decline. Another to say it aloud.

"Be that as it may, Bluebird was a good man," Trick said. "I'm sorry."

"Me too."

The men playing pool walked up to the bar to settle their tabs, so while Trick put some cash in the register and checked on the bearded regulars, I ate in silence.

I was halfway done with my dinner when a group of four men came inside, their thick-soled boots heavy on the floor. They were younger than the others, about my age, and dressed in heavy coats and oil-stained jeans.

"Hi, Trick." The tallest of the men jerked up his chin as he unzipped his jacket.

"Chris." Trick's eyes narrowed as he watched the group pull out stools at a table in the center of the room. His focus was locked on a man with a shaved head and cool blue eyes.

My gaze darted between them, a prickle running down my spine as the temperature in the room seemed to drop. Whoever these men were, especially the guy with blue eyes, they weren't exactly welcome at Trick and Sully's.

Chris came up to the bar, hands planted on its edge. "Four Buds. Thanks, Trick."

Trick nodded, grabbing them from a fridge. As he took off the caps, he lowered his voice. "You shouldn't have brought him, Chris."

"He'll behave. I'll make sure of it. I told him not to fuck around."

"Any trouble and you can find another place to drink. Got it?"

"Understood." Chris nodded, tossing a ten-dollar bill on the bar and collecting all four beers for the table.

Trick's jaw flexed.

"Everything okay?" I asked.

"Yeah." He moved closer, leaning on the bar again like everything was fine. Though the clench in his jaw said otherwise. "Guy with the shaved head isn't from Dalton. He works with Chris and the others at the railroad. This past summer, he got into a pool game for money. Lost. Didn't like that. Met the guy who beat him in the parking lot. And did his own kind of beating."

I flinched. "Did he go to jail?"

"Yeah. Raynes hauled him in. Honestly, I'm shocked Jackie has the balls to come back to Dalton."

I picked up another fry but my appetite was gone. Between the stories about Dad and the strange tension in the bar, this date with myself was over. It was time for me to go home. "Thanks for dinner. It was great."

"Glad you liked it." His eyes crinkled at the sides when he gave me that crooked smile.

Yeah, this guy was cute. If we were in Phoenix, I'd make it a point to visit this bar more often.

Except this was Dalton, and while Trick was good-looking, he had nothing on Sheriff Cosi Raynes. A man whose face popped into my mind more often than I liked.

For so long, the man who'd invaded my thoughts was Troy. Strange how easy it was to forget now, since I'd stopped answering the phone on Sundays.

"How much do I owe you?" I asked.

"On the house."

"What? No."

"I insist. Let me buy you dinner. For Bluebird. Just promise you'll come back. No offense to your dad, but you're much prettier to look at."

"Thank you." My cheeks flushed as I finished the last swallow of my drink, then stood. "Night."

"See ya."

I crossed the room, fishing my keys from my purse, but before I could make it to the door, the man with the shaved head came to stand in front of me.

His blue eyes drilled into mine. "Hey."

"Hi," I drawled. "Can I help you?"

"Leaving already? I was going to buy you a drink."

"Darn. I'm all done." I sidestepped him, but he shifted, blocking my path.

"Come on, beautiful. Don't run off." He inched forward, crowding my personal space enough I had to step back.

"You're in my way." I leveled him with my best glare, but the asshole didn't budge.

He came closer, his head cocking to the side as he stared down at me. "I like a challenge."

"Goodbye," I said through gritted teeth.

He grabbed my elbow, moving so fast it made me gasp.

But I was quick too, and I yanked my arm free, refusing to cower to this man. I jutted up my chin, holding his stare. There was something wrong with this man's eyes. They were too cold. Too calculating. "Do *not* touch me. Got it? There's no challenge here. Just me driving my knee into your dick if you don't move. Now."

There was a commotion at my back, the scrape of stool legs on the concrete floor.

"Chris," Trick barked.

More chairs scraped until Chris appeared at the man's side, pulling at his arm. "Come on, Jackie. Leave her alone."

"Don't fucking touch me," Jackie snapped, and before I knew what was happening, his fist plowed into Chris's nose.

Blood sprayed as chaos erupted.

I leapt back, searching for an escape route. I was about to race for the door, but Chris recovered fast from the punch and barreled into Jackie, tackling him to the ground.

They tussled for a moment, but then both managed to scramble to their feet, fists raised and ready to throw punches.

I got the fuck out of the way, shying away until a table was between me and the brawling idiots.

Trick leapt over the bar, a baseball bat in hand.

And then came a flash of light. The door opened, a tall, broad figure filling the frame. The music from the jukebox faded to the background as Cosi Raynes strode into the bar.

He scanned the room, taking in the brawlers and Trick with his bat. The regulars had swiveled on their stools, beers in hand, to sit back and watch.

When Cosi's eyes landed on me, my knees wobbled. My heart skipped.

This man was breathtaking. Definitely too handsome for my own good.

His stony expression was fixed in a glower.

A glower he'd definitely taught his son.

A glower that said I was in trouble.

Shit.

Chapter 9

Cosi

This goddamn bar. Ninety percent of the calls that came into the station dragged me to Trick and Sully's. There was always some sort of trouble.

And Ilsa was standing in the middle of it.

Why was I not surprised?

I'd deal with her after I handled Jackie.

About ten minutes ago, Archie Lee had radioed the station. He'd been at the bar playing pool after work. He and a buddy were talking in the parking lot outside before heading home when Chris and a few of the railroad guys pulled up.

Jackie included. The dumb shit.

I'd told Jackie after the last bar fight he'd started that the next time I saw him in Dalton, he'd be spending more than one night in jail. But had he steered clear? Of course not. The son of a bitch never listened.

Larry and Alan were already on their way over with a cruiser. I hadn't waited for Trick to call about a fight. I'd just assumed it would happen. And I was right.

Well, Jackie had picked the wrong day to come to my town. I was in a shit mood and my patience was gone.

Trick walked over and killed the jukebox. Without the music, the bar became so quiet I heard the faint sizzle of burning cigarette paper as Leon, one of Trick's regulars, took an inhale from his Marlboro.

Jackie had shaved his head since the last time he'd been in town. But those blue eyes were the same. Always too mean. Always too angry.

"I'm done with this, Jackie." I pointed a finger at his nose as I kept my voice low. Steady. Shouting wasn't really my style and it usually only made things worse. "Third strike. You're done."

He'd be a fool if he didn't heed the warning in my tone.

His answer was to spit on the floor.

Fool.

I crossed the room, my steps measured and deliberate, letting the thud of my boots fill the silence. My gaze stayed locked on Jackie even as Chris lifted up his hands in surrender and inched away.

Chris was a decent guy, but we'd have words later about why the fuck he'd thought it would be a good idea to bring this asshole to Trick's.

I stopped in front of Jackie, holding his gaze.

It would make my life a hell of a lot easier if he came quietly and didn't make a scene, but I wasn't holding my breath.

He was at least five inches shorter than me with a stocky frame. As I stared down at him, he began shifting his weight from foot to foot. His jaw locked and his face started to turn pink. So did his head. It was like watching a pot of water begin to boil.

Definitely not going quietly. *Fine.*

I'd let him make a big fucking mess. We'd lock him up. I'd get the county attorney involved. Jackie would probably face a felony charge and likely lose his job at the railroad station.

His choice. I'd warned him the last time I'd been called to deal with his bullshit.

It was at the café. He'd tipped over a table when a waitress dumped a glass of water on his head after he grabbed her ass.

Jackie seemed to lose his cool whenever there was a beautiful woman around. And Ilsa put beautiful to shame.

I wasn't sure what I'd missed in the moments before I'd walked through the door, but I'd find out. After he was behind bars. If he'd touched her, well . . . I might enjoy this a little bit.

"You're spending the night in jail." My tone brooked no argument, but I knew he was going to argue anyway.

"The fuck I am." He puffed up his chest, stepping close enough to almost touch me.

"Outside," I ordered. "Don't make me drag you."

The pink in his face turned to red. Rage sparked in his eyes.

Here we go.

He was quick. He stepped back, and a moment later, his fist slammed into my gut.

It was a strong punch but not exactly a surprise. My muscles were locked, my abs contracted. Other than curling my lip, I didn't so much as move.

A flicker of panic filled his blue eyes. He probably would have hit me again, but he was too damn slow.

As his other fist flew toward my face, I sidestepped, catching his wrist with my hand. I spun him around, using his own momentum against him, and with a quick stomp on the back of his knee, he buckled, slamming into the floor on his belly.

He let out a pained *oof.*

I kept hold of his wrist, twisting his arm behind his back as I dropped to my knee at his side. With my other hand, I took out my handcuffs. "You have the right to remain silent."

"Fuck you!" Jackie bucked and flopped, shouting at me as my grip only tightened.

I ignored him, snapping on the cuffs while I recited the rest of his rights. By the time Larry and Alan burst through the front door, I had Jackie on his feet and was pushing him across the room.

"He's all yours." I transferred him to Larry, letting my deputies take a still cussing and spitting Jackie to the parking lot.

My heart was pounding, adrenaline coursing through my veins, when the door closed behind them.

"Cosi," Chris said, taking a step closer.

I held up my hand, palm out. "Any damage Trick finds, you're on the hook."

"Yeah." He gulped. "I didn't think . . . We were finishing up a shift. He's only here for one night and staying at my place. He offered to buy me a beer. I told him not to cause any problems. He swore he'd keep his cool."

"The next time I see him, you'll be right beside him in a cell. Understood?"

"Yes, sir." Chris's frame slumped as he dropped his gaze to his boots.

"Go home."

He didn't need to be told twice.

A nice kid, but he'd always been gullible, especially when it came to the influence of his friends. His senior year in high school, I'd busted a party in the mountains. When I'd pulled up, all the kids had taken off to hide, but they'd left Chris behind with a case of beer because he was the only one who'd been nineteen at the time and of legal age to drink.

When I'd told him that he could be charged with giving alcohol to minors, he'd started to cry and begged me not to take him to jail. Apparently, he still needed to find better friends.

The other guys at the table stood, pulling on coats as Chris collected his jacket. Then the three of them streamed out the door.

Leon and the other old timers at the bar swiveled their stools forward, returning to their smoldering cigarettes and beer bottles.

I exhaled, the air hot in my nostrils, as I faced Ilsa.

We stared at each other for a long moment, neither of us moving.

She didn't look frightened or upset or on the verge of tears. She actually looked calm, like this little display of testosterone had barely ruffled her feathers. If anything, she looked mildly irritated and slightly pissed off.

I liked that. A lot. She'd been more visibly rattled after calling the station about a masked figure outside her house.

Which made me wonder if maybe I'd missed something. *Damn.* The idea that I'd failed didn't sit right and my stomach knotted.

Trick appeared at her side, still holding his baseball bat. He put his free hand on her elbow, leaning too close. "You okay?"

Why was he touching her? That, I didn't like. Not a fucking bit.

"Fine." Ilsa shifted to face him, gently freeing her elbow as she stepped away. "I guess I had that coming, didn't I?"

He let out a dry laugh. "Guess so."

"I'm sorry."

"Not your fault."

She forced a tight smile, then with a small wave, walked away. The sharp click of her heels filled the bar as she brushed past me for the door.

I turned and followed, like there was a damn leash around my neck.

The magnetic pull when she was around was as unsettling as the notion I'd spent weeks not believing her about a stalker.

"Ilsa," I called as she reached Ike's truck.

Chris and his coworkers hadn't wasted any time and their vehicles were pulling out of the snow-covered parking lot. Larry and Alan were already rolling down Main in the cruiser.

Ilsa opened the driver's-side door and tossed her purse inside before turning to face me. "Yes, Sheriff Raynes? Here to give me a warning like the others?"

"Cosi," I corrected. Again.

She'd only said my first name once, and I'd liked it. Wouldn't mind hearing it more often.

"Yes, Cosi?" She crossed her arms over her chest. Definitely pissed off. And I still liked it.

"Trick's attracts a certain crowd."

"The kind of crowd that likes an occasional drink and a burger for dinner?" She arched her eyebrows. "Is this the part where you tell me to be careful? Because as I see it, *Cosi*, I'm in just as much danger at my own home as I am here, so I might as well live my life."

That attitude shouldn't be attractive, but damn if it didn't make her that much more intriguing. "Trouble seems to follow you around."

She huffed. "Apparently only when I'm in Montana. Can I go home now?"

"Why'd you really come to Trick's?"

Ilsa didn't seem like the bar-going type. Maybe I was wrong, but my intuition said there was more to her Thursday evening visit than a burger and fries.

She dropped her gaze to the snow beneath her heeled boots. When she sighed, her entire body seemed to sag against the truck's door, like the weight of a thousand bricks settled on her shoulders. "My dad came here."

"Most people in Dalton come to the bar from time to time."

"It was more than time to time, wasn't it?" When she met my gaze, there was a sadness in her chocolate irises. "Trick called him Bluebird."

"Most around town called him Bluebird."

"You don't."

I shook my head. "I don't spend a lot of time at Trick and Sully's."

"Ah." She turned to stare down the street. "It's been a long time since I heard that nickname. Not since I was a kid."

"When was the last time you were in Dalton?"

"Ten years ago. I was sixteen. Dad and I didn't, um . . . talk. Often."

So she'd come to the bar hoping to get to know her father. That made more sense. "Trick knew him pretty well."

Trick knew most people in town pretty well. Part of the reason people loved this bar was because he was a constant. A friend to anyone who came in the door. A confidant for those needing a listening ear. When it came to secrets, he was a collector.

Chances were, he had some of Ike's.

"I'm sure he'll tell you whatever you'd like to know," I told her. Maybe he already had.

"Have a good evening, Sheriff."

"Cosi."

She gave me the same tight, dismissive smile she'd given Trick before climbing in her truck. Her sad, pretty brown eyes met mine before she drove away.

Something pinched in my chest. I watched until her taillights disappeared, then let go of the breath I'd been holding.

Shit. That woman was on my mind, and I couldn't seem to shake her loose.

The right thing to do would be to head to the station, make sure Jackie was booked, then write up a report. We'd be adding assault of a peace officer to his list of charges today. But first, I wanted to know more about what Trick had told Ilsa. I wanted to know if this was the first time she'd visited his bar. And why he was touching her damn elbow.

I marched inside, giving my eyes a moment to adjust to the light. Then I went to stand at the corner of the bar, waiting for Trick to come over.

"How'd you know Jackie was here?" he asked.

"Archie Lee."

"Ah." He nodded, his gaze flicking to the pool table. "I owe him a beer next time he's in. I owe you one too. What do you want?"

"I'm good." I waved it off. I'd stopped drinking at Trick's a long time ago. Not that I didn't want to share a beer with my friend. But it was best that when we had that beer, it was in my living room.

Though it had been a long time since Trick and I had hung out. Over the years, our lives had just gone in different directions.

We'd gone to high school together. When I'd left for the police academy, he'd used the money he'd gotten from his grandmother's inheritance to go in with Sully on the bar.

It had been a dive in those days. At first, all they'd been able to do was change the name. But over the years, they'd fixed it up. The building no longer looked like it might collapse on a windy day.

The door opened and a couple of guys who worked at the hardware store came in, waving at Trick. He'd be busy soon, so it was time for me to ask a few questions and leave.

"What did Ilsa want?" I asked.

Trick's eyes narrowed, not by much, but enough I caught it.

He liked her, didn't he? Not a surprise. Trick always had a thing for brunettes. "She asked a few questions about Bluebird. I got the impression they weren't close."

"Anything else?"

"Not really." He shrugged. "I heard she called in a couple of times about someone poking around her place."

He was fishing for information, but he'd have to get that from someone else.

The corner of his mouth turned up and he chuckled, shaking his head. "You never change. Always tight-lipped."

"Something like that." I rapped my knuckles on the bar. "I'd better head to the station. Let me know if you need anything."

"Sure you don't want to stay for a burger?" he asked.

"Next time. Promised Spencer I'd make him dinner."

"How's he doing?"

"He's fourteen. So he's pissed at me at least half the time."

Every day was a gamble. I'd go home to a son itching to pick a fight or a kid who wanted to talk to me for hours about basketball practice.

"How's your mom?" he asked.

"Also pissed at me." Yesterday, she'd found out about Gwen's letter and was furious that I hadn't told her about it a month ago.

"Anyone not pissed at you?"

"Are you?"

"Not today." He stretched his hand across the bar.

I shook it, then left him to his customers.

After stopping at the station to ensure Jackie was locked up for the night, I went home to find Spencer's bedroom door shut.

"Hey." I knocked. "How about some dinner?"

"Not hungry."

I hung my head. Guess tonight wouldn't be a good night. "Can I come in?"

"I'm changing."

Was he really? He changed clothes a hell of a lot. Mostly, it had become his way of getting rid of me because I didn't want to invade his privacy.

So I ate dinner alone. I watched a game on TV alone. And when I finally went to bed, I should have slept until morning. Except every time I drifted off to sleep, a pair of sad, chocolate-brown eyes would haunt my dreams. Would snap me awake.

What was really going on at Cotters Lake? How far downhill had Ike gone before his death?

And what the hell would it take to get Ilsa out of my damn head?

Chapter 10

Ilsa

Dad's journal rested on my lap. The fire I'd started after getting home from school was crackling, and the lasagna I'd put in the oven was beginning to fill the house with scents of garlic and tomatoes. I was sitting on the couch, my fingers poised on the journal's cover, ready to flip it open. But for the past ten minutes, all I could do was stare at the scratched leather surface.

That letter he'd written to Donnie after her death had been . . . excruciating. If this book was filled, cover to cover, with those letters, I wasn't sure I could read them.

Donnie hadn't just been Dad's special friend. He'd called her the love of his life.

All these years, I'd thought he'd been in love with Mom. That he'd never moved on because she'd been his soulmate. But what if the reason he'd never come to visit me in Phoenix, what if the reason he'd stopped calling on Sundays, wasn't because he'd been heartbroken over their divorce?

What if he simply hadn't cared? What if his life in Montana had always been more important than his daughter?

What if it hadn't been hurt keeping him away, but choice?

I was terrified of what I'd learn from this journal. Not just about Donnie, but everything Trick had told me yesterday had been rattling around my brain for twenty-four hours, and I couldn't decide what was worse.

Knowing? Or not?

His cryptic letter delivered by his equally cryptic friend, Jerry, wouldn't point me to a journal where Dad confessed to being happy his child lived three states away, right? Dad wouldn't have begged me to visit if he didn't care, right?

"Just read it," I whispered.

I closed my eyes.

And opened the journal.

There was a very real chance that by the time I finished, I'd have more questions than answers. But there was also a chance I'd understand my dad. That this journal could help me say goodbye.

I flipped past the first entry, glossing over Dad's letter to Donnie. I expected to find another on the following pages, but instead, there were no words, just a line drawn on the page annotated with tiny numbers.

"What the hell?" The details were so small I bent forward, squinting at the paper.

There were a few smudged eraser marks and some of the numbers were blurry, marred by finger smudges.

"What is this?" I asked the empty living room and flipped to the next page.

It was another line with another set of numbers, this one even messier than the last. But the line and numbers seemed to be the same as on the previous page.

Another flip, another line with numbers. Seven pages later, I still had no idea what Dad was trying to draw.

I squinted at the page, wondering if something would jump out at me. It wasn't the profile of a person. It wasn't a plant or animal or structure. It was just a winding line on a page sprinkled with numbers.

"Huh." Well, this certainly wasn't giving me confidence in Dad's mental state.

I turned to the next page and found it filled with random words. It was four columns of impossibly small print, each letter capitalized.

BUCK KNIFE
LICENSE
CHISEL
MIRROR

My head began to throb as I scanned the rest of the list. This one wasn't on a napkin. And nothing was crossed out. Maybe this had been the first of many packing lists for his move with Donnie. As I scanned the items, they were all familiar. All things I'd found in various boxes.

The knife and a compact mirror had been in his hunting backpack along with five vacuum-packed MREs. That bag had also included his hunting license and an unused deer tag, both sealed in a plastic baggie.

As I stared at the tiny letters, so neatly organized in columns, my stomach sank.

"What was going on with you, Dad?" More than anything, I wished I could ask him in person.

The next two pages weren't filled with handwritten notes or sentiments, but old newspaper clippings he'd glued into the book. Each and every one was about the ghost town of Garrack. One was how the state of Montana had taken over the abandoned town and would be administering it as a state park. Another was a list of old mining towns throughout the state. He'd circled Garrack.

The same town he'd told me about in my letter.

I set the journal aside and shot off the couch, racing to my purse on the kitchen counter. I lifted out both letters that I'd tucked inside. The note he'd given Jerry to give me. And the letter he'd sent right before his death.

Maybe it was silly carrying it around with me all the time, but since I couldn't make sense of it, there was always the wild hope that it would sink in through osmosis.

Carefully taking out the single sheet of paper inside the envelope, I read Dad's letter for the hundredth time.

It was only a story. It was another of Dad's tales, like those he'd make up when I was a kid, out fishing with him on his boat. I'd get bored and want to go home to swim, but he'd keep me out there for another hour by making up something fanciful.

This letter was only a story. He said so himself, right at the top.

But what if . . .

No, this wasn't real. It couldn't be real. Lost gold from the mining days? That would be impossible. Wouldn't it?

I paced the length of the house, walking back and forth between the fireplace and the stove, worrying my bottom lip between my teeth.

What did all of this mean? How did those articles tie to this letter? Unless . . .

Had Dad convinced himself that this legendary gold from the Garrack ghost town was real?

Was there something in that journal to explain the letter Jerry had given me? I took it from its own envelope, reading it for the millionth time.

"Find the atlas and the key," I murmured, speaking the words aloud. Then I stared at them until they began to blur on the page.

What was I missing? Somehow, these pieces all linked together, but how? There had to be a missing piece. Dad was trying to tell me something, but what?

My gaze drifted to his closed bedroom door. I'd organized and cleaned that room, but I hadn't gone in there since. I doubted I would until the spring, until it was time to take his ashes from the trunk where they were stowed and scatter them on the island.

Was there something tucked away beneath a floorboard in that room? Possibly a hidden compartment in his closet?

If so, I wasn't finding it tonight.

On a sigh, I went to the couch and tucked both letters into the journal, closing the button snap. The timer beside the stove had a soft tick as it moved. There were still ten minutes to go on my lasagna. Time enough to talk to Mom.

I went to the phone, taking it off the cradle and pressing the numbers to my childhood home.

"Hello," she answered.

"Hi, Mom."

"Oh, hi, cutie. What a surprise. How are you?"

"I'm good. How are you?"

"Great. Just got home from aerobics."

Mom loved her aerobics class. The exercise. The friends. The outfits. She had leotards and leg warmers in every color of the rainbow.

"How was class tonight?" I asked, leaning against the counter.

"A butt kicker." She laughed. "What are you doing?"

"Making your lasagna." The recipe was one of my favorites, and tonight, after a long week of school, I'd wanted a dinner that reminded me of home. It took forever to make, meaning I was eating much later than normal, but it would be worth it.

"Yum. You know, I created that recipe in that house."

"You did?"

"I did. Your dad got so sick of lasagna by the time I had the recipe exactly the way I liked it. But he never complained. He'd just eat whatever I made and tell me it was delicious, even when it wasn't."

The tenderness in her voice made my heart squeeze. "That's sweet."

"He had his moments."

"Did he, um . . . give you anything? Recently?"

"Other than a headache?"

"Mom." I rolled my eyes. "Please."

"Sorry, I'm kidding. And no. I haven't gotten anything from him in a while. Though he did send me a box a while back."

I stood straight. "When?"

"Gosh. It was over a year ago. After Thanksgiving. It was just some of my old things that I'd left behind."

Damn. "Like what?"

"Some pictures. A diary I kept from before you were born. A few trinkets. Honestly, I didn't really give it much attention. After I opened it, I kind of got mad. I thought he'd actually remembered to send you a Christmas gift, early even, and when I realized it was just some old junk he could have tossed or given to me years ago, I put the box on a shelf in the garage and haven't thought much of it since."

Over a year ago, after Thanksgiving, Dad must have been packing to move in with Donnie. He'd probably found Mom's things and wanted to get rid of them.

"Would you send me that box?"

"Why?" Mom asked.

"I don't know." It was the truth. That box would likely be another I'd end up cleaning out. But what if there was something Mom had overlooked? Something that might trigger a few answers to the questions that kept multiplying? "I guess I'm just trying to understand him, Mom."

"But it's my stuff," she said. "Not his."

"Did you write about him in your diary?"

"I suppose. I can't really remember what's in that diary."

"Would it be weird if I read it?" Probably. For all I knew, she'd written about their sex life.

I gagged.

Mom hesitated, like she was mentally rewinding to that time, to whatever she'd written. "Okay, fine. I'll stick it in the mail tomorrow."

"Thanks. There's, um, nothing about you and Dad being *together* together in it, right?"

She burst out laughing. "No. I wouldn't send it to you if there was. And I certainly wouldn't have left that behind for your father to find."

"Thanks, Mom." I smiled, leaning against the counter again, staring down at my blue wool socks. "People around here call him Bluebird."

"Still?"

"Yeah."

She hummed. It was a peaceful note like she was glad Bluebird hadn't faded away. "You know I gave him that nickname."

"I remember."

"That man loved bluebirds. He said they meant good fortune. The first time I called him that it was only a joke, but he liked it, so I kept using it." A hint of sadness crept into her tone.

Mom and Dad might have been divorced, but a decree didn't make the feelings stop. She was mourning his loss too.

The timer dinged, loud enough Mom heard it.

"I'd better let you get to that lasagna. Love you."

"Love you too, Mom. Bye."

I hung up and took my dinner out of the oven, giving it time to cool before I sat down alone and ate my meal. There was plenty left over, so I covered the pan in foil and stowed it in the fridge. Then I did the dishes, put the house to rights and added another log to the fire before shutting off the lights and retreating to my room with Dad's journal tucked under my arm.

Reading it before bed would probably give me strange dreams, but for some reason, I didn't want to leave it in the living room.

"Paranoid much, Ilsa?" I asked, tossing the journal on my bed. "Yes. And apparently, also talking to yourself."

I ducked into the bathroom to wash my face, but instead of turning on the water, I took a long, hard look at my reflection. At my dark hair. My brown eyes. My nose and forehead and chin.

All features I'd inherited from Dad.

Was this paranoia his doing too? Was I imagining people looking through my windows? Spying on my life? Would I be sharing my own conspiracy theories with Trick the next time I stopped at the bar?

My grandmother—Dad's mom—had died in Dalton's nursing home with Alzheimer's. I'd never met my grandma, but Mom had known her well enough. If I asked, she'd tell me about my grandmother's disease, but I wasn't sure I wanted to know the hard truths yet. I wasn't ready to admit that all signs pointed to Dad succumbing to the same.

I shook it off and turned on the faucet, letting it run for a moment until the water was hot. Then I washed the makeup from my face.

Once I was dressed in my warmest flannel pajamas, I climbed into bed, foregoing the Danielle Steel romance novel I'd been reading each night—it was after eleven and well past my bedtime. A yawn pulled at my mouth as I flipped off the lamp and snuggled beneath my quilts.

Except as I relaxed into my pillow and closed my eyes, I couldn't seem to shut off my brain.

Garrack.

G-A-R-R-A-C-K.

The letters seemed to wink behind my eyelids, like the countdown wheel at the beginning of an old black and white movie.

I squeezed my eyes shut tighter, trying to block them out, but no matter how long I lay there, I couldn't fall asleep. By midnight, I gave up on sleep.

"Ugh," I groaned, sitting up and stretching for the book on my nightstand. But before I could flip on the lamp, a flicker of light flashed on the wall.

I froze, hand poised above my paperback, as I stared into the darkness.

The flicker came again, faint and white, but enough to stir the shadows in my bedroom. I sat upright, my face whipping to the window.

The snow still covered most of the glass, but the drift had settled enough that there was a three-inch sliver at the top of the frame where I could peek outside.

The flicker came again, silver and subtle. Like moonlight.

Except on the drive home from work, the sky had been blanketed in clouds. There was no moon tonight.

My heart climbed into my throat as I whipped the covers from my body and rose to my knees, inching across the mattress toward where it was pushed up against the wall. I lifted to my feet and carefully peered through the window's narrow slit.

A circle of white bounced across the snow, stretching and shortening—a flashlight held at a person's side, swinging with a steady stride.

Someone was walking through the forest, heading straight for my house.

I gasped, clapping a hand over my mouth as I dropped to my knees. Then I flew off the bed and out the door, hurrying to the kitchen to take a knife out of a drawer.

With it clutched tight, I inched through the living room, toward the windows that I'd covered with quilts. The windows that overlooked the yard.

Carefully peeling the blanket away from the glass, I peeked outside, waiting for whoever was walking to pass the house and cross into the yard.

My pulse boomed in my ears as I held my breath, gripping the knife's handle until my knuckles were white.

Who was out there? Why were they creeping around my house at night? What if they tried to come inside?

My head whipped toward the door, squinting at the deadbolt. It was too dark to make out, but it had to be locked. I'd been locking myself inside for weeks. But if this person wanted to get inside, all it would take was a rock through a window.

Was this the person in the black mask? Maybe it was just someone walking by, out for a late-night stroll along the lake in below-zero temperatures.

It could be Jerry on his way to wherever it was that Jerry lived. Maybe it was Robert or Sue Anne, those neighbors Cosi kept telling me to meet but I'd been avoiding. But why would anyone be out at night when prolonged exposure meant hypothermia?

Oh God. This was bad. This was really, really bad. I was stuck out here alone, in my pajamas with nothing more than a knife. Yes, Dad had guns, but they were all in his bedroom closet, and I hadn't fired a gun since the last time he'd taken me target shooting the summer I was sixteen.

My head was spinning so fast my vision skipped.

"Breathe," I whispered, forcing air into my lungs. I shifted on my toes, keeping low. The yard was covered in gray, the only light coming from the single bulb outside the front door. I squinted into the night, breath lodged in my throat as I waited for that white flashlight. Every second was agony and my muscles trembled.

But the light never came. I clutched the windowsill, holding it tight as a minute passed, then two.

Where were they? Had they shut off their light? Or was this a dream? Was I imagining this entire episode, and any minute now, I'd wake up, warm in my bed, with all the knives shut in their drawers?

Sweat beaded at my temples as I set the knife on the floor, slowly rising to peer around the edge of the house. As I shifted, a glow caught my eye. Not white, like the flashlight, but orange and red.

I stood tall, my mouth falling slack as the flames grew higher and higher, smoke curling into the night. And with my cheek pressed against cold glass, I stared at Dad's tiny shed.

Burning to the ground.

Chapter 11

Cosi

Tonight was one of those dark nights where the world was black and white and every shade of gray in between. The clouds had parted enough to let through a sliver of light from a crescent moon. It was a night meant to be colorless.

It was one of those quiet and peaceful dark nights ruined by red and blue flashing lights.

The bright strobes from Chuck's cruiser colored the snow in Ilsa's yard. Every light was on in the cabin, the yellow hue seeping from her windows. The heap of orange coals—what used to be Ike's shed—was smoldering, the hot red fading beneath charred clumps. The lingering flames wouldn't survive to see the dawn.

Ilsa's call to the station had come just after midnight. But by the time Chuck and the volunteer firefighting crew had made it out to Cotters Lake, there'd been no point in trying to extinguish the fire. Not only was the lake covered in a thick sheet of ice, making it difficult to get to water, but that shed had gone up like dried kindling.

The crew had made sure the fire didn't spread to the house, and with all of the snow, it had been easy to contain. The guys had been standing around the blaze, each with a shovel in hand, when I'd arrived at the scene ten minutes ago.

Chuck had radioed me at home after Ilsa had called in the fire. It had taken me a few minutes to get dressed and wake up Spencer, letting him know I had to leave. Years ago, I would have had to load him up and take him to Mom's. Now, he was old enough to stay home alone for a couple of hours, not that I liked leaving him in the dead of night.

But this was not a call I was going to delegate to my deputies.

I hadn't seen Ilsa yet. Chuck had told her to wait inside, to get out of the cold. As soon as I finished getting an update, I'd head inside myself.

"Did you look around?" I asked.

"Not yet. Wanted to wait until you got here. Once we realized there wasn't anything to do but keep the fire contained, I asked everyone to limit where they walked."

"Good." Still, there were footprints everywhere around the shed.

According to Chuck's recap, Ilsa had been in bed, the cabin dark, when she'd seen a flicker of light on her wall. Someone had approached the house carrying a flashlight. The next thing she'd known, the shed was on fire, and she'd called the station.

"I'll take it from here," I told Chuck. "Head back to the station. Write up a report. Leave it on my desk. I'll review it in the morning."

"I'm happy to stay and help you look around," Chuck said, his teeth chattering. He was tall and lanky, almost six nine, and naturally thin. Even standing close to the fire, the cold had probably already seeped to his core. All he was wearing were a pair of jeans and his black department coat. No hat to cover his red hair. No gloves for his bony fingers.

Chuck was only twenty-four, and I'd told him no less than a hundred times to wear long johns this time of year, but he griped that they chafed. Some days, I felt more like a parent than employer to these younger deputies.

Part of me wanted to leave him out here. Let him get so cold that he'd heed my advice from now on. But as his lips began to take on a blueish tint, I jerked my chin toward his cruiser. "I'm sure. Go warm up."

"Thanks, boss." He hurried to his car, shutting himself inside the cab. The engine was still running, and his hands immediately lifted to the air vents.

"I think we're good to take off, Cosi," one of the firefighters said.

"Yeah." I lifted a hand. "Thanks for hurrying out."

"No problem."

With that, the three-man crew trudged through the snow for their truck.

I waited until both vehicles disappeared down the road. Once the sound of their engines faded to nothing, all that remained was the pop of the fire and the slight rustling of evergreen branches.

Tugging a pair of leather gloves from my coat pocket, I fitted them over my hands. Then I crouched to the snow, studying the tread of Chuck's boots so I could rule it out from the others. I did the same with the tracks left behind by the firefighters. And once I had their prints memorized, I inched toward the fire, assessing and dismissing any familiar prints as well as taking in the rubble.

The snow was trampled in a ring around the fire, about five feet away from the blaze. They'd worn a path between the shed and house. But the rest of the area was mostly undisturbed. Good thinking on Chuck's part to limit foot traffic. The kid might not be great at taking details over the phone, but when he was on a scene, he had strong instincts.

The smell of smoke and gasoline filled my nostrils as I moved closer to the shed's dwindling remains. A metal gas can was tipped on its side, the lid nowhere to be seen. The sides were intact, so there must not have been much fuel inside. Otherwise, it would have exploded.

My boots sank in the snow as I circled the shed, getting close enough to see metal debris buried in the ash. The side of a toolbox. The head of a rake. The blade of a shovel. With the toe of my boot, I pushed a charred board aside, finding nothing beneath.

As sparks floated into the night, I inched around the building's footprint toward the back, where a different smell hit my nostrils.

Not gas, but diesel. Fresh. Pungent. It mingled with the smoke.

I pulled a small flashlight from my pocket, illuminating the snow. It was mostly undisturbed, pristine and smooth.

The walls of the shed had all collapsed inward, folding toward the center of the blaze. The roof had capsized into the heart of the fire too. There was a single corner post that hadn't completely fallen. It was broken in half and the outer edge was still brown, unmarred by the fire.

Around that corner post, the snow wasn't the smooth blanket like it was in the yard. It was mottled and dimpled. The trees above had suffered the heat from the fire, and the snow on their branches had melted, plopping to the ground.

I swept my light back and forth over the area, searching for tracks. The scent of diesel was stronger, and it was only by chance that my light caught a string of red dots. I bent, touching my finger to one of the dots before lifting it to my nose.

Dyed diesel.

As far as I knew, Ike didn't have any equipment that would need dyed diesel. His boat's motor was gas.

My heart rate spiked, my senses going on full alert, as I stood and followed the direction of those dots as they disappeared into a nearby bush.

The branches were bare, the heat defrosting them too. The underbrush was unruly and dense, left wild to grow on the shoreline.

I swept my flashlight back and forth, my gaze following the beam, as I searched through the bramble for any sign of another person. Except it all looked the same, and in the night, it was nearly impossible to make out anything but clumps of snow.

"Damn it," I muttered. Not again. This couldn't be the third time I'd come up here because of Ilsa's call only to tell her there were no signs of another person.

This wasn't a hoax. This wasn't a paranoid woman living in the wilderness alone. There was a knot in my gut that screamed something was wrong.

But this investigation might have to wait until daylight.

I was about to turn back, to check on Ilsa and get her side of the story for myself, when two grooves in a narrow space between bushes caught my attention.

They could have come from an animal. A deer or elk cutting through the foliage. Or they could have come from a person. The lines in the snow stopped three feet away from the far edge of the shed, from that post that hadn't entirely burned and the drops of dyed diesel.

It could have been close enough for someone to toss diesel on a shed wall, then strike a match.

I traced the trail through the bushes, away from the cabin and the lake, toward the edge of Ike's property and the taller trees of the forest. "Gotcha."

A surge of adrenaline raced through my veins as I set off to follow, picking up the trail about fifteen yards away.

I sidestepped the tracks, making sure I didn't disturb them as they made a straight line to the trees. The snow came up to my knees, giving a slight *whoosh* as I walked. It was so cold that the flakes were light, holding no weight from water. It was deep, but it didn't take much effort to wade through the drifts. Behind me, my path began to collapse on itself, hiding some of the evidence of my footsteps.

If the wind picked up tonight, it would blow the featherlight snow everywhere and cover up these tracks by morning. Maybe the person who'd been sneaking around Ilsa's was counting on it.

The trail neared a towering tree where the branches had shielded the ground from some of the snow. Enough that there was a single, perfect imprint in the snow.

A boot with horizontal treads about the same size as mine pointed the opposite direction. He'd followed the exact same path to and from the cabin.

Not a deer. Not an elk. Some fucker tormenting Ilsa.

I picked up my pace, following the trail deeper and deeper into the forest. My pulse pounded in my ears, my eyes continually shifting from the ground to my surroundings. Sweat beaded at my temples beneath my wool cap and my muscles warmed. I wasn't sure how far I'd gone, but when the trail turned toward the lake, it didn't take long before I hit the shoreline.

And that's when the trail stopped.

The snow had blown off the lake enough to reveal wide, clear stretches of ice. Whoever had gone to Ilsa's knew this area well to know there'd be nothing to follow once they hit the lake.

"Fuck." My chest heaved as I planted my hands on my hips. A breeze hit my face, the sheen of sweat turning cold. And the hairs on the back of my neck stood on end as a shiver trickled down my spine.

My entire body tensed with the feeling of being watched. My breath lodged in my lungs as I shut off my flashlight. Then I flipped open the clasp on my holster, hand poised over my gun.

Ears straining for any noise, I let my eyes adjust to the night as I spun in a slow circle. Whoever had set fire to her shed was likely long gone. But what if they'd stayed close to watch it burn? Or worse?

Another shudder rolled over my shoulders as I let the darkness settle over my body like a cloak.

What the fuck was happening on Cotters Lake?

I waited for a few long moments, heart thundering in my chest. If someone was out here, there'd be no finding them tonight. So I set off toward the cabin, turning my flashlight back on to follow my own tracks.

The sound of an engine cranking echoed in the night as the house came into view. The lights were all off save for the single bare bulb in a sconce beside the front door.

I found Ilsa in the driveway, sitting in the driver's seat of Ike's truck, the door open. Her right hand was on the key in the ignition. Her forehead was on the steering wheel, her shoulders curled forward.

"Hey," I said.

She startled, shooting upright as her hand slapped over her chest. "Shit, you scared me."

"Sorry."

"It's okay." She sighed. "I'm just . . . on edge. And I can't get this fucking truck started."

It was damn cold tonight, the coldest we'd had all winter, and I didn't see an extension cord from the house to keep the truck plugged in. Maybe Ike hadn't installed an engine block heater for his Ford.

She sniffled, reaching for the key again. And once more, the engine turned over but didn't start.

"Come on." I waved her to my Bronco. "I'll drive you into town."

"All right." She closed her eyes, frame sagging like she didn't have the energy to get out from behind the wheel. It took a moment before she swung her legs out and hauled out the bags she'd loaded inside. A duffel bag. A purse. A purple briefcase and an empty jar.

"I'll carry this." I took the duffel from her hand, then escorted her to my truck, opening the passenger door for her.

"Thanks," she murmured, hopping inside. She tried to hide it, but I didn't miss the quick swipe she made at the corner of her eye.

Damn. That tear was partly my fault.

The drive to town would be over thirty minutes. That would give us plenty of time to talk. Plenty of time for me to apologize.

I carried her bag around the hood, putting it in the back. Then I got in and started the truck, cranking the heat.

Ilsa wrapped her arms around her waist. She leaned against the door, her eyes trained outside as I turned us around and headed toward Dalton.

Her sweet, citrusy scent filled the inside of the cab as the heater chased away the cold.

When we passed Robert Aaron's place, Ilsa sat straighter. And by the time we reached Sue Anne's A-frame, her spine might as well have been a steel rod.

Every light was on in both houses.

Had one of them burned the shed? I couldn't see it. Neither had a reason to torment Ilsa like this. And the tracks I'd found led away from their houses, not toward them.

"I found a trail of footprints leading away from the shed," I said.

Ilsa faced me, her expression blank. Not the curiosity or outrage I would have expected. She just looked empty. Tired. "So all it took for you to believe me was a case of arson. Noted."

Hell. "I deserve that."

"Yes, you do."

"I'm sorry."

She dropped her gaze to her lap. "I'd be lying if I said I hadn't had my doubts too. When you couldn't find any tracks, especially the first time, I was worried that maybe . . ."

The rest of her sentence hung in the air, but she didn't need to finish it. She'd been doubting herself, hadn't she? Wondering if her own imagination had run wild. The stress of that worrying was my fault too.

"I don't know what the hell is going on," I said. "But I'll find out. I promise."

I made it a rule to be careful making promises. I rarely made promises to my own kid, let alone people in the middle of an open case. A broken promise was a wound. I'd suffered enough of those from my own father—I wasn't going to inflict that pain on others.

But for this? Like it or not, I owed Ilsa. I'd fucked up.

This was a promise I'd make. And keep.

Ilsa stayed quiet as we rolled through the dark. It took a while, but about fifteen minutes after leaving the cabin, her posture relaxed and the stiffness in her shoulders eased.

The temperature warmed enough that I tossed my hat and gloves in the back. And as we wound down the road, following the curves and corners that would take us to the highway, it took an active effort not to steal glances to her side of the truck.

Other than my mother, I'd never had a woman in this truck. Strange how I hadn't noticed the dust on the dash on the way up to Cotters tonight. Or the dirt on the floor or the coffee cup I'd left in the console this morning. Tomorrow, I'd beg Spencer to clean the Bronco and pay him a few bucks.

When we reached the highway, I was grateful for the loud whir of the tires on the asphalt. The noise was a welcome distraction from the beautiful woman at my side. I loosened my grip on the wheel and breathed deep for the first time since leaving the lake.

How many minutes, how many hours, would it take until I could relax when she was around? When I wasn't so on edge in her presence?

"How long have you lived in Dalton?" she asked.

Small talk was never my favorite, but I'd take idle questions to fill the silence. "Twenty years. Mom and I moved here when I was ten. After my dad's accident."

"I wonder if we ever crossed paths when we were kids. I used to spend my summers in Dalton. Dad and I mostly stayed at the lake, but we'd come into town from time to time. Sometimes I see faces that are familiar."

"Maybe we did." Though I had a feeling if I'd seen her at the ice cream shop or café, I would have remembered.

Hers was not a face I'd ever forget.

Granted, the years after Spencer was born, the years when I'd been old enough to notice girls, they'd been the farthest thing from my mind. I'd been too busy changing diapers, trying to graduate as a teenaged parent and working at a local ranch to make money.

"You're thirty?" she asked, earning a nod. "So you had Spencer when you were sixteen?"

"Yeah. His mom was my high school girlfriend. We were . . . stupid kids." Kids too caught up in each other to practice safe sex. "Not that I regret Spencer. But the timing wasn't ideal."

"That's fair."

"His mom, Gwen, isn't in the picture."

Maybe she heard the tightness in my tone because she said, "You don't have to explain."

No, I didn't. But for some reason, I wanted her to know. "Where did you move from?"

"Phoenix."

"Ah. Bet you're missing the warm weather right about now."

She let out a soft laugh. "I don't mind the snow. My mother, on the other hand, was not made for Montana winters."

"Is that why she left?"

"It was the reason she could articulate," Ilsa said. "It was easier to blame the seasons and a tiny town and a remote cabin for her leaving."

"What was the real reason?"

"I don't know if she ever figured that out. But if I had to guess, I'd say, deep down, she and Dad were very different people. And when you put love on one side of the scale and their differences on the other, no matter what, they were never going to balance."

"That's the harsh reality of life, isn't it? That love alone isn't enough."

"I hope you're wrong about that," Ilsa whispered. "I hope that when love is real, it's always enough."

Considering the only time I'd convinced myself I was in love, I'd been a teenager, I was no expert.

The lights of Dalton glinted ahead, drawing an end to our conversation. Probably good timing. I didn't need to be talking about relationships and love with Ilsa.

"Where are you staying?" I asked.

She shrugged. "The motel, I guess."

The motel? Well, fuck. I'd assumed that while I'd been trekking through the woods, she'd called a friend and found a place to stay.

My grip on the wheel tightened as my foot let up on the gas, just a bit. "The motel is closed."

Her entire body jerked. "W-what?"

"The owners spend January and February in Palm Desert."

"But their sign says vacancy."

"Yeah, they never change it."

"Of course they don't." She pinched the bridge of her nose. "Shit."

"We can radio a friend."

"I don't have any friends in Dalton." Her dry, humorless laugh sounded a lot like the one Mom gave at times. The times right before she burst into tears.

I wasn't sure I could handle seeing Ilsa cry tonight. Not when I should have done more to stop this in the first place.

She swallowed hard. "If you could take me back, I'd appreciate it."

"You're not staying in that cabin." Not until I was sure it was safe.

"If I can get my car unburied or Dad's truck started, I'll drive to Helena. Stay at a motel there."

"And school tomorrow?"

"I don't mind getting up early."

Helena was over an hour away when the roads were clear. But in the middle of winter, after a massive storm? It could take her two.

Not an option. So I kept driving.

Toward home.

"Where are we going?" she asked as I turned off the highway and onto Pine Street.

"You can crash at my place."

"What? No. That's . . ." She shook her head. "That's too much of an inconvenience. If you need to get home to Spencer, maybe your deputy can drive me back to the cabin."

I tapped the button on the garage remote hooked to my visor, slowing as I pulled into the driveway. "You're not going home."

"But—"

"It's either here or I'm sure there's a cot free at the station." I parked, facing her as I shut off the Bronco. "You could probably bunk in the cell beside Jackie's."

The glare she shot me was lethal. There was the spark, that fire in her brown eyes. And damn if it didn't make her even prettier. I hit the garage remote again to close it behind us and opened my door.

"Sheriff Raynes—"

"Cosi." What the hell was it going to take to get her to use my first name?

"You're the sheriff. And you're my student's parent."

"Both true statements. Neither of which means you can't crash in my guest bedroom."

She didn't move.

"It's late." I waved her out of the Bronco. "Let's argue about this after we've both slept for a few hours."

Still nothing. God, she was stubborn. I wished I didn't like it.

"Fine. Stay out here." I took her bag from the back seat and carried it to the side door.

I was three steps onto the sidewalk when I heard the truck's door open, then close. Then her footsteps sounded behind me, and I bit back a grin as I led the way to the front door.

Fitting my key into the lock, I walked inside, waiting for her to join me in the entryway before I closed out the cold. I set down her duffel and unzipped my coat to hang it on a hook.

She eyed the bag as if she was about to snatch it and bolt outside.

"Ilsa. Please," I murmured, my voice low.

Her gaze lifted to mine. Her mouth parted and something flashed across her expression, but in the darkness of the house, it was impossible to make out. She looked away too fast, dropping her chin as she set down her purse, briefcase and that jar to unfasten her coat.

I didn't analyze why I liked seeing it hanging on the hook beside mine.

Maybe this was a bad idea.

But she had nowhere else to go, and I wasn't taking her home. So I picked up her bag and led the way to the guest bedroom, turning on the overhead light as I set her duffel inside the door. "My mom stays in here whenever she's watching Spencer and I've got to work late. Sheets are clean. There's an extra quilt in the closet if you get cold. Bathroom is down the hall. It's Spencer's, but he's used to sharing. And he just cleaned it after dinner as part of his chores. Towels are in the cupboard. Make yourself at home."

Ilsa glanced into the room but didn't move out of the hallway as she hugged her purse, briefcase and jar tighter. "I'm sorry. I didn't realize the motel was closed, and I've only been here for a month and haven't really had a chance to make friends."

"The only person with an apology to make is me. I should have taken your calls more seriously. That's my fuckup, not yours. I'm sorry."

Her gaze lifted, her pretty eyes filled with exhaustion and frustration and fear. It was a dagger to the heart. She pulled her bottom lip between her teeth, worrying on it as a lock of hair slipped free, falling across her temple.

My hand lifted automatically, fingers splayed to push those strands off her face. Except this woman wasn't mine to touch.

I raked the hand through my own hair instead, clearing my throat as I took a step away. "Get some rest. We'll talk in the morning."

She nodded, slipping into the bedroom and easing the door closed, the light dimming as it swung shut. Except before I could retreat to my end of the house, she opened it again and whispered my name. "Cosi?"

I shouldn't like the way it sounded. Not this much.

Yeah, this was a horrible fucking idea. There was no maybe about it.

"Yeah?"

"Thank you."

I dipped my chin. "Good night, Miss Poe."

A faint smile ghosted her lips. "Good night, Sheriff Raynes."

Chapter 12

Ilsa

Cosi's guest bedroom smelled like my mom. Like Mary Kay emollient night cream and Caress soap. Sweet and floral and clean. His mother must use the same products as mine. Those familiar, comforting scents were the only reason I'd managed a few hours of sleep.

Even then, sleep hadn't come easy. In my rush to pack a bag and leave the cabin, I'd only grabbed my chartreuse silk nightgown with thin straps and a lace hem. Not something I would have thought twice about wearing to bed in the privacy of a motel room, but in this house, sharing a roof with the incredibly handsome sheriff and one of my students?

I hadn't wanted to risk an accidental encounter in a nightgown that barely covered my ass and showcased the peaks of my nipples. So I'd slept in the Levi's and Nebraska State Fair T-shirt I'd pulled on after calling the police. I hadn't even bothered taking off my bra, something I regretted this morning. The underwire was stiff and unforgiving, denting the skin next to a rib.

Sitting on the foot of the mattress, I stared at an invisible spot on the floor as my toes flexed and unflexed in the tan shag carpet. Beneath me, the bed was made, the patchwork quilt smoothed and pillows fluffed.

The room was simple and clean, with beige walls and white curtains. The furniture was the same shade of brown as the closet's bifold doors. My duffel was on the floor of that closet, the bag stuffed with enough clothes to get me through the weekend and a few days of school.

My hands were wrapped around an empty glass jar. Why I'd grabbed it during my panicked packing last night, I wasn't sure. But I'd snagged it at the same time I'd grabbed my briefcase.

Toddlers carried around security blankets. Apparently, this was my security jar.

Now what? Where did I go from here? Sooner or later, I'd have to return to the cabin. I couldn't exactly stay in Cosi Raynes's guest bedroom until the motel owners returned in March. But just the idea of going back, of seeing the charred remains of Dad's shed, churned my stomach.

Who would do this? That shed had been full of tools and a rusty old lawnmower. A few empty gas cans. Items I'd planned to sell in the spring. What was the point of burning it down? Why?

If someone was trying to scare me, it was working.

A shiver rolled down my spine, forcing me to my feet. The house was quiet, not a sound coming from the hallway. I padded to the door, carefully turning the knob to avoid making a sound. I tiptoed into the hall, about to go to the bathroom, when the scent of fresh coffee hit my nose.

It was like inhaling magic, the tension instantly easing from my shoulders. I followed that delicious smell to the kitchen, where I found a sight that made my mouth go dry.

Cosi leaned against the counter with a mug lifted to his lips. He was dressed in a hunter-green flannel shirt, the snaps open and the hem untucked. Beneath was a cream Henley, the buttons undone to show the hollow at the base of his throat and a sliver of taut skin. He wore faded jeans that molded to muscled thighs, the hems pooling at his bare feet.

His hair was damp, the strands curling at his nape. His mustache was a smooth, dark band above his mouth that would undoubtedly feel incredible against my lips. He hadn't bothered shaving this morning and his cheeks were dusted in stubble of the same shade.

My knees wobbled, not enough to make me trip over my own feet, but enough I came to an abrupt stop.

No man had any business looking that good.

I really, *really* needed to get out of here. Riding to town in his Bronco last night had been hard enough. With everything that had happened, the very last thing I should have been thinking about was how good he smelled, woodsy and fresh. How the corners of his jaw were sharp and chiseled. How much I liked the shape of his hands. How he had the most balanced, striking profile I'd ever seen—the line from his forehead, down his nose to his chin, was nothing less than flawless.

In all my years of stealing glances at Troy, not once had I noticed his hands or chin.

I could study Cosi's features for days on end and still want more. That scared the hell out of me.

"Morning," he said, lowering his mug from his mouth.

My cheeks flushed as his gravelly voice filled the kitchen. "Morning."

His eyes dipped, taking in my clothes.

This T-shirt was my favorite. A souvenir from the trip Mom had taken me on for my twenty-first birthday to watch Dolly Parton sing at the Nebraska State Fair. It was threadbare with a small hole in my left armpit. The letters and logo were faded and the fabric that had once been black was now a dark gray.

This shirt was as comfortable as my own skin, and as Cosi's gaze drank in every detail, I fought the urge to tug at the hem and smooth down the front. I'd never met anyone with such a natural intensity. It was as potent as the scent of coffee.

Something flared in his hazel eyes before he looked away. It almost looked pained. Guilty, maybe? He turned his back to me, reaching for the coffee pot to refill his mug.

"Coffee?" he asked.

"Please."

"Cream and sugar?"

"No, thanks. Just black." I set my jar on the round table in the corner of the kitchen.

He opened a cabinet, taking out a simple white mug. After filling it, he brought it over, his feet a gentle thump on the floor. Also something that shouldn't have been attractive. Male feet were supposed to be gross.

His? Not gross. Not at all.

Damn it.

I could not, absolutely not, have a crush on Cosi Raynes. He was a student's parent, and while I wasn't sure if that was against Dalton School District's code of conduct, it was against mine.

Yet when I took the cup from his hand and our fingers brushed, the sensation that zinged up my forearm to my elbow was impossible to ignore.

This had all the ingredients of a mess.

And I had enough messes to worry about at the moment.

"What's with the jar?" he asked, retreating to the coffee pot again.

It felt safer with the entire kitchen between us, so I took a seat at the table, at the chair in the farthest corner. "My dad didn't have drinking glasses. He saved jars and used them instead."

Cosi hummed, quietly sipping his coffee.

I hadn't been around him often, but I liked that he was okay with quiet moments in a conversation. That he wasn't the type to fill every moment with idle chatter.

Troy chattered. Mom chattered. I couldn't remember a time when I'd gone out for dinner and drinks with my friends in Phoenix and the entire evening hadn't been filled with chatter.

The one person in my life who'd always been okay with quiet was Dad.

I missed my dad.

Especially today. Especially after last night. He would have given me a bear hug—a *honey bear* hug, those tight, all-encompassing embraces he saved only for me. He would have told me not to worry about the shed, that it was old and full of junk anyway. Dad wasn't the emotional type. Even when Mom had left, I'd never once seen him angry.

Though I had a feeling this fire would have pissed him off.

The sting of tears pricked my nose, so I sniffed it away, distracting myself by studying Cosi's kitchen.

It was exactly what I'd expect from a single dad. Simple. Clean. No ornaments or frills in sight.

Mom loved chickens, so her kitchen was crowded with ceramic hens and roosters. In Arizona, I'd kept every graduation announcement from my high school seniors tacked to the fridge with magnets. Troy kept empty beer growlers and whiskey bottles above his cabinets.

Cosi's kitchen was functional to its core. Beige countertops. Hickory cabinets. White appliances. Taupe linoleum floors.

Its lack of character *was* the character. Sturdy. Reliable. Manly.

Exactly what I would have expected from a guy like Cosi.

"You sleep okay?" he asked.

I lifted a shoulder. "Not really. Too much on my mind."

"Yeah. Same here."

I took a sip from my mug, savoring the strong, bitter taste. "What now?"

It was the same question I'd asked last night. And it was time for an answer.

"I'm heading out to your place."

"All right." I nodded. "Can I finish this coffee before we go?"

"You're not going."

"It's my house."

"So?" He tipped his cup to his mouth for a gulp. Then he set it in the sink before stalking out of the kitchen.

I scoffed as his broad frame disappeared down the hallway opposite the one leading to the guest room.

Cosi was dreaming if he thought I'd just stay behind like a dutiful citizen. Something I would make explicitly clear when he came back.

I guzzled more than sipped my coffee, letting the warmth and caffeine seep into my bones. When my mug was empty, I helped myself to a refill from the pot. But just as I was about to go to the bedroom and find a sweatshirt to wear to the cabin, the sound and vibration of a door slamming made me pause.

Breath held, I listened for footsteps or movement. The distant sound of a garage door opening unglued me from my spot in the kitchen, and I raced through the front living room to the entryway, yanking open the door just as Cosi's Bronco rolled down the street.

He didn't so much as glance at the house as he drove away.

"You did not just leave me here." I huffed, my breath a puff of white as the cold seeped into the house.

"Miss Poe?"

I whirled, heart leaping into my throat. *Damn it.* I'd forgotten about Spencer. What kind of a teacher forgot about her student?

A teacher who needed to drink more coffee and have a very stern discussion with the local sheriff.

Spencer stood at the mouth of the entryway, his feet partly on the burnt umber tiles, partly on the plush shag carpet. He was dressed in sweatpants and a Dalton High sweatshirt, his brown hair sticking up at odd angles. His toothbrush was in his mouth, the teal handle dangling off his lower lip.

"Oh. Um. Hi, Spencer." *Shit.*

He raised his eyebrows, gripping the toothbrush. A silent *what the hell are you doing in my house* hung between us.

"There was a problem at my place last night. The motel is closed, so your dad let me crash in your guest bedroom. It was here or jail."

Spencer blinked.

"I, um . . . I'm new in town, so I don't know many people."

Except I wasn't new in town, not really. I'd been coming here my entire life. But it was easier to use it as an excuse for the reason I hadn't made any friends. It was easier to blame my isolation on frosty teachers and Principal Harlan and the remoteness of Dad's cabin.

The truth was, I hadn't tried. When it came to Dalton, I'd always kept one foot out the door.

Maybe it was time to stop hiding on Cotters Lake and find a place in this town, even if it was only temporary. A problem to solve later, when my student wasn't staring at me with his toothbrush hanging out of his mouth.

"This is weird, isn't it?"

Spencer scrubbed at his molars, giving me an eye roll as he walked away.

What were the chances he wouldn't tell people at school about this? I could already hear the rumors in the teachers' lounge.

My groan filled the entryway before I poked my head out of the still open doorway to glance down the street. *Empty.* Cosi was long gone.

I slammed more than shut the door. "So I'm just stuck here?"

"Do you always talk to yourself?"

I flinched, turning to once again find Spencer staring at me with raised eyebrows. "Yes?"

We stared at each other, my confidence withering under his unwavering gaze. Teenagers really were brutal.

"This is awkward," I said.

"Pretty much."

"I don't have a car. Mine wouldn't start last night."

"'Kay," he drawled.

"I don't know when your dad is coming back."

"He said a few hours."

"Oh." When? "He talked to you before he left?"

"Duh. He doesn't just leave." With an eye roll, he walked away. Again.

"Right."

I hated when students rolled their eyes.

Though I probably deserved at least one of those.

Standing in the entryway for hours, waiting until Cosi returned, wasn't a great way to spend a Saturday, so I made my way to the living room, where I found Spencer on the couch, the television remote aimed at the screen.

I plopped on the opposite end of the leather sofa, sinking into the soft cushions as Spencer turned up the volume to the music video playing on MTV. "Is this what you're doing today?"

"It's Saturday."

"So, yes?"

He nodded. "Yes."

I shivered, rubbing at the goose bumps covering my forearms. I'd left the door open too long and now I was cold.

Spencer stretched to snag a plaid throw blanket from the back of the maroon corduroy recliner next to the couch. He tossed it on my lap. "Want me to build a fire?"

There was a neat stack of wood beside their stove.

"No, this blanket is enough. Thanks." I spread it out, drawing it up and over my shoulders.

"Want to watch a movie?" he asked.

"Sure."

He was already flipping through the channels.

"When it's over, we're going to do your homework." If I was going to be stuck here, at least I could do something productive.

He scoffed. "It's the weekend."

"And it's due on Monday."

That scored me another eye roll. Three in less than ten minutes. My new personal record.

"My favorite student of all time lives in Arizona. His name is Richie, and he's in a wheelchair. He was in a car accident and got a spinal cord injury."

Drunk driving. I had a feeling that Cosi had already covered that lesson.

Spencer kept flipping channels, but I knew he was listening.

"Richie is not the smartest kid. And I'm not saying that to be mean. He'd tell you that himself. Some people, like you, are simply born with more intelligence than others. But the reason Richie is my favorite student of all time is because he worked his ass off to be the best. He was valedictorian and earned a full-ride scholarship to Notre Dame. He always did his homework on Saturdays."

Richie did homework every day. What would take Spencer twenty minutes, would take Richie two hours.

Spencer glanced over, expecting more to the story.

But I let it end there. He could glean the morals for himself.

He kept flipping the channel, pushing the same button over and over and over again.

"Fine," he muttered. "We'll do my homework after a movie."

I snuggled beneath the blanket, drawing my legs toward my chest. "Nothing gory and scary. I don't like horror movies and thrillers give me nightmares."

Eye roll number four. It actually made me smile.

Chapter 13

Cosi

In all the years I'd lived on Pine Street, I'd never once avoided my own house. Especially on a Saturday.

But I couldn't seem to close my notebook and set my pen aside. I couldn't stand up from my chair and get out from behind this desk. I couldn't seem to make myself walk out of the station and go home.

Probably because home meant Ilsa, and Ilsa meant questions. Questions I couldn't answer.

This morning, I'd scoured her property, searching for any hint as to who could have torched her shed. I'd poked and prodded at the charred rubble, desperate for a lead. I'd followed the track of footprints through the woods twice, hoping there'd be a clue only daylight could reveal. I'd taken photos of the shed and the single footprint I'd found, but beyond that, I was stuck.

I'd left the cabin with cold fingers and wet boots.

There'd been no trail to pick up on the lake, and no evidence left behind by the house.

I was already starting to regret the promise I'd made her last night.

She wasn't going to like it, but she'd have to stay another night in the guest bedroom. I refused to take her back to the cabin until I could guarantee it was safe.

That was, if she was even still at my place.

There was a good chance she'd already left.

While I'd been at the station making notes about her cabin and shed, she could have found a ride out to Cotters Lake. She could have walked to the bar and asked Trick to drive her home.

Given the way he'd looked at her on Thursday night, he wouldn't tell her no. Hell, he'd probably offer up his own guest bedroom. Then he'd be the man pouring her coffee, trying not to drool at the sight of her in his damn kitchen.

"Fuck." I tossed my pen aside and dragged both hands over my face. Then I pushed to my feet and walked out the door, snagging my coat from its hook as I turned off the lights.

As much as I didn't want to deliver bad news, to see the disappointment on her face, I couldn't avoid home forever. And I wanted to see Spencer.

He'd barely cracked his eyelids when I'd popped into his bedroom earlier to tell him I was leaving. Probably should have warned him his teacher was in the house.

I'd realized that mistake halfway to Cotters Lake. But I'd been in too much of a hurry to leave the house before Ilsa could convince me to bring her along.

Spencer would have every right to be pissed. It wasn't my finest move.

Poor kid. I'd find a way to make it up to him.

Someday, when he was older, maybe he'd understand what it felt like to be so twisted up over a woman you couldn't think straight.

It wasn't going away. Why wasn't it going away? This whole situation would be easier if I could just get her out of my head. But the more time I spent around Ilsa, the more I wanted.

I liked that we took our coffee the same way. I liked those fancy clothes she wore to school, but when she'd walked into the kitchen in a casual tee and jeans, my heart had nearly stopped. I liked the way her cheeks flushed when she'd checked me out this morning.

For the last fourteen years, I hadn't *liked* many women.

There'd been the occasional hookup. A one-night stand if I was out of town for training or a meeting and didn't have to worry about crossing paths with a woman I'd screwed in a hotel room. But even those who'd managed to briefly catch my eye had been quickly forgotten.

Until Ilsa.

Maybe all I needed was to stop fighting this attraction. To scratch the itch and move on. To invite her into my bed and fuck her out of my system.

Give in to the temptation that was Ilsa Poe.

I made sure the door to the station automatically locked behind me, then hustled to the Bronco. The short winter days meant the light was already fading, and it would be dark before dinner. The temperature was about to plummet, dropping like it had last night.

It would be a good night for burgers. There was food in the fridge, chicken and potatoes, but a detour to the grocery store gave me a few more minutes to delay going home.

The lights were all on as I pulled into my garage. Hopefully, Spencer was still at home and hadn't run off to spend the day with Mom or a friend. He'd be a great buffer with Ilsa.

I'd definitely owe my kid after this ordeal.

With my paper grocery bag in one hand and this morning's empty coffee mug in the other, I steeled my spine and went inside. After hanging up my coat, I passed through the living room. The intoxicating scent of Ilsa lingered in the air. Orange and vanilla. Fresh and sweet.

I liked that perfume. Way too much.

"Hey," I said as I made my way toward the kitchen, expecting Spencer to come out of his room.

Assuming Ilsa was hiding in hers too.

But as I walked into the kitchen, I came to an abrupt halt, my brain struggling to comprehend what my eyes were seeing.

Spencer and Ilsa were sitting at the table, hunched over a textbook and worksheet.

This woman was doing homework with my son. On a Saturday.

I was fucked. Entirely.

Spencer was dressed in jeans and a button-down, his hair washed. It was a far cry from the frayed sweats he normally lived in on the weekends.

Ilsa had changed too. Gone was that tee from this morning, replaced by a thick burgundy sweater that brought out the cinnamon flecks in her eyes. She glanced up first, and the soft smile on her face was enough to stop my heart.

"Look." Ilsa nudged Spencer's elbow with her own. "We've shocked him."

Spencer glanced up from his schoolwork. "Hey, Dad."

"Hey, pal." My voice cracked as I unglued my feet and walked to the fridge to unload. When the bag was empty, I folded it in half, setting it on the counter. "What are you working on?"

"Math," he grumbled.

"We saved the best for last," she said.

"Yeah right." He rolled his eyes but there was a grin on his face as he focused on his paper.

I couldn't remember a time that he'd actually smiled when there was homework within a fifty-foot radius.

He wrote something with his pencil, sliding the paper over for her to inspect. "There. Done. Is it right?"

"You tell me."

Spencer's eyes narrowed at the page. "It's right."

"It's right." Ilsa beamed, and it was like a sledgehammer to the chest.

That smile was mesmerizing. The kind of smile a man would do just about anything to see on a regular basis.

"Can I be done now?" Spencer asked.

"Yes. But no more sloppy work. You're too smart to do a half-ass job. Deal?"

"Deal." He blushed. My kid actually blushed as he closed the textbook.

He looked like he'd never been told he was smart before. Maybe all he'd needed was to hear it from someone other than myself or his grandma.

Spencer stood, the chair's legs scraping on the floor. "Okay, I'm leaving."

"Wait. What?" The jolt of panic was instant. Spencer couldn't leave. He was the buffer. "Where are you going?"

"Grandma called and asked if I'd have a dinner date with her. Then we're going to watch a movie or something. I'm going to sleep over and go to church with her in the morning."

Oh, hell. "But I was going to make burgers. Thought we could hang out."

"Well, you should have told me that before you left this morning." The glare he sent me was as sharp as my kitchen knives.

So he was pissed at me. Fair.

"All right." I crossed the room and put my arm around his shoulders, hauling him into a quick hug.

He wiggled free after a heartbeat and disappeared down the hall for his bedroom.

Leaving Ilsa and me alone.

The smile she'd had for Spencer vanished as she leaned back in her chair, crossing her arms over her chest. She didn't exactly glare but she was pissed too.

Definitely should have stayed at the station longer.

"Bye," Spencer called as he cut through the house. The front door opened and closed a moment later.

Ilsa stood, sidestepping the chair to push it into the table. Then she did the same with Spencer's. "Did you find anything at my house?"

"No."

Her shoulders slumped, her eyes turning sad. Her disappointment filled the kitchen.

It was exactly the reaction I'd expected. So was the feeling of failure.

"Sorry."

"It's fine." That was a damn lie. "Give me five, and I'll be ready."

"Ready for what?"

"To go home."

"Just because I didn't find anything doesn't mean you can go home."

"Why not? Is it dangerous?"

"It could be. And I'm not willing to risk it."

"So, what? I just stay here?"

"Is here really so bad?"

"No, it's just . . ." She worried her bottom lip between her teeth as she trailed off.

It was impossible to look anywhere but at her mouth. A rush of heat flooded my veins. My dick twitched behind my zipper, and I clenched my fists, willing my body to stop screwing around. This was not the time for a fucking hard-on.

"I guess I'll take my chances anyway," she said.

"No." Nonnegotiable. She was dreaming if she thought I'd take her to the cabin tonight.

"It's not really your decision." She crossed her arms over her chest again.

"Actually, it is." I turned and walked out of the kitchen.

I'd been cold all damn day, but five minutes in her presence and the two shirts I'd pulled on today was one too many. Unbuttoning my flannel as I headed down the hall to my bedroom, I didn't realize that I wasn't alone until I was nearly at my door.

"That's the second time today we've been in the middle of a conversation and you walked away."

I stopped and turned, still working free the buttons on my shirt. "That's because the conversation was over."

"It definitely isn't. I want to go home."

"And I said no." I finished with the last button and stripped the flannel off my shoulders and arms, tossing it through my bedroom's door.

Her nostrils flared. "Excuse me?"

I bent closer, my gaze locked with hers. "No."

A fire sparked in her irises, a defiance that was quite possibly the sexiest thing I'd ever seen in my life.

"I will walk home if I must." There was a challenge in her voice, her mouth forming each word deliberately, making sure I didn't miss a single syllable.

The corner of my mouth turned up.

"You think I'm joking," she said, chocolate eyes flaring.

"I think you're dead serious. And I think if you really wanted to leave, you'd be long gone. We both know you don't really want to go back to that cabin. But if you want to keep pretending, baby, then go right on ahead."

She clenched her jaw, shifting closer to jab her finger into my chest. "Don't call me baby."

Fuck, she was something special.

She'd stand here, go toe-to-toe with me, and never back down. That stubborn streak was sexy as hell, and that flush in her cheeks said she did, in fact, like being called baby.

"Take me home, Cosi."

"You're staying, Ilsa."

Her gaze darted to my mouth, like she enjoyed watching me say her name. Her lips parted and any shred of control I had vanished.

I wasn't sure who moved first. But one moment, we were locked in a standoff, the next, my mouth was crushed to hers, and she had my shirt balled in her fists.

A whimper escaped her throat, the sound shooting straight to my cock. I framed her face with my hands, holding her in place as I licked the seam of her soft lips.

The moment she opened for me, I tangled my tongue with hers, slanting over her to delve deep.

She melted against me, another moan echoing in my ears as I tasted every corner of her mouth. Sweet. So fucking sweet.

I sank into the kiss, alternating strokes of my tongue and licks of her lips, loving how she met me, beat for beat.

Damn, this woman could kiss. She nipped at my lower lip. She slid her hands around my ribs, her palms molding to my back as she looped her arms around my middle. Her nails dug through the fabric of my shirt, hard enough to bite into my skin.

It took everything I had to tear myself away. To let go of her face and step back.

My chest heaved as my breaths came in labored pants. My entire body was on fire, my muscles locked and trembling.

Ilsa stared at me, her mouth wet. Eyes hooded. Cheeks flushed.

Fucking stunning.

"I don't want to take you home," I admitted.

"I don't want you to take me home. But you're a student's parent."

"Yeah. That kiss was probably a mistake." Or the best kiss of my damn life.

"A big mistake." She nodded. "It can't happen again."

"Agreed."

We were two miserable liars.

"I should go," she said. "To my room."

"Me too."

Neither of us moved.

One kiss . . . it wasn't enough.

"Fuck it."

We collided, mouths fusing as our bodies crashed together. I banded my arms around her and lifted her up off her feet.

Would I regret this?

Probably.

But the moment she smiled against my mouth, I didn't fucking care.

Chapter 14

Ilsa

Stop kissing him. Stop kissing him. Stop kissing him.

The rational, responsible part of my brain was screaming at me to make this stop. This was reckless and rash. This could cost me my job and would likely be something I regretted come morning.

But as Cosi's tongue twisted with mine, as he hauled me off my feet, the very last thing I wanted to do was to stop.

My arms were wrapped around his shoulders, my breasts pressed against the broad plane of his chest, but it wasn't close enough. I needed more and more and more. This was a kiss I wanted to last a lifetime.

Cosi's lips were soft, yet firm. He fluttered his tongue against mine and every nerve ending in my body tingled. That perfect mustache tickled my skin, and when he nipped at the corner of my mouth, my insides liquified. Desire coiled in my lower belly as a dull ache bloomed between my legs.

His spicy, rich scent surrounded me as he carried me into his bedroom and kicked the door closed behind us. His arms shifted lower, his hands pressing into the curves of my ass before they slid lower and lower. With a quick tug at the back of my knees, he hooked my legs around his waist.

I crossed my ankles and ground my center against the bulge behind his zipper.

"Fuck," he hissed, tearing his lips free.

"Off," I panted, pulling at the cotton of his Henley until it came free from where he'd had it tucked into his jeans.

"Ilsa . . ."

I really liked how my name sounded in his voice. Gravelly with a hoarse rasp. Like he was on the verge of ravishing me for hours.

Not once in my life had I been ravaged. Sex had always been . . . fine. Enjoyable but not toe curling. I'd convinced myself that the reason I couldn't fully relax during sex was because it wasn't with Troy.

At the moment, I couldn't even picture Troy's face.

Not with Cosi's hazel eyes locked on mine. I wanted him. Only him.

"Kiss me," I breathed.

He walked us to the bed, then planted a knee on the mattress to lay me down. He came down on top of me, bracing on an elbow to not crush me beneath his weight.

His other hand lifted to my face, his fingers tracing a line across my cheekbone, then along my jaw until his thumb was at my mouth. With his eyes locked on mine, he tugged my lower lip free from between my teeth.

I'd never met a man with such beautiful eyes. Green and gray, flecked with gold. For one night, I was going to lose myself in those eyes. Just once.

Cosi captured my mouth, his tongue giving a languid swirl before he did another flutter.

Heat swept through my veins, my nipples pebbling beneath my bra, and all I wanted was to strip him bare. To feel his skin against mine.

I pulled and yanked at his shirt, trying to work it free. My hands reached between us, unclasping the button of his jeans. But before I could work the zipper down, he abandoned my mouth to latch on to my pulse, his tongue hot and wet as he kissed a trail down my throat.

His hand moved to cup my breast, and I arched into his grip, aching to feel those fingers against my flesh. To feel him everywhere.

I looped my leg around his, grinding against his muscled thigh, desperate for some friction. Some relief to the throb that was building in my core.

My hands roved the hard muscles of his back, my fingertips dipping into the small indents along his spine. Then I flattened my hands, skimming beneath his jeans, expecting boxers or briefs beneath. All I found was taut skin over sculpted cheeks.

A smile stretched across my mouth as I dug my nails into his ass. "No underwear?"

Cosi lifted up, a smirk on his mouth as he shook his head. "Not today."

That was so damn hot. My smile widened as I lifted to graze my lips along his.

He pressed his leg against my center, making me gasp at the pressure against my clit. "This is going to be hard and fast. Take the edge off. Then we'll take it slow. Good?"

"Yes." I managed a nod before he hauled me up to sit. My sweater came up and over my head in a whoosh, sailing to the floor as he reached behind his neck, yanking off his Henley and tossing it aside.

My mouth watered as I drank in the sight of his bare chest. Chiseled arms roped with muscle. Broad shoulders and firm pecs dusted with dark hair I wanted to feel against my nipples. And a washboard stomach that made my belly dip.

Cosi wasn't just built, the man was a dream. A flawless blend of smooth, strong lines and rugged, masculine edges.

His hands dove into my hair, pushing it away from my face and over my shoulders as his gaze swept over my chest. His Adam's apple bobbed as he swallowed and his eyes darkened.

With a quick flip of his fingers on the clasp of my nude bra, it came free. Then his fingertips were gliding across my skin as he pulled the straps from my arms. He took my bra off with such ease I didn't want to think about how much practice he must get, only that I was reaping the rewards.

There was something sexy about a man who knew how to undress a woman. No fumbling fingers. No awkward questions.

He wanted me bare and made it so.

As my bra joined our other clothes on the floor, Cosi swept down, capturing a nipple in his hot mouth, sucking hard as he flicked it with his tongue.

"Yes." My hands dove into the soft strands of his hair, holding him to me as I arched into his mouth.

He released my nipple to give the same treatment to the other, the cool air on my wet skin a delicious contrast to the heat in my veins.

The throb in my core matched my pulse, beating harder and harder. I ached for him so desperately it wasn't going to take more than a touch and I'd explode.

My hands drifted down his corded neck to explore his body. Over his arms and shoulders and chest, fingertips digging into his skin to feel that strength beneath.

He laid me down, his chest covering my own before his mouth moved lower and lower, that mustache tickling my ribs as he kissed his way to my navel. He freed the button and zipper on my jeans, then as he stood from the bed, he dragged them and my lace panties over my hips, slowly easing them down my legs, inch by teasing inch. By the time he made it to my ankles, I was trembling.

Was this foreplay? I'd had boyfriends undress me before, but it had felt nothing like this. The attraction, the raw chemistry, seemed to crackle in the air. Weeks of stealing glances at his handsome face, denying this magnetism between us, heightened every look. Every touch.

It had always been inevitable, hadn't it? I might as well have been a foregone conclusion. I loathed being predictable. But at this moment? I didn't care. I just needed this man inside me.

I didn't want a sweet, tender night. I wanted him to fuck me senseless. To satisfy that ache that doubled as the sound of his zipper lowering filled his bedroom.

Pushing up to my elbows, I stared, heart racing, as he pushed off his own jeans, his length bobbing free.

Holy fuck. His cock was long and thick. Huge. Cosi gripped his shaft, giving it a few hard strokes as his gaze drifted over my breasts, lowering to my pussy.

"Spread for me, baby," he ordered, and I obeyed.

Baby. There was that nickname again. He'd probably called a dozen women baby, and I shouldn't like it. But my core clenched, my pulse skipped.

Right now, he could call me anything he wanted.

His tongue darted out, licking his bottom lip. Then he released his erection, rounding the bed for his nightstand. He took out a condom from the drawer, lifting the packet to his teeth to tear it open. He sheathed himself, and a new wave of anticipation washed over me as he climbed onto the bed, settling between the cradle of my hips.

With his elbows bracketed beside my head, he stared down at me, eyes roving my face before his mouth came down on mine, his tongue sweeping inside. He licked and sucked, rocking his cock through my soaking-wet slit.

I tilted my hips, urging him inside, but he tore his lips away and gave me a devilish grin.

"I want to taste every inch of this body." His hand cupped a breast, kneading and massaging as his thumb flicked my nipple.

"Yes." I didn't care what he did as long as it ended with an orgasm.

"Later." He planted a hard, firm kiss on my mouth. Then he lined up at my entrance and rocked inside. He worked himself in slowly, giving me time to adjust to his size. But once he was rooted deep, he thrust his hips forward, stealing my breath.

"Cosi," I gasped, fingers digging into his shoulders as my body stretched around him, the breath gone from my lungs as every muscle began to quiver.

"Fuck, Ilsa." He gritted his teeth, jaw flexing as he groaned.

"Move," I panted.

He sucked in a sharp inhale as he eased out, then pumped forward again, hitting even deeper than before.

I melted into the mattress, my eyes drifting shut, sinking into the pleasure as he fucked me, his strokes slow at first, teasing and torturous.

Cosi fucked like he kissed, with intention. With dominance. He moved like he was on the verge of losing control but not quite. He kept it leashed.

"God, you feel good." He dropped his mouth to my ear, his breath tickling the shell only driving me closer to the edge. "You're so fucking tight, baby. Like this pussy was made for me."

"More." I looped my legs around his hips, changing the angle of my hips. "Oh, God."

"Look at me."

My eyes fluttered open, meeting his hazel gaze.

He took my hands, lacing our fingers together as he lifted them above my head, keeping me pinned. "You're mine. All night."

"Yes," I moaned as he fucked me harder, faster, bringing us together, stroke by stroke as the headboard slammed into the wall, a steady thud that matched the beat of my heart.

Each time he thrust forward I saw stars. My inner walls began to flutter as he took me higher and higher.

"Cosi," I whimpered, my limbs shaking. My body writhed beneath his and my nipples scraped against his chest as my breasts bounced, up and down.

"Come, baby. Come on my cock." He rolled his hips, the root of his cock hitting my clit, and the rush of heat and ecstasy sent me over the edge.

I exploded, my back arching off the bed as my incoherent cries filled the room. Stars burst behind my eyes. My toes curled.

"Fuck." The grip he had on my hands tightened as he buried his face in my hair, and on a ragged roar, his frame went taut as he succumbed to his own release.

Pulse after pulse, I clenched around him as he continued to fuck me, drawing out the release until every cell in my body shattered. Until I was boneless.

Destroyed for any other man.

When he was spent, he collapsed on top of me, his heavy breaths a mirror of my own. Cosi rolled us to the side, shifting to his back and taking me with him, draping me across his chest, our bodies coated in a sheen of sweat.

We lay there for a few moments, waiting for our hearts to stop thundering. Then Cosi slipped out from beneath me, tugging back the covers. He draped them over my naked body before walking away.

The sound of a faucet turning on echoed from his bathroom, and I knew I should get up. Get dressed.

But I couldn't keep my eyes open, and when he returned to bed after dealing with the condom, his large frame curling around my body, I was already asleep.

The sound of a car's engine woke me from sleep. The flash of headlights illuminated the room as it passed by outside.

In such a short amount of time, I'd grown used to the stillness at the cabin. The darkness. There was no noise of traffic to wake me from a dreamless sleep.

It took me a moment to remember where I was. Cosi's bed.

I lifted off the pillow, letting my eyes adjust to the night.

Cosi was sprawled on the other side of the mattress, his naked back on display. He'd kicked off most of his covers and only a sheet covered his lower half.

Even in the dark, the definition in his back was tempting. My fingers itched to touch the strands of hair that were curled at the nape of his neck. To touch the dimples at the base of his spine, right above that sculpted behind.

A quick glance at the clock on his nightstand said it wasn't even midnight. After he'd fucked me into oblivion, I'd crashed. It had only been hours, but that was the hardest I'd slept in weeks. Months.

Flashes of us together looped through my mind. His mouth. His hands. His dick.

My eyes squeezed shut. What the hell was I doing?

I couldn't get tangled up with this man. He was a student's parent. This could cost me my job. My reputation as a teacher. And I was leaving Dalton. Even if I were staying in town, Cosi Raynes should have **COMPLICATED** tattooed across those broad shoulders.

And now that we'd had sex, it was only going to get worse.

Shit. My stomach knotted as I carefully lifted away the covers and slipped out of bed. Tiptoeing toward the door, I snatched the first piece of clothing I came across, clutching it to my naked chest—Cosi's Henley.

Easing the door open, willing it not to make a sound, I held my breath until I was in the hallway. Then with the door closed at my back, I brought his shirt to my nose, inhaling his scent in a moment of weakness before I pulled it over my torso and moved on silent feet for the kitchen.

The lights were still on. Spencer's textbook and homework were still at the table.

I smacked a hand to my forehead. "Stupid, Ilsa."

Stupid and incredible. I'd never known sex could be that way. My nipples rubbed against the cotton of his shirt as I walked to get my jar from the table and fill it at the sink. There was a tenderness between my legs along with a lingering desire. Stupid or not, I wanted to do it all over. Again and again and again.

I sipped my water, willing that desire to fade. Once had to be enough.

Unless . . .

No. I wouldn't let myself go down that path. In the morning, we'd talk. Reestablish some boundaries. I'd return home to the cabin. And hopefully, he'd agree that last night had to stay between us.

My stomach knotted tighter, already dreading that conversation. He would agree to keep this a secret, right? Cosi didn't seem like the type to publicize his conquests to the community, but I didn't know him well enough to be certain.

That was the real problem, wasn't it? He was basically a stranger. And I'd never had casual sex before, not once. The only men I'd let into my bed were boyfriends. Men I'd dated for weeks before inviting them into my body.

But I didn't regret last night. Not at all.

"Damn it," I whispered.

"Sneaking out on me already?" Strong arms wrapped around my shoulders.

I yelped, jumping as my heart leapt into my throat.

"Easy." Cosi caught the jar in my hand before I dropped it.

"Shit." I twisted and glared up at him before sagging into his chest as the moment of panic faded. "You scared me."

"Sorry. Thought you heard me." He took a drink of my water, then set the jar on the counter. "Freaking out?"

"Maybe a little." *A lot.* "You're my student's parent."

"No one needs to know about this, Ilsa. It's not their business. It's ours."

The relief was instant. But there was a twinge, deep down, that I didn't want to admit felt a little bit like disappointment.

"Good. I think this would be best if it stayed between us. A one-time thing. A lapse in judgment."

Cosi's frame tensed. "Yeah."

Except it didn't feel like a mistake. At all.

Just once. I'd told myself this was a one-time deal. So I stood taller, about to wiggle free from his arms.

But instead of letting me go, he spun me around, so quickly I didn't have a chance to fight it as he hoisted me up and plopped me on the counter.

He stood between my knees, forcing my legs apart. He'd pulled on his jeans but hadn't bothered with the button and they hung low on his narrow hips, showcasing the sculpted V and dark trail of hair that disappeared beneath the open waistband.

The counter was cool against my bare ass as the heat from his chest radiated to mine.

His hand skimmed up my thighs, dipping beneath the hem of his shirt. He leaned forward, his mouth a whisper against mine as his fingers traced higher and higher.

My breath hitched when he reached my inner thighs, and when his middle finger dipped into my core, a mewl came from my throat.

"What did I tell you earlier?" he asked, his lips and that fucking mustache tickling my cheek as he spoke against my skin. "You're mine. All night."

My hands settled on his shoulders, holding tight as he pushed my legs even farther apart. The shift brought me to the very edge of the counter, and if not for his body, I would have toppled off the edge.

His finger circled my clit once, then twice, before dipping inside, curling to the spot that made me whimper.

"Want me to stop?" He nibbled on my earlobe as his fingers continued to tease my pussy. "Call this a mistake too?"

Yes. The answer was yes.

But instead, I shook my head and let him finger fuck me in the kitchen before he carried me to his bedroom. And when he fucked me again, he made sure I was exhausted enough to sleep until dawn.

Chapter 15

Ilsa

"Is this weird?" I asked Spencer as we walked along Pine Street's shoveled sidewalk.

He lifted a shoulder.

"It's weird." I frowned. "Do you want me to hurry ahead so people don't see us together?"

"Nah, it's cool."

Not the answer I'd expected from a teenager walking to school with his math teacher. "Really? You're not embarrassed to be seen with me?"

"No." He tucked his hands into his coat pockets.

"Okay. Well, if you change your mind when we get closer to school, I'll stop to tie my shoe."

He glanced down to my caramel, knee-high boots. Boots without laces to tie. The corners of his mouth turned up, and it made him look so much like his dad that I couldn't help but smile back.

"I'm overthinking this."

"Just a little." He laughed and hitched his backpack higher over his shoulders.

Spencer wasn't quite as tall as his dad, but he stood well above my height, and every few steps, he'd glance down. Probably because I was staring up at him.

Did he know about Cosi and me? So far, I hadn't noticed him acting strange, and I had to believe that if he knew I'd slept with his father, he'd act strange. But this morning, he'd seemed his normal teenage self.

Not that I knew his normal teenage self very well.

"What?" he asked.

"Nothing." I waved him off as we reached Main Street and turned the corner to continue on to Dalton High.

I'd been overthinking for hours and couldn't exactly shut it off, no matter how hard I'd tried to stop.

The gossip was inevitable. Sooner rather than later, people would learn that there'd been a fire at the cabin, and afterward, I'd spent the weekend at Cosi Raynes's house. If they suspected I'd spent the weekend in his bed too, they wouldn't be wrong.

Cosi had fucked me again yesterday morning after we'd woken up, then he'd carried me into his shower. I'd never had this many orgasms in a week, let alone a twelve-hour period. And while I was *entirely* satisfied, I still wanted more.

But the minute Spencer had come home from his sleepover at his grandmother's house, I'd made sure to keep at least three feet of personal space between Cosi and me. I'd spent a solid hour freaked out and convinced Spencer could smell Cosi's Zest soap on my skin.

The three of us had spent an awkward afternoon in the living room. Well, it had been awkward for me. Neither Cosi nor Spencer had seemed to care.

Spencer had come home and flopped on the couch to watch basketball on TV. Cosi had taken the recliner, alternating between watching the game and getting up to do laundry or tidy up around the house.

My plan had been to read through Dad's journal and attempt to make sense of its chaos. Except every time Cosi stood from his chair, my gaze automatically went to his ass. Then I spent the next ten minutes worrying that Spencer had seen me ogling his father's very sculpted behind.

By the time Cosi had gone to the kitchen to make burgers for dinner, I'd been a ball of nerves.

Thankfully, as far as I could tell, Spencer hadn't been the wiser. Just like he didn't seem to know that after he'd gone to bed, his father had stolen me away to his. Again.

So much for just one night.

That plan had disintegrated like wet tissue paper the moment Cosi's hand had captured mine, and he'd jerked his chin toward his bedroom.

But the weekend was over. It was Monday and time to get my shit together.

I'd slipped out of Cosi's bed this morning at four o'clock, and as I'd showered and pulled on a black sweaterdress for work, I'd made myself a new promise.

No more. The sex was fucking fantastic, but this could not continue. And tonight, it was time for me to go home.

"My grandma said you used to live here," Spencer said. "When you were a kid."

"Yeah. It was a long time ago. I used to come every summer to stay with my dad. His house is on Cotters Lake."

"That's cool. Dad takes me out there sometimes in the summer."

"It's a nice spot," I said as we passed Ted's Taxidermy. There was a stuffed jackrabbit in the window holding a sign that read CLOSED. "When I was a kid, that jackrabbit also had antlers."

Spencer laughed. "It still does in the summer. Ted puts them back on for the tourists."

Dalton was located a bit too far off the beaten path to be a popular travel destination, but enough people flocked to this area on their way to Glacier National Park that Dad used to grumble about the abundance of out-of-state license plates every summer.

This town had a unique charm beneath its rugged exterior. Most of the buildings and signs were familiar from my youth, and in a way, it was like stepping back in time. To the days when life seemed simpler. Happier.

The IGA was the same sage green it had been painted when I was young with the same shopping carts with red handles. Every other building had wooden siding that blended in with the surrounding trees. The new businesses had a shine that both clashed and balanced the older, weathered establishments.

"Dalton hasn't changed much since I was a kid," I told Spencer. "Does the ice cream shop still make homemade huckleberry ice cream in the summer?"

"Yeah. It's my favorite. Dad's too."

I'd have to stick around long enough for that. I'd have to stay in town long enough to see Dalton emerge from these piles of snow. To see if they still put flags and hanging flower baskets on each streetlight. To wander up and down Main Street with a bag of popcorn from the popper at the hardware store.

A yellow school bus passed on the road, its back tires covered in chains.

"Are you coming back to our place after school?" he asked.

"I'm hoping I can go home. Give you back your house. Stop making you share a bathroom with me."

He watched the ground as we walked, his stride shortening to match mine until we were in sync. "We don't mind. If you have to stay. Especially if your cabin isn't safe. Don't feel like you have to go. It's cool. It doesn't bother me."

I wasn't sure where the glowering, grumpy version of Spencer Raynes had gone this weekend, but I also didn't want him back. This kid was quickly becoming my favorite person in Dalton. He was funny. Kind. Considerate. Smart, even though he didn't like to show it for some reason.

"Thanks, Spencer."

"Yeah. Sure. Whatever."

The bus pulled into the loop at the school, its doors opening. As the students streamed out, Spencer adjusted the brim of the baseball hat he was wearing. He'd have to take it off once we got inside, but it was clearly part of the teenage male dress code. Every boy came to school wearing a hat along with jeans and cowboy boots.

A couple high school boys walked off the bus, one of them lifting a hand to wave at Spencer.

He jerked up his chin.

"Need me to stop and tie my boot?"

He rolled his eyes. "Come on. Let's cross the street."

The students in my last period of the day flew out of their chairs at the final bell. As they streamed past me for the door, each dropped today's pop quiz on my desk.

Maybe it was wishful thinking, but I didn't seem to get as many angry looks as normal. No one threw their quiz in my face.

Was I actually making progress with these kids?

I was taking it as a win and calling today quits. Opening the drawer of my desk, I took out my briefcase, stuffing the quizzes inside to grade later. Then I pulled on my coat and, after collecting my purse and jar of water, flipped off the classroom's lights and hurried down the hallway, dodging students as I made my way to the exit.

"Miss Poe." Principal Harlan's voice bounced off the walls, mingling with the sound of lockers slamming and kids laughing. *Mizzz Poe.*

"Ugh," I muttered, turning to find him strutting my way, his chest puffed. I feigned a happy smile. "Hello, Principal Harlan."

He made a show of checking his watch. "Leaving already?"

"Yes, I'm so sorry. I've got an errand to run." Not exactly an errand but he didn't need to know the details.

"I heard about what happened at your house. The fire."

Already? News was traveling fast in Dalton. "Oh. Yes. It was rather . . . unsettling."

"I imagine. You're staying with Sheriff Raynes?"

What the hell? How could he possibly know *that* already? "Yes," I drawled. "It was just for the weekend. I didn't realize the motel was closed for two months."

He stepped closer, lowering his voice. "I don't need to remind you that he is a parent."

"I'm well aware." Where was he going with this?

"While relationships between teachers and parents are not explicitly against our rules, they are frowned upon."

Heat crept into my face, more anger and embarrassment than guilt.

This was not a conversation that should be happening in a busy hallway full of curious students. Harlan must really dislike me if he couldn't even call me into his office for a modicum of privacy.

"Understood. Good day, Mr. Harlan." My hands balled into fists as I turned and walked away.

The few students who glanced my way read the murderous expression on my face and shied away. Smart kids. I stormed to the door, pushing it open with too much force.

God, he was *such* an asshole. At least I knew how long it would take for rumors to swirl around town. Less than one business day.

The gossips must have been working at light speed for word to have reached the school already. "Shit."

People must be speculating that Cosi and I had something going on. They were right. But that didn't make it any easier to know strangers were talking about me behind my back.

It was definitely time for me to get out of Cosi's house and go home.

But first, I had a stop to make. Frustration fueled my steps as I marched down Main to the bar. Trick and Sully's parking lot was empty, not a single vehicle parked out front. Good. It would be easier to talk to Trick without an audience.

Just like the last time I'd visited, music from the jukebox greeted me as I opened the front door and stepped into the dimly lit room. The scent of cigarettes wasn't as strong but a faint cloud cloaked the air, a haze I suspected was permanent. Beneath it all was a hint of bleach and citrus.

"Hey there, trouble." Trick gave me a crooked grin from behind the bar. In front of him was a cutting board loaded with lemons and limes.

"Hey, Trick."

"Wait." He pointed at me, setting down the knife in his other hand. Then he spun for the shelf at his back and picked up his baseball bat, setting it beside that cutting board. "This time, I'll be prepared."

I laughed, the anger from my conversation with Harlan fading as I slid onto a stool. "Sorry."

"I'm just teasin'. Don't worry about the other night. Beautiful woman in town, everyone takes notice."

"No, I jinxed it by talking about a bar fight."

"This is true." He laughed. "I hope Paul Johnson knows you were looking out for him."

"Uh, no. That kid hates me."

Every day, Paul called me Miss Crone. And every day, he'd make a veiled threat about me being sorry. I had a feeling that when Harlan did eventually fire me, Paul Johnson—or his father—would be the driving force behind that termination.

"His loss," Trick said.

"Thanks."

It would have been so easy to flirt with Trick, except after this weekend with Cosi, all I could muster was a wobbly smile.

"I was wondering if you wouldn't mind answering a few more questions about my dad."

"Of course. Want anything to drink?"

"No, thanks." I picked up my jar and set it on the bar. "I've got water."

He barked a laugh. "You know, Ike used to carry a jar around everywhere. Left a few behind from time to time too. I think I've got a marinara sauce jar around here somewhere. Not a conventional water bottle but it worked for him."

"Works for me too." I unscrewed the brass lid and took a sip. "I was wondering if Dad ever mentioned anything about an atlas or a key."

"An atlas or a key." Trick's forehead furrowed. "Like the keys to his truck?"

"I don't know." I sighed. "Hence why I'm here. He left a few letters behind and, in one of them, mentioned a key and an atlas. There was no context to the note, so I can't tell if it actually means something or if it's nonsense."

"Sorry." Trick reached out like he was about to touch my hand, except a bright flash filled the bar and his gaze drifted over my head to the door. "Hey."

"Hey." Boots thudded as a rugged voice sent tingles down my spine.

My heart skipped.

That voice had kept me awake most of last night.

I didn't bother turning as Cosi came to stand beside me, stretching a hand across the bar to shake with Trick.

He was dressed in the same clothes he had been this morning when he'd left the house for the station. Wrangler jeans that molded to his ass and hugged his thighs. A dark green button-down shirt that brought out the mossy flecks in his eyes.

"Can I get you anything, Raynes?" Trick asked.

Cosi shook his head. "No, I'm good but thanks."

"You two are bad for business." Trick winked at me. "Though maybe I can convince Ilsa to stick around and have dinner with me. Sandi should be in shortly to bartend tonight. We could even hit up the café if you haven't been there yet. What do you say?"

Oh, hell. Trick was cute and sweet, but the only man I was interested in dating was currently wearing a gun and a scowl. "Oh, um—"

"No." Cosi didn't so much as look at me as he answered Trick's question, but the possessiveness was clear.

Trick's gaze swung between us. "Ah. Got it. I'm too late."

"Sorry." I gave him a sympathetic smile.

"Don't worry about it." He winked at me again, picking up his bat to stow beside the cash register.

As Trick moved away from the bar, I looked up at Cosi with my own scowl, lowering my voice. "So much for not broadcasting this. Whatever *this* is."

"*This* is me coming to pick you up from school only to find out you walked to the bar."

"Well, I would have driven except you won't take me home to get my truck." If that truck would even start. It was still cold, but the temperature had warmed a little. I was keeping all of my fingers crossed I could get Dad's pickup going. "Wait. You came to pick me up. Why? Does that mean I can go home?"

"No."

That momentary glimmer of hope died a quick death. "Why not?"

He took the stool beside mine, sitting sideways to face me. The moment I looked into his eyes, my stomach dropped.

Cosi wasn't here to make some macho claim on his latest romantic fling. He was here because something bad had happened.

"What's wrong?"

He put his hand on my thigh, and in true Cosi fashion, he didn't hesitate. "Someone vandalized the cabin."

Chapter 16

Cosi

Chuck and Larry were still at the cabin when I parked the Bronco in the driveway beside Ike's Ford Ranger.

Ilsa's anxious energy had been our invisible passenger on the drive to Cotters Lake, coiling tighter and tighter the closer we came to her house. She'd insisted on coming up here to assess the damage, and while I hated that she was dealing with this bullshit at all, I admired her for facing it head-on.

She'd been fairly quiet on the drive, listening as I'd explained what had happened. Asking a few questions. Mostly, she'd looked like she was trying not to cry.

When I found the person who did this, they'd better pray I was in a merciful mood.

This morning, after checking in at the station, I'd wanted to take yet another look around Ilsa's place with the head of the fire department. We'd met at the cabin, planning to walk around the shed and glean any other information possible. I'd hoped he would be able to tell if someone had poured diesel on the shed before lighting it on fire.

Except when I'd arrived, the front door to the cabin had been ajar. When I'd stepped inside, it had been entirely ransacked.

I'd radioed for Chuck and Larry to come out immediately, and we'd been here most of the day, taking photographs and dusting for fingerprints. Then while they'd finished up, I'd returned to town to tell Ilsa.

It was sheer good luck and good timing that I'd seen her walk into the bar as I'd driven by.

Later, we'd talk about why she'd gone to Trick's. We'd also talk about him asking her on a date. But first, we needed to deal with the cabin.

"You don't have to go inside," I told her. "Just tell me what you'd like, and I'll get it."

She shook her head. "I need to see it for myself."

"Okay. Sit tight." I shut off the engine and got out, rounding the hood to open her door for her. Then I walked with her to the house, my hand on the small of her back.

It was more possessive than necessary. So was my insistence on opening her door. But at the moment, after what I'd seen today, after last night, I was feeling fairly fucking possessive.

"How'd they get inside?" she asked.

"From what I can tell, through the front door." There were no broken windows. No signs of forced entry.

"Shit." She slowed, forehead furrowing. "I can't remember if I locked up."

"No one in Dalton locks up. Especially out here." This was a safe town. A break-in was practically unheard of.

The door swung open and Larry stepped outside, zipping up his coat. "We're all done, boss."

"Thanks."

Chuck followed him out carrying a fingerprint kit. "Sorry, Miss Poe."

"Me too." She blinked too fast, her eyes lowering. "Can I go inside?"

"Yeah." As she stepped across the threshold, I hung back, dropping my voice as I spoke to my deputies. "This is priority."

"Understood." Chuck nodded, then walked to his cruiser as I joined Ilsa in the cabin.

She stood in the small entryway, her arms wrapped around her middle as she surveyed the mess.

The kitchen cabinets were all open, dishes and jars pulled from their shelves and smashed on the hardwood floor. Their broken pieces were scattered with the silverware and utensils that had been thrown from drawers.

Ilsa's boots crunched on glass and ceramic shards as she picked her way toward the living room, where the couch was turned on its back. Every cushion had been sliced through, the upholstery split to reveal the yellowed foam stuffing.

The television was upended, the black cord's prongs barely clinging to the outlet. The coffee table had been stomped so hard it had cracked down the center. The stack of chopped wood beside the fireplace had been strewn throughout the space.

"Why would someone do this?" she whispered.

"I don't know." I dropped to a crouch, picking up the phone. It was off its cradle, the spiral cord stretched so far it would never coil tight again. But I fitted it to the base, picking the entire thing up and setting it on the countertop.

The rage I'd felt earlier returned with a vengeance. It was even stronger now that I was here with her. Without question, the motherfucker who did this was going to pay.

Ilsa had told me the other night she hadn't made many friends. But an enemy who'd resort to this? It screamed immature. Emotional. Revenge.

It had to be a pissed-off student. Some kid hell-bent on punishing her.

She moved deeper into the living room, bending to pick up a smashed picture frame and shake away the broken glass. The faded picture she lifted out was of her as a kid, her two front teeth missing as she smiled at the camera, holding up a fish she'd caught. Her mouth twisted as she caught a tear at the corner of her eye.

“I’m sorry, Ilsa,” I said.

“I think . . .” She spun in a slow circle, taking in the destruction. Her spirit, that tenacity and strength, withered before my eyes until her face went blank and distant. Like she was seeing someone else’s home destroyed, not her own. She didn’t finish her sentence as she set down the broken frame and carried that photo to her bedroom.

It was as bad as the rest of the house. Her clothes had been yanked off hangers. Her underwear had been pulled from the dresser drawers. That someone had touched her bras and panties only stoked my simmering rage, but I kept a lock on that anger.

Tomorrow morning, during my daily workout at the station’s weight room, I’d take it out on a heavy bag.

Ilsa didn’t need me to lose my cool on top of everything else.

I stood in the bedroom’s threshold, watching as she snatched clothes from the floor, stuffing them into a suitcase she’d set on the bed’s frame. The mattress had been tossed against the wall, sliced through to the springs and stuffing.

“What else do you need?” I asked. “Let me help.”

“I don’t even know.” She paused packing, scanning the room. There was a single high heel in one hand, a pair of sweats in the other as her gaze shifted to the wall behind her bed. “There’s a small white box in the other room. In the trunk. It’s Dad’s ashes. If it’s still intact—”

A fresh wave of tears filled her eyes as her entire body shuddered. Probably at the thought of someone tossing her father’s remains around his bedroom.

“They didn’t open it. I’ll grab it.”

Her frame sagged. “Thanks.”

“Anything else?”

“No.” She returned to collecting her things as I made my way to Ike’s bedroom. It was a mess, like the rest of the cabin, but there was a stale taste to the air, like Ilsa had kept this door closed.

Ike’s clothes had been ripped from his closet, his mattress upended and slashed too. Whatever contents he’d kept in the cedar chest at the foot of the bed had been strewn around the room. Except for the box Ilsa was after. It was still at the bottom of the trunk.

The person who'd done this had probably read the **CREMATORY** label and backed off. Or they'd taken one look under the lid and realized the plastic bag lining the box wasn't filled with dirt, but ash.

I tucked it under my arm, then picked my way back to the door, stepping over books and blankets and shredded feather pillows, meeting Ilsa in the hall.

She was lugging an overfilled suitcase out of her room.

"I'll take that."

She dropped it, like the handle was hot, and spun for the bathroom to keep packing.

By the time I'd loaded the box and suitcase into the Bronco, she was finished, walking out the door with a bag hung over each shoulder. She wouldn't meet my gaze as she walked to Ike's truck.

"Fuck," I muttered, hustling over to grab the bags. "Hold up."

"I need a vehicle, Cosi. I can't—" Her attention landed on the rear tire, and she did a double take.

What she hadn't noticed when we'd pulled up were the tires. All four had been slashed and the bench seat inside sliced apart. They'd slashed the tires on the Rabbit too.

The despair that settled over her beautiful face was unbearable, like someone had a fist around my heart and wouldn't stop squeezing.

Ilsa's chin quivered, and she didn't try to stop the tears as they cascaded down her cheeks. Her bags slipped off her shoulders, plopping on the snow.

"It'll be okay." I framed her face, using my thumbs to catch them for her. "I've already called the garage. They're coming up tomorrow to bring the truck into town. We'll get it fixed. We'll put the house to rights. I know it's bad, but it'll be okay."

She nodded, but the tears only came faster and a ragged sob broke free. She slapped a hand over her mouth to quiet the next one.

I pulled her into my chest, holding tight as she cried. What did I say? Nothing seemed like enough, so I just held her and kissed the top of her hair.

She only gave herself a few moments to cry before she shifted out of my arms.

My hands hovered beside her elbows, ready to catch her in case she crumpled to her knees. But I should have known better. Ilsa wasn't the crumpling type.

She wiped her face dry and sniffled, squaring her shoulders as she bent to pick up her bags.

"I've got them." I snatched them up, then followed her to the Bronco.

As I loaded the rest into the back, Ilsa climbed in and slammed the door too hard.

The furious set of her jaw said we were done with the sad portion of the afternoon. Those tears would likely return. This was the type of violation that would haunt her for years. But if she wanted to be mad right now, I'd work with mad.

I was fucking mad myself.

Where my anger was a hot, boiling fury, hers was an icy, silent wrath. The kind of fury that chilled me to the bone.

The person who did this had better pray I got to them before she did.

Neither of us spoke on the drive to town, and it took the entire ride for her fists to loosen, her jaw to unclench.

The lights were on in the house as I pulled into the garage—Spencer's practice must have finished early.

"Tomorrow, I'll find another place to stay," she said.

I parked and shut off the Bronco, not bothering with a reply.

She wasn't going anywhere, but if she needed to believe she'd find another place to stay, I'd let her think that tonight.

I grabbed her suitcase, then motioned for the door. "I'll bring the rest of your stuff in after a bit. Come on."

With my hand on the small of her back, a constant touch I couldn't seem to stop, I walked at her side along the sidewalk to the house.

The scents of garlic and tomatoes and onion greeted me as I pushed through the door. *Oh, shit.* The smell of dinner meant we had company.

My mother appeared in the opening between the living room and kitchen with a wooden spoon in one hand and an oven mitt covering the other.

Not once in my adult life had I ever been disappointed to come home and find Mom in the kitchen and smell her spaghetti. But tonight, I wished she would have called me first.

"Hey, Mom."

"Hi." She took off the mitt as she walked through the living room. "You must be Ilsa. Spencer told me all about you. I'm Linda Raynes. It's so lovely to meet you."

"It's nice to meet you too." Ilsa smiled as she shook Mom's hand, doing her best to hide the exhaustion in her eyes.

But Mom wasn't the type to miss much. "Long day?"

"Yeah," I said.

Mom had spent plenty of evenings and nights in this house, watching Spencer during the times when I got called in. I'd come home on more than one occasion to find her in the recliner, knitting as she waited up.

Over the years, we'd developed an unspoken sort of language to convey just how bad things were. A sad look. A shake of my head. A shrug of my shoulder. This wasn't a fatal accident or an emergency that had ended at the hospital, but yeah, it had been a long day.

Mom studied my face for a heartbeat and nodded. "Then you don't need me here when you're trying to wind down. But I wanted to make you dinner."

And meet Ilsa.

Word that I had a houseguest was already spreading around town. Pamela had come into my office this morning to let me know she'd heard about the fire. Apparently, Ilsa staying here had been a topic of conversation at yesterday's quilting club after church.

Mom was in that quilting club.

I should have called to talk to her first. And I should have expected this spaghetti dinner and warned Ilsa about it on the drive home.

"The noodles need another five minutes, then I'll skedaddle."

"Please don't feel like you need to leave," Ilsa said. "I'll get out of your hair, and let you enjoy a family dinner."

"No one is skedaddling or getting out of anyone's hair. We can all eat together." I brushed a kiss to Mom's cheek, then sidestepped past her to carry Ilsa's suitcase to the guest bedroom.

When I returned to the entryway to lose my coat, Mom was in the kitchen, but Ilsa was still right where I'd left her.

"I'm intruding," she said, voice low so Mom wouldn't hear.

I took off my coat, hanging it on a hook. Then I unzipped hers, stripping it off her shoulders, putting it up beside mine.

"Cosi." She frowned. "I should go."

With my hand on her elbow, I steered her away from the door and through the living room, straight for the table in the kitchen where I pulled out a chair.

She was still frowning but took the seat.

I went to the cabinet where I kept my whisky, taking out the bottle. Then I grabbed two tumblers, filling each with a shot.

"Not just a long day," Mom said from her spot in front of the stove, eyeing the glasses.

"No. Not just a long day."

"Sorry."

"Me too." I sighed, then brought Ilsa her glass, setting it on the table as I took the chair across from hers.

Mom turned down the burner on the stove and wiped her hands on a towel. "I washed a load of Spencer's laundry. I'll go stick it in the dryer, then we'll be about ready to eat whenever he gets home from practice."

"Thanks, Mom."

She patted my shoulder as she walked toward the hall.

Ilsa lifted the tumbler to her nose, taking a sniff. "Promise when you catch the person who did this, they'll pay."

It was another promise I had no business making. But I did it anyway. "Promise."

"Good." She tossed the whisky back, downing every drop. She grimaced as she swallowed and set the glass on the table. "Eww. I don't know what that was, but it's not for me."

"Noted." I chuckled, taking a sip as the front door opened.

Spencer walked into the kitchen a moment later, still wearing his coat with his backpack over a shoulder. His cheeks were flushed from the walk home. The longer strands of his hair were damp beneath the band of his hat, either sweat from basketball or he'd actually taken a shower in the locker room.

"Hey, pal," I said.

"Hey, Dad. Hi, Miss Poe."

Ilsa's smile wasn't as tired when she looked up at my son. "Hi."

"Is Grandma here?" he asked.

"Yeah. She's doing your laundry."

"Really?" Spencer's eyebrows rose.

I nodded to Ilsa.

"Oh." Realization dawned on his face. "Right."

Mom hadn't done his laundry in over a year. The day after he'd turned thirteen, she'd spent an hour teaching him how to do it himself because any teenager should know how to wash their own clothes. And while it wasn't uncommon for her to cook us dinner, this was definitely an excuse. Mom had come here for Ilsa, not us.

Spencer plopped down in the seat beside Ilsa, dropping his backpack to the floor. "Good thing you decided to stay. Grandma's spaghetti is the best."

"It's just for tonight," she said.

Spencer's gaze shifted to mine. Worry flashed in his hazel eyes.

I winked.

He relaxed.

Yesterday, I'd pulled him aside to give him the abbreviated version of the situation. That I wasn't sure the cabin was safe for Ilsa, and that she needed a place to stay.

My kid—my wonderful, protective kid—hadn't even blinked. He'd nodded and promised to keep his bathroom clean.

Whatever had happened on Saturday, Ilsa had won him over. Entirely.

"How was school?" I asked.

"School." He shrugged. "Want to watch something on TV later?"

"Sure," I said, taking another sip. "Do you have homework?"

"Yeah." He gave Ilsa a sheepish smile. "Think you could help me?"

"Spence—"

"Yes." This time, Ilsa's smile reached her eyes. "I'd like that."

Chapter 17

ILSA

Cosi didn't wake as I slid out from beneath his arm, plucked his T-shirt off the floor to pull over my head and tiptoed out the door. The house was dark and quiet as I made my way to the kitchen. The air had a chill that raised goose bumps on my bare forearms and legs.

The clock on the microwave lit my way to the sink and the jar I'd washed after dinner, left to dry in a wire rack.

The last jar.

I hadn't inspected every cupboard at the cabin, but at a glance, they'd all looked empty. I doubted there'd be any jars left unbroken. Whoever had vandalized my house had been thorough and ruthless.

A slimy, sickening feeling spread beneath my skin. It melded with the overwhelming urge to cry. I couldn't decide if I was more sad than angry at the moment. It was like a set of scales never quite balancing, the emotions shifting back and forth until I was sick to my stomach.

The hatred it took to be so destructive. So cruel. Why me? What had I done to make someone so mad? Was it a student? A parent? Was this over some silly grade on a math test?

The lump in my throat was hard to swallow past as I took a drink of water. The sting in my nose was sharp. But I blinked away a fresh wave of tears and carried my water to the couch. My briefcase was on the coffee table where I'd left it after dinner.

Linda hadn't stayed long tonight after we'd eaten spaghetti. She'd peppered Spencer with questions about school and basketball during the meal, filling the silence. As Cosi had washed the dishes, Spencer and I had knocked out his homework. Then while they'd watched basketball, I'd worked on grading papers.

Anything to distract myself from the reality of this situation. Anything to not feel entirely disappointed in humanity.

Cosi had done his best to distract me too. The three orgasms he'd given me should have been enough to wear me out until his four a.m. alarm went off. But I just couldn't sleep.

My mind was whirling over what to do next.

That cabin was my home. I still had to live there. I'd have to buy furniture to get me through the semester. It wouldn't have to be much, a couch and a new mattress and a handful of dishes, but it was money I didn't have to spend. Every dollar would cost twice its worth in an emotional toll.

Cleaning the cabin would take days. It would be hour upon hour of heartbreak. Most of Dad's belongings were ruined, and I'd have no choice but to toss them out. I'd always planned to say goodbye to his things, but I'd hoped to sell or donate them. Now it was all destined for the trash.

There was a different level of hopelessness in taking all of a man's possessions to the trash. It broke my heart all over again.

When it was done, there was a good chance all I'd have left was a single glass jar. And a journal I still hadn't finished reading.

The clasps on my briefcase popped free with two soft clicks. The hinges had a slight squeak as I opened the top to lift out Dad's journal.

My hand skimmed the cover, fingers sliding along soft leather before I reached for the lamp on the end table, flipping it on. Then I opened the book.

Dad's letter, the one he'd mailed to me in Phoenix, was tucked before the first page.

> *Dear Ilsa,*
> *Remember those days when you were little, and I used to tell you stories?*

Behind it was the note Jerry had given me.

I flipped past the pages I'd already read, Dad's letter to Donnie and those weird lines and numbers. I paused on the list he'd made of endless, random words.

> *BUCK KNIFE*
> *LICENSE*
> *CHISEL*
> *MIRROR*

Beyond this point, it would all be new. Once I read it all, it would be over. My fingers trembled as I turned the page.

> *I miss you, Donnie. I don't know how to live without you. The color has bled out from the world. It's gray and dark and there's a hole in my chest. I miss you so much it hurts. I don't want this life, not without you.*

My hand came to my sternum, pressing against the ache as I turned the page.

This was the place where he'd tucked a Polaroid into the spine. I didn't recognize the woman in the photo, but it had to be Donnie.

She was so different than Mom. Where my mother was blond with blue eyes, this woman had silky black hair and dark eyes. She looked younger than I'd expected, but maybe that was because in this photo, he'd captured her smiling. It was such a raw, beautifully vivid picture I could practically hear the sound of her laughter.

A tear pooled at the corner of my eye, and I dabbed it away.

Was I really crying over a woman I'd never met? *Yes.* I sure was.

I flipped the page, expecting something else to pull at my heartstrings, but it was empty. So was the page after that and the page after that. I kept flipping, finding more empty pages. Until finally I reached a page with a note written so close into the spine I had to flatten out the journal to the point it nearly cracked to see the ink.

Box 286

"Oh my God," I whispered, closing my eyes.

Those boxes in Dad's house. Had he numbered them all? I hadn't noticed during the cleanup, but I hadn't exactly been paying attention to the boxes themselves, more to the contents within.

And now those boxes were gone. All emptied and flattened down. Most were loaded in the Rabbit for me to haul away.

Shit. My head began to throb. I closed my eyes and pressed my fingers to my temples, rubbing in slow circles, wishing any of this would click and make sense.

The couch dipped and my eyes flew open as Cosi sat down at my side. He was shirtless, only wearing his jeans. The dim light and lingering shadows accentuated the honed definition in his arms and shoulders and stomach.

"I'm getting tired of you sneaking out of my bed."

"Sorry." I leaned against his strong arm, soaking in the heat from his body. "I couldn't sleep and didn't want to wake you."

"It's all right." He dropped a kiss to the top of my hair. It was only a chaste kiss, less than a second. But it was sweet and affectionate. It gave me butterflies.

What did we call this thing between us? It wasn't a relationship, but it felt more serious than a casual fling. I guess until we figured out that label, I'd have to settle for kisses on my hair and the warmth that spread through my body when he was near.

He leaned forward, elbows to knees, and nodded at the journal. "What's this?"

"Oh, it was Dad's." I closed the cover, handing it over. "The letter in the front is one he sent right before he died. I got it two days later. It's a story about a lost treasure from the Garrack gold mining days. He was always into Montana history and ghost towns."

"Mind if I read it?" Cosi asked.

"Not at all." I stayed snuggled into his side as he pulled it from the book and envelope, reading over Dad's neat script.

"Interesting story. Is that what he's got in this journal? More stories?"

"No." I let out a quiet, dry laugh. "The rest is a jumbled mix of sadness and nonsense. It's all as weird as how I found the journal in the first place. That's what the second letter is all about."

He took out the note, reading it quickly. "This makes no sense."

"Nope, not a bit. A friend of his brought it to me at the cabin. I was on the dock one day, looking out over the lake. Then this man walked up, across the ice."

"What man?" Cosi's frame stiffened.

"Jerry. I think he lives on Cotters."

Twin lines formed between his eyebrows. "There's no Jerry who lives out there."

"Are you sure?"

"I'm sure." Cosi nodded.

"Huh." I replayed that conversation with Jerry, trying to remember the exact words and details. That day seemed so long ago, even though it had been less than a month. "Now that I think about it, he never said he lived out there. I guess I just assumed because he was so comfortable on the lake. He walked from my dock to the island."

"Did he give you a last name?"

"No. Do you know who it is?"

Those lines between his eyebrows deepened. "No."

Then who was Jerry? Unease spread through my bones as Cosi turned the note over, examining the back.

"What else did he say?"

"Not much. He said Dad asked him to give me that note. That Dad knew I'd be coming to Montana. Which is strange because I never told Dad I'd visit."

"When was this?"

"Three weeks? Before the storm. It was on a Saturday. I'd been talking to a friend on the phone and it put me in a strange mood, so I went outside."

I hadn't spoken to Troy since that day. And I hadn't thought much about him either. Strange how quickly he'd faded from my mind. My life. I owed him a phone call and an explanation, but I just didn't have it in me to make that call right now.

"I have no idea what key Dad was talking about and I never found an atlas in the cabin. But there was so much junk, there's a chance I threw it out."

"And a tap dance?"

"That's how I found this journal." I touched the spine. "I was talking to my mom, trying to figure this out. I guess when I was a little girl, I'd tap dance in the middle of the living room. Dad would move the coffee table out of the way so I had space. I moved the table and found a loose floorboard. The journal was underneath."

"He hid this book beneath the floor?"

"Yep. It's all very strange. There's not much in there of substance. Some odd sketches. A list I think he made when he was packing. He wrote some letters to Donnie, after she passed. They're hard to read. And it feels a bit like I'm invading his privacy."

"Do you care if I read it?"

"No." I shook my head. Maybe he could make sense of it where I couldn't.

He ran a hand over his jaw, his gaze narrowing on the journal. "Describe Jerry for me."

"Well, he was older. Probably Dad's age. He was wearing a hat, but the hair that was sticking out from underneath was white. Blue eyes. His lips were really chapped."

"Did he say anything else?" Cosi turned to face me, and even though he wasn't wearing a shirt, he looked every bit the cop in interrogation mode that I'd met weeks ago.

"He, um . . . he said Dad's death wasn't an accident. That Dad wouldn't have drowned."

Understanding dawned on his face and he loosed a sigh. "That's why you came to the station."

"Yeah." Jerry had been the person to plant those seeds of doubt. "I needed to hear it from you."

Cosi set the journal aside to put his arm around my shoulders, hauling me close. "It was an accident. I went and reviewed the file after you came in that day. Read through the notes and the medical exam three times. There's always the chance that we missed something, but from everything I've got, everything I saw with my own eyes, it was an accident."

"I know." I snuggled against him, loving how easily I fit into his side. "This journal, that letter, is nonsense. A part of me was just clinging to the hope that Dad hadn't entirely fallen apart. But all the signs were there. When I came to the cabin, every room was filled with boxes. I think Dad must have packed to move in with Donnie, and after she died, something in him broke. Maybe his sanity. I found box after box filled with empty cans. Lists made on napkins. It's been hard knowing he was suffering, alone."

"For what it's worth, people around Dalton loved Ike. He was a good man."

"But he was still alone."

"That's not your fault." He buried his nose in my hair, breathing it in, before he hauled me into his lap, cradling me against his chest.

Cosi held me like he had no intention of letting me go.

I curled into him, resting my cheek on his shoulder. It had been a long, long time since a man had held me like this. Since I'd *let* a man hold me.

But Cosi wasn't the type to ask for permission. I was in his arms because that's where he wanted me to be. End of story.

There was no fighting him. There was no keeping him at arm's length. Not that I'd even tried.

How many men had I dated who'd let me push them away? How long had I used Troy as an excuse not to get too close to someone else?

I loved my dad. I missed him. But our relationship had left its scars. And I'd been protecting myself from getting close to others for too long.

This thing with Cosi might fizzle out in a week. I might leave Dalton with a shattered heart. But I had enough to worry about right now. At the moment, it just felt nice to be in his arms.

"Who do you think trashed my house?" I'd been too angry to ask on the drive to town. And it wasn't anything I wanted to discuss in front of Spencer.

"A student. Some idiot teenager who's going to learn a hard lesson when I catch them. Tomorrow, I'm going to ask you to give me names."

Paul would be at the top. If it was him, I almost felt bad for the kid. Almost.

This seemed like such an extreme reaction to a new teacher, but I'd spent enough time around teenagers that I'd learned not to underestimate their emotions and hormones. And Paul had not made my life easier.

Maybe I should have taken his threats more seriously.

"I don't want to go to school tomorrow," I murmured.

"Then don't. Call in sick. Take a day or two."

"No." I sighed. "Then they win."

Cosi kissed my forehead. "Atta girl."

I tilted up my chin until I met his hazel eyes. "Thanks for letting me stay. I promise I won't intrude forever. I'll see if there's a rental or—"

He silenced me with a soft kiss. "You're not leaving. I'm not done with you yet."

I wanted to ask what happened when he was finished. How long until he'd grow tired of me in his bed. But I'd had enough disappointment for one day. Those questions would have to wait.

"Almost everything he left behind is ruined," I said.

Cosi took my face in his hands, his thumbs tracing my cheekbones. "Not everything. He's still in you, baby."

If I wasn't careful, I was going to fall for this man. I was going to drown in Cosi Raynes and probably end up broken and alone.

At the moment, I didn't really care.

So I leaned in, taking his mouth and dragging my tongue across his lower lip. I swallowed his moan, pressing my palm over his heart to feel its steady beat. And then I sat up, my mouth never breaking from his as I straddled his lap.

His hands slid beneath the hem of his T-shirt, molding to my ass cheeks and pulling me down until my core rocked against the hardness growing in his jeans.

We kissed on the couch, exploring each other's mouths. Grinding. Groping. Making out like teenagers until my lips were swollen, and I was soaking wet. Then he swept me up and carried me to his bed, fucking me so hard that there'd be no chance I woke up before his alarm.

Cosi wasn't finished with me yet.

Good. I wasn't finished with him either.

Chapter 18

Cosi

Pamela stood in the open doorway to my office, staring at me with eyebrows raised like I was in trouble.

"What? What did I do?"

"I've been standing here for a solid minute."

I cocked my head to the side. "Really?"

"You were completely lost in your own head. Should I be worried about why you've been so distracted all day?"

"No. Sorry. Just a lot on my mind. Come on in."

"Like Ilsa Poe?" She tried—and failed—to hide a sly smile as she took the chair across from my desk.

If I had to guess, she'd wanted to ask me about Ilsa all day. I was actually impressed she'd waited until the afternoon.

"You're as bad as my mother," I told her. "Was it your idea that she ambush us with a spaghetti dinner last night?"

Pamela feigned insult, pressing a hand to her chest, palm flat against the pearl buttons on her white blouse. "Me? I'd never suggest spaghetti. You know I get awful heartburn from tomato sauce."

"Right." I chuckled. "What was I thinking?"

"We're all just wondering what's happening there. It's all over town that she's staying with you and Spencer."

Hell. I'd expected as much, just not so soon. If we were in the middle of summer, people would be occupied by vacations and outdoor activities. This would fly right under the radar. But in the winter, gossip was the preferred pastime in Dalton.

"I don't know what's going on," I admitted. "She needed a place to stay."

"You could have called me. We've got that little loft above the garage."

"It was late."

We both knew it was only an excuse. There were other places Ilsa could have stayed. Maybe not the night of the fire, but afterward, there were options. Pam's loft. Mom's house. Larry had a basement apartment he wasn't using.

I just didn't like any of those options. For her. Or for me.

And now that she'd been in my bed, I definitely wasn't letting her go.

I'd fooled myself into thinking a few nights together, and I'd fuck her out of my system. But every kiss, every touch, only left me craving more. I had no goddamn clue what we were doing.

All I knew was that I couldn't stop.

Spencer suspected something was going on. This morning, before school, I'd offered to give them both a ride, but they'd opted to walk. Before they'd left the house, Spencer had given me a knowing look when he'd caught me checking out Ilsa's ass in the slacks she'd worn for work.

We'd have to talk about it soon. Not only was she his teacher, but in his entire life, he'd never seen me with a woman. I simply didn't date.

Maybe a better father would have run this by his kid first. Maybe I was afraid he'd ask me to stop, and I'd have to disappoint my son.

Whatever was happening with Ilsa, I couldn't stop. Not yet.

Especially after last night.

She'd passed out after that last orgasm, sleeping soundly on my chest, while I'd stared at the dark ceiling, mind whirling around everything she'd shared about Ike.

I couldn't put my finger on what was bothering me, but there was something poking the back of my mind. Something that made my blood run cold.

"Cosi." Pamela snapped her fingers.

I blinked, jerking myself out of my thoughts. "Yeah?"

"There you go again."

"Sorry." I dragged a hand over my face.

Her mouth flattened in a thin line. "What are you doing? She's a beautiful, unmarried woman in your house. Your son is her student. The person who suffers most from this is not you."

Fuck. "How much talk?"

"Enough. You're not doing her any favors."

Pamela was right—this gossip wouldn't impact me, the man in the relationship. It wasn't fair, but it was reality. Ilsa, on the other hand, would be labeled and judged. "We'll figure it out."

"Good. The loft is hers if she needs it."

"Thanks," I said. "Changing subjects . . . do you know anyone in town named Jerry? Someone around your age."

Pamela was a walking Dalton directory. She'd lived here her entire life and there weren't many she didn't know by first, middle and last name.

"Jerry." She hummed, thinking it over for a minute. "I went to high school with a Jerry. But he left Dalton thirty-something years ago."

"Anyone else?"

"Not that I know of."

"And no one named Jerry who lives on Cotters Lake?"

"No. Why?"

"Just curious." Ilsa either got the name wrong or this Jerry hadn't told her the truth. I was betting on the latter. "Could you do me a favor? Would you bring me Ike Poe's file?"

She frowned. "This is the fourth time you've asked for that file since she stopped by the station."

"I'm aware. Would you please just bring it in?"

"What are you thinking, Cosi?"

"I don't know yet," I said. "Something doesn't feel right."

"It was an accident. You said so yourself."

"It was an accident." I'd meant what I'd told Ilsa. There was nothing that pointed to foul play. Nothing that hinted another person had been on that boat with Ike. We had a witness statement that Ike had been fishing alone. The examiner had confirmed that gash to his head would have knocked him out before he'd fallen in the lake. Ike had drowned.

It was an accident.

But everything that had happened since? Intentional. And whoever was tormenting Ilsa was going to pay.

"Would you bring me a fingerprint kit too?" I asked. "Please?"

"Of course." She smacked her knees, then stood, leaving the office. Minutes later, she returned with both Ike's file and the kit.

"Thanks, Pam."

"Welcome." She closed the door as she left me alone to open the file.

Like I had before, I reviewed every note, every photo. I had all but memorized them, but I forced myself to read the words aloud in case my ears picked up on anything I might have missed. By the time I reached the end, I was as annoyed as I was sick of my own voice.

Every detail pointed to this as an accident.

Besides that, I couldn't name a soul in this town who'd want to hurt Ike.

Maybe I was looking in the wrong place for more clues.

I opened my desk drawer, taking out the journal Ilsa had lent me this morning. And for the next hour, I studied every page.

She'd warned me the letters to Donnie were tough to read. She hadn't been wrong. The lists were odd, the blurry lines and numbers strange, some completely unreadable. And then there was the page with *Box 286* in the spine. Whatever the hell that meant.

By the time I closed the journal, I was ready to get the hell out of my chair and this office. So I pulled on my coat, tucked the journal in the zippered pocket beside my ribs, snagged the fingerprint kit and headed to find Pamela.

"I'm taking off," I told her. "I've got a couple errands to run."

"All right. Are you coming back?"

"No, I don't think so. I'll probably head home. Call me if anything comes up."

"Will do."

With a wave, I pushed out the door and walked to the Bronco. Then I drove to the school, parking in a visitor's space before going inside.

The final bell would ring in five minutes, but for now, the halls were quiet. Most classroom doors were closed, and through their small windows, I saw students squirming in their chairs, antsy to be set free from desks and teachers writing on chalkboards.

When I reached Ilsa's classroom, I lingered in the hallway, not wanting to bother her until school was out. Through the door's window, I watched her teach.

She was standing beside an overhead projector, writing out an equation in blue marker. Her hair was twisted into a sleek chignon. She'd pushed the sleeves of her navy cardigan up her forearms, revealing the delicate gold bracelet I'd helped clasp on her wrist this morning.

She looked up, toward the door, and her eyes lit up the moment she spotted me. A smile stretched her lips, and the colors around us faded to gray.

Beautiful. So beautiful. I couldn't look away.

My world seemed to change in an instant. It toppled end over end, and when the spinning stopped, the pieces of my universe had been rearranged. All from a single smile.

For so long, it had only been Spencer, Mom and me. My life was full. Complete. Except what if it wasn't? What if there'd always been a vacant hole?

It was like pushing all of the hangers in my closet to one side and realizing that, all along, I'd had space for more.

For fancy clothes hung beside mine. For makeup and hairbrushes on my bathroom counter. For a woman who'd sit with my son and do homework every night. Who'd sleep on my chest at night and kiss the corner of my mouth each morning.

It had only been days. But Ilsa was so deep under my skin she was sinking to the bone.

The bell rang, and I jolted, torn from the moment as doors flew open and students hurried into the hall.

"Quiz tomorrow," Ilsa called after them. "Please spend five minutes studying."

A couple kids gave me a nod as I shuffled past them and into her classroom.

When the last kid was gone, she flipped off the projector's light. "Hey."

"Hi." I took a seat on the corner of her desk. "How's it going?"

She shrugged, rounding the projector to perch beside me. "What's that?"

I lifted up the fingerprint kit. "I hate to ask. But we need to rule out your fingerprints from the cabin. Can I take your prints?"

Her lip curled. "Fine."

It didn't take long to collect them all, and while she went to wash the ink from her fingertips, I packed up the kit to drop at the station.

Larry and Chuck would go through everything they'd collected yesterday and compare prints to hers. We had Ike's fingerprints on file from his autopsy, so we could sort those from the mix too.

"This is very surreal," Ilsa said when she came back to the room, drying her hands on a brown paper towel. "I didn't think I'd ever get fingerprinted. But at least it was you."

"Sorry."

"It is what it is." She shrugged. "What will you do next?"

"We'll see if whoever trashed the cabin wasn't smart enough to wear gloves. I'll warn you it's not a fast process. In the meantime, I'll be asking questions around the school. Talking to the kids you told me about."

Kids like Paul fucking Johnson, who'd been harassing her for weeks without my knowledge. That little asshole.

"I was going to start today," I said, "but thought you might need a normal day without me stirring things up."

"I did." She gave me a sad smile. "Thanks."

"You got it, baby."

She came to stand in front of me, looking up with those pretty brown eyes. "You keep calling me that."

"Yep." I traced a finger over the freckles sprinkled across her nose.

"What if I asked you to stop?"

"I won't."

The corners of her mouth turned up. "If you keep calling me baby, I might get the wrong idea about what's going on here."

Or maybe she'd clue in to the right idea.

"People around town are talking about us," I told her, already loathing this conversation.

"Great." She groaned. "Do I want to know what they're saying?"

"Probably not. I didn't ask for specifics myself. But I'm sure we can both imagine what they're saying."

"I've been labeled Dalton's newest harlot, haven't I?" She scrunched up her nose. "So much for improving my reputation."

"I'm sorry. I should have warned you about it."

"Meh." She shrugged. "Let them talk. I don't care."

"Really?" That was not at all what I'd expected her to say.

"It's no worse than what Paul Johnson says in my classroom. At least he's got the guts to say it to my face. People will find something else to talk about once I'm back at the cabin."

She wasn't going back to the cabin, but we'd talk about that another day. For now, if she wasn't worried about leaving my place, then neither was I.

"Here." I opened the flap of my jacket, taking out Ike's journal and handing it over.

Her body seemed to relax once it was back in her hands, like she hadn't wanted to let it go. "Did you read it?"

"I did."

"Did you make any sense of it?"

"Beyond those letters to Donnie? No," I said. "You about done for the day? I'll give you a lift so you don't have to walk."

She frowned at the papers on her desk. "I need to grade papers and plan a new lesson for tomorrow, since my juniors are clearly not comprehending the material. But I can bring it along. Would you care if we stopped at the post office on the way? I'm expecting a package from my mom, so I'd like to see if it's here."

"Not at all, baby. Whatever you need."

"Another baby?"

"I like it. And so do you."

Her cheeks flushed as she fought a smile. She could pretend all she wanted, but we both knew I was right. "Give me five."

"Take your time." I wandered around the classroom, taking in the posters on the walls that depicted various algebra functions. "When I went to school here, this was Mrs. Hamilton's room. She taught English."

"There's a Mrs. Hamilton who works in the office a few days a week. Same lady?"

"Sure is."

"I wonder if she doesn't like me because I'm in her former classroom."

"What do you mean, she doesn't like you?"

Ilsa shrugged. "She doesn't like me. No one here really does."

What the fuck? "Why not?"

"No idea." Ilsa closed her briefcase. "I'd ask, but no one talks to me. Granted, I haven't exactly gone out of my way to get to know the other teachers. This school feels very much like the Good Ol' Boys Club. And if I had to guess, I'd say most of the boys are irked that there's a girl in the sandbox."

I wished I could tell her that people in our small town were welcoming to outsiders. But they weren't, not always. And the teachers at this school had their noses in the air. The men would judge her if they'd heard the rumors around town. And so would the women. There weren't many female teachers—Harlan made a point of hiring men whenever possible. And those women who did work here had an impenetrable clique that included Mrs. Riley.

Ilsa had come into this school and, based simply on what I'd seen from Spencer, proved that Mrs. Riley had not been doing a good job.

That clique was threatened by Ilsa. It was horseshit. It was unprofessional and rude. But Principal Harlan was a wimp of a man who wouldn't put a stop to it. That, and he was Mrs. Riley's cousin.

I went to the hook beside the door, taking down her coat and holding it open for her to slip on. "I don't like this."

"I'm stubborn. I'll wear them down eventually."

Yes, she would.

Still, I didn't like that she was getting flak from teachers and students alike.

"Ready?" She turned off the light and led the way down the hallway.

As we walked side by side, I stuffed my hands in my pockets to keep from trying to hold hers. When we reached the Bronco, I opened her door, shutting her inside before I went to the driver's side.

She fiddled with a ring of keys from her purse as I drove to the post office.

"What's your mom sending you?"

"It's a box of stuff Dad sent her. I was curious about it, and she said I could look through it. Now I'm glad I didn't get it sooner or who knows what would have happened to it." She grimaced. "Every time I think about the cabin, I want to scream."

"Then scream."

She looked over and smiled. "Maybe later tonight."

"Promise?"

That smile widened.

Better. If all I could do to help her through this until I found the person responsible was distract her with sex, then so be it.

Ron, the postmaster, was sitting behind the desk when we walked inside the building. His thick pop-bottle glasses were perched on the end of his nose, and his long, black braid was draped over a shoulder.

"Ron." I shook his hand as Ilsa went to the wall of boxes, fitting her key into number 392.

"Cosi." Ron's dark eyes shifted to Ilsa. He stared at her long enough that I glanced over my shoulder.

She had a red slip of paper in her hand, probably for the package that wouldn't fit into the mail slot. The small metal door to her box was open, but she'd moved down the row.

She was standing in front of PO Box 286.

I held up my finger to Ron, leaving the desk to go and stand at her side.

"What if this is the box he meant?" she asked, voice lowered. "I thought he meant one of the boxes in his house, but I don't remember seeing numbers on any of them."

She returned to her box, locking it up to retrieve her keys. Then she flipped through them, shaking her head the entire time. "Most of these are from Dad's key chain. I don't know where half of them go. But I kept them in case. Do you think one might be another post office key?"

I bent over her shoulder, inspecting each of the keys as she looped through them. "The small gold key probably goes to a padlock."

Ilsa paused on a larger brass key with *D* scratched into the metal. "It's different than the one for Dad's box. His is gold."

"The boxes are different sizes. His might have been rekeyed at some point."

"D for Donnie?" she asked.

"Probably."

"Do you think this was her post office box? Would he tell us?" She tilted her head toward Ron.

"Not without a warrant."

"Should I just try this key?" she asked. "What if it's someone else's? Think he'll get mad?"

"Can I help you with something?" Ron asked, standing from his chair.

Ilsa worried her bottom lip between her teeth.

I took the red slip of paper from her hand and walked it to the counter. "She's got a package, Ron."

He gave me a pointed stare from over the rim of his glasses before he disappeared into the back room to get her parcel.

The sound of a key sliding into a lock filled the lobby.

Ilsa opened the box, wide eyes finding mine as the door opened. There was another red slip inside.

Ron emerged, a box tucked under his arm. He paused, staring at her for a long moment. "Wondered when you'd finally clear out that box. Was going to mention it but you usually come in after the lobby is closed."

"That was Ike's box too?" I asked.

"Used to be Donnie's. After she passed, Ike took it over. Never changed the name on it. I think he liked to see mail come in with her name. Pretend she wasn't really gone." Ron pressed a hand to his heart. "Donnie was a good friend. We went to school together in Browning. After she moved here in '74, we'd get together from time to time. She was real close with my wife. Now they're both gone, but I like to think they're in heaven together, making beaded earrings and talking about *Days of our Lives*."

"You knew Donnie?" Ilsa asked, coming to stand by my side.

"Sure did."

"I never got to meet her, but I think my dad loved her. Very much."

"That he did." Ron nodded. "You don't remember, but I knew you when you were just a little thing. When you'd come visit your dad in the summers."

"I'm sorry, I don't remember."

"No apologies. Glad to know you now."

"You too." Ilsa gave him a smile that brightened the lobby.

I hadn't seen Ron smile in years. But damn if she didn't make him grin.

It was impossible not to be pulled into this woman's orbit. Eventually, the assholes at Dalton High would realize it too. Like Ilsa said, she'd wear them down, one magnificent smile at a time.

Ron held out a hand for the slip of paper she'd taken from Donnie's box. He set down the box addressed to Ilsa, then went to the back again, returning with a large stack of mail kept together with three rubber bands.

Most looked like fliers and junk mailings. But folded around the smaller pieces was a large goldenrod envelope.

"Thank you." Ilsa took the bundle, then gave him a wave as we walked to the door.

She clutched the mail to her chest as we got into the Bronco and immediately started unfastening the rubber bands. The first piece she tore into was the large envelope.

And the second she pulled out an atlas, my stomach dropped.

"Cosi." She reached her hand across the center console.

"What the hell?" What had Ike been up to?

"What does this mean?" she asked.

"I don't know." I threaded our fingers together, staring blankly through the windshield as my mind whirled.

The spying. The fire. The vandalism.

What if this had never been about Ilsa?

What if this was all tied to Ike?

Chapter 19

ILSA

The table was scattered with a mix of my parents' belongings. Dad's journal, his letters and the atlas. Mom's diary and a pile of photos he'd sent her, memories from the life they'd shared before she'd left Dalton.

In the hours since Cosi had brought me back to his house, we'd both pored over everything we'd found at the post office.

If Dad had meant for me to understand any of this, he would have been disappointed.

The atlas was just an atlas, outdated by ten years. Each page was a map of different areas in Montana. There were no markings or annotations or dog-eared corners. Nothing to give us a hint why Dad would have sent this to himself through Donnie's post office box.

"There's nothing here." I leaned back in my chair, disappointment heavy on my shoulders. "It makes as little sense now as it did this morning."

Cosi propped his elbows on the table, staring blankly at the wall. He'd had that faraway look since we'd left the post office.

"What? What aren't you telling me?"

He shook his head. "Nothing."

"That's a lie."

"It was just a thought I had earlier. I can't make any sense of the fire and vandalism. I can't figure out motive."

"To punish me, clearly, for trying to teach children math."

"Most likely, it was a student. Vandalism is an emotional crime. It fits that it would be a pissed-off kid." Cosi's jaw worked as his forehead furrowed. "But when we found that atlas, I started to wonder if it wasn't about you at all. What if it's about all this?"

"This?" I waved a hand to the table. "This is a conspiracy theory from a man losing touch with reality. I think my dad convinced himself he found some lost treasure from the Garrack gold mining days. That's why he sent me the letter before he died. It's why he's left what he must have thought were clues. But none of it points anywhere. None of it makes sense. And the more we find, the more I worry about his mental state in his final days."

"He never said anything about this Garrack gold legend?"

"No. Not until that letter." And by then, it had been too late to ask.

Cosi sighed. "In my head, the most logical explanation for vandalism is an angry student or parent. But my gut says this is all connected. That Ike was the reason behind it."

"You think Dad told someone about all of this and they believed him."

"It's possible. The fire might have been a way to get you out of the house."

"Which it did," I said, my stomach tightening.

We were only tossing out a theory, but I hated the way it clicked. Maybe that was simply wishful thinking. My tender heart not wanting to take the blame for alienating a student so completely.

But what if . . .

"So while I was out of the cabin, someone came in to search for this stuff?"

Cosi lifted a shoulder. "Could have."

"Why destroy everything? Why not just poke around?"

"Could have been worried you'd notice. And you've got a history of calling the cops." He put his hand on my knee. "Saying it out loud . . . it sounds like a stretch. Fuck, I don't know what to think."

"Neither do I." I traced a fingertip up and over each of his knuckles. "Well, if someone was looking for this, they'd be disappointed. It's a cluster."

Cosi chuckled. "No shit. Not worth the jail time they're going to get when I track them down."

The confidence in that statement eased some of my fears. It might take him time, but the more I learned about Cosi, the more I was starting to see the man behind the handsome face and sexy mustache.

He was determined and resolute and unwavering. He'd turn himself inside out to keep that promise he'd made me.

"I think I might read my mom's diary." It was the one piece in this that I hadn't delved into yet.

"I'll make us some dinner. Spencer should be home—"

The front door burst open before Cosi could finish his sentence. Then a moment later, it slammed shut so hard the entire house rattled.

We both stood from our chairs as footsteps pounded through the living room, then Spencer came storming through the kitchen, ignoring us both as he threw a ball of white across the room. It bounced off the counter and landed in the sink as he stomped down the hallway.

"Hey, what's wrong?" Cosi asked.

Spencer kept walking, his bedroom door banging closed a moment later.

"What the fuck?" Cosi followed his son, knocking on the door before he tried the knob. But it was locked. "Spencer, open this door."

"I don't want to talk, Dad."

"Spence—"

"Go. Away!"

I flinched, my stomach dropping as I moved for the sink, lifting out the ball.

It was a crumpled envelope, and as I smoothed it open, I saw Spencer's name on the front and the back flap open.

He hadn't bothered putting the letter inside again. A single sheet of lined white paper was wrinkled with the envelope. The handwriting on the page was pretty and swirled in blue ink.

A single word jumped off the paper.

Mom.

Cosi hadn't shared many details of Spencer's mother, only that she wasn't in the picture. If he'd wanted to share more, he would have. But here I was, intruding again.

I let the letter drop into the sink and backed away like it was poison, only to run into a hard, solid body. I glanced up and over my shoulder, finding Cosi's gaze locked on the paper. "I'm sorry. I shouldn't have looked."

"It's all right." He reached past me, snatching it up.

I kept my eyes on the counter as he scanned the page.

Then like his son had done, he crumpled it into a tight ball, only he threw it in the trash, not the sink.

"Son of a bitch." He planted his hands on his hips, pacing the length of the kitchen. "She couldn't help herself."

"His mom?"

Cosi nodded. "She wants to see him. He doesn't want to see her."

There was more to that story, but it wasn't my business. Besides, I wasn't sure I wanted to hear about the woman who'd had his child, his high school sweetheart. A woman who had more of a claim to both Cosi and Spencer than I did.

A green, slimy feeling crawled up my neck. Damn it, I hated being jealous.

But in just days, they'd both become mine.

Cosi took out a pan, filling it with water and putting it on the stove. Then he went to the fridge, opening the door to take out a pack of chicken breasts. He rinsed them at the sink, then patted them dry. And as he put a skillet on the burner, adding a dollop of oil, I leaned against the counter.

"Can I help?" I asked.

"I've got it."

No man had ever cooked for me before. Each time I'd offered to help, Cosi had turned me down. So I stayed against the counter, mesmerized as he moved around the kitchen, preparing a meal for his son. And for me.

"His mom's name is Gwen," he said. "We grew up together. Started dating when we were fourteen."

"Young."

"Too young." He came to stand in front of the sink, staring through the window to the snow-covered yard, like he was staring into the past. "When Gwen got pregnant, it was rock bottom."

"You were fifteen?"

"Yeah. Sixteen when he was born."

Too young. When I was fifteen, I'd been too shy and awkward to even consider kissing a boy, let alone having sex.

"Her parents were furious. They disowned her and kicked her out of their house, so she moved in with her aunt."

"Not you?"

He shook his head, walking to the pantry to take out a box of dried pasta. As the water came to a boil, he dropped in the noodles with a sprinkle of salt. Then he put the chicken into the pan, the sizzle filling the kitchen as he added some seasoning.

"Mom offered to let her live with us," he said. "And she did for a couple of months, right after Spencer was born. But after he was about two months old, Gwen moved back in with her aunt."

"Why? Did you break up?"

"No." He shook his head. "We were still together. At least, that's what I thought. She said she wanted her own space. That her aunt really wanted her back and she owed it to her. I figured we'd stick it out and get married when we turned eighteen. Looking back, I can replay so many moments and see her pulling away. She dropped out of school to stay home with him and it was like the light dimmed in her eyes. We stopped talking unless it was about Spencer. We didn't kiss or sneak off to my truck to be together. She was unhappy, and in the thick of it, living in the fog of a newborn baby and juggling school with work, I was clueless. All I could manage was surviving one day to get to the next. So no, we never broke up. I thought I was in love with her up until the day she left."

The day she'd broken his heart.

"Gwen turned eighteen when Spencer was eighteen months old, and she'd planned this trip with a couple of friends to Missoula to celebrate. She dropped him off at my house on a Saturday morning. We haven't seen her since."

My gasp filled the kitchen. "What?"

"Yeah. The only reason we knew she was okay was because she called her aunt and told her she wasn't coming back."

"Wow." That was not at all the story I'd expected to hear.

Cosi yanked a drawer open to take out a pair of tongs and flip the chicken. He gripped the utensil just a bit too hard, oil splattering on the stove. "Honestly, I never expected to hear from her again. But right around Christmas, she wrote me a letter. She wants to visit and see Spencer. Except he doesn't know her. He couldn't pick her out of a crowd."

"Really?"

"Really. I've got pictures of her in high school yearbooks. I kept them in case he ever asked what she looked like. But he's never asked. Not once. Not even when he was little."

Because Cosi was enough. Spencer hadn't needed anyone but his father.

I was going to fall in love with this man, wasn't I? It was inevitable.

Cosi pulled ingredients from the fridge to make an alfredo sauce, setting the chicken on the cutting board to rest. He rolled his shirt sleeves up his forearms, and I nearly swooned. His muscles flexed as he whisked the sauce in the pan, veins popping beneath smooth skin.

God, that was sexy.

I could spend a lifetime in this kitchen, watching this man cook. Tonight, I wouldn't need any foreplay. Everything about him was a turn-on.

Gwen was a fool. Her loss was my gain.

"I wrote her back," Cosi said. "Told her he wasn't ready for that. But apparently, she thought another letter would change his mind."

"Can she demand time with him?"

"No. I went to the county courthouse when he was three and made sure I had all the rights when it came to my son. Her parents moved away around that time, not that they ever had anything to do with him. If we accidentally bumped into them around town, they'd pretend like we didn't know each other. Wouldn't so much as make eye contact with their own grandchild."

Assholes. "And Gwen's aunt?"

"Also gone. When everyone realized Gwen wasn't coming back, I think she felt guilty. Like she could have been a better influence. From what I heard, she moved to Texas."

"Which means she has no reason to come here other than to see Spencer. She can't fake a visit to a relative. Hence the letters."

"Yes." His jaw clenched. "The first letter was to me. I could understand that one. But the second? Addressed to him? Damn her."

"What are you going to do?"

He took a long breath, then pulled a colander from the cupboard. "It's Spencer's call. Whatever he decides, I'll support him."

The perfect answer.

Cosi didn't want Gwen around his kid. But he'd set his own feelings aside. He'd let Spencer make that decision.

"My parents had a strained relationship," I told him. "My mother didn't want to live in Montana, and my father didn't want to live anywhere else. There were times when I know Mom wanted to strangle

Dad. He never visited me after we moved to Arizona. He made very little effort. So she made it for him. Every summer, she'd drive me up here to spend a few months in Dalton. Not because she wanted to live without me for three months. Not because the trip was all that easy to make. But because it's what I wanted." I walked over and put my hand on his arm. "Spencer is lucky to have you."

Cosi stared down at me, the flecks of green in his hazel irises brighter tonight. "Thanks, baby."

"That's three times today."

"You're counting?"

"You were right. I like it."

"Good." His eyes crinkled at the sides as he smiled. Then he dropped a kiss to my forehead and nudged me aside so he could drain the pasta.

I went to the cabinet where he kept his plates, opening it, as movement caught my eye.

Spencer stood in the mouth of the hallway, his boots gone, his socked feet quiet on the floor. Without a doubt, he'd seen Cosi kiss me.

My cheeks flamed, but all I could do was offer a guilty smile.

He rolled his eyes, clearly unsurprised.

I guess Cosi and I hadn't been as discreet as I'd thought. *Damn.*

"You okay?" Cosi asked as Spencer walked into the kitchen.

"Did you read her letter?"

"I did."

Spencer raked a hand through his hair, a move that made him look so much like Cosi it was uncanny. "I don't know what to do."

Cosi crossed the room and put his hand on Spencer's shoulder. "No need to decide tonight. Let's eat. Sleep on it."

"Okay." Spencer fell into Cosi's chest.

Cosi wrapped him up, holding tight. "Love you, pal."

"Love you too, Dad."

A part of me felt like an intruder again. The other part felt like I was exactly where I should be.

After a quick kiss to his son's hair, Cosi let Spencer go and went back to the food.

Spencer shuffled to the table, staring down at the mess. "What's all this?"

"The ramblings of a depressed man who was giving in to his own delusions," I said, taking out three plates.

"Huh?"

"Stuff of my dad's."

He picked up the letter that Jerry had given me, reading it before setting it aside. Then he touched the open page of the journal. It was one of the pages with a squiggled line and random numbers.

"So you have the atlas." He picked up the book of maps. "I don't get the tap dance thing. But where's the key?"

"On my key chain."

"No, to this." Spencer picked up the journal, separating a page with a line and numbers. He bent back the rest of the journal, so that single page was alone. Then he flipped through the atlas, to the page that included Dalton.

With it open, he overlayed the page on the map.

"What do you mean?" I walked over to see that line match up perfectly on the atlas.

It wasn't a line at all. It was the Blackfoot River.

My jaw dropped. My knees buckled so quickly I nearly dropped the plates, but then Cosi was there, taking them from my hands to set aside.

The blood drained from my head so fast I got dizzy, but Cosi's arm banded around my back, holding me to his side as he bent over the atlas.

"No fucking way," he murmured.

Spencer pulled the page away and traced his finger over the river in the same shape as the line on the page.

"How did you know that?" Cosi asked.

"We're learning Dalton history this month in social studies."

"And you paid attention in class?"

I elbowed him in the ribs. "Cosi Raynes."

"What?" He didn't even flinch. "I'm just asking."

I shot him a frown as Spencer placed the page back on the atlas. "These numbers must mean something. Miles, maybe?"

No, not miles.

FIND THE ATLAS AND THE KEY

A key.

"Can I see that?" I took the journal from his hand, flipping to the list of items Dad had made. Then I took my favorite red pen from my briefcase and wrote a number next to each line.

1. BUCK KNIFE
2. LICENSE
3. CHISEL
4. MIRROR

One of the numbers along the line was *1,2,4*. The commas were small ticks on the page.

"Buck knife. License. Mirror." I looked to Cosi. "I don't know what that means."

He stared at the map, his face hardening before he pointed a finger to the place where the numbers would have lined up against the page. To a section of forest without any roads or markers. "This is BLM land."

"B, L, M," Spencer repeated. "First letter from each line."

The key. It wasn't a physical key. It was a key to Dad's strange code.

I sank into a chair, my heart racing so fast it felt like it would gallop out of my chest. "Does this mean what I think it means? Are we staring at a treasure map?"

Chapter 20

Cosi

Spencer yawned, covering it with a hand.

It was nearly eleven, and we'd been sitting at this table for hours. After scarfing dinner, the three of us had settled in to slowly decode Ike's map.

We'd just finished with the last line—a creek so small it had taken us a while to place and highlight it. There were still five more numbers to decipher, and while some of the number sequences hadn't been as straightforward as the first, others had meant piecing together different items from the key.

Ike's logic had made sense to him, but it had taken us hours to muddle through.

Even when we were finished with the numbers, we'd have three different lines and series of dots on this atlas to reconcile. I wasn't sure how long it would take for us to make sense of this map.

If there was sense to make.

When Ilsa yawned, I knew we'd be more productive with fresh eyes in the morning.

"Okay, time for bed," I said.

Spencer's eyes bugged out. "But, Dad, we're not done."

"It's late. This will be here tomorrow. No arguments. We could all use some rest."

"Fine," he pouted, slumping in his chair. "Can I skip school?"

Ilsa laughed. "Because you want to work on this or because you have a math test?"

"Both?" He grinned, looking to me with pleading eyes. "Please?"

"Not a chance." I nodded to his hall. "Off to bed."

"You never let me skip school," he grumbled.

"Get straight As and we'll talk."

"Working on it." His gaze lifted to Ilsa. "Is Richie still your favorite?"

Who was Richie?

Ilsa threw her head back and laughed. "Yes, but you're catching up."

"Good." He grinned again and stood.

I wasn't the only Raynes enamored with her, was I? If impressing her was the motivation behind this newfound effort he was putting toward school, I wasn't going to complain.

"Hey, pal?" I stopped him before he could disappear down the hall. Before he went to bed, I wanted him to know Ilsa was going to be in mine. If anyone deserved to know the truth, it was Spencer. "Ilsa is sleeping in my bed. You okay with that?"

"Cosi." Ilsa's jaw dropped as she smacked my arm.

I chuckled, catching her hand and holding it against my chest. "He already knows."

She grimaced. "Since you saw him kiss me earlier?"

"No, since Dad was checking out your ass this morning and he winked at me before we left for school."

Ilsa's face flamed. "You weren't meant to see that."

"Just like I wasn't meant to see that kiss." Spencer smirked, teasing her.

"Is it going to be weird now?" she asked, genuine concern etched on her face. "I don't want anyone to give you a hard time at school."

"I don't give a shit about what people say." He puffed up his chest.

That was a lie. All teenagers cared what other kids said. But he'd withstand any taunting to make her feel good about this.

Pride swelled in my chest, making it hard to breathe. God, I loved my kid. I loved the young man he was becoming.

"Are you sure you don't care?" she asked.

If he said it bothered him, if he asked us to stop, she'd spend every night in that guest bedroom. And I'd let her. We'd put this on pause until he was comfortable.

"You can date my dad," he said. "It's cool."

The breath I'd been holding rushed from my lungs as a shy smile lit up Ilsa's face.

"Okay." She winked at him.

"So can I skip school?" he asked.

I burst out laughing, tipping my face to the ceiling as Ilsa threaded her fingers with mine.

"Worth a shot," Spencer said. "Night."

"Good night." I stood, keeping Ilsa's hand in mine. As Spencer went to his bathroom, I shut off the lights in the kitchen, pulling her with me down the hallway.

"Cosi?" She tugged on my hand, slowing me as we reached my doorway. "Do you think we should talk about what we're doing?"

"What are we doing, baby?" I pulled her into my dark bedroom and closed the door, sweeping her into my arms. Then I dipped to skim my lips across her cheekbone.

"I don't know. You tell me." She was already working the buttons on my shirt free.

"This." I kissed the corner of her mouth.

She melted against me, her fingers splaying across my chest. "And what is this?"

Everything. This had the potential to become everything. But it was too soon for that answer, so I latched my mouth to her pulse, sucking hard enough to leave a mark that she'd have to hide with a turtleneck tomorrow.

"Cosi," she hissed, knowing exactly what I was doing, but she didn't try to tear away.

I grinned against the column of her throat, trailing my lips along the underside of her jaw.

Her fingers slipped under the collar of my shirt, nails skimming along my collarbone. Her touch was light but it felt like fire, stoking the desire that burned through my veins.

"Strip for me."

She pulled away, her eyes dark, her breaths coming in short pants. She unfastened her slacks, shimmying them down her hips and legs. Stepping out of them, she kicked them aside and lifted up her sweater to reveal a sexy white lace bra that matched her panties.

The silvery moonlight that streamed through the windows made the fabric glow as it accentuated the slender curves of her hips, the swell of her perfect breasts.

My cock throbbed behind my zipper, desperate to sink inside her body, but it would have to wait. Tonight, I wanted her on my tongue.

She reached to unclasp her bra, but I took her wrist, pulling her closer. Then I sealed my mouth over hers, savoring that sweet moan as my tongue licked her pout.

With a quick tug, I pulled her against me and carried her to the bed, laying her on the mattress. Her hair fanned out over my pillows, and as I came down on top of her, she wrapped her legs around my hips, her hands diving into my hair.

The way she pulled on my hair made me never want to cut it again. Made me never want to leave this bed.

I kissed her until she was breathless, then I tore my mouth away from hers, trailing my lips along her throat and through the valley of her breasts.

Lower and lower, I worshipped the flat plane of her stomach, licking her navel, until I reached the top of her panties.

She pushed up to her elbows, meeting my gaze.

I gave her a wicked smirk, dropping to the apex of her thighs to suck her clit into my mouth, panties and all.

Ilsa nearly bucked off the bed, falling backward and slapping a hand over her mouth to stifle a cry.

Reaching for her bra, I tugged the cups down below her peaked nipples, giving each a flick that made her back arch.

"Are you wet for me?"

She nodded, her hand still over her mouth.

"Let's find out." I eased her panties off her hips, kissing the sensitive flesh of her inner thigh as I dragged them down, revealing a mound of neatly trimmed, glistening black curls. "So fucking wet."

I climbed off the bed, taking her panties with me until they slipped off her feet. Then I yanked off my shirt, tossing it aside before I stripped out of my jeans.

She liked that I rarely wore underwear, and I sure as hell didn't miss the extra layer at moments like this.

"Look how hard you make me." My cock throbbed, aching to sink inside her perfect pussy.

She sat up, tongue darting out to lick her lower lip as I stroked myself, spreading the drop of come at the tip along the shaft.

I hadn't fucked her mouth yet, but soon. I'd take her in every way she'd let me. "Spread your knees."

She obeyed, widening her legs, letting me take in that gorgeous pussy.

"Touch yourself."

She gulped, hesitating for a moment. But then she skimmed her hand over her hip, dropping it to her center. Her fingers toyed with her slit, timid and teasing.

"After I fuck you with my tongue, I'm going to flip you over and take you from behind. Hard."

Her fingers moved faster, sliding her wetness to her clit.

"You like that idea? Me pounding into you as you hold on to the headboard?"

"Yes." She rocked her hips against her hand, fingers working faster.

"Then I'm going to carry you to the shower and put you on your knees so I can fuck your mouth and come down your throat."

"Cosi," she whimpered, her middle finger circling her clit. "I need you inside me."

"Not yet." I gripped the backs of her calves, dragging her to the edge of the bed. Then I dropped to my knees and took hold of her hand.

Finger by finger, I took each into my mouth and licked them clean. By the time I was done, her legs were trembling.

"Cosi. Please."

"Not yet."

Her frustrated growl filled the bedroom.

It was delicious, torturing her. Kissing along her center, giving her playful licks. Fluttering my tongue along her clit but only for a second. I played with her until she was so desperate, she pulled and pinched at her nipples, lifting her hips to my mouth.

I was rock hard, my arousal pressed against the foot of the bed, when I finally fucked into her with my tongue, letting my mustache tickle her clit until I drew the bundle of nerves into my mouth.

One hard suck and she came apart, bucking against my mouth so hard I had to hold her down, feasting on the sweet taste of her release until she collapsed.

The most intoxicating sight was this woman coming apart on my bed.

I'd known it the first night we'd met. She was something special, and I was in trouble. So much fucking trouble.

"Oh God." She draped an arm over her eyes, the aftershocks of her orgasm still shaking her body as I lifted her higher and spun her over onto her belly.

I went to the nightstand for a condom, but before I could take one from the drawer, she reached for my hand.

"I'm on birth control." Every muscle in my body locked as she twisted onto her side and gave me a shy smile. "If you want."

I wanted to feel her bare more than I wanted my next breath.

"I know that's probably a big step. After everything with Spencer's mom and—"

I silenced whatever else she was going to say with a kiss, my tongue sliding between her teeth.

If she'd read my hesitation as doubt rather than shock, we'd settle that right now.

I came down on top of her, rolling her to her belly and covering her back with my chest. Then I let my cock nestle into the crack of her ass. "All fours, baby."

She obeyed, our bodies moving in tandem as she lifted to her hands and knees. Then she flipped her hair out of the way, looking over her shoulder at me with those magnificent chocolate eyes.

"You're perfect." I grabbed the globes of her ass, spreading her cheeks as I lined up at her entrance. Then with a single thrust, slid into her tight, wet heat. "Fuck."

It was better than I could have ever imagined. Heaven. And with nothing between us, I felt every flutter of her inner walls, every shudder in her body as she adjusted to my size.

"Oh God," she moaned. "You feel . . ."

"Made for me. You were fucking made for me." I pulled out and thrust forward again, sinking as deep as I could go.

With a flip of the clasp, her bra was free, the straps sliding down her arms until she tossed it aside.

Her breasts bounced with every piston of my hips. As I pumped forward, she sank back, matching my rhythm, driving me wild.

Ilsa's back arched, her eyes squeezed shut as she chased her second release. It hit like a lightning bolt, toppling her forward and into the pillows where she could hide her scream. Her body clamped around me like a vise, pulsing over and over and over again as she gave in to her orgasm.

Any hope I had of drawing this out vanished as the build at the base of my spine spiked. I let go, toes curling, muscles shaking, and gave in to the sheer pleasure of fucking this woman.

This remarkable woman who'd ruined me for anyone else.

My woman.

The white spots in my eyes stole my vision, and the world seemed to tilt sideways, like it had in her classroom earlier. More of those pieces rearranging, making space for a new reality. When I finally came down from my release, I collapsed, our bodies tumbling into the bed, slick with sweat.

"Wow." She let out a soft giggle. "It keeps getting better. Every time."

I jackknifed to a seat, then stood and held out my hand. "And we're just getting started."

She pushed up to her side, looking up at me from beneath long lashes. "Thought you were going to carry me in there."

"Right. My mistake." I chuckled, then swept down and hauled her over my shoulder, giving her ass a smack as I carted her to the shower, where I did exactly as promised.

I fucked that pretty mouth, and when she swallowed every drop I had to give her, it was my turn to drop to my knees.

Ilsa toyed with the damp strands of hair beside my ear as she lay naked, draped across my chest. Her own hair was still wet, combed out of her face, hanging in sleek panels over her spine. "Cosi?"

"Ilsa?" My hand drifted down her ribs to her hip, keeping her pinned against me. Maybe if I kept her close enough tonight, I wouldn't wake up to find her side of the bed empty.

"What do you think it all means? Dad's map?"

"I don't know. I've never seen anything like this before."

"Do you think it's possible he found the Garrack gold? Or do you think it's a wild idea he convinced himself was real?"

I rolled her onto her back, needing to see her face. "That we're even talking about a lost treasure is a wild idea. I wish I had an answer for this, but I don't."

She nibbled on her lower lip, her hand lifting to absently trace the line of my nose. "If we figure out this map, I want to follow it. It will have to wait until the snow melts, but even if it leads to nowhere, I want to try. Will you come with me on a treasure hunt this spring?"

"Try to keep me away."

A smile lit up her face, and my heart nearly beat out of my chest. Hair tousled. Cheeks flushed. Lips swollen. Eyes shining like moonbeams. She was magnificent.

My lips found hers, kissing that smile as my body stirred, ready for another round. But a distant ringing broke through the moment, halting any chance of a decent night.

"Damn it." I frowned and swung out of bed, pulling on my jeans before I hurried through the house to answer the phone in the kitchen.

No good ever came from a phone call after dark.

"This is Cosi," I answered.

"Hey, boss," Chuck said. "Sorry to bother you so late."

"It's all right." With any luck, we could solve this over a call, and I wouldn't have to leave. But that kind of luck was rare, so I sandwiched the phone between my shoulder and ear to zip and button my jeans. "What's going on?"

"A guy just came to the station," Chuck said. "Pounded on the front door like the sky was falling."

"Who?"

"Guess he's a friend of Ilsa Poe's."

Every muscle in my body went rigid. "What friend?"

She'd told me she hadn't made any friends. So who the hell was this?

"I, uh . . . didn't catch his name."

"Chuck," I barked. "This is the last time you call me without a damn name."

"Sorry. I asked but it slipped my mind. His last name started with a *b*. Brady or Bradley. I didn't recognize him, and his truck had Arizona plates. He'd gone out to her place on Cotters Lake, and when he couldn't find her, he came here. He was upset, worried something happened to her. I guess he's been trying to get ahold of her for a while. Anyway, I assured him she was fine and that she was staying in town for the time being until the arson and vandalism at the cabin could be sorted. He, um . . . well, he didn't know about the fire or realize her place had been wrecked."

Hell. Those were details Chuck hadn't needed to share, but he had a tendency to say too much when he was rattled, and clearly, this friend of Ilsa's had shaken him up. I could picture him at the door, sharing detail after detail that only made the situation worse.

"What else did you tell him?" Before I left to calm down this friend, I'd like to know what I was walking into.

"I might have, um . . . I didn't mean to say it but it sort of slipped out."

"What?" I said through gritted teeth.

Ilsa walked into the kitchen wearing my T-shirt and a flannel from my closet. Its sleeves hit well past her fingertips.

"Everything okay?" she mouthed.

I held up a finger. I'd have questions for her too once I was done with this call.

She leaned against the wall, covering a yawn.

"He asked where she was staying," Chuck said.

"And you gave him my name."

"Sorry," he murmured. All this friend would have to do is swing by the gas station, flip through the phone book, and he'd have my address. "He was determined. And he said he was more than just her friend."

More than a friend? The jealousy was instant. "So you're saying I should be expecting a late-night visitor."

"Sorry, Cosi."

"Yeah," I clipped at the same moment the doorbell rang. I hung up the phone too hard, making Ilsa stand straight, her gaze swinging to the entryway.

"What's wrong? Who's here?"

"A *friend* of yours." I marched past her for the door, pulling it open with too much force.

The cold was a blast against my bare skin, my nipples tightening.

A man stood on the stoop, his dirty-blond hair stylishly combed to one side, not a strand out of place. He was tall, about my height, wearing light-wash jeans and a thick, navy parka. Behind his black-frame glasses, his brown eyes narrowed when he took in my bare chest.

What the fuck did he expect me to be wearing this late at night?

"Can I help you?" I crossed my arms.

"I, uh . . ." He leaned back to look at the numbers tacked on the house. "I'm looking for Ilsa Poe. I was told she was staying here."

She appeared at my side a moment later, eyes wide. "Troy?"

"There you are." He exhaled, and for a moment, I thought he might cry. Then he barged into my house and hauled her into his arms.

Who the fuck was Troy?

Chapter 21

Ilsa

Never in my life had I been quite so aware that I wasn't wearing pants. Or underwear.

As Cosi shut the door—a little too hard—I wiggled out of Troy's hug and pulled down the hem of his flannel to make sure it was covering my bare ass. "What are you doing here?"

"Me?" Troy jerked away at the accusation in my tone. "You're asking *me* what I'm doing here? What are you doing *here*?" He pointed to the floor where the snow clumps on his boots were already melting on the tile. "I went to the cabin. Your car was full of junk and the tires were slashed. The house was dark, and I've been calling you for over a week. What the fuck is going on, Ilsa?"

Shit. With Troy's rising voice, irritation radiated off Cosi's frame in hot waves.

"There's a lot to talk about," I told Troy. "Let's get away from the door. Come in."

Troy frowned but trailed behind me to the living room.

I expected Cosi to join us, but no. He stood in the entryway, his arms crossed and legs planted wide. *Stubborn.* Why was I even surprised?

"Give us a minute," I told Troy, turning on an end table lamp, then motioned to the couch. "Please, have a seat."

Did he move? No. Neither did Cosi. These two weren't going to make this any less awkward, were they?

"Fine." I pinched the bridge of my nose. "Don't sit."

"What is going on, Ilsa?" Troy planted his hands on his hips, his voice rising.

I shot him a scowl. "Not so loud. Cosi's son is asleep down the hall. Would you just sit down? Give me sixty seconds to pull on some pants, and I'll explain."

Still, nothing.

"Please." I clasped my hands together.

His nostrils flared, but finally, he moved to the maroon recliner, sitting on its edge.

"Thank you." I turned toward Cosi and found his hazel eyes waiting. After giving him my best pleading look, I walked to the hall, hoping I'd hear his footsteps behind me. Except when I made it to his bedroom, I was alone.

My growl filled the room. This could not be more uncomfortable.

How did Troy even know where to find me? I was missing whatever had happened on the other end of that phone call.

My stomach knotted as I snatched my panties from the floor. The scent of sex still lingered in the air. The bed was rumpled and pillows strewn. My hair was wet. Cosi's hair was wet. Troy was a smart man and had no doubt realized there was a reason Cosi and I were both half clothed.

Not that it was any of his business. I was a single woman with every right to enjoy earth-shattering sex with a single man. But I still felt a little guilty for not letting him know where I was staying.

Cosi came into the bedroom, closing the door behind him. "Who is that, Ilsa?"

"Troy. He's a friend from Phoenix," I said, searching the floor for my pants. "I had no idea he was coming up here."

Well, sort of. He'd mentioned a trip, but I'd assumed after many, many instances of me telling Troy not to come to Montana, of me not answering his calls on Sundays, he would have gotten the hint. Apparently not.

"I'm sorry. I'll take him . . ." Where? Where the hell could we go?

Earlier tonight, when we'd been sitting at the kitchen table, I'd had a momentary thought of how lucky I was that the Dalton motel was closed until March. I wouldn't be here otherwise. I wouldn't have started this thing with Cosi.

But now there was no place for Troy to stay. No place for us to have a private conversation except Cosi's living room. It was late and the café wasn't open. But we could go to Trick's.

I wouldn't mind a drink for this conversation.

"We'll go talk at the bar. That way you and Spencer can sleep," I said.

Cosi scoffed, planting his hands on his hips. "You are not going to the bar."

"Then where should I go? I can't just send him away."

"Why not?"

I gave him a flat look. "Cosi."

"Ilsa."

I stepped into my pants, pulling them on too fast, my fingers fumbling with the zipper before I finally managed to drag it up and fasten the button. "What do I do?"

Cosi glowered for a moment, then sighed. "He can crash on the couch."

I walked over, putting my hands on his waist as I stood on my toes to kiss the underside of his jaw. "Thank you."

"I don't like this."

"I'm not happy about it either." I patted his washboard stomach, then returned to the living room, sitting on the couch to face Troy.

We stared at each other for a few long moments, the silence stretching between us.

He looked tired, with dark circles under his eyes and genuine concern on his face.

"I'm sorry for making you worry," I said.

"Don't ever do that to me again." He scowled, but it softened after a heartbeat. "Hi."

"Hi." I smiled. "I can't believe you drove all the way up here."

He shrugged, the stiffness in his frame relaxing. "I needed to see you. Make sure you were okay. That *we* were okay. I miss you, sweetheart."

Once upon a time, I'd lived to hear him call me sweetheart. But now it felt too intimate, too far past the line of friendship we'd never crossed.

Because we were only meant to be friends. It was the reason Troy and I hadn't found a way to be together. Timing and circumstance were simply my favorite excuses.

I'd come to Montana to let him go. One look at his face, and I knew, any feelings I'd harbored for Troy were long, long gone.

Now we could simply be the friends we'd been for years.

"I missed you too."

His gaze softened and he stood from the chair, moving to sit next to me on the couch. He put an arm around my shoulders, hauling me into his side for a hug. "What the hell is going on?"

"Oh, well, that's a long story."

"I drove for two days to get here. Let's hear it."

I blew out a long breath and groaned. Then I shifted out of his embrace, curling into the corner of the couch with my knees drawn up to my chest as I told him everything that had been happening at the cabin.

When I was finished, he tore off his glasses to rub his eyes. "So Cosi went out there and found the place trashed?"

"Yes." I didn't like the way he said Cosi's name with a sneer.

"Are you sure he didn't trash the cabin himself to force you to stay with him?"

Wait. What? Had he just said that? "Excuse me?"

"It's rather convenient, isn't it?"

"Oh my God." I shook my head, struggling to believe this was happening. "After everything I just told you, your first response is to accuse Cosi? Are you kidding?"

"Like I said, it's rather convenient."

"Stop it, Troy," I snapped, standing from the couch, too pissed off to sit beside him. He sure as hell wasn't going to stay here tonight. Not after this. "He's the sheriff. He's a good man. How dare you say otherwise. You don't know him."

"Do you?"

"I know what counts. I know he let a man into his home tonight who just accused him of a crime. Rather than question his integrity, you should be more worried about your own."

Troy flinched. "You're right. I'm sorry. This is . . . it's been a long day. A long trip. And this is a lot to take in."

The vandalism? The fire? Or Cosi and me? I didn't ask. He could figure that out on his own.

"You can't go back to that cabin, Ilsa."

"That's my decision to make. And I will have to go back eventually." Just not yet. Avoiding the cabin for a few days should soothe the frustration and heartbreak about the vandalism, but sooner or later, I'd face the mess. "I'm not going to leave it like that."

"Then I'll help. That's what I came up here to do. I'll go out there tomorrow and start cleaning while you're at school. When you're done, we can work together. Might mean a few long nights, but I bet by the end of the week, we could have it all empty and ready to sell. Do you have a realtor you could call?"

"No, I don't." Even if it was clean, I wasn't letting it go, not yet. Troy didn't get to dictate my timeline.

But that was Troy. He pushed and pushed and pushed for what was most convenient for him.

Did I like his favorite martini bar? Not really. But that's where we always went. Did we ever have dinner at a restaurant on my side of town? No. We'd go to a place close to his house or firm because I was only a teacher, and he didn't have the time to drive.

"I'm not ready to sell the cabin yet," I told him.

"Why not? I get that winter isn't the most ideal time to list a house, but the sooner you can come home, the better."

It was my fault that he still thought I was coming back. A mistake I'd remedy tonight. "I'm not moving back to Phoenix."

His forehead furrowed. "What are you talking about? Of course you're coming home."

"I don't want to live there anymore."

"You can't be serious. Instead, you're going to stay in *Dalton*?" Another word he said with a sneer.

"No, I'm not—I don't know what's next yet, Troy."

A week ago, I would have sworn that Dalton was only a temporary stop. Now? I wasn't so sure. I hadn't really given this town a chance.

Maybe if I wasn't planning my exit, I'd remember why I'd loved this town when I was a girl. I'd see all the reasons Dad had chosen to stay in Montana.

"Ilsa, where is all of this coming from?" Troy stood, rounding the coffee table to pace in front of the TV. "It's this guy you're tangled up with, isn't it?"

Troy was searching for a villain, and he'd chosen Cosi.

"It's not about him. I left Phoenix knowing I wasn't coming back."

He stopped walking. "You never told me that. Why? What is going on?"

I almost gave him a vague answer about needing a change of scenery or trying out a new city. But it was time for the truth. The whole truth. "If I come home to Phoenix, everything will go back to the way it was, and I don't want that life anymore. You are my closest friend, but I can't fall into our old routine. I spent too many years convincing myself I was in love with a man who I knew could never love me back. Because it was safe. If I loved you, then I didn't have to fear my heart getting broken. That's not living. That's going through the motions."

"Ilsa." Troy's jaw slackened, and he stared at me with unblinking eyes. "What do you mean?"

"Oh, come on. Don't act surprised."

The pain creeping into his expression made the world stop spinning. In the span of five heartbeats, as we stared at each other, I rewound time to the day we met. To the days in between then and now.

He knew how I'd felt. He had to know. Everyone knew I'd been enamored with Troy.

"You really think I could never love you back?" He pressed a hand to his chest. "Of course I love you."

He believed it, to the bottom of his heart. Except the love between us wasn't enough.

It wasn't real. It wasn't lasting.

It was like Mom and Dad. They loved each other on the surface. It was a layer of ice on a winter lake. But all it would take was a change of season and that love would melt away.

I wanted a love that went bone deep.

"I know you do," I said, as gently as possible. "But not the way we both deserve to be loved. You love me because I'm safe. Because I'm familiar. Because I'm comfortable. You love me because I'm your friend. And you love me when it's convenient. But I want to be loved recklessly. I want the kind of love where the idea of someone else is unfathomable. I want love that's easy. This is too hard. It's always been too hard."

"And you don't think I can give you easy?" He shook his head, holding up his hands. "I have always loved you. I have waited and waited for you. Every time I turned around, you were in another man's bed. Just like now."

I tried not to laugh. "You haven't waited."

"You really think that? I call you every week. I'm nice to your mother even though she drives me up the fucking wall." He fisted his hands. "I could have married any of my last three girlfriends. They all wanted a ring, but I ended it with them instead. How obvious can I make it that I want to be with you someday?"

Someday. Wow. That was so, *so* much to take.

God, I was such a fucking idiot. Troy had been stringing me along for years, not waiting for me, but doing what Troy wanted for Troy.

Done. I was completely done. I'd known it for weeks, but tonight's visit was the closure I'd needed to say farewell. And I certainly wasn't going to offer him Cosi's couch.

"I think you'd better go, Troy."

He blinked, the confusion in his eyes fading as annoyance took its place. He scoffed, his jaw working back and forth. "That's it?"

"Yeah. That's it."

He looked me up and down. "What a fucking waste you turned out to be."

It knocked the wind from my lungs. It was the first truly mean thing he'd ever said.

I stood there, stunned, as he marched to the door, slamming it too hard as he left.

The person who'd been my best friend, gone.

"Goodbye, Troy," I whispered, walking to the lamp to switch it off.

The room went dark. Outside, an engine roared to life. The sting of tears pricked my nose.

Damn it, I didn't want to cry. But it hurt. The rumble of the engine faded to nothing.

As my best friend—former best friend—drove out of my life.

I pressed a hand to my heart, rubbing at the ache. Did it hurt because our friendship was over? Or because I'd spent so many years on that friendship?

Troy was right.

What a fucking waste.

I swallowed the lump in my throat and turned away from the living room.

Cosi was leaning against the wall, still shirtless. Still glowering. "You okay?"

"Ask me tomorrow." I lifted a shoulder. "I'm sorry about Troy."

"Yeah." He looked away, staring blankly across the room. "It's fine."

"Is it?"

His jaw worked as he stayed locked on the opposite wall. "You should get some rest."

"What about you?"

"Not tired."

I stilled at the cold, aloof detachment in his voice. He wouldn't look at me. Why wouldn't he look at me?

I stared at him for a long moment, willing him to look at me. To take my hand and come with me to bed. But I could feel him pulling away. Shutting me out. Putting a wall between us.

How much of that conversation had he heard? All of it?

From his standpoint, from the outside looking in, that must have been an ugly conversation to overhear. Not only Troy's accusation, but it probably sounded like I'd been in love with another man all this time. Like I'd been using Cosi as an escape.

There was so much to say. So much to explain. But the burn in my throat warned that tears weren't far away. "I'm sleeping in the guest room tonight. I need . . ."

Him. I needed him. But I was too wrung out to talk. All I wanted to do was cry. And I couldn't ask Cosi to hold me together while I wept over another man.

So when I walked down the wrong hallway for the wrong bedroom, Cosi didn't stop me.

When I cried myself to sleep, it was alone.

Chapter 22

Ilsa

Spencer sat hunched over a bowl of cereal at the kitchen table the next morning. He was still dressed in his pajamas from last night, his hair sticking up at odd angles. As he shoveled corn flakes into his mouth, he studied Dad's atlas.

It seemed like days, not hours, had passed since we'd all sat around the table studying that map. I hadn't felt this exhausted and emotionally drained since, well . . . since after Dad had died.

This was a mild heartache in comparison, and it wouldn't take me long to mourn the loss of Troy's friendship. Still, this morning, I was raw.

"Hi," I told Spencer, walking to the coffee pot.

"Hey," he said as he chewed.

After pouring myself a mug, I joined him at the table, glancing down the hallway toward Cosi's room.

"He left while you were in the shower," Spencer said.

"Oh." I swallowed the disappointment with a sip of coffee that scalded my tongue.

"He told me to tell you he had to get to work early."

"Ah." Was that the truth? Probably not.

"Want some cereal?" Spencer asked. "I'll pour you a bowl."

"No, thanks." No matter what happened with Cosi, I was glad I'd had the chance to see this sweet, considerate side of Spencer. "I'm not hungry yet."

"Okay." He shrugged and picked up the bowl, guzzling the last of his milk before he carried his dishes to the sink. "I'll get showered and dressed, then after I make my bed, I'll be ready to go."

"All right."

"Cool." He left for his room while I stared blankly at the mess on the table and contemplated the mess of my life.

Even though it hadn't ended the way I'd hoped, with our friendship intact, that conversation with Troy had been long overdue. It was as sad as it was freeing.

I had months left at Dalton High before the semester was finished. It was time to stop avoiding the teachers' lounge. It was time to eat Trick's cheeseburgers. It was time to meet those neighbors on Cotters Lake. It was time to make some friends.

If I left someday, I wanted one or two people here to remember Ilsa Poe as more than the harsh substitute who'd forced their children to learn math.

While Spencer got ready for school, I finished my coffee, then collected all of Dad's belongings and stowed them in my briefcase. Maybe stashed inside, the puzzle pieces would shuffle themselves into a complete picture. Then I filled my water jar and grabbed my purse, waiting in the living room until Spencer emerged with his backpack on a shoulder.

"Ready?" His hair was damp at the ends and covered in a baseball hat. He was dressed in jeans and a Dalton High sweatshirt.

"Are you going to wear a coat?"

"No."

"It's freezing."

He rolled his eyes but dropped his bag to put on his jacket. "Happy?"

"Yes." I winked, then headed outside.

We started down the sidewalk, and as we took the familiar path along Pine Street, I let my mind replay last night.

I wished we had never heard the phone. I wished we hadn't answered the door. Just thinking about everything Troy had said, accusing Cosi of vandalism, made me cringe.

"You okay?" Spencer asked.

"Great." The feigned enthusiasm in my voice fell like a snowball on the concrete, going splat.

"Really? You seem . . . off."

Definitely off. But Spencer wasn't the Raynes who could put me to rights.

All I had to do was survive this day, then Cosi and I could talk. I'd tell him about Troy. I'd find out exactly what he'd overheard. And maybe, we could talk about us.

"Are you worried about your dad's stuff?" Spencer tapped the side of my briefcase with his knuckle. "Because you shouldn't be. We'll figure it out. I know it. We can't really hike in the mountains until the snow melts, so we have time."

"You're right. We do."

His hazel eyes lit up. "How cool would it be if we found a lost treasure this summer?"

"Very cool." I laughed and took a deep breath, letting the cold, crisp air fill my lungs and give me a boost of energy. "Where's the mechanic's garage in town?"

"Second and Maple. Why?"

"I was going to walk over during my lunch break and check on my truck."

"Dad said it wasn't working."

Because the tires had been slashed.

Cosi must not have told Spencer about the vandalism, and I certainly didn't have the energy to give him those details. Besides, if there was an active investigation, if Cosi or his deputies started asking questions around the school, it would be best for Spencer to hear about this from his dad.

"Yeah, it's not working. But hopefully they've been able to fix it."

"Are you going back to your house?"

"Well, I can't share your bathroom forever. Aren't you sick of my makeup taking up your counter space?"

"I don't care. It doesn't bug me."

I bumped his shoulder with mine. "Thanks. But I do need to go home."

It was time to get the cabin in order. Again.

When we reached Main, an older man with a cloud of black and gray hair waved from the parking lot of the Grizzly Café across the street. "Howdy, Spencer."

"Hey, Mr. James."

"Thanks for shoveling my walk."

"Welcome." Spencer tipped the brim of his hat. "That's Mr. James. He lives next door to Grandma."

"That's nice of you to shovel for him."

"No big deal."

"You're a good kid, Spencer Raynes."

"Your favorite?"

I laughed. "Is that what this is about? The newfound focus on school. The good behavior. You wanting to beat Richie for the top spot?"

The flush of his cheeks was confirmation enough.

"You're my favorite student in Montana. He's my favorite student in Arizona. How's that?"

Spencer nodded, that blush turning a deeper shade of pink.

Most teenage boys with a hint of humility didn't know how to receive compliments, so I changed the subject. "Is the café good? I haven't eaten there yet."

"I like it. The hot beef sandwich is my favorite."

"I don't know if I've ever had a hot beef sandwich."

"Dude, you have to. They're the best."

I laughed. "I think that's the first time I've ever been called dude."

"It's a good thing. Trust me."

"I trust you."

This kid was good for my heart. I might have to stick around Dalton just so I could see him graduate.

Buses and cars rolled past us, most destined for the school. The lot was busy when we arrived, parents dropping kids off as teachers and students pulled into parking spaces.

A navy blue Impala was parked in the teachers' lot. I hadn't seen it before and would have noticed because it was almost identical to the car my mom drove.

A woman about my age with blond hair stood in the open driver's side door, scanning faces like she was searching for someone in the crowd.

When her gaze shifted toward us on the sidewalk, she did a double take. Then her eyes widened.

I slowed, checking over my shoulder to make sure she wasn't looking at someone behind me. But when I turned back, she was already inside the car, reversing out of the spot.

Weird. Who was that woman? I didn't recognize her, but I definitely would have remembered that car. Was she a parent? Did I know her child? Did her kid hate me enough to vandalize my house?

That thought nearly stopped me cold.

Paranoid much, Ilsa? That poor woman was probably wondering why *I'd* been staring at *her*.

After everything that had happened at the cabin, I was clearly on edge and searching for villains around every corner. I tracked the Impala, watching it pull through the exit on the opposite end of the school. The exit that parents used after dropping off their kids.

"Ilsa?" Spencer touched my arm. "Are you sure you're okay?"

The smile I gave him was wobbly, but I didn't want him to worry. "Peachy."

"Dad says that when he's really not. You can tell me what's bothering you."

"I'm fine. Promise. Just a little tired today." I yawned to reinforce my point. "What do you have going on today?"

"Dad does that too."

"Does what?"

He gave me a knowing look. "Changes the subject when he doesn't want to admit something is wrong."

Well, damn. "You are too observant for your age."

But my troubles were too big for a kid. I wasn't going to explain that I was stressed and upset about the vandalism. That I was sad about the end of an important friendship. That I wasn't sure what to make of my relationship with his father, but the more I was around Cosi, the more I never wanted it to stop.

"I really am fine. Don't worry."

That only earned me a teenage side-eye, but as we got closer to the front doors, he let it go. "I have a pretty normal day, I guess. I have to meet with the career counselor this morning."

"And when she asks what you want to be when you grow up, what's your answer?"

"I don't know." He lifted a shoulder. "Probably a job at the railroad or something. My grades aren't good enough for college."

"And whose fault is that?" I quirked an eyebrow. "Think of how far you've come with just a teensy bit more effort lately. Imagine what you could do if you gave it your all."

"Yeah," he mumbled.

"What do you *want* to be?"

"Maybe . . . a cop. Like Dad."

Because Cosi was his hero. "Put those observation skills to good use. For the record, I think that's a very noble profession, and you'd make a great police officer."

"Thanks, Miss Poe."

"If you want, you can call me Ilsa when we're not at school."

"'Kay." He gave me a shy smile. "I have a basketball game tonight. It's about an hour away. Dad usually drives to our away games. Want to come?"

"Um, maybe." I wasn't sure if Cosi wanted to be stuck in his Bronco with me for an hour both ways. And arriving at a game together wouldn't exactly be keeping our relationship out of the public eye.

Rather than run off to meet his friends, Spencer walked with me to the front door, opening it and waving me inside. Then he headed for the hall that would take him to the freshman lockers. "See ya."

"Bye." Normally, I went straight to my classroom, where I'd mentally prepare for first period. Where I'd spend thirty minutes convincing myself it didn't bother me when Paul Johnson called me Miss Crone.

But today, after a shitty night, I needed more coffee, so I walked to the teachers' lounge.

Two ladies were sitting at the small table, laughing and talking. Mrs. McNally, the home ec teacher, and Mrs. Hamilton from the office. Their happy chatter died a swift death the moment I walked into the room.

"Good morning." I smiled and poured myself a cup of coffee.

Neither of them spoke a word until I was gone, then their whispers followed me into the hall.

It wouldn't always be like this, right? Eventually, they'd realize I wasn't the enemy.

Don't quit. Don't give up.

I carried my coffee to my classroom and repeated that mantra over and over and over again.

Even when Paul Johnson took his normal tormenting up a notch and called me a cunt when I handed him his latest failed test.

I didn't bother trying to keep control of the first period seniors. Mostly, I simply tried not to cry. When the boys spent the hour whispering behind my back every time I turned to the chalkboard, sending the rest of the class into a fit of giggles and cackles, I ignored them and kept going with my lecture. During second period, everyone might as well have been asleep. And by third period, it had started snowing outside, changing my plan to walk to the garage during my break.

I was finishing the banana and yogurt that was my lunch when a knock sounded at the door, and Cosi filled the threshold.

"Hey." He didn't step into the classroom. And the serious expression on his face only made the ache in my chest pinch harder.

"Hi." God, he looked good.

I wanted to walk into his arms, wrap my arms around his waist, bury my face in his chest and breathe in his masculine scent until I no longer wanted to cry. But he looked every bit the Dalton County sheriff at the moment and this visit wasn't for fun. He was here on business, so I stayed in my chair.

"I'm meeting with Harlan in five. We're going to be calling in parents and bringing in the students you've been having trouble with for questioning. Wanted to give you a warning."

It wouldn't take long for news that the sheriff was asking kids questions about Miss Poe to leak through the building. If I wasn't already hated, this would tip the scales.

But I wanted justice for my father's cabin. For those possessions of his that someone had carelessly destroyed. Even if I decided to let this go, Cosi would not.

"Okay," I whispered, setting down my spoon, my appetite gone.

"Spencer has an away game tonight," he said. "I'll leave a spare key to the house under the door mat."

Meaning I wasn't invited to the game. It was probably for the best. I didn't understand basketball. And showing up together would only fan the flames of the gossip fire. Except it hurt, almost as much as my fight with Troy.

"Sure. Thanks," I murmured, biting the inside of my cheek to keep from crying.

Cosi opened his mouth, like he wanted to say something. But then he closed it and, without a goodbye, walked away. The clop of his boots faded as he headed toward Harlan's office.

The last half of the day was as frustrating as the first. Maybe it was the students. Or maybe it was me. My bad mood had infected the air.

It took until eighth period for the students to find out the sheriff was asking questions. Every kid in the room stared at me like I'd betrayed them. Every kid called me Miss Crone.

When the last bell rang, I wanted to be anywhere but Dalton, Montana.

I called the mechanic after school, hoping that by some miracle my truck was finished, but the seat replacement hadn't come in yet and wouldn't arrive until Friday. So with nothing else to do, and nowhere else to go, I packed up my briefcase and walked through the snow to the café for dinner at four thirty in the afternoon.

The hot beef sandwich was delicious. I ate my meal and bonded with the waitress, Dawn, over her unfortunate encounter with that asshole from the bar—Jackie. And when I couldn't avoid it any longer, I walked down Pine Street to Cosi's house.

The porch light was on and the key was tucked beneath the mat.

Part of me wanted to curl up on the couch, to watch TV until they came home. To ask Spencer about his game. To beg Cosi to take me to his bed and help me forget a bad day.

But I wasn't Spencer's mother. I wasn't Cosi's girlfriend.

And it was time to stop playing house.

So I shut myself in the guest bedroom, and by the time Cosi and Spencer made it home, I was already asleep.

Chapter 23

Cosi

The phone rang as I waited for my morning coffee to brew. I hurried to answer before the second ring, not wanting it to wake up Spencer or Ilsa this early on a Saturday. "Hello?"

"Hiya, Cosi. It's Marty. Just wanted to let you know Bluebird's truck is ready. Finished it up last night."

"Thanks. We'll swing by later to pick it up."

For Ilsa's sake, I was glad. For mine? This was a call I'd been dreading for days.

How long would it take her to get in that Ford Ranger and leave Dalton? Leave me?

"Good deal," he said. "I'll be here until about four. Hey, did you ever find out who did it?"

"Marty, I can't tell you anything about the case."

"Sure sure sure. Understood. Sorry, was just being nosy."

Marty, and everyone else in Dalton.

It hadn't taken long for word to spread about the vandalism or the questioning I'd done at the school this week. People were already speculating and pointing fingers.

Maybe someone could point me in the right direction, because I was stuck.

"We'll see you in a bit," I said and hung up the phone as the coffee pot began to gurgle.

Beyond the window overlooking the sink, the yard was blanketed in fresh snow. We'd added another three inches over the last few days, and every morning, I'd woken up early to shovel the driveway and sidewalks.

It had been a long, shitty week, and I was blaming it on *Troy*.

His visit had fucked everything up, namely my headspace.

I hadn't meant to eavesdrop. When Ilsa left my room to go and talk to him, I'd forced myself to leave them alone. I'd lain on my bed, eyes glued to the ceiling, teeth grinding so hard I'd given myself a headache.

It was when Troy had gotten loud, when Ilsa had told him to stop, that I'd gotten off the bed. And when I'd made it to the hallway, I'd overheard her tell him she was leaving Dalton.

She might as well have taken me out at the knees.

All this time, I'd assumed she was staying. That she'd cleaned up Ike's cabin to live there. But no, she was leaving.

And I didn't have it in me to be left by another woman.

I didn't want Spencer to watch someone he cared about walk away. My heart couldn't handle the heartbreak of falling for a woman who was not long for this town.

Too bad it was too late.

So now what? Where did we go from here?

Ilsa and I needed to have a long talk. Except she'd been avoiding me, sticking to that guest bedroom like the floor outside the door was made of lava.

On Wednesday, we'd come home from Spencer's game and she'd already been asleep.

Thursday, I'd planned to leave the station early but then Dean Johnson had marched into my office and told me that the woman I was fucking was fucking up his kid's life. We'd gotten into it, and when I'd finally had enough of his bullshit and told him to get the hell out of my office, I'd hit the gym to take out my fury on a punching bag.

Spencer had been at Mom's for dinner after practice, so I'd swung by to pick him up. When we'd finally made it home, Ilsa had been asleep early. Again.

Last night, I'd made it home by five. She and Spencer had already been home, walking home together after school since he hadn't had basketball. She'd been locked in that fucking guest bedroom with a headache—according to Spencer.

She was avoiding me. And I was avoiding her. But today, it had to stop. Today, we were going to talk.

"Morning," Ilsa said as she walked into the kitchen. She was dressed in a pair of jeans and that Nebraska State Fair tee I liked so much.

The world outside the kitchen faded to a blur. I saw nothing else when she was in the room. She plagued my thoughts, day and night. It took everything I had not to take her hand as she passed me for the coffee pot. Not to pull her into my arms and bury my nose in that soft hair.

Fuck, I missed her. And it had only been days. What was I going to do when she left for good?

"Want some?" she asked, taking out a cup from the cabinet.

"Sure."

She lifted out another mug—blue with **World's Greatest Dad** on the front—and filled it nearly to the brim. She set it aside while she poured her own, then carried it to the table, sinking down into a seat. Then she twisted to stare at the wall.

Anywhere, but at me.

It was a gut punch. A punch I deserved for not breaking down my own guest bedroom's door. For being a coward.

"Ilsa, I'm so—"

"Did the garage call? I thought I heard the phone ring. When I talked to them on Wednesday, the guy said Dad's truck would be fixed by this morning."

"Yeah, it was Marty. The truck is done."

"Great." She stood, taking her cup with her. "I'm going to walk over and pick it up."

"No need to walk. I'll take you."

"That's okay. I'd like to get some air. Maybe run a few errands."

No, she wanted to get out of this house. Away from me. Also my fault. "Ilsa—"

"Did you finish questioning everyone at school?"

Clearly, she knew I wanted to talk. And clearly, she didn't.

Maybe she didn't know what to say either.

"Yes, I finished at the school. I was going to give you an update last night but Spencer said you weren't feeling well and went to bed early."

"Headache." She tapped her temple.

That was a damn lie, but I let it slide. "All but one of the kids had an alibi for the time of the fire. They were each at home. And all but one was at school on the day your place was ransacked."

"Let me guess. The one outlier here is Paul."

I nodded. "Melody swears he was home sick that day. But she was at work from nine to five, so she can't be sure. Dean was working too. Since they refused to let me take Paul's fingerprints, I'm working with the county attorney to get a warrant from the municipal judge."

"And how long will that take?"

"It's not a fast process. Especially where minors are concerned."

She dropped her gaze to her cup. "We're never going to know who did this, are we?"

"Don't give up. I promised you I'd find out." And I'd keep that promise, even if it took a lifetime. "Chuck and Larry are still sorting through prints."

"Have they found any that aren't mine or Dad's?"

"Three partials. One full." It wasn't much. But it was enough to keep my hope alive.

She closed her eyes, breathing deeply. Then she turned and disappeared to her room.

I took a step to follow, to say to hell with it all and just take whatever time I could get with Ilsa, no matter how short. But before I could chase her down the hall, Spencer shuffled into the kitchen, his hair a mess and his eyes heavy with sleep.

"Hey, pal."

He walked right to me, right into my chest for a hug, like he used to when he was little. Half asleep and cuddly.

I wrapped an arm around him, letting him sag against my shoulder.

When was the last time he'd done this? It was getting harder and harder to remember the lasts.

The last time I'd tucked him into bed. The last time I'd picked him up and carried him on my hip. The last night I'd rocked him to sleep.

If this was a last Saturday morning hug, I wanted to savor it.

When Ilsa returned, wearing a coat, hat and gloves, she took one look at us and the softness in her eyes, a sweet smile, was enough to take my breath away.

Was that my last Ilsa smile?

The twist in my chest was so fierce I couldn't fill my lungs.

She mouthed, "Bye."

Then she was gone, quietly leaving the house while I hugged my son.

With a sweeping arch, I brought my axe down on a round of wood. The sound of the log splitting echoed through the backyard. It was followed by a thump as the smaller piece dropped to the ground.

Sweat beaded at my temples. The cold air was crisp in my lungs. The coat I'd pulled on earlier was draped over our chain-link fence, leaving me in only a flannel and jeans, but I was plenty warm.

This past spring, Spencer and I had gone up to the mountains to cut a cord of wood. The pieces had been stacked against the backside of the garage for months, waiting to be split. After Ilsa had left for the garage, after Spencer had fully woken up and gone to take a shower,

I'd eaten a quick breakfast and decided chopping wood would help clear my head.

Except it wasn't working. As the pile next to the chopping block kept growing, the knot in my gut only twisted tighter. At this point, I was afraid I'd puke up my coffee and toast.

I positioned a new log and split the piece in half. Ironic I was splitting things today when I felt torn in two.

"Uh-oh." The crunch of boots came with Mom's voice. She walked into the yard, bundled in a coat and knitted stocking hat. "What's wrong?"

I set the axe down, leaning the handle against my thigh as I wiped the sweat from my brow with a sleeve. "Nothing."

She scoffed. "You chop wood when something's wrong. Your father was the same way. And when I asked him what was wrong, he'd say *nothing*. So many *nothings* that I had five years' worth of firewood by the time he died."

Mom knew exactly how to use my father against me. Because in every way, he was the last man I wanted to become.

Detached. Obstinate. Difficult.

My memories of him had faded with time, but I remembered the feeling of our house from the years before he died. It had always been tense and sullen and angry.

Dad hadn't been a bad man. But he hadn't been a happy man either. The war had left many scars on Harvey Raynes. The emotions he'd kept inside, the suffering he'd endured alone, had taken their toll on all of us, but especially Mom.

When he'd died in that hunting accident, she'd been devastated. Not only because she'd lost her husband and I'd lost my father, but because she'd wanted so, so badly to be there when he found his smile again.

"Talk to me," she said. "Is it Ilsa?"

That pleading look was one I didn't see on her face often, but it conjured memories that hadn't faded. Times when Mom would beg Dad to share the load, and instead, he'd shut her out.

I didn't really feel like talking, but it would hurt her more if I kept quiet than it would for me to get this shit off my chest. "Yeah, it's Ilsa."

"I heard about the cabin and her truck." There was a note of accusation there.

It irritated Mom to no end that she typically learned about happenings around town through the rumor mill rather than directly from me, the source. But she also respected my job and knew I'd share what I could. And usually, it wasn't much.

"Do you have any idea who did it?" she asked.

"We're still sorting it out."

She frowned. "So no, you don't. Damn."

"Pretty much."

"How's she holding up?"

I lifted a shoulder. "She's taking it in stride."

"She's got gumption, that girl. I like that. She's not afraid to push back. We need someone like that in Dalton. Especially at that school."

"Well, don't get attached." I pulled off my leather gloves, tucking them into the back pocket of my jeans. "She's leaving."

"Because of what happened at the cabin?"

"No. She was never planning to stay." I waved her toward the sidewalk so we could head inside and get out of the cold.

"And how do you feel about that?"

Like my soul was being crushed. "It's fine."

"Is it?"

"At least I know this time around. I can take care not to get attached."

Mom stopped walking to face me. "I'll never forgive Gwen for making you this way."

"What way?"

"Scared." She put her hand on my shoulder. "Ilsa isn't Gwen."

"She's leaving too, Mom. And I can't do it again." Even if I wanted to try. Even if I wasn't ready to see the last of Ilsa's smiles.

"When we first moved here, I'd hear the occasional story about Ilsa's mother," she said. "How she ran from this town so fast it gave poor Ike whiplash. I always felt bad for him. But I remember how he'd become a different man during the summers when Ilsa would visit. He'd parade her around town and wear this beaming smile wherever they went."

It hadn't really occurred to me that Mom might have remembered Ilsa from decades past. I wish I had known her back then too.

"There's a lot working against her right now," Mom said. "Ike's death. The cabin. A school full of men and that little shit, Tim Harlan. The women who do work there are snotty and awful. They're all probably making sure Ilsa knows she's not welcome. But someday, Ilsa's going to remember those summers. And how her smiles were just as bright as Ike's. She loved it here. Don't give up on her. Not yet."

Was it really that simple?

"I like her, Mom. A lot."

"As you should."

"And Spencer? How does he take this if she leaves?"

Mom rolled her eyes. "You've used that boy as an excuse to avoid relationships for far too long."

"It's not an—"

"It is an excuse. We both know I'm right."

She was right. *Damn it.*

"When was the last time you reviewed his homework?" she asked. "Made him show you what he's been doing this week? Whether she stays or leaves, that girl is good for Spencer. And she's good for you too. Pull your head out of your ass, Cosi Raynes." Mom smacked my arm and walked away. Not to the house, like I'd expected, but along the sidewalk.

"Where are you going?"

"I'm meeting a friend for lunch at the Grizzly. Love you."

"Love you too." I waved as she continued on, and I headed inside.

It smelled like bacon and burnt toast. Someday, I was going to have to teach my son how to cook.

I found Spencer in the kitchen, carrying plates to the table. Three instead of two. "Lunch?"

"BLTs." He shrugged. "I burned a piece of toast."

"I'll eat it." I went to the fridge, taking out a jar of Mom's strawberry jam she made each summer. "Your grandma just walked by. She said something about your homework from this week."

"Oh, it's, uh . . . nothing. She was looking at it when I went over there yesterday after school."

"Can I see it too?"

He hesitated before setting down the last plate. Then he walked down the hallway to get his schoolwork while I checked the bacon on the stove to make sure it wasn't burning too.

It was. So I shut off the stove and took out the strips to dry on a paper towel.

"Here." Spencer handed me a stack of papers before going to the silverware drawer.

I flipped through the worksheets and quizzes, focused on the grades circled on each page. As and Bs. Not a single C or D. If not for his name—Spencer Raynes, not a Spencer Michael in the bunch—I would have thought these were from other students.

"This is . . . Wow. Good job, pal."

These were the best grades he'd gotten since fourth grade. Fifth was the year he'd stopped applying himself. Ironically, Mrs. Riley had been his fifth-grade teacher before she'd moved up to the high school.

"It's no big deal." He shrugged, setting out forks.

"It is a big deal. I'm proud of you."

He tried to hide a shy smile. "Thanks."

I had no clue what Ilsa had done to inspire this change, but I'd kiss her for it later. A kiss that lasted all night long. A kiss to say I was sorry.

Yeah, it was time to pull my head out of my ass.

"Hey, Dad?" Spencer's eyebrows knitted together. "Did you find out if Paul was the person who trashed Ilsa's cabin?"

"No, not yet."

On the drive back from his basketball game Wednesday, I'd been real with him about what was going on with Ilsa's place. He'd already heard the rumors going around school. So I'd told him everything I could, including how I suspected it was Paul, trusting him not to share.

Paul hadn't said much when I'd questioned him with his parents. They'd brought their lawyer, who'd advised them to stay quiet.

But the other kids had been much more forthcoming. Most had been terrified to sit across from me and be questioned, their parents too. From them, I'd learned that Paul harassed Ilsa almost daily. That he called her Miss Crone. That he used every insult possible, from bitch to cunt.

Ilsa and I would also be talking about how she hadn't told me this was happening.

"Paul was talking shit about her after practice," Spencer said. "In the locker room. He was being really loud, like he knew I was in there and wanted to make sure I heard."

Paul was on the basketball team with Spencer, and being a senior, he was a kid Spencer looked up to. The last place I wanted my son was in the middle of this mess, but like it or not, he was in the middle.

"Sorry."

"Screw Paul. He's a dickhead if he did this."

I barked a laugh. "Definitely. But I don't know if it was Paul. So let's not say he's guilty yet."

"'Kay. But you're going to find out who did it, right? And if they burned down her shed too?"

"Promise."

"Good." His frame relaxed. "Is Ilsa going to be okay? Where is she, anyway?"

"Her truck was fixed, so she went to pick it up."

"Should we wait for her?" he asked as the sound of his growling stomach filled the kitchen.

"You go ahead and eat. I'll wait until she's back."

He heaped his plate full of bacon, taking the burnt toast for himself and making a sandwich so thick it barely fit in his mouth. But he still inhaled it in less than five minutes.

I checked the clock as he rinsed his dishes, walking to the living room window to peer out over the street.

The garage was a ten-minute walk from my house. Marty was chatty, but Ilsa had been gone for over an hour. What errands had she needed to run?

I waited another thirty minutes before I ate a piece of toast. I waited another thirty before I put the bacon in a Tupperware container. And I waited another thirty minutes before I stopped ignoring the sinking feeling in my gut.

She wouldn't go out to the cabin, would she?

Fuck. She definitely would.

"Spencer," I hollered. "I gotta go."

Chapter 24

Ilsa

The cabin smelled like dust and winter.

It was almost as cold inside as it was outside. One of the deputies, or maybe Cosi, had turned off the baseboard heaters in the bedrooms and bathroom after the house was vandalized, not wanting anything loose to catch fire. I couldn't even see the fireplace in the living room because too many things had been overturned or tossed in the way.

It probably wouldn't take long to clear a path to the fireplace in the living room. But I couldn't seem to move myself out of the kitchen. Every crunching step on broken glass and shattered ceramic felt like a crack through my bones.

Was it a mistake to come to the cabin? Maybe I should have stayed locked away in Cosi's guest bedroom, hiding from him. From the world. But after I'd picked up Dad's truck, it had practically steered itself to Cotters Lake.

As much as I wanted to avoid this mess, it was inescapable. And when Cosi eventually asked me to leave his home, I'd have nowhere to go unless I picked up the broken pieces beneath my boots.

I turned toward the entryway closet where I kept the dustpan and broom. The vandals had snapped the stick in half, but I used it to sweep a clean path from the door to the cabinet under the sink, where I found the roll of garbage bags intact.

One by one, I filled them up until the kitchen floor was clean. Then I hauled the bags to the back of Dad's truck.

The chill I'd felt earlier was gone, and I took a few moments to let the air cool the sweat on my brow. The sky was clear today, blue and bright. Not a breath of wind stirred the treetops.

The fresh snow we'd gotten this week covered the charred remains of the shed. But beneath that blanket of white, there'd be another project for me to tackle. Another mess not of my making.

Maybe it was fortunate that I could stress over cleanup projects and ignore the mess that was my life.

Not wanting to go back inside quite yet, I trudged a path in the snow toward the lake, stepping onto the dock and walking to its edge. The cold was starting to sink through my sweater, so I pulled the sleeves over my fingertips, wrapping my arms around my waist as I let my gaze sweep across the lake and forest.

I inhaled through my nose, filling my lungs to the point it burned. Then I held the air in my chest, one heartbeat, two, before I exhaled, releasing a bit of my worries into the Montana wilds. Five more of those deep breaths and the tension eased from my shoulders.

So much had changed in the past few months. These past weeks had been the hardest and saddest of my life. Yet as I stood here, in Dad's place, it felt like this was where I was supposed to be. That a divine force had brought me here so I could finish whatever it was that Dad had started.

"What are you trying to tell me, Dad?" I closed my eyes, hoping for an answer if I listened hard enough.

The world went silent. No birds chirped. No trees creaked as they swayed. No pinecones clacked against limbs as they dropped to the ground.

It was the most peaceful moment I'd had in years.

A peace I wouldn't have found in a city. A peace I'd known as a kid, sitting on this dock with my father.

A peace that came when you were home.

I opened my eyes, smiling at the sky. As much as I wanted to stay out here longer, the cold was too much. I turned, about to go inside, when movement across the lake caught my eye.

A plume of gray smoke snaked into the sky.

It was almost directly across the lake from where I was standing, past the closest end of the island, then over to the other shore. Almost exactly the way Jerry had gone the day he'd given me Dad's note.

Was that where he lived? I didn't think anyone lived on the other side of the lake, but maybe things had changed. Did he have a cabin on the lake too?

If I could just talk to Jerry for a little bit, someone who Dad had clearly trusted, maybe I could understand.

I spun around, running up the dock and through the yard, bursting into the cabin to grab my coat. Then I raced back outside, yanking the door closed behind me. As I ran for the lake, I fitted my arms into my coat and zipped it closed.

The first step onto the ice made my heart seize, and for a moment, I was sure it would break. I froze, listening for any sign it was cracking. But the surface held firm as I took another step, then another, my strides tentative at first. Then, once I was sure I wouldn't plunge into the freezing water, I squared my shoulders and locked my eyes on that smoke, not wanting to lose sight of it as I moved toward the center of the lake.

Oh, God, what was I doing? My heart was beating so hard it was difficult to breathe. If it wasn't Jerry across the shore, then this was going to be incredibly awkward.

In all my time out here, I'd never seen smoke on that side of the lake. If this was my only chance to find Jerry's house, then so be it.

A shiver raced down my spine, from nerves and the cold. My entire body vibrated with anxious energy. The tips of my fingers were beginning to sting, so I tucked my trembling hands into my pockets and burrowed my chin into the collar of my coat. Then I glanced over my shoulder to see how far I'd gone.

The cabin looked so dark and lonely from out here. So small.

My foot slipped and I nearly fell, only catching my balance at the last second.

"Shit," I hissed, heart in my throat.

I stopped, giving myself a moment. This was a horrible decision. Jerry didn't seem like the type who liked surprise visitors. But I kept moving forward, taking caution with every step. Beneath the snow, the ice was a sheet of translucent white, too thick to see the water beneath.

As the island loomed ahead, I took another glance back. The snow-covered dock was almost impossible to make out against all of the white. The trees seemed to move in on the cabin, the branches hanging lower and lower, like they were warning me to stop. That if I kept going, they'd hide it from me so I couldn't find my way home.

Another chill zinged through my veins as I kept walking, eyes locked on that thin band of white smoke.

I gave the island a wide berth as I passed by, not wanting to get too close to where the ice might be thin. Then, before I was ready, I reached the other shore.

Stepping into the forest, into knee-deep snow and the shade of a thousand trees, felt like crossing a veil into another realm.

There were no trails or paths cut through the trees. This side of the lake had a steeper incline than the other, meaning I had to hike up the slope. Every step was an effort, and by the time I reached a flat spot where the trees thinned, my lungs and legs were on fire. Sweat made my clothes sticky against my skin.

I stopped to catch my breath, searching the sky for any hint of that smoke. It would be impossible to see now that I was in the trees, but I could smell its faint bitter aroma. Every twenty feet, I stopped to scan past tree trunks, hoping to find the source.

Nothing. Farther and farther, the longer it took, the more and more I realized this was a mistake.

I wouldn't get lost out here. All I had to do was walk downhill to the lake. But these woods were crawling with predators. The last thing I wanted was to cross paths with a mountain lion or wolf.

Another twenty steps and I was about to give up this asinine quest. To go home before I became an animal's midday meal.

"Jerry," I called. It was timid and raspy. I cleared my throat, cupping my hands around my mouth, and tried again. "Jerry!"

My voice ricocheted off the trees. A bird burst out of a nearby bush where it had been hiding, and I leapt back, nearly falling on my ass.

"Fuck." It took a moment for the jolt of panic to fade. When my heart climbed down from my throat, I tilted my face to the sky.

If Dad was watching me from above, I doubted he'd like me out here alone. If Cosi found out, he'd be livid.

"Damn." Time to go home.

Except before I could turn, a faint wisp of smoke wafted above, past the treetops.

I whirled, eyes wide as I stared in the direction from where it came. I started moving, a surge of energy pushing me through the snow.

A tiny log cabin with a snow-covered roof nearly blended into the evergreens. It was more of a hut than a home, no bigger than a single room. The square windows were dark, and the smoke from the chimney was shrinking.

"Jerry." It was no more than a murmur. I couldn't seem to speak any louder.

A chill raced down my spine, and I twisted to look behind me. The only tracks in the snow were mine, but I couldn't shake the feeling that I wasn't alone. It was the same feeling I'd had the day Jerry had given me the letter on the dock.

"Hello," I called. "Is someone there?"

When no one answered, I moved closer to the shelter, and with every step, my pulse spiked.

This was a bad idea. Such a bad idea. "Hello?"

The cabin was a perfect square with a single wooden door. The snow in front was tamped down with footprints that led in the opposite direction, winding through the trees.

I knew no one would answer, but I knocked anyway. "Jerry?"

That uneasy feeling doubled as the silence of the forest wrapped around my shoulders like a blanket of ice.

Someone was out here. I couldn't see them, but I felt it. I felt them watching me.

Was this Jerry's cabin? Or someone else's? Someone who did not want me at their doorstep.

I held up my hands in surrender, then backed away from the door, glancing left and right. Then I whirled and followed my tracks the way I'd come, through the trees and down the slope to the lake. Every few steps, I checked over my shoulder.

Still alone.

And not alone.

The eerie feeling stayed with me like it was my own shadow. Not just someone watching, but someone following. I walked faster and faster, adrenaline pumping through my veins until I was running.

The fear was a living, breathing monster on my heels, biting and snapping at my feet. When I reached the tree line, I leapt off the bank to the lake, my feet sweeping out beneath me and sending me onto my ass.

I landed with a hard jolt, and the ice beneath me creaked but didn't break. Scrambling to stand, I took a last look over my shoulder before I kept on running. I slipped and skidded every other step. Twice, I fell to my hands and knees. And by the time I was almost to the other side, tears pricked at the corners of my eyes.

The shore was about fifty feet away when a loud crack echoed through the air. My entire body flinched, my hands flying to cover my head as I dropped to a crouch.

The echo of the gunshot was drowned out by my thundering pulse.

A tear dripped down my cheek as I stood, not bothering to search for the person shooting. When I made it to the shore, I jumped the last few feet into the yard.

Another gunshot rang out, a loud pop that split the air.

I looked back, toward where the smoke had been, expecting to see a person in a black mask over my shoulder. But the lake was empty.

If someone was out there, they'd have to follow me into town because I was getting the fuck away from Cotters Lake.

Except before I could make my escape, I whirled and collided with a body.

A strong body that belonged to the very handsome, very irate sheriff of Dalton County.

Chapter 25

Cosi

Ilsa yelped as she crashed into me and pitched backward, about to tumble into the snow, but I caught her by the arms, keeping her from falling on her ass.

"Ilsa, what the fuck are you—"

"Cosi." A sob broke free as she clung to me, burying her face in my chest.

My arms wrapped around her automatically, holding her tight. The irritation and worry that she was out here alone, that I'd gone into the cabin and couldn't find her, vanished in a blink.

Instead, all I felt was fear.

Her entire body was trembling as she fisted the front of my coat, like she was afraid I'd let her go—I wouldn't.

"Breathe, baby. I've got you."

She sucked in a jagged inhale, the air catching in her throat. But aside from that one cry, she kept it together, holding tight to me as she calmed down.

I pressed my lips to her hair, smelling her shampoo and the winter cold. The strands at her temples were damp with sweat, but her coat was cold, the fabric stiff. How long had she been out here? Why was she coming off the lake?

A pop came from behind us and Ilsa's entire body jerked, her hold on me tightening.

"It's just Spencer," I said.

My stubborn, stubborn son had insisted on coming along when I'd told him I was driving out here to get Ilsa. He was worried I wouldn't be able to convince her on my own—he was probably right to worry. That kid was too damn perceptive for his own good and knew it had been a tense few days. I'd decided it was safe enough for him to come along, and I could use his help with cleanup.

"I sent him off to do some target practice with his pistol so we could talk alone." Except she'd been nowhere to be found until I'd spotted the tracks in the yard and followed them toward the lake. "What were you doing out there?"

She eased her face away to look up at me, but the grip she had on my coat didn't loosen. Another gunshot rang out and she nearly jumped out of her skin.

I lifted my fingers to my lips, turned over my shoulder and let out a piercing whistle.

Spencer knew when he heard that whistle to come back.

"Just relax," I told her, running my hands up and down her arms.

"Shit." She sighed, closing her eyes for a moment. "Sorry."

"Talk to me. What's going on?"

When she looked at me, the fear in her gaze was enough to make my stomach drop. "I was cleaning and came outside with some trash. I saw a plume of smoke across the lake and thought it was Dad's friend Jerry. So I went to try and find him."

"Where?" I tucked her into my side and walked us to the shore. "Show me?"

She pointed to the other side of the lake. "There."

I narrowed my eyes, trying to make out smoke, but all I saw were snow, trees and blue sky. "I'm not seeing it."

"It's gone now." She slumped, bringing her hands to her mouth to blow hot air on them. Her knuckles were practically blue from the cold. Where were her gloves?

I took her hands, putting them palm to palm, then covered them with my own, slowly rubbing back and forth, building some friction and warmth.

"It was there. I swear," she said, eyes pleading for me to believe her. "And I found a cabin."

"I believe you."

Her face crumpled, like this time she really was going to cry. And when she fell into me again, her forehead resting over my heart, I let go of her hands and wrapped her up again.

Over her head, I stared across the lake, hoping I'd find that plume of smoke.

"Dad," Spencer called.

I turned, keeping Ilsa against me, as Spencer rounded the side of the cabin.

"Head on inside, pal," I told him. "We'll be in soon."

He gave me a single nod, concern clouding his expression, before he ducked into the cabin.

"Tell me about Jerry again," I said.

She turned her face so she could talk but not move away. "He gave me the short letter. The one about the tap dance. And he said Dad wouldn't have drowned. That it wasn't an accident."

"You're sure he said his name was Jerry." I'd asked her this already but wanted to hear the answer again.

"Yes."

Then he must have lied. "And he came to you from across the lake?"

"From the island. At least that's where he walked to after he gave me that letter. I didn't notice where he came from before that. He just sort of . . . appeared. And I know how that sounds and that this all seems like some big, fabricated mess that I'm making up in—"

I pressed my finger to her lips. "Ilsa, I'm not asking because I don't believe you. I just want to make sure I've got the details right."

Relief filled those beautiful brown eyes. "Thank you."

"But do me a favor? Don't walk across the lake again."

The little color remaining in her cheeks blanched. "Why? Is it unsafe?"

"Considering how cold it's been this winter, it's probably fine. But there's always the chance of weak points, and I don't want you out there, especially alone."

The idea of her falling through the ice, of getting hypothermia or drowning, made my blood run cold.

It must have hers too because she shivered, head to toe.

"You said you found a cabin over there?" As far as I knew, there weren't buildings on that side of the lake. But I guess I was wrong.

"Yes. It's small, more like a hut. Almost the size of Dad's shed. There were footprints in the snow, and I knocked, but no one answered. And . . ." She shivered again as she trailed off.

"And what?"

"I got the feeling that I was being watched. Like they saw me coming and left."

Whoever this Jerry was, he didn't want to be found. But he was going to have a harder time avoiding me.

He was likely long gone today. Ilsa would have scared him off. But tomorrow, I'd come back with Larry and Chuck. If we were lucky, Ilsa's tracks wouldn't get snowed over tonight and they'd be easy to follow. But even if we had to search every square foot of land around this lake, I'd find that cabin and figure out who owned it.

"All right. Let's get out of here. Go home. Get you warmed up." Except when I took a step away, toward the house, she didn't move.

"I'm staying out here. I need to come back and get my stuff, but it's time for me to come back to the cabin."

"No." *Fuck no.*

"Cosi—"

"You told Troy you were leaving Dalton. It fucked with my head." I took her face in my hands. "The last woman I cared about was Gwen. And she left."

Understanding filled her eyes. So did guilt.

"When you told Troy you were leaving, it brought back a lot of shit I never dealt with. I'm sorry. Since Gwen left town, I haven't wanted anyone else. I've avoided anything that resembled a relationship. Until you. Any other woman, I wouldn't have cared if she left. But you? I don't want you to leave. And that's fucking with my head too."

Her eyes softened. "I don't know what I'm doing. I don't know where I belong. I just know that this"—she motioned to the cabin—"is hard. Dalton is hard. Work is hard. My friendship with Troy was always hard. But when I'm with you, it's easy. It's so easy it terrifies me."

I dropped my forehead to hers. "I'm in this with you, Ilsa. I don't know how to do it any other way."

"I'm in it too."

I dropped my mouth to hers, kissing away the cold from her lips. Kissing away the tension and stress from the past few days. My tongue slid inside, tangling with hers, but before I could delve deep, a loud *thwack* sounded from the house.

Ilsa and I broke apart as Spencer marched outside with a piece of ruined furniture under each arm. He chucked them in the back of Ike's truck, brushed his hands on his jeans, then walked back inside.

"Come on." I held out my hand. "Come home with me."

"Just one more night," she said, lacing her fingers with mine.

I was getting more than one night. But we'd worry about that tomorrow.

Another crash came as Spencer yanked a mattress through the front door. He hefted it into the truck, his face hard and angry. "She can't stay here, Dad."

I'd warned him it wasn't good. Now that he'd seen it for himself, it came as no surprise he was furious. Hopefully he'd cool down before he went to school on Monday. Even if he didn't, we'd have a talk because the last thing I needed was him getting into it with Paul.

Spencer sent a glare across the yard the likes of which I'd never seen from him before. It was more man than boy. "You're not staying here."

Ilsa nodded. "Okay."

"Good." Spencer kicked a tuft of snow, then stomped into the house.

"I love that kid." She let out a quiet laugh. "I'd better help him before he throws out something I want to keep."

She walked ahead, clueless to the fact that she'd just snatched another piece of my heart. Another week, maybe two, she'd own the entire thing.

She couldn't leave Dalton. I wouldn't allow it. Whatever was making her life hard, I'd move mountains to make it easy. Starting now.

I tucked my hands into my coat pockets and headed for the house, but halfway across the yard, a prickle crept up my neck.

Slowing, I turned in a full circle.

Nothing but trees and snow.

But I'd bet my badge that someone was out there, watching.

Whoever it was, their days were numbered.

I was done with this bullshit on Cotters Lake.

Chapter 26

Ilsa

The guest room's floor was littered with my clothes. My suitcase and duffel bag were empty and open on the bed.

Every article of clothing I owned was in this room, and somewhere in my wardrobe was a kelly green sweater. I'd left Arizona with a kelly green sweater. "So where is my goddamn kelly green sweater?"

I bent to pick up a black shift dress, making sure there wasn't anything hidden beneath. But all I saw was carpet and clothes that were not kelly green.

Balling up the dress, I tossed it onto the bed and plopped down on the floor, sitting amid the mess.

Dalton's school colors were bright green and white. And tonight, while I cheered on the Lynx in their basketball game against the Calamity Cowboys, I wanted to wear bright green. I wanted to fit in with the crowd.

Since I couldn't find my sweater, I'd have to settle for a white blouse instead. But a blouse was too fancy for basketball. A blouse said teacher and city girl. It screamed I did not belong. Clothes made a statement, and all I wanted tonight was for that statement to be as quiet as possible.

"Ugh." I rubbed at my temples, wishing I could shut off my brain and stop overthinking this outfit. Except I'd been nervous about this game all day.

The front door to the house opened, then closed. I checked my watch. It was time to go. But I took one last look through my clothes, pushing and tossing them around, frantically searching for that green sweater.

"Ilsa," Cosi hollered.

"Two minutes," I called back, throwing a red silk nightgown on the bed.

God, I owned a lot of red. And cream. And tan. And blue. At this point, I'd settle for any shade of green, except apparently, I didn't have a stitch of green in this room.

Cosi appeared in the open doorway, eyebrows raised. "Do I want to know what happened in here?"

"I can't find my green sweater."

"Just wear the one you have on."

"This is blue." I plucked at the soft navy fabric.

"So?"

"So I want to be supportive."

"You going to the game is supportive."

He wasn't wrong. But he also was. "Do you see anything green?"

"Baby, no one cares what you're wearing."

"I care." I picked up a brown button-down I'd forgotten I even owned and tossed it into the corner. "Damn it. Where's my sweater?"

Cosi muttered something under his breath I couldn't make out and walked away while I kept searching on my hands and knees, crawling across the floor.

My face felt too hot and sticky. Great, now I was sweating off my makeup.

"Damn it." I tore off my blue sweater and fanned my face as the air cooled my torso. Then I stood and snatched the white blouse from the bed, about to pull it on when Cosi walked into the room with a gray sweatshirt in hand.

"What are you—" My question was cut short as he pulled the crewneck over my head.

"There. Now you're supportive."

I pushed my arms through the sleeves, tugging down the hem. A Dalton Lynx logo adorned the front. It was perfect. And it wasn't. "I can't wear this."

"Why not?"

"Because it's obviously yours." The hem hit my thighs and the sleeves were too long.

Cosi studied me for a moment, then he took my face in his hands and sealed his lips over mine in a kiss.

The panic instantly faded. Like magic.

"Better?" he asked, pulling away.

"Yes."

"Then can we go?"

"After I change."

"Baby—"

"Everyone is going to be watching us tonight," I said. "They're going to talk about us."

"They already are."

"I know." My lip curled. "But this is gossip with me sitting in the middle of it. I don't want them to say I'm not dressed right or that I don't belong. Or that I'm not good enough for you."

I'd made myself a promise on Saturday when we'd been standing beside the lake. If Cosi was real with me, then I'd be real with him. No pretending. No sugarcoating. No hiding.

And no leaving Dalton, at least for now.

Not until Cosi and I had a chance to explore this thing between us. For him, I'd stay in Montana. Even if an entire gymnasium of people judged me and my clothing tonight.

"Ilsa." His hazel eyes softened before he pulled me into his arms. "I want you to walk into that gym wearing my sweatshirt. I want everyone to see us holding hands, sitting together. I want all of Dalton to know you're mine. That's what I want them talking about."

Easy. This man made my life easy. "Then I guess I'm ready to go."

He took my face in his hands again and pressed his soft lips to the corner of my mouth. "Found out some stuff today about that cabin on the lake. Want me to tell you now or save it for later?"

"Tell me now."

On Sunday, Cosi had taken two of his deputies to Cotters Lake and found that tiny cabin. The door had been locked and the windows all covered, so there hadn't been much to find without going inside, which he couldn't do without a warrant.

So first thing Monday morning, he'd gone to the county courthouse to find out who owned it and to request that warrant. Except there'd been no title record to find.

No one owned that cabin or the property it rested upon.

That land was designated as public land and managed by the BLM, and whoever had built that place had done so illegally. Meaning no need to wait for a warrant.

He'd gone back yesterday, only to find the door open and cabin empty. If there had been something inside, it was gone now.

"We're working through fingerprints," he said. "It'll take a few days. But the photos I took yesterday are developed. And I matched the tread on a few tracks to the same tread on those from the shed at your place."

"So it's the same person." My stomach dropped. "And I waltzed across the lake like an idiot to say hello."

Cosi was gracious enough not to rub it in.

"Okay, now what? You start asking to see the bottom of people's boots?"

He chuckled. "Well, no. But it's another way to confirm a suspect."

A suspect like Paul. That kid hated me, but despite the name-calling and threats, something about him as the culprit felt wrong.

"Do you still think it's Paul?"

He tucked a lock of hair behind my ear. "Up until I found that matching boot print, yes. But now? No, I don't."

"Then who?"

"I don't know. There's someone on Cotters and has been this whole time. There's a chance it's been different people. Maybe Paul was the person who trashed the house. But the fire, the person spying on you. I'm thinking they're different."

"But why?" I wiggled free, pacing over my clothes. "What did I ever do to anyone?"

"Maybe it's not about you at all. Maybe it's the property. Places on Cotters don't come up for sale often. Maybe once a generation."

"If that." Dad's cabin had been passed down to him from his parents. "So you think it could all be a scare tactic."

"It's a new theory," he said.

I wrapped my arms around my waist, playing through everything over and over again. "I'm going to call my mom and find out if she knows anyone who ever asked to buy the cabin from Dad."

"Good idea."

I owed my mother a call anyway. It was time to tell her about the disaster that was Troy's visit. And that I was still not staying at the cabin, not until we found out who was doing this.

"Do you think it could be this Jerry?"

Cosi rubbed a hand over his jaw. "Could be. But no one knows a Jerry. I've asked around."

"Damn," I mumbled. "Maybe I heard his name wrong."

"At this point, I think the only person who knew what was going on over there was your dad."

"That doesn't help us, does it?" I groaned. "Do you think it could be about Dad's journal and atlas?"

"Maybe. But if Ike was going around town talking about some lost, legendary gold, that's something that would have made people talk. Someone at the station would have heard about it."

"And knowing Dad, he kept all of it to himself." Well, except sharing clues with me. "Now what?"

"Now we go to a basketball game." He held out his hand for mine, then led me through the house.

I rolled up the sleeves of his sweatshirt and tucked the hem into my jeans so it was a bit more flattering. With my coat on and my purse over a shoulder, we hurried to the Bronco and drove to the school.

The parking lot was filling up quickly when we arrived and a line of people were filtering through the doors to the gym. The sound of bouncing basketballs and the pep band playing mingled with the hum of conversation as people shuffled into the bleachers.

Cosi and I walked inside hand in hand, and for a brief moment, all of the noise seemed to stop. The people lingering inside the door gave us a double take, but it was more out of curiosity and surprise than pointed stares.

I plastered on a smile despite my growing nerves and tightened my grip on Cosi's hand.

"Howdy, Cosi." A man I didn't recognize stepped into our path.

"Hi, John." Cosi shook his hand. "Have you met Ilsa Poe?"

John quickly took off his cowboy hat, holding it over his heart as he gave me a slight bow. "Nice to meet you, ma'am."

"You too."

"We're going to find a seat." Cosi moved past John, only to get stopped by a man named Luke.

Introduction after introduction, by the time we made it to the center of the bleachers, I'd met at least fifty people and their names were beginning to blur. But they'd all been kind and genuine. Most had welcomed me to Dalton. An older couple had said they knew me when I was a girl.

The nerves were still there but they were calming, handshake by handshake.

We climbed the stairs of the bleachers to the third row, taking a seat and saving one for Linda. Once we were settled, our coats tucked beneath us, Cosi leaned his elbows to his knees, eyes locked on Spencer as he warmed up on the floor.

Spencer dribbled in to make a layup, and as he jogged to the end of the line of players, it put him directly behind Paul.

Both boys looked over at the same time, one with a smile, the other with a glare.

Paul lifted a hand, raised his middle finger and pretended to wipe his eye.

Cosi's body went rigid.

"It's okay." I put my hand on his knee, but we weren't the only ones who'd noticed.

Spencer's nostrils flared, and he leaned in closer, saying something in Paul's ear. Despite their age difference, both boys were about the same height, though Paul had grown into his frame.

The muscles in Paul's arms flexed as his hands fisted, his face turning red.

"Oh, Spencer," I whispered.

Cosi stood, body primed and ready to jump to the floor to break up a fight.

But Spencer, that wonderful, brave kid, sent his dad a look that screamed *don't even think about it.* This was his fight.

A fight for me.

Spencer crossed his arms over his chest and leveled Paul with a stare that begged him to do it. To fuck it all up by throwing a punch.

Paul was a shithead but he wasn't stupid. If he hit Spencer, he could kiss basketball goodbye and say hello to a school suspension. After a mouthed *fuck you*, he turned toward the basket and caught the ball as it was passed to him.

"Phew." I exhaled, taking Cosi's wrist, urging him back to his seat.

Spencer looked over and grinned. Then he went back to warmups like nothing had happened. Like he hadn't just been ready to throw down with a teammate to defend my honor.

If every person in Dalton treated me like crap, it didn't really matter, did it? Not when I had the Raynes men on my side.

"Good?" Cosi asked, putting his arm around my shoulders.

There were people watching us. I could see them from the corner of my eye. I heard the whisper of my name along with "that math teacher." But they could look and talk all they wanted.

"Good." I leaned into his side as we watched the teams run through drills and stretches.

With only two minutes left before the game started, as the cheerleaders ran out to the floor, I slipped away to use the bathroom. I was washing my hands at the sink when a woman emerged from another stall.

It was the same woman who I'd seen in the parking lot a week ago. The blond woman who drove a navy Impala like Mom's.

She met my stare in the mirror, eyes blowing wide, then went to a sink to wash her hands. When she looked up, I was still staring.

Like a creep.

"Sorry." I shut off the water at my faucet. "I don't mean to stare. I saw you last week in the parking lot. Your car is exactly the same car that my mom drives. That's why I noticed."

"Oh." She relaxed a bit, giving me a sideways glance as she hurried to finish washing.

"Excited for the game?"

"Yes." She beat me to the paper towel dispenser, barely drying her hands before she tossed her damp towel into the trash. "Have fun."

"You too."

She was out the door before I could ask who she was here to watch.

A loud buzzer echoed.

"Shit." I hurried to dry my hands, then rushed out, making it back to the bleachers just as everyone stood for the national anthem.

One of the senior girls belted "The Star-Spangled Banner" along with the band, and as the last chord rang out and applause filled the gym, Linda came up the stairs, taking the seat beside Cosi that he'd saved for her.

She was missing her usual smile.

"You okay, Mom?" Cosi asked.

"Fine," she lied, lips pursed.

"Are you—"

"I said I'm fine, Cosi. Let's just watch the game."

"Okay." He held up his hands, the two of us sharing a look before we focused on the game.

We watched the Lynx beat the Cowboys by thirty points, with Spencer scoring twenty of his own. The kid was on fire. Paul had a horrible game and sat out the entire last quarter.

I scanned the crowd, trying to find that woman from the bathroom to point her out to Cosi and ask her name. But I never saw her again.

And Linda never found her smile.

Chapter 27

Ilsa

As the kids from fourth period streamed out of the classroom, I opened my desk drawer and took out my Yogi Bear lunchbox, flipping open the lid to pull out the matching thermos.

I'd found the set in Cosi's kitchen cabinet, tucked away next to a jar of lard. The lunchbox had belonged to Spencer, but obviously he was too cool for Yogi Bear these days.

Not me. I'd asked to borrow it, and every time I pictured a younger Spencer toting this around the elementary school, it made me smile.

A puff of steam escaped as I twisted off the thermos's lid. The scent of salty broth filled my nose from the chicken noodle soup I'd made for dinner last night.

In the past two weeks, I'd started cooking more often for Cosi and Spencer. I still felt like a guest in their home, but between cooking and cleaning and laundry and grocery shopping, the guilt of imposing was slightly less.

I couldn't stay on Pine Street forever, but at the moment, I had no furniture at the cabin, so I couldn't exactly live there either.

It had taken ten total trips to clean out Dad's house, but everything that had been destroyed was now gone. The cabin was nearly empty and walking through the front door was unbearable.

So I hadn't spent much time on Cotters Lake, preferring to stay in town. To make homemade chicken noodle soup or lasagna or tater tot casserole for my guys. To enjoy a couple weeks of easy.

My stomach growled as I crumbled a stack of saltine crackers into my soup. Both Cosi and Spencer had teased me last night for using so many crackers, but I hated the sensation of slurping. Ever since I was a kid, if there was soup, I'd add so many crackers that it became a stew.

Dad had been the same way. We'd use an entire sleeve of saltines for a single can of Campbell's soup.

These memories of Dad were bittersweet, but the pain was fading, day by day. I missed him. I would carry the regret of our strained relationship for the rest of my life. But being in Montana was healing too.

I'd forgotten just how much I loved the mountains. How many stars came out at night. How every sunset was a kaleidoscope of pastel colors.

I'd forgotten the things I'd learned from Dad and the habits we'd shared. Now when I crushed a handful of crackers into my soup, I did it with a fond smile. The same was true when I drank from his water jar.

A jar that I'd forgotten on the kitchen counter this morning.

My coffee cup was a poor replacement. The taste of coffee had infused itself into the ceramic mug, and no matter how many times I'd washed it out today, every sip came with a bitter tang.

I stirred my soup with a spoon, about to take a bite, when the sound of footsteps in the hall pulled my gaze to the door. Cosi walked into the classroom.

With my water jar in hand.

"Hi." I smiled, soup and spoon pushed aside as he walked over to my desk.

"Hi, baby." He set the jar down and bent to kiss my forehead. "Thought you might want that."

"Thanks."

He took a seat on the edge of my desk, stretching out his legs to cross them at his ankles. Comfortable. Familiar.

I put my hand on his thigh, feeling the muscles flex beneath. "I like that you come to visit me at work. I've never had a boyfriend do that before."

"Boyfriend?" His eyebrow arched. "Makes me sound like I'm fifteen."

I shrugged. "I'm surrounded by teenagers all day. Besides, what else should I call you?"

Cosi leaned in close until his mouth hovered over mine. "Yours."

How I loved this man. Without question. It didn't matter that our relationship was new. That we were still getting to know each other. My heart knew his. Belonged to him.

"Mine." I put my hands on his face, pulling him in for a kiss, licking the seam of his lips until he parted for me and took control.

His tongue tangled with mine as he delved deep, exploring every corner of my mouth. He worshipped my lips, and though he didn't touch me anywhere else, I felt him in every cell in my being.

It was reckless. It was claiming. It was a kiss that spoke the words neither of us were ready to say quite yet.

The sound of footsteps in the hallway tore us apart.

I cleared my throat, pulling in my lips to hide a smile as I put a few feet between us. The last thing I needed was to be caught kissing the sheriff.

Mrs. McNally walked by, her silver hair pulled back so tight the bun had to be giving her a headache. She paused at my doorway and gave a haughty puff when she saw Cosi perched on my desk.

"Hello, Mrs. McNally," he said.

"Sheriff Raynes." Her eyes narrowed on me before she continued down the hall.

"Self-righteous, old bat," I muttered.

Cosi tossed his head back and laughed, the rich, carefree sound filling the classroom. It was mesmerizing, watching him laugh. His hazel eyes sparkled, and when they met mine, I fell a little deeper.

I wasn't leaving Dalton, was I? Which meant I was going to have to kiss Harlan's ass and beg him for another job. Damn.

"What's that look?" he asked, running his thumb across my bottom lip.

"I was just thinking that I need a job in town. For next year."

He blinked, taken aback for a moment. Then his mouth was on mine again, his hands framing my face, urging me out of my chair and onto my feet so he could wrap me in his arms.

So he could kiss me until we were breathless.

When he pulled away, his gaze searched mine. "Ilsa, I . . ."

"Me too," I whispered.

He dropped his forehead to mine, keeping me close until the five-minute bell rang, warning that students would be returning to class soon.

"I wanted to give you some news, but it can wait."

I shook my head, easing away and back to my seat so I could eat lunch while he talked. "No, tell me now."

"We got the warrant this morning."

My spoon fell out of my hand, clattering on my desk. "For Paul? He's not in school today."

"Chuck was able to catch Dean and Melody before they left their house this morning. They kept Paul home so we could take his prints there instead of at school."

"Was it him?"

The defeated look on his face was answer enough.

"It wasn't," I said on an exhale. "That's actually a relief."

Paul was still a pain in my ass, but it would have broken something inside me if a student hated me enough to destroy my house. And I didn't want a kid saddled with a record for his entire life because of a stupid dccision hc madc whcn hc was cightccn.

"If it wasn't Paul, then who?"

Cosi dropped his chin. "I promised you I'd find out. And I'm terrified I'm going to break that promise."

I took his hand, threading our fingers together. "Maybe all of this happened for a reason. Maybe breaking this promise means you can make me others that you'll keep."

His thumb drew a circle around my knuckle. "I'm not giving up."

"I know you won't."

"I actually just came from Trick's. Stopped in before he opened today to talk while it was quiet. See if he knows anyone named Jerry or a friend of your dad's who matched your description."

"And?"

Cosi shook his head. "Nothing. But Trick was just my first stop, not my only."

"Okay."

"I'll get out of here so you can eat. See you at home?"

I liked how *home* sounded. Too much. "I think tonight we need to talk about my living situation."

"Your living situation?"

"Well, yeah. I can't live out of your guest bedroom forever."

"Then move your stuff into ours."

Ours? I liked how that sounded too. But that wasn't my bedroom. Unless . . . "Are you asking me to live with you?"

"You already do, baby. Catch up."

"But don't you think it's too fast?"

"Nope."

"What about Spencer?"

Cosi glanced over his shoulder as kids started to filter into the hallway from their lunch break. "What about Spencer?"

"Don't you think we should talk about this? Give it some time? Make sure it's not weird for him?"

"Tell you what. If you want to talk to Spencer about your *living situation*, you go right on ahead. And if he says you can leave, then you can leave."

I frowned at the arrogant smirk on his face. "Then I guess there's a chance I won't be at the house when you get there. The motel is open again. Maybe I'll stay there until I buy a bed for the cabin."

"See you at home." Cosi chuckled. With a chaste kiss on my lips, he stood and pointed to my soup. "Got enough crackers?"

"Har har." I picked up my spoon and took a bite, smiling as I chewed.

"Bye." He winked and was gone.

Did we really just agree to live together? In less than five minutes? Shouldn't big decisions, like an address change, take more than five minutes? Apparently not.

But that was Cosi.

Easy.

Happy.

I was still shoveling soup into my mouth as my fifth-period students filed into the room, taking their seats and pulling books and pencils from their backpacks.

As the bell to start class rang out, I swallowed the last of my lunch and chased it down with a gulp of water from my jar. Then I stowed my thermos and lunchbox before going to the chalkboard to write out the first equation for my juniors.

"Any volunteers to solve this one?"

Not a soul raised their hand.

"Don't everyone rush to the chalkboard at once," I teased. "Five points extra credit."

Every kid raised their hand.

"Much better."

Bribery truly worked wonders.

Don't puke. Don't puke. Don't puke.

By the final class of the day, my soup was about to make a reappearance.

My stomach roiled as I sipped my water, hoping I could just make it to the last bell and not vomit in front of these kids.

I'd given them free time to get a head start on their homework so I wouldn't have to speak. All I could do was breathe through my nose, enduring wave after wave of nausea.

Oh God, I was going to puke. My insides cramped so hard I wanted to cry. When the bell rang, I let out a huge breath, forcing a smile until the kids were gone. Then I grabbed my trash can and threw up my lunch.

When I was finished, I groaned and sagged in my chair, feeling better for a moment. "Gross."

That was not something I expected the janitor to deal with, so I let myself have two minutes before I took the can to the bathroom, cleaning it out before returning to my class to pack up for the day.

Spencer walked through the door as I was pulling on my coat. "Um, you look like shit."

"Don't say shit in school," I chided, zipping up my coat. Though I felt better after puking, the chills were setting in and my skin felt clammy. "I don't feel very good. I think I might have that flu going around. Or last night's soup made me sick."

"Want me to call Dad to come pick you up?" he asked.

"No, he's busy. I'll just walk."

The weather had changed this past week. A chinook had blown in and the warm wind had begun melting the snow. The mild temperatures wouldn't last. Winter would be slow to loosen its grip on Montana, but for now, the streets were clear of ice and the snowdrifts were shrinking by the hour. And since it wasn't freezing outside, the fresh air might clear my head.

"Are you sure?" Spencer asked.

"I'm sure."

"'Kay. If you're feeling up for it, maybe we could look at that map again tonight."

"I'd like that."

We'd finished decoding Dad's number key, but we hadn't spent much time trying to understand the atlas in the past two weeks. Mostly because there didn't seem to be too much to find. Not until the snow melted and we could hike the trails he'd plotted.

But even though we couldn't act yet, Spencer was enamored with the lore of a lost treasure. If he wanted to scatter all of Dad's things on the kitchen table tonight, I'd gladly sit by his side just to watch his face light up.

"Are you sure you're okay to walk home?" he asked.

"Yes. I'm sure. What are you doing here anyway? Don't you have practice?"

Spencer shrugged. "Just wanted to say hi."

"Hi." I looped my arm with his and let him walk me to the door. Then I sent him to the locker room to get changed for practice while I made my way down Main Street with my briefcase in hand.

The walk should have given me a boost of energy, but by the time I turned on Pine Street, the queasiness had returned. My head was spinning and sweat dripped down my temples.

Shit. Something was wrong. This couldn't just be a flu.

I needed to get inside, call Cosi for help. Every step ached and my stomach pinched so hard it hurt to breathe. But I kept moving, my gaze locked on the house, putting one foot in front of the other. My legs wobbled and I nearly tripped on a crack in the sidewalk.

White and black spots burst in front of my eyes, too bright and too dark at the same time. It was a miracle that I made it to the house, and it took the last shards of my strength to make it to the front door. When I reached the welcome mat, I dropped to my knees, unable to stand.

I breathed through my nose as saliva pooled in my mouth. My fingertips were tingling and I couldn't get my hand into my coat pocket to take out my keys.

Cosi had made me my own key to the house so I wouldn't have to use the spare. Except I couldn't lift my arm. Why couldn't I move my arm?

Help. I opened my mouth but nothing came out.

The world was spinning too fast. My heart was beating too hard. A cough tore through my chest, and I tasted the metallic tang of blood when I swallowed.

A new wave of dizziness sent me sideways, falling to my shoulder. My throat was dry and burning.

If I could just get some water, if I could clear my throat and call for help . . .

Except my water jar was on my desk at school. I'd forgotten it again. That was my last thought before the world went black.

Chapter 28

Cosi

Commotion outside my office made me look up from the file I'd been reviewing as Pamela and Chuck appeared in the doorway, their faces pale and panicked.

"What?" I shot to my feet, rounding the desk as my worst fears began running through my mind. "Is it Spencer?"

"It's Ilsa," Pamela said.

No. The world tilted beneath my feet. "What happened?"

"Aunt Helena called," Chuck said. "She's on shift in the emergency room and was there when they brought Ilsa in. Thought you might want to get down there. Fast."

I was already moving, pushing past them for the hall. Icy dread pooled in my bones as I shoved through the door and sprinted for the Bronco, digging my keys from my jeans pocket. The squeal of the tires was a dull screech beneath the blood roaring in my ears. With a flick of a switch, I turned on the light bar and siren, then stomped on the gas.

This wasn't happening. It couldn't be real. It had to be a mistake.

She was fine. I just saw her at lunch. She was fine. She was at school, probably grading papers, sitting at her desk drinking water from her jar.

She had to be okay. I wouldn't survive it otherwise.

My vision blurred at the fringes as I sped through town, my heart in my throat, not knowing what I'd find when I reached the ER.

The ambulance was parked out front, its back doors open. I took the space reserved for first responders and ran inside.

"Cosi." Mom was waiting beyond the double doors, arms wrapped around her waist.

"Where is she? What happened? Is she okay?"

The tears in Mom's eyes made my stomach drop.

"Mom." My voice cracked. "Where is Ilsa?"

"With the doctors. I don't know what happened."

I moved around her, marching toward the nurses' station. It was empty. Where the fuck was everyone? There was a bell on the counter. I hit it three times fast, the ding filling the lobby.

Nothing. I pounded a fist into the desk and pushed away, marching for the door that led to the ER rooms. Except before I could reach for the handle, it blew open and Helena came out, dressed in teal scrubs, her gray hair twisted into a severe knot.

"Come with me," she ordered. Her footsteps were muted on the thin blue carpet as she led the way along a hall.

Behind me, Mom jogged to catch up.

We turned one corner, then another, winding past closed doors and empty waiting rooms. With every step, the strength in my legs waned, making it harder and harder to pick up my feet.

"Helena." I could barely speak past the lump in my throat. "Please."

She slowed and turned, giving me a tight smile.

Chuck's aunt had been a nurse at this hospital for years. She was stern, her face set in a permanent pout, and she didn't believe in sugarcoating bad news.

I'd always respected that she was a straight shooter. But today, I wasn't sure I could handle a blunt truth. Not if it meant losing Ilsa. "Is she okay?"

"We don't know yet. Dr. Harris is in with her now. He thinks she's been poisoned."

My knees buckled.

"Cosi." Mom caught me by the arm, holding me up.

"I'm okay." I found my balance, swallowing the terror, and met Helena's cool blue eyes. "Is she . . ."

I couldn't finish the sentence. I couldn't bring myself to ask if she was going to survive this.

"It's going to be a while before we know anything," Helena said. "What I need is for you to remain calm. Come and sit in a waiting room before you pass out. I don't have time to deal with you too. When I know more, I'll know exactly where to find you."

"Come on." Mom urged me forward, keeping her arm looped with mine as we followed Helena to a waiting room.

She left us to sit in stiff, tweed-upholstered chairs.

"Fuck." I scrubbed my hands over my face. At any minute, I'd wake up from this awful dream. Ilsa would be asleep beside me in bed. I wouldn't be in this damn hospital.

I hated the hospital. I hated being tucked away in a room where doctors delivered bad news. The last time I'd been back here was when Spencer was eight.

He'd built a skateboard ramp in the driveway, then proceeded to break his arm. Since then, I stuck to the lobby.

Doctors didn't deliver bad news in the lobby. No, they saved the bad news for private waiting rooms. This was where they told people that the love of their life was dead.

"I can't—" I pushed my palms to my eyes, pushing so hard black spots broke out. Thinking about losing her was too much. So I shut it out. I pushed all of the fear, the dread, into a dark, dusty corner of my mind and let the cop inside me take control.

"Did you find her?" I asked Mom.

"No." She shook her head. "I was leaving the mail room after my shift. I saw them bring her in on a gurney."

My hands were trembling, every muscle in my body shaking and tense. My knees started to bounce and sitting in this chair only made the anxiety worse. So I stood and paced the small room, raking my hands through my hair. “You don’t have any idea what happened?”

Mom’s chin quivered. “No. But I do need to tell you something.”

I stopped moving. “What?”

“There was a woman with her.” She swallowed hard. “I think she rode in the ambulance with Ilsa. And she might have been the person who found her and called the hospital.”

That cold, icy dread seemed to double. “Who?”

“Gwen.”

I rocked on my heels so hard I took a step backward. “What? Are you sure?”

“I’m sure. She’s in the lobby. You walked right past her.”

“The fuck I did.” My hands fisted, and I marched out of the waiting room.

“Cosi,” Mom called, chasing me into the hallway.

I whirled, glaring down at my mother. “What the hell is going on?”

“I don’t know.” Mom’s eyes filled with tears. “Remember that game against the Cowboys a couple weeks ago? I thought I saw her at the school that night, but it was quick. And then I started second-guessing myself. It’s been so long.”

Mom had been in a horrible mood that night. Now the reason made sense. “Why would she come in with Ilsa?”

“No idea. I was about to confront her when you stormed into the ER.”

“She better not have left,” I snarled, retreating to the lobby.

Anger surged, and I let over a decade of rage and resentment toward Gwen chase away the fear of losing Ilsa. I gave that fury all of my energy, craving it instead of the terror. I let that anger keep me together.

Gwen was in the far corner of the hospital lobby, sitting stiffly in a wooden chair. She was dressed in jeans, white tennis shoes and a beige sweater that blended with the color of the walls. Her eyes lifted from her lap as I walked into the room. She gulped and rose to her feet.

She was pretty, like she'd always been. Older, like we both were. But her blond hair paled in comparison to my favorite shade of silky brown. Her blue eyes didn't hold a candle to chocolate irises flecked with gold and cinnamon.

I'd wondered for a long, long time what it would feel like to see Gwen again. I'd wondered if it would hurt. If I'd still find her as beautiful as I had when we were kids. If I'd have this overwhelming urge to scream and yell for the pain she'd caused me. If I'd throw every good memory I had of Spencer's life in her face.

But as I came to a stop in front of her, I felt nothing. It all disappeared. There was no anger. No compassion. No regret.

Nothing.

Gwen was nothing but a source of information so I could figure out why the only woman who mattered was in the fucking ER.

"Why did you come in with Ilsa?" I asked, crossing my arms over my chest.

"Hi, Cosi," she said, glancing past my arm to Mom. "Linda."

"Answer the question, Gwen."

She gulped again, her gaze dropping to the badge and holstered gun on my belt. "I, um . . . I saw her walking home from the school. I was going to talk to her."

"About what?"

She hesitated. "Spencer."

Part of me wanted to tell her that she had no right to speak my son's name. But that argument would come later. "Why?"

"I got your last letter. I know I shouldn't have reached out to him. I'm sorry. I really am. I understand I lost my chance with him a long time ago."

"That you did."

Her eyes filled with tears before she ducked her chin to stare at the floor. "I just wanted to see him. Even if it was only from a distance."

"You were at his basketball game," I said.

She nodded. "I met her that night. I saw you together and then she was in the bathroom. You said her name is Ilsa?"

"Yes."

"She had no idea who I was."

"Why would she?"

Gwen flinched.

If she expected me to be gentle about this, she was sorely mistaken. At the moment, she was nothing more than a witness. And she was lucky I hadn't called Chuck to take her to the station for questioning.

"I, um . . . I thought maybe if I got to know her—"

"She could put in a good word for you to see Spencer."

"Yeah." She nodded, eyes still locked on the floor.

"If you knew my son, you'd know that this manipulative bullshit isn't the way to win him over. And using Ilsa? Guaranteed to piss him off. He's about as protective of her as I am. So tell me why the fuck we're in the emergency room, Gwen." I didn't care that I was shouting. I didn't care that tears began dripping down her cheeks. I didn't care that Mom put her hand on my arm because she knew I was seconds away from losing my goddamn mind.

I only cared about the truth.

"I've, um . . . I've been coming to town for a while. I'd go to the school in the morning and wait in the parking lot to see Spencer. He looks just like you."

"Because he's mine."

She wiped at her cheeks, sucking in a shaky breath. "I saw her walking with him one morning and realized you were together. So I started following her. When I saw her in the bathroom and she didn't know me, I thought maybe I could meet her. And then today, she was walking alone and I decided it could be my chance. I drove to the station to make sure your truck was there. Then I went back to your house. I was going to introduce myself. Explain why I was here. Tell her that I was sorry and trying to make amends."

Gwen was going to play on Ilsa's heart to soften Spencer's. And mine.

The hell of it was, it would have probably worked.

"I was just pulling up when I saw someone running away from the house with the purple briefcase Ilsa was carrying."

"Who?"

"It's been a long time, so I can't be sure. But it looked like Trick."

For the second time today, the world tilted beneath my feet.

Trick? No. Fuck no. He was one of my oldest friends. Why would he want to steal Ilsa's briefcase?

Gwen had to be lying. She had to be wrong.

"I found Ilsa on the porch, unconscious. There were keys in her coat pocket, so I opened the door and called the hospital for an ambulance."

Gwen had gone into my house. The last place I wanted her to be.

But it might have saved Ilsa's life.

"Why did you come to the hospital?" Mom asked. "Why did you stay?"

Gwen sniffled. "I wanted to make sure she was okay."

But Ilsa wasn't okay. None of this was okay. I hadn't done my job to keep her safe.

The pressure in my chest made it nearly impossible to breathe. That paralyzing fear returned tenfold.

I went to the closest chair and sat down before I fainted. Then I put my elbows to my knees, clasped my hands and prayed that Ilsa would survive this. That I'd get the chance to tell her how I felt. To make the rest of her life easy.

After an hour, Mom left to meet Spencer and take him to her place for the night. After two hours, Gwen slipped away, murmuring something about staying at the motel. And after three hours, Helena finally returned.

She wasn't happy to find me in the lobby instead of the waiting room, but she waved for me to follow her into the hospital, past empty beds and open curtained walls. We walked to a room with a glass wall where the most beautiful woman in the world was hooked up to too many tubes, too many wires, and too many machines.

Her skin was pale, her eyelids blue and her lips leached of their normal pink. They'd changed her into a greenish-gray gown and covered her torso and legs with a thin white blanket. She lay utterly still, and the only reason I knew she was still alive was because of the beeping machine monitoring her heart.

The burn in my throat was so fierce I choked. The only thing keeping me from coming apart at the seams was that little green line bouncing on a black screen.

"Dr. Harris is on his way." Helena pointed to the lone chair positioned by Ilsa's side.

I took a seat and lifted Ilsa's hand, clasping it between my own. Her knuckles were too cold, so I blew my warm breath on them, holding them against my lips.

Wake up, baby.

"Sheriff Raynes." Dr. Harris walked into the room with a clipboard in one hand. His white coat was open, revealing teal scrubs like Helena's. His salt-and-pepper hair was clipped high and tight with a square style on top.

Dr. Harris was the man who'd delivered Spencer. He'd set my son's broken arm. I hoped and prayed he'd save Ilsa's life.

"Is she going to be okay?" I asked, my throat ragged, the words raspy.

"I can't tell you much since you aren't immediate family," he said, stepping closer until he stood at the foot of her bed. "The next forty-eight hours are critical. We're lucky she was brought in so quickly. We've notified her mother. She said she'll leave Phoenix immediately and be here as soon as possible. Once she gets to Dalton, I can share more."

He'd abide by his protocols. And I'd abide by mine.

I let go of Ilsa's hand, placing it gently at her side, and stood. "What happened to her? I'm asking as the sheriff."

Harris hesitated.

"If you need me to get a deputy down here to ask the questions, I'll call the station right now. Or you can tell me why the hell Ilsa Poe is in this hospital bed."

He frowned but plucked the reading glasses from his coat's pocket, fitting them to his face as he looked at the clipboard. "Every indication leads me to believe she was poisoned. We've treated her with activated charcoal and we're trying to flush it from her system with intravenous fluids."

"What poison?"

"I don't know yet. We've taken urine and blood samples. They're not always definitive."

"Ingested, inhaled or injected?"

"Ingested."

Fuck. My molars ground together so hard they cracked. "Anything else you can tell me?"

"No." Harris gave me a tight smile. "Given the circumstances, we'll limit visitors to—"

"Me. And only me. Until her mother arrives. Even then, every visitor is cleared through me."

"Very well." He nodded and took off his glasses. "Sheriff Raynes."

I gave him a nod. "Doctor Harris."

The moment he left, I used the phone next to Ilsa's bed and called the station.

Chuck answered on the first ring. "Dalton County Sheriff's Department."

"Chuck, it's Cosi."

His exhale was audible. "How is she?"

"Alive." And if I had to will her to stay that way, so be it. I brushed the hair off Ilsa's temple before I sank into the chair. "Got a pen?"

"Yes."

"There's a glass jar, a Mason jar, either at my house on the stoop or at the school. Find it. Print it." Hopefully, no matter where it was, no one had touched it. And that the prints I was looking for weren't entirely smudged.

I suspected that the fingerprints on that glass would match those found at the tiny cabin Ilsa had found across Cotters Lake.

Fingerprints that belonged to one of my oldest friends.

When I'd gone to ask Trick today if he knew anyone named Jerry, he'd looked me dead in the eye and said he had no clue. Then he'd offered to fill up Ilsa's water jar when I'd said I was taking it to her at school.

That motherfucker must have laced it with poison.

I wasn't sure exactly why yet, but I had ideas. I suspected it had everything to do with the contents of Ilsa's briefcase. When he hadn't been able to find Ike's journal at the cabin, he'd poisoned Ilsa so she'd be out of his way.

"Got it," Chuck said. "Anything else?"

"If there's water in that jar, don't toss it. Bring it to the hospital."

"All right, boss."

"I'll be at this number." I pressed the button in the cradle once to end the call, then waited until I had a dial tone. After a quick call to Mom to check on Spencer and give her an update, I put the phone aside and clasped Ilsa's hand.

Her knuckles were cold again.

"Ilsa." I waited, hoping those eyes would flutter open. That she'd gift me with a small smile. But she didn't move, so I kept her hand warm in mine and stared at the monitor, knowing that if her heart stopped, mine would too.

For three days, I stayed at Ilsa's side.

When Chuck came to the hospital to give me an update on his investigation, I listened from her room. I learned that Trick's prints were on the glass along with mine and Ilsa's. That the water had tested positive for ricin, a poison derived from castor beans. And that a man I'd once called *friend* was nowhere to be found.

When Ilsa's mother, Florence, arrived in Dalton, I had the nurses bring in another chair because I wasn't giving up mine.

And when Spencer came to visit, he sat at the foot of Ilsa's bed while I told him the whole truth about what had happened, including how his mother might have saved Ilsa's life.

For three days, I stayed at her side, holding her hand.

Until finally, those beautiful brown eyes opened. And the nightmare came to an end.

"Hey, baby," she whispered.

I clutched her hand as tears filled my eyes. "That's my line."

Chapter 29

Ilsa

The most popular place on Saturday mornings in Dalton, Montana, was the Grizzly Café. Something I'd learned in the past three weeks.

Breakfast here had become a fledgling tradition for Cosi, Spencer and me. We'd sleep in and enjoy a cup of coffee on the couch. Then whenever Spencer rolled out of bed, the three of us would walk to the café for eggs and bacon and their famous banana bread French toast.

Conversation filled the restaurant with a boisterous buzz. Every seat was taken. We'd been lucky enough to snag a booth this morning, which meant I got to sit tucked into Cosi's side. His arm was draped over my shoulders, his fingers idly drumming on the booth's caramel vinyl.

The wall of windows beside us overlooked Main, and as cars and trucks rolled down the street, Spencer built a pyramid out of the individual jelly packets.

A couple of his classmates were in the café this morning. Amanda was sitting with her family at a table in the center of the room. Nicole was at the counter with her grandpa. Both girls had given Spencer shy smiles when we'd walked into the café, but other than a jerk of his chin, he'd hardly acknowledged either.

Those poor girls probably thought that cool attitude was their doing, when really, it was because he had a lot on his mind.

"You don't have to go," Cosi told him. "If you're nervous."

"I'm not." Spencer added a grape jelly to his stack.

Cosi and I shared a look, both hearing that lie.

That kid was a ball of nerves.

"So I've been thinking about my car," I said as Spencer kept stacking, totally lost in his own head. "I'm giving it to you for your birthday."

Spencer's eyes whipped up, and he bumped the table with his elbow, his pyramid crumbling. "W-what?"

While I loved my little green Rabbit, I mostly drove Dad's truck. So over our morning coffee, Cosi and I had talked about giving the car to Spencer.

He was almost fifteen, and when they gave him that shiny new driver's license, he'd need a vehicle. It didn't make sense for me to sell a perfectly good car.

"If you want it, then it's yours," I said.

"I want it." His smile was contagious.

"Happy Birthday."

"Thanks, Ilsa."

I winked. "Welcome, bud."

Even though his birthday wasn't until Tuesday, Cosi and I figured telling him today might chase away the sullen mood we'd been dealing with for weeks. And we hoped that it might give Spencer and Gwen something to talk about when they met later today.

We were all grateful Gwen had been there that horrible day three weeks ago. Had she not found me so soon and gotten me to the hospital, I might not have survived the poison.

But three weeks was a short time to overcome years of abandonment.

Gwen and Cosi had met once, last week, to talk. She'd asked if Spencer would be up for a picnic lunch over the weekend.

When Cosi had posed the question, Spencer had shocked us all by agreeing. Though given his grumpy mood today, I suspected he wanted to take it back.

"Dad?" Spencer went back to stacking jellies. "Did she tell you where she was? After she left Dalton?"

"Yes."

"Where?"

Cosi gave his son a sad smile. "Not in a good place."

During their meeting, she'd told Cosi about the years she'd spent away from Dalton. She'd moved from place to place, coast to coast, sampling a variety of drugs along the way. Until a year ago, when she'd gone to rehab and turned her life around. After she'd climbed up from rock bottom, Gwen had realized it was time to face her mistakes. It was time to apologize to her son.

"Do you think she'll stay in Montana?" Spencer asked.

"I don't know, pal. I think right now, she's just hoping for a nice picnic."

"Whatever," Spencer muttered with an eye roll.

We'd had a lot of *whatever*s and eye rolls this week.

"Morning, Sheriff." Dawn, the waitress, appeared, setting down three glasses of water. "Hi, Ilsa. Sorry for the wait."

"Hey, Dawn. No problem. We're not in a rush."

"Still up for pinochle tomorrow?"

"As long as you promise to be my partner."

"Deal." She smiled, tucking a lock of her strawberry-blond hair behind her ear.

Dawn and I had bonded that afternoon that I'd come to the café for the first time and had a hot beef sandwich at four thirty in the afternoon. She'd called earlier this week to invite me to her pinochle club.

The girls met on Sundays for a few hours, and though I hadn't played the card game in ages, I really liked Dawn and wanted the chance to meet her friends. Women who might become my friends too.

"Okay, are you ready to order?" she asked, taking out her notepad.

We rattled off our breakfast orders, and as she rushed away, Cosi picked up a water.

He took a sip, eyes narrowing as he gave it a good taste.

Now it was my turn to roll my eyes. "Give me that."

He deemed my water safe and handed it over.

"This is getting ridiculous, Cosi."

Ridiculous, considering ricin was tasteless and there would have been no way to know Trick had poisoned my water. Still, Cosi had been drinking my waters for three weeks. Unless he filled the glass himself, he took the first sip.

But despite my grumbling, Cosi would keep tasting my water and my food until the day that Trick Dougan was found and put behind bars.

We were each healing in our own ways.

According to Dr. Harris, there'd been no permanent damage to my internal organs, and he expected me to make a full recovery. I felt fine, physically. Emotionally? I was still coming to terms with it all.

Now that the journal and atlas were gone, along with my briefcase, I could no longer read the last letter Dad had written to me. I couldn't look at his handwriting or touch the pages he'd filled himself. I couldn't drink out of a jar, not that Cosi would have let me. Those pieces of Dad were lost and ruined.

All because of Trick. Even thinking his name sent me into a rage. If I had to drive past the bar, well . . . I didn't. I used the back roads because I couldn't even look at the dark building without getting angry.

The bar was closed at the moment. It had been since the day Trick filled my water jar and handed it to Cosi, knowing he'd deliver it to the school.

The rumor around town was that someone was trying to track down Sully, Trick's partner, but even if they reopened, even if there was a different face behind the bar, I doubted I'd ever set foot in that building again.

Cosi wouldn't tell me everything they'd found when they went to Trick's house, either because he couldn't share details of an open investigation or because he was trying to protect me. Given just how tight-lipped he'd been, it couldn't have been good.

So I was doing everything in my power to put it behind me. I was trying, every day, to move on.

"What time is your meeting?" Spencer asked, sliding the cup of coffee creamers over to add to his creation.

"Twelve thirty," I answered. "We'll go out after we drop you off."

While he was with Gwen, Cosi and I were going to Cotters Lake to meet a realtor about Dad's cabin.

Part of me couldn't fathom letting it go. The other part, the practical part, knew that I'd never again call it home.

I lived on Pine Street.

And as of now, I had no prospects of a job come next fall. When I'd asked Principal Harlan about a position for the upcoming school year, he'd basically laughed in my face. He told me that hiring a young woman was his very last choice because obviously I'd get married and pregnant soon, then leave them high and dry.

Asshole.

Unemployed teachers didn't need to be paying taxes and utilities for vacant, lakefront cabins. Though I was certain Cosi would make it work if I wanted to keep it.

For now, I was simply getting information. I wanted to hear what the realtor had to say. Then I'd decide if I could stand letting it go.

"Do you think your mom will come back?" Spencer asked.

"Oh, I'm sure. Though probably not until summer."

"Good. I like your mom," he said.

"She likes you too."

Florence Poe had taken one look at Spencer Raynes and fallen in love. She'd already claimed him as her grandchild, and she was enamored with Cosi. Mostly, she loved that he was enamored with me.

Mom hadn't stayed long in Dalton, only a week. Once I'd been discharged from the hospital, and she'd realized that Cosi was going to hover over me for weeks on end, she'd returned to Arizona.

But the short trip had given Mom a new perspective on Dalton. A fresh look from her daughter's eyes. A daughter who'd fallen in love in this town and had no plans to leave.

"Do I have to meet with Gwen today?" Spencer asked, so quietly the question was almost lost in the noise of the café.

"No," Cosi answered. "We can call her at the motel. Tell her plans changed."

Gwen would be heartbroken, but her feelings weren't the priority at the moment.

Spencer looked up from his jelly-creamer creation. I expected him to stare at his father, to wait for Cosi to give him guidance. But instead, he looked to me. "What would you do?"

I picked up the saltshaker, positioning it at the top of his pyramid. Once it was balanced, I let go, my fingers splaying wide in case I needed to catch it. But the shaker held fast.

"Ilsa, what would you do?" Spencer waited for me to answer his question, but I stayed quiet. This was a decision he had to make on his own.

"Fine," he grumbled—with an eye roll. "Whatever. I'll go. Do you think she even remembers it's almost my birthday?"

"Yes, I do." At least, I hoped so.

When we dropped him off, I'd find a way to bring it up, just in case.

"She better bring me a birthday present," he grumbled. "Hopefully it's cash."

"Spencer," I hissed.

"What? I need gas money." He shrugged. "I'm broke."

Cosi threw his head back and laughed while I balled up my napkin, tossing it into Spencer's face, earning a laugh as beautiful as his father's.

Easy. Exactly the way it should be.

~

Cosi's fingers tapped on the wheel as we drove down the highway. He'd been tapping ever since we left Spencer with Gwen for the picnic.

"He'll be okay." I reached over to put my hand on his thigh. Worst-case scenario, they'd have an awkward lunch and Spencer would walk home early.

"I know." He sighed. "This is hard. I've never had to share him."

"What about me?"

He clasped my hand, lifting it to his lips. "Doesn't feel like sharing. Feels like how it was always supposed to be."

This man. He stole my breath away. I rested my temple against the seat, twisting sideways to smile at him as he slowed for the turnoff to Cotters Lake.

"I love you." Saying it felt like the thousandth time, not the first.

Cosi pressed my hand to his heart, holding it against his chest. "I love you too, baby."

Like how it was always supposed to be.

We eased off the highway, taking the gravel road into the mountains. The weather had warmed enough that the thick layer of snow and ice had melted, leaving slushy twin tracks. The noise of the tires and hum of the engine was like a lullaby.

"Don't fall asleep on me," Cosi murmured, his warm hand still holding mine as he drove with the other.

"It's your fault I'm tired." I yawned. "You kept me up too late last night."

He grinned. "Planning to do the same tonight."

I laughed, drawing my knees to the seat as I closed my eyes. Another yawn pulled at my mouth, and I was seconds from drifting off when Cosi dropped my hand.

Not a gentle loosening of his fingers. He let it go so quickly that my eyes flew open and I sat upright.

"What?"

Cosi's gaze was narrowed at the road ahead, both hands gripping the wheel as he took his foot off the gas pedal.

"What's wrong?" Was there an animal or something out there? A bear or moose or elk?

I stared through the windshield, trying to make out whatever it was that he saw. But before I had the chance, he floored it, sending us fishtailing for a minute as the tires spun to get traction. Then we were racing down the narrow road, bouncing over dips and bumps.

"Cosi." I gripped the handle on the door and the console between us.

"Hold on, Ilsa."

My fingers dug into the seat, my hand clutching the door's handle, as he kept going faster and faster. Too fast for a rough country road. My body flung side to side in the seat, up and down, as panic set in, my heart climbing into my throat.

Cosi stayed wholly focused ahead, his jaw set in a determined line at whatever he'd seen.

We hit a bump that sent my elbow slamming into the door, making me wince. But as the sting in my arm faded, I saw movement ahead.

A green Chevy truck was speeding backward almost as quickly as we were moving forward.

"Who—" I didn't finish my sentence. There was only one person Cosi would risk chasing after with me in the passenger seat.

Trick.

The engine revved as he slammed on the gas and the distance between us and Trick shortened. Closer and closer until I could see Trick's face. It was covered in a beard, a hat pulled low on his head. In passing, I wouldn't have recognized him.

How Cosi knew it was him, I wasn't sure, probably the truck.

Trick alternated between looking forward at us and backward at the road, searching for an escape. But the trees blocked him in. There wasn't enough room for him to turn. If he stopped, Cosi would have him.

Tree trunks streaked by my window. Clumps of snow flew up from the road, sloshing on the windows. And not once did Cosi look away from Trick.

We got so close that our fenders bumped.

Trick's eyes went wide as Cosi laid on the horn. But it only seemed to spur Trick on, pushing him to go faster, inching away, still driving in reverse, until we came to a small clearing.

Trick spun his Chevy around, and even though we were right behind him, even though he had to know that this was a dead-end chase, he kept driving, off the road and into the forest. His tires cut tracks in the snow as he dodged trees and crashed through drifts.

"I'm not losing him." Cosi didn't hesitate to follow. He yanked the wheel, taking the same path as Trick, until we were so close to the lake that I could make out the shoreline.

"Fuck," Cosi clipped. "He's going to try and cross the lake."

"But the ice." Jerry's warning from weeks ago not to drive on it came rushing back.

Trick didn't slow as he shot for the lake. For a moment, I was sure he'd fly across the ice and be gone forever. But then the front corner of his truck lurched in the air, like he hit a rock or tree stump. It sent him careening sideways, skidding to a stop ten feet from the shore.

Cosi slammed on the brakes. The Bronco came to a stop nearly touching Trick's bumper, blocking him in. Moving faster than I'd ever seen a person move, Cosi was out the door, his hand flicking free the clasp on his holster.

Two quick, deafening pops filled the cab as he shot out Trick's front tire.

"Out and on the ground," Cosi bellowed, gun leveled at Trick as he sidestepped for a better angle.

My pulse pounded as I watched Trick slowly open his door. He swung out one leg but didn't shift from behind the wheel.

"Out. Now, Trick," Cosi shouted, gun still raised. "Shut off the truck."

Trick hung his head, his shoulders curling forward as he obeyed. When he looked to Cosi, it was with a sadness that almost made me pity him. Almost.

"It's over," Cosi said.

Trick shook his head, looking up. "I didn't mean for this to happen."

Above the hum of the Bronco's idling engine, I strained my ears to hear.

"Trick," Cosi warned.

Trick twisted so he could meet my gaze. "All Bluebird ever talked about was the gold. How he was sure he could find it. How he was onto something big."

So when I'd gone to the bar to ask Trick about Dad, he'd known all along.

"I'm fucking sick of tending bar. Dealing with drunk assholes. Living off shitty tips and struggling to pay the bills."

"Get the fuck out of your truck," Cosi yelled.

But Trick didn't move. He kept his eyes on me as his lip curled, and his stare morphed into a sneer. "You didn't even know him. You weren't here for him when Donnie died. You didn't drive him home when he'd drown his sorrows in a bottle of bourbon. You didn't listen to him cry because his goddamn heart was broken. You didn't deserve Ike."

It was every insecurity, every truth, I felt bone deep.

He was right. I hated that he was right.

"Trick," Cosi barked. "Shut your fucking mouth and get out of your truck."

"She knows I'm right." His gaze swung to Cosi. "She should have stayed away. But she came here, slid right into your bed and started asking questions about the day he died."

Oh God. I covered my mouth with a hand, knowing where this was going.

Cosi took a step closer.

Trick swallowed hard, his gaze shifting toward the lake. Toward the snow-covered island where Dad's body had washed ashore. "I came out to go fishing with him that afternoon. We fished together a lot last year. He was talking about the gold. How he wrote you a letter and was sure you'd come home. How he was going to give it all to you. And I told him that a daughter who couldn't even visit after Donnie died didn't deserve a thing."

Except I didn't know about Donnie. Dad had never told me. Dad had rarely spoken to me.

"What did you do?" Cosi asked.

Trick's eyes were full of tears when he turned away from the lake. "It was an accident. I didn't mean to push him so hard."

My heart stopped. "You killed him."

The whisper was too quiet for Trick to hear but the guilt on his face was confirmation enough.

"Out and on your knees, Trick. Nice and easy."

He only shook his head, reaching for the key in the ignition. "I'm sorry, Raynes."

"Patrick."

"You'll have to shoot me." Trick turned the key, the truck roaring to life.

He was going to force Cosi to shoot him. To end his life or let him drive off.

"Cosi, don't."

Maybe Trick would get away today, but I couldn't let Cosi live with Trick's death. It would haunt him for the rest of his days.

Cosi's jaw clenched, and before I knew what was happening, he shot out Trick's other front tire.

But it was too late. With the door still open, Trick threw the truck in drive and stomped on the gas. It lurched forward, on flat tires, over the shoreline and onto the frozen lake.

Cosi opened fire on the back, bullet holes littering the tailgate.

But Trick kept driving, swerving and sliding, the door slamming closed and the rubber loosening on both his front tires.

Cosi lowered his gun, running toward the shore.

I leapt out of the Bronco, hurrying to his side.

Together, we watched in horror as the metal rims of Trick's wheels began cutting into the ice, sending white flakes spraying up behind him as he drove.

He would never make it out on the other side of the lake. If he doubled back, Cosi would stop him. Trick had nowhere to go.

Except into the water.

Trick wasn't going to leave this lake alive. He knew what would happen if he drove out there. He'd made his choice.

The ice cracked. One moment, the green truck was skidding over the surface. The next, the front end dropped, followed shortly by the back.

Then Cotters Lake swallowed Trick Dougan.

Chapter 30

Cosi

Ilsa, Spencer and I stood side by side on the island at Cotters Lake. We'd hiked to a small outcropping of rocks where we could overlook the lake and the mountains beyond.

Ilsa was about to cry. She was fighting it. Doing her best to blink away those tears and keep her chin from quivering. But six sniffles in a row and I knew it was coming.

"Spencer." I jerked my chin toward the aluminum boat we'd tied up on the shore before scattering Ike's ashes.

He nodded, giving Ilsa a hug before following the same path we'd taken to this spot, through the towering trees and green grasses and blooming bushes to the rocky shore.

I pulled Ilsa into my arms. "You can cry."

"I don't want to cry today."

"Why not?"

"I don't know. I guess I feel like I've cried enough at this lake."

She swallowed hard before leaning her head on my shoulder as the sun streamed down on us from a cloudless sky.

It had been three months since the day Trick had died on this lake, and in that time, we usually spent our Saturday mornings at the Grizzly

Café. But this morning, Ilsa had poured a cup of coffee and asked if we could scatter Ike's ashes today.

Not once since she'd moved in had she mentioned Ike's ashes. She'd put that box in the closet of the guest bedroom and closed the door. So when she'd asked, I'd picked up the phone and called Chuck to see about borrowing his rowboat.

She'd chosen this spot, though I wasn't sure when. Maybe during one of the afternoons we'd visited the cabin and she'd sat quietly on the dock to stare out over the lake. It was exactly the place Ike would have chosen for himself.

The water was a sheet of crystal-clear glass reflecting the trees and the mountains beyond. We had a perfect view of the cabin and the dock so he could see home.

"Goodbye, Dad." Ilsa lost her fight against the tears. Her shoulders began to shake, so I turned her in my arms and held her while she cried.

But my girl wasn't one to stay sad for long. After a few minutes, she stood straight and dried her eyes. "Thanks for coming with me."

"Wouldn't miss it." I brushed a kiss to her temple.

She turned to the lake, taking in the view as she pressed a hand over her heart. She let her eyes wander over the shoreline, giving herself one last moment—I doubted she'd ever set foot on this island again.

"Okay, I think I'm ready to—" She gasped, her entire body tensing as she reached for my hand. "Cosi."

"What?"

"Jerry." She nodded toward the shore, to the area where we'd found that tiny cabin of Trick's.

A man stood on the shore, hands tucked in his coat pockets. His head was entirely bald on top with a ring of white tufts that circled from ear to ear. That white was a sharp contrast to the green and brown forest around him.

Even from across the water, I recognized him. His name wasn't Jerry. It was George.

"I'll be damned," I muttered. "That's the guy who gave you your dad's letter?"

"Yes. Do you know him?"

"Yeah." I'd seen him three months ago at Trick's funeral. No one I knew called him Jerry. "His name is George Dougan. He's Trick's great-uncle."

"So he lied about his name," Ilsa said, her spine stiffening. "Do you think he knew about Trick? That he—"

Killed Ike? "I don't know."

I wanted to give George the benefit of the doubt. People in this town respected George Dougan, but people had respected Trick too.

Maybe George had seen Trick fishing with Ike. He'd warned Ilsa that Ike wouldn't have drowned. He had to know something. Maybe Trick had confessed to pushing Ike.

But rather than give Ilsa the whole truth, a truth that would have condemned his great-nephew, George had offered only vague hints. And then she'd gotten hurt.

That was on him. The bastard. As far as I was concerned, he was just as guilty as Trick.

Though I suspected that when I showed up at George's place on Monday morning to ask some questions, he wouldn't be there.

Like he could sense my darkening mood from across the water, George turned and walked into the trees, disappearing from sight.

"Was he friends with my dad?" Ilsa asked.

"Yeah. He was."

"We'll never see him again, will we? We'll never have all the answers."

As much as I wanted to tell her otherwise, I couldn't lie. "Probably not."

That was probably the last I'd ever see of George.

There'd be no catching him today. I'd never be able to row across the lake quickly enough, and he'd grown up in this area. He was an avid hunter and fisherman. Hell, he'd probably helped Trick build that illegal cabin.

George had spent his lifetime prowling around these mountains, learning them like the back of his hand, with Trick as his companion. No doubt the reason Trick had been able to sneak up to Ilsa's cabin windows without leaving tracks was because George was good at covering his own.

"Fuck you, Jerry." Ilsa stared into the forest for a moment, then she turned her back on George. She faced the water, closing her eyes as she drew the earthy, clean air into her lungs. And then on an exhale, she slipped past me and headed to join Spencer at the boat.

I took a moment to stare over the water, to the depths where Trick had met his end three months ago.

He'd drowned in his truck. He could have swum to the surface, but he'd made his choice while we'd stood on the shoreline and watched.

We'd had to send a diver into the lake to retrieve Trick's body, but with the ice, getting the truck out had proved to be more of a challenge, so we'd opted to wait until it melted. By the time we'd finally fished that Chevy from the lake, it had been down there for nearly two months.

And tucked behind the bench seat was Ilsa's purple briefcase. Everything inside, the journal and atlas and letters, was ruined.

His house had been full of maps and pictures—too many of Ilsa for my comfort. I'd found his stash of poison and enough cocaine to question our every interaction over the past year.

The man Trick had become was not my old friend.

It was only by chance that we'd met Trick on the road to Cotters Lake that day. He must have come up to search the cabin for more information because the front door had been kicked in, the lock shattered.

At this point, Ilsa and I were both convinced there was no gold. That Ike's obsession with the legend had been a way for him to survive the grief of losing Donnie.

But he'd been convincing. Trick had certainly believed. Enough to nearly kill Ilsa over a journal and atlas, things she would have given him had he only asked.

I'd replayed it all a million times and likely would for the rest of my life, wondering if there was more I could have done. Maybe someday I'd be able to come to Cotters Lake and not think about Trick's death. I hoped so, considering Ilsa had decided to keep the cabin.

She'd lost enough of Ike already.

Eventually, this would be a happy place for her. For our family. We just needed time. And thankfully, we had it. So I turned away from the lake and hurried to catch up to Ilsa.

After helping her into the boat, I pushed us off the shore and climbed inside, taking the center seat. With the oars in hand, I rowed us for the cabin, facing Ilsa and Spencer as they sat side by side on the back bench.

"Can we get our own boat?" Spencer asked.

"No."

"Yes."

Ilsa and I spoke in unison.

Spencer looked between the two of us, then pointed to her. "I like her answer better."

Ilsa laughed, looping her arm through his. "I think we should definitely get a boat. But maybe not until we have more than a couch in the cabin."

That couch was the one and only piece of furniture in the cabin. Mom had wanted to get something nicer for her living room, so we'd volunteered to take her orange plaid couch for the cabin.

It was hideous. I'd always hated that couch. But it looked oddly right inside Ike's cabin.

"I'll pitch in for the boat," Spencer said. "With lawn-mowing money."

That kid had finished the school year with decent grades and a plan to make a pile of money this summer mowing lawns. He'd lined up twelve houses around town already, and every week, he seemed to add another to his schedule.

"How about you save your money for gas?" I stroked the oars through the water, glancing over my shoulder to gauge the distance to the dock.

"Or college," he murmured.

Ilsa and I shared a look. College? That was new. The light that sparkled in her eyes made my heart swell.

"I think we should get you a checking account," she told Spencer. "Then you can deposit your earnings and save them to use when you're ready. I'll teach you how to balance your checkbook. And budget your money for gas."

"We're doing that in Mrs. McNally's home ec class next year."

"Oh." Ilsa turned to the side, hiding a lip curl from Spencer.

Most of the teachers at Dalton High had finally fallen victim to Ilsa's charm. Most, but not all. Mrs. McNally was one of the few holdouts who still barely acknowledged Ilsa when they passed each other in the halls.

As far as I was concerned, McNally could piss off. She was just bitter that Ilsa was now the official math teacher at Dalton High, a job McNally had apparently wanted but hadn't gotten.

Mrs. Riley was not returning from maternity leave after all, and though I doubted Principal Harlan would ever openly praise Ilsa's efforts, the rumors floating around town were that the standardized test scores the students had taken at the end of this school year were the best they'd been in a decade.

Strong test scores meant state funding, so when Mrs. Riley had decided to become a stay-at-home mom, Harlan had changed his tune about hiring Ilsa. She'd been a shoo-in for the job.

She had the summer off, but she was already brainstorming ideas on how to refresh the curriculum.

And I, for one, was glad that the shithead seniors like Paul Johnson were graduated and gone.

Ilsa needed easy for a while. We all did.

The only real stress we had at the moment was Gwen. She was trying with Spencer, I'd give her that. She'd moved to Missoula, and any chance she could get, she came to Dalton. Sometimes they'd go out to lunch. Sometimes he'd call an hour before she was supposed to drive over and cancel their plans. Once, she'd made it all the way to town and he'd blown her off entirely.

That was the one and only time I'd intervened. He didn't have to see her, but he needed to be courteous. Otherwise, I was staying out of it, even when every paternal instinct screamed to take charge, to fix this.

My mother hated that Gwen was in Spencer's life. She was terrified Gwen would disappear again and crush Spencer's spirit—it was my biggest fear too. But Ilsa was unbending in her faith that Gwen wasn't leaving.

For Spencer's sake, I hoped she was right.

I doubted Spencer and Gwen would ever be close, but Gwen's return was teaching him some important lessons for life. That people could change. That we could forgive those who gave us scars. And that no matter what, he had me. He had Ilsa.

"Want to hop out and tie us up?" I asked Spencer as we approached the end of the dock.

"Got it." He stood, waiting until he could jump out.

Then after I stowed the oars, I helped Ilsa, keeping a hold of her hand as we made our way to the cabin.

My thumb skated over her fingers, over her knuckles and the flat spots in between. There was something missing on her left hand. Something I'd fix soon enough with the diamond ring hidden in my desk drawer at the station.

"Ready to go home?" I asked Ilsa.

She stared at the cabin as we meandered across the yard, our linked hands swinging between us. "I guess. There's really nothing else to do out here."

"Or we could go for a hike." Spencer dug a folded piece of paper out of his jeans pocket. "I, um . . . I made this."

As he unfolded the paper, Ilsa and I moved closer, peering down at the map he'd drawn.

The map that was a close replica of the atlas Ike had left for Ilsa.

My observant, clever boy had committed it to memory.

"Spencer." Tears flooded Ilsa's eyes as she took in the incredible detail on the map. "How long have you been working on this?"

"Since your stuff got stolen." He shrugged. "I don't know if it's even right. It's probably not."

"Even if it's not, who cares? We could still go on a treasure hunt." Ilsa smiled up at me. "I'm up for it. You?"

"Let's do it." I nodded to Spencer. "Then lead the way, pal."

"Okay." Spencer waved us to the Bronco, spreading out the paper and telling us his theory that the cabin was the starting point. He'd clearly thought about this because, unbeknownst to me, he'd brought along a hiking pack complete with bear and bug spray.

"I'm going to fill up our canteens, then we can go," he said, jogging for the cabin.

I waited until he was gone to take Ilsa's face in my hands. "You okay with this?"

"If it makes him happy, then I'm happy."

Fuck, I loved this woman. I dropped my mouth to hers, swallowing a moan as I licked her lips, then slid inside, nice and slow, just how she liked it.

Her hands skimmed around my waist, dropping into the back pockets of my jeans so she could squeeze my ass.

The dreamy smile on her face when I broke the kiss was more beautiful than any Montana scenery. Prettier than a watercolor sunset or a blanket of diamond stars.

"How are you holding up?"

"I'm good. I think doing this, searching for Dad's lost gold, is the perfect way to end the day. Do you think we'll find a lost treasure?"

No, I doubted we'd ever find gold. Not that I needed it.

Ilsa was my treasure. "Already did, baby."

Epilogue

Ilsa

Seven years later . . .

"Ilsa Raynes." Cosi's voice was mixed with a crackle of static as it came through the CB radio. It was usually a bit dicey on the gravel road to Cotters Lake.

I picked up the microphone, pressing the button as I spoke. "Cosi Raynes."

No matter how many times I told him we needed more creative radio handles, we still hadn't come up with anything new. I thought Cosi's should be Mustache Ride—he hadn't found my joke funny.

"Where are you?" he asked. "Over."

"Ten minutes away. Over."

"All right. Over and out."

I hung up the microphone and sat taller to look through the rearview mirror of the Bronco. My two beautiful girls were asleep in the back seat with their new puppy sprawled between them.

Summer sunshine streamed through the windows, kissing the freckles that decorated their noses.

Madeline always seemed to fall asleep on the drive to the lake. No matter what time of day. No matter if she'd slept twelve hours the night before. Since she was a baby, if we ever had a hard time getting her to sleep, we'd load her up and go for a drive. It usually only took one lap around Dalton and she'd conk out.

Her dark hair had fallen in her face and her mouth was agape. But even though she was out, she kept a firm grip on the furry black ball beside her.

Bear had been her shadow since the day Spencer had walked through the door with a puppy in his arms for Madeline's sixth birthday present.

Cosi had about strangled Spencer—a puppy had been a surprise for all of us. But when it came to his little sisters, Spencer would gladly face his father's wrath if it meant making the girls happy.

Spencer had already warned me that we should expect a kitten for Chloe's fourth birthday in October.

A cat would fit Chloe's personality perfectly, just like a dog fit for Madeline. Where Maddy was sweet and cuddly and shy, Chloe was my spitfire, and she filled our lives with noise. If she wasn't laughing or screaming, she was singing or shouting. She didn't understand the meaning of quiet, and there wasn't a timid bone in her body.

The girls were night and day, yet the best of friends. That would probably change as they became teenagers, but for now, watching them together was like magic.

Chloe rarely slept in the car. She loathed naps and had her entire life, always too afraid she'd miss something. But she'd fallen asleep today, slumped sideways on the seat, her hand resting on Maddy's arm.

Always linked, my girls. I hoped that never changed either.

After Spencer had graduated from Dalton High and moved away for college, we'd given the girls their own rooms. But night after night, Maddy would sneak into Chloe's room and curl up on the floor beside her sister's crib. After a month of fighting it, we'd given up keeping them apart.

Now they had bunk beds, and whenever Mom came to visit from Arizona, she could stay in the guest bedroom.

I reached for the window crank, rolling it down so I could rest my elbow on the sill. The warm breeze washed over my face as the scents of trees and earth flooded into the cab. The mountain air filled my lungs, crisp and fresh.

Our house on Pine Street was home. But the cabin on Cotters Lake was our escape. This road was like leaving reality behind and driving into a dream.

It had taken a few years to put the trauma of that first winter behind me. To let the bad memories fade away. But after so many happy times on the lake, Dad's cabin had become our getaway.

While I was on summer break from teaching, the girls and I would drive out a few times a week to go swimming while Cosi was working. On the weekends, we'd all come out to motor the boat around the lake. After every dinner, we'd sit around a campfire to roast marshmallows. The times when we'd stay overnight, Cosi and I would watch the sunrise from the dock.

As I drove by Sue Anne's A-frame, every window was dark. She'd moved two weeks ago to be closer to family in Idaho, and it was still strange not to see her face in the window. Robert Aaron had also left his cabin this past winter after some health scares.

At the moment, the only person living on this part of Cotters Lake was Spencer.

He'd graduated from Montana State this spring with a teaching degree, and in the fall, he'd be joining me at Dalton High School.

Somewhere along the way, he'd decided not to become a cop like Cosi, but a teacher like me. And when an opening had come up at the school, he'd been the first to apply.

Eventually, he'd probably move into town, but he loved this cabin more than anyone. He loved hiking in these mountains, searching for that lost Garrack gold. He still hoped that one day, he'd stumble onto whatever my dad thought he'd found.

Maybe that lost legend was the reason he'd decided to become a history teacher.

The sound of a power saw echoed through the trees as we pulled up to the cabin, and the moment I shut off the Bronco's engine, Cosi came walking around the corner.

He'd left the house early this morning to come help Spencer with the remodeling they were doing together.

Sweat gave his forehead a sheen, and his jeans were dusty. A pair of leather gloves was tucked into his pocket, and his white T-shirt molded to his body, stretching over that broad chest I slept on every night. The smile on his face still gave me butterflies.

"Girls, we're here." I twisted to the back seat as Cosi opened my door.

"Hey, baby." He kissed the corner of my mouth as I got out. Then he flipped the driver's seat forward to reach back and unbuckle Chloe's seat belt, lifting her out.

"Hi, cricket." He brushed the brown curls off her forehead as she rested her head on his shoulder.

"Hi, Daddy." Chloe wasn't the snuggling type, not like Maddy. She always preferred to chase around. But the one person she'd cling to without fail was Cosi.

He tucked her into his arm, then went to open the back for the cooler and tote I'd brought, along with a change of clothes.

I rounded the hood for the other side to get Maddy. "Time to wake up, honey bear."

Her eyes fluttered open as I settled her on my hip. She took a groggy look around, then wrapped her arms and legs around me, clinging tight as I made way for Bear to jump out.

"Did you have a good nap?" I kissed her temple, then shut the door, carrying her toward the cabin.

Spencer came from around the back side of the cabin, wiping his brow with a red handkerchief. At twenty-two, he looked so much like Cosi it was uncanny. They had the same hazel eyes. The same tall, muscled frame. All Spencer was missing was a mustache.

Bear spotted him and tore off running, tail wagging as he crashed into Spencer's shins.

"Hey, pup." He bent to scratch Bear's ears as we walked over to join them. "Hey, Ma."

From the day Cosi and I had gotten married in the Dalton courthouse, a month after he'd slid a ring on my finger, Spencer had called me Ma.

Gwen was still living in Missoula, and they'd see each other from time to time. She called him every week, and this past Christmas, he'd invited her to join us for dinner. Their relationship had evolved from strangers to acquaintances to something akin to friendship.

But she would always be Gwen. And I would always be Ma.

He was as much my son as he was Cosi's.

"Hi, bud." I scrunched up my nose as he stood and gave me a sideways hug. "Eww. You stink."

"I was waiting to jump in the lake until the girls got here."

Maddy lifted up, staring at her big brother. The smile they shared was identical. Both girls had my brown eyes, my nose and the shape of my face, but their smiles were Cosi's.

"Hey, Mads." He touched the tip of her nose. "Wanna go swimming?"

"Yeah."

"Me too." Chloe squirmed out of Cosi's arms, ran to Spencer, grabbed his hand and pulled him toward the yard. "Whet's go."

"Life jacket, Chlo." Cosi pointed to where they were hanging on a hook outside the cabin.

"Get yours too," I told Maddy, setting her down.

She nodded, but rather than following Chloe and Spencer, she walked straight into Cosi's arms. "Daddy, will you swim with me?"

"Of course, baby girl. But I need to show Mama something first, okay? You get ready. I'll meet you on the dock."

With a kiss on her hair, he sent her off after Chloe, who was already taking off the sundress that I'd pulled on over her swimming suit.

"What do you have to show me?" I asked.

"Baby." He put his hands on his hips, shaking his head as he laughed. "You're never going to believe this."

I groaned. "What now?"

So far, this remodeling project had been one unexpected problem after another. The roof had started to leak this spring, and when they'd gone up to patch the shingles, they'd realized the entire thing needed to be replaced.

Spencer wanted new appliances in the kitchen, which had led to completely rewiring the cabin. And when they'd brought in a new toilet, they'd realized the old lead pipes were a disaster waiting to happen, so they'd been working to replace them all with copper.

"Come on." Cosi held out a hand, threading his fingers with mine as he led me around the side of the house.

The access panel to the crawl space was open. And beside it was a pile of cans.

Campbell's Tomato Soup cans. Western Family Whole Kernel Corn cans.

Years ago, when I'd moved into this cabin after Dad died, I'd been up to my elbows in those cans.

Each of them was capped at one end in silver duct tape.

"He put empty cans under the house? What on earth?"

"Better take a closer look." Cosi nodded to the pile.

"Okay," I drawled, walking over to pick one up. Something rattled inside as I peeled away the tape. Something like rocks.

Except it wasn't rocks.

The can was full of nuggets.

Gold nuggets, stowed in empty cans and hidden under my father's cabin.

My jaw dropped as I stared at the gold in my palm. "Cosi. Is this . . ."

"Yeah, it is." He laughed, still shaking his head. "I can't believe it. I'm guessing he made the atlas and left those clues behind in case he never found it himself."

Except Dad had found the gold. Probably right before he died. Probably at the time he'd sent me the letter about the legend of Garrack's gold. And after he'd found it, he'd kept it hidden in these empty cans beneath his house.

All those hikes Spencer had taken us on, his treasure hunts, scouring these mountains. The gold had been here in this cabin all along.

"Oh my God." I threw my head back to the bright sky, and when I laughed, I was sure that Dad was somewhere looking down on me, laughing too.

Watching me and my family in his favorite place.

Watching as we discovered Bluebird's gold.

Acknowledgments

Thank you for reading *Bluebird Gold*!

I am forever thankful for having such incredible readers. Thank you for coming along with me as I give voice to the imaginary characters rattling around in my brain.

This is a story I have wanted to write for years. In fact, I started it in 2022 but had to set it aside for other commitments. I am a firm believer that stories are meant to be told when the time is right, and this was one of those books that came at the perfect moment. I hope you enjoyed reading Ilsa and Cosi's story as much as I loved writing it.

Thank you to the entire team at Montlake. My amazing editor, Maria Gomez, thanks for being such an incredible and supportive partner who didn't even bat an eyelash when I said I wanted to write a book set in 1983.

Thanks to Logan Chisholm for being the person I can always count on to tackle whatever gets thrown our way. I am so lucky to have you as head cheerleader and assistant extraordinaire. Thank you to Georgana Grinstead for all you do. I am so lucky to have you in my corner.

A huge thanks to my editors, Elizabeth Nover and Kelli Collins. Thank you to Julie Deaton, Judy Zweifel and Vicki Valente. And thanks to Hang Le for this gorgeous cover.

I am so grateful to God for blessing me with the opportunity to write these stories and the gift of this career. And last but certainly not least, thanks to my friends and family for filling my heart each day. Your love and support never cease to amaze me.

About the Author

Photo © 2024 Hailey Booth

Devney Perry is a #1 *New York Times*, *USA Today* and Amazon bestselling author of over fifty romance novels. After working in the technology industry for a decade, she abandoned conference calls and project schedules to pursue her passion for writing. She was born and raised in Montana and now lives in Washington with her husband and two sons.